"My dear Virginia," Jim replied, adopting her speaking-to-an-idiot voice, "I appreciate that this is alien territory for you, but in the realm of thought there is no such thing as mainstream."

"Truths are constantly forgotten and constantly rediscovered, which is why history is not a straightforward slide to hell, but a rollercoaster."

"Foreigners should be recognized as an emerging new nation. They already outnumber most nations and they are growing faster than the population of China. They should have a seat on the UN Security Council."

"They stood in the crowded foyer with less than a foot between them and as their blood speeded up, they watched its ebb and flow on each other's faces. Alert, their nerves drawn, they were like cats smelling fish, twisting this way and that way, with widening eyes and flaring nostrils, smelling happiness."

"It was at the back of their minds from the start that whatever happened, it would be brief, and they abandoned themselves to each other all the more freely. He knew there wouldn't be enough time to get bored; she knew there wouldn't be enough time to be hurt."

"'Oh, God, let him be bright!' she prayed, as she got into his car."

"All through August Lesley felt she was the most beautiful woman in the world. She was no longer unhappy about her small breasts."

"I'll be damned if I let our jobs go to Malaysia," he swore. "I risked jail to keep them here."

"He was in charge of all the pain yet he felt helpless."

to Gloria

Fifty years ago I published In *Praise of Older Women* myself because no publisher believed in it as much as I did. Now I'm publishing If Only because no publisher believes in it as much as I do.

If Only is the story of Jim Taylor, a gifted young man who dreams of becoming a great musician, but tired of poverty and homelessness, gives up his vocation. "I want to enjoy life before I'm too old for it,' he says when he finds a well-paid job working with the first computers. He meets Lesley at a concert and they have a disastrous affair, but "each felt guilty, each felt the other was innocent – they were in love" and they get married. Lesley is the sun of Jim's life, the light of this otherwise dark story.

'You turn your head and a decade is gone." Jim is the Senior Vice-President of the UK's biggest software company. A decent but weak character, ('he had a mortgage – he wasn't a free man') he became the best of the worst kind of villains. If only he had stuck to music! If only he had known, if only he had understood.

I love books that breathe freedom, inspiring us to imagine that we are freer than we actually are, for this is the only way we can avoid becoming depressed automatons. More than drugs, what we need for mental health is the constant exercise of our imagination. A young boy lands in the story to give Jim and Lesley a second chance to be young again and remake their lives, with the knowledge and regrets of their past. I believe that If Only will strike a chord with readers who can conceive a better world, who wish that they could undo their blunders and start again.

STEPHEN VIZINCZEY

Stephen Vizinczey

If Only

Books by Stephen Vizinczey
In Praise of Older Women
The Rules of Chaos
An Innocent Millionaire
Truth and Lies in Literature
If Only

Technical Director: Predrag Tomašević

Paperback ISBN: 978-0-9935837-1-1
Hardback ISBN: 978-0-9935837-0-4

1st Edition, June 2016

Financed by readers through Kickstarter
http://bit.ly/kickstarter-if-only

Thanks are due to the writer and astronomer William K.
Hartmann and law professor Philip Anisman for their advice and
comments on the novel.

Published by The Happy Few Ltd. Timber Lodge, School Lane,
Farnham, Surrey GU10 3PE
thehappyfew@btinternet.com

Printed and bound in Great Britain by Clays Ltd, St Ives plc

Contents

1

2

1

1. Statistics

I am i' the way to study a long silence.
WEBSTER

More people commit suicide during their holidays than at any other time. It's strange but it makes sense. The rest of the year they are too busy, too harassed, too tired to think seriously about anything. Only when they get away from home and work do they have the leisure to reflect at length on their misery and abandon themselves to despair. It's only then that they have the energy to rouse themselves without the aid of habit and do something out of the ordinary.

James Taylor, senior Vice-President of Quantum Systems, the biggest UK computer company, hadn't had a holiday for over a year. In addition to his regular workload, he had been put in charge of downsizing and sacked 4,153 employees, including his deputy who wrecked his hands by trying to tear his fingers from their sockets and a line manager who hanged himself in his garage with his daughter's skipping rope. James Taylor, mentally and emotionally drained, was about to leave his office on Christmas Eve for a three-week break in the sun, when he himself was sacked with immediate effect.

James Taylor was married. His wife, Lesley, had only the salary of a teacher; his own salary and bonuses were offensively high, but they hadn't saved, and with an outstanding mortgage of 4.5 million they could no longer afford first-class air fares and a long stay at a five-star apartment hotel on a resort island off the Gulf Coast of Florida. Still, everything was prepaid, so they went. Magdalena Island was an isolated and old-fashioned place, without drug dealers, muggers or killers. The long, narrow strip of land with sandy beaches on both sides and a road in the middle was connected to the mainland by a causeway manned by security guards, and undesirable visitors were made to feel unwelcome. There was also a ban on motorboats and jet-skis that foul the beaches elsewhere with the noise of combustion engines and exhaust fumes. This additional measure, almost unique at seaside resorts, transformed the island into a cultivated paradise of peace and tranquility.

As soon as the Taylors got into their suite in Gulf Views, they went out to the terrace. Ahead of them lay the immense expanse of glittering water and the limitless sky; they breathed in the soft air and let the mild breeze stroke their skin. The hotel was full for the Christmas holidays, yet there weren't too many people on the mile-long stretch of powdery white sand. The sound of lapping water mingled with children's shrieks of excitement, the raucous cries of seagulls and the muted slap of round wooden bats hitting rubber balls. Most adults were lying on sun-loungers or were walking on the sand. Lesley counted only four heads in the water. A couple below the Taylors' terrace who were sunning their backs suddenly got up, marched into the sea, splashed about for a moment and then came out to lie down again.

"That wasn't much of an exercise," commented Lesley.

As they stood on the terrace, leaning on the railing, a pelican cruised by right in front of them. They could have touched the tip of its large brown wing if they had reached out in time. The big bird tilted, catching an air current, and, without moving its wings, glided upward and out to sea, scanning the waves with its radar eyes. Pelicans can see a fish, register how fast it is moving, and with their small but sophisticated brains, calculate exactly where it will be when they come down for it. The bird cruised at a height of some forty feet until it suddenly closed its wings, hit the water with incredible speed and emerged an instant later with a glittering silver fish flapping in its beak.

Thrilled by the pelican's amazing vision and aim, Lesley stood on tiptoe and spun around, her eyes flashing with pleasure. "Let's not bother to unpack. Let's just go for a swim."

Within hours of their arrival on the island, two incidents occurred which plunged the ex-executive into deeper depression. He felt light in the water during his swim, but walking on the beach afterwards with Lesley and seeing a number of sleek, lithe people, he was hit by the realization that he had become repulsive. He knew that he had gained thirty pounds in the last nine months, but it was abstract knowledge, it wasn't backed up by comparisons with other bare bodies. Few people over forty can keep in shape unless they confront the whole of their bare bodies every day. Jim Taylor's clothes had hidden a great deal and it was only on the beach that it dawned on him that he was a revolting fat old wreck.

"You shouldn't have kept telling me that I looked wonderful," he told his wife angrily.

"But you do look wonderful, my darling," she replied in the reassuring voice she used with her anxious pupils at school. "Stop fussing about your weight. You are the handsomest man I ever saw." And she meant it too, proving that conjugal love, when it exists, is the strongest love there is.

He took her soothing remark with bad grace: she was deceiving him. "You're still beautiful, you never put on any weight, so what do you care!" he grumbled.

Lesley didn't mind that either and smiled contentedly. She still looked like a girl in the growing stage on account of her small breasts and her springy walk. With her red hair and freckles, she seemed to be on fire with life. Jim Taylor counted five men, each younger than himself, who eyed her with intent. And who took any notice of him? Attempting to recover a sense of his manhood on this international beach alive with sexual sparks, he focused his eyes on a tall, slim, elegant brunette in a black bikini, strolling at the edge of the water. She was as stunning as a film star. She might have been a film star.

Jim stared at the long-legged beauty with all the desire he could muster. She glanced at his belly and looked back at him with an expression of amazement which he understood as clearly as if she had spelled it out in words. *How could you even think of it?!*

2. Luke

Child? Mother? Either grief will do.
W.H. AUDEN

Just a few minutes later, James Taylor received another blow: Lesley fell in love with a little boy in a red and white baseball cap. The boy's head practically disappeared under the cap as he stood on the wet sand at the water's edge whimpering, while his father splashed about in the shallow water, coaxing him to come in. The boy didn't move, continuing his weak, plaintive cry. The Taylors walked past him but after a few steps, Lesley turned around, hurried back and crouched down beside the child to say hello. Surprised, the boy fell silent. He was a strikingly fragile, subdued little fellow; his ribs showed and his shrunken face made his big, dark, watchful eyes seem even bigger. When Lesley managed to make him smile, she fell in love with him. Jim saw the change on her face and was jealous. He felt rejected, discarded, thrown over.

"His name is Luke," said the father, stepping ashore. "We brought him here for his fifth birthday." A fleshy man with a wide, ruddy face, straw-coloured hair and pain in his pale blue eyes, he didn't wish to disturb Luke's encounter with a sympathetic woman and stayed in the background, striking up a conversation with Jim instead.

"By the way, I'm Lewis Mayberry." He reached out to shake hands. Desperate to talk to somebody, he forced Jim into a conversation. Jim told him that the redhead was his wife and he worked with computers.

"It's good of your wife to make friends with Luke," the man said in a low voice. "Most people give him a wide berth." A landowner with an estate in Kent, much of it apple orchards, he envied Jim's simpler life with computers. "You're lucky. You don't have to worry about worms eating your programs."

"We do, we do. We have computer bugs."

"We didn't spray this year and we lost half our apple crop."

"Not even a third," interjected Anita Mayberry, a slender, tawny-skinned woman in a purple swimsuit, jumping up from a nearby sun lounger. She had a beautiful but disturbing face. She didn't look at Luke's father.

Mayberry's face tensed when he heard her voice: he didn't look at her either.

"May I introduce my wife, Anita," he said grimly. "She knows everything better than I do."

She had her back to her husband, addressing him through their new acquaintance. "I do know many things better than you do, but you never listen to me," she snapped, smiling at Jim to show that the hostility in her voice wasn't meant for him.

Mayberry moved his eyebrows up and down in mock

horror, commenting in a sarcastic whisper. "She thinks I'm a murderer."

"And you are, you are a murderer," she said in an equally low voice, flashing another smile at Jim. "He thought I'd spare him in front of strangers."

"I don't see how I could possibly think that, considering the way she goes on about me to everybody."

A yellow beach ball fell at their feet and they had to move to give way to the girl who was running after it. But the Mayberrys still managed to look in different directions. Though they spoke in low voices to spare their son, they had the compulsive, unrestrained volubility of people under great strain, unburdening themselves to anyone who would listen. The mother blamed the father for the boy's leukemia, believing that it was caused by Mayberry's pesticides and herbicides.

"I'm a murderer, because I try to protect my crop like any other farmer." Mayberry's voice and expression conveyed all the comment he felt was necessary. "Needless to say, she knows nothing about chemicals."

"I read the newspapers."

"Exactly," Mayberry said, sounding drained. "I have a wife who reads the newspapers to find something she can torment me with."

She moved her head and hands rhythmically from side to side to suggest what nonsense he was talking.

"Of course," Mayberry went on, "Luke has never been near any spraying. He has never had any contact with anything even remotely toxic ..."

"He's a farmer, and he doesn't know anything about

winds," she interrupted, still talking only to Jim.

Mayberry made a face. "There you are. There you have it. The winds. We stopped spraying to humour her, but it's no use. She has to blame somebody nearer than God."

Just then an extraordinary thing happened. As Lesley said something to Luke and pointed to a heron flying by, the boy started laughing. His thin, weary laugh, so different from the confident shrieks of other children on the beach, had something eerie about it. It was an old man's laugh in a child's voice. It made Jim shiver, but it produced a miraculous change in the parents: their tense faces smoothed out, their eyes flashed with joy, and they exchanged glances.

As they joined Luke and Lesley, Jim finally took a good look at the boy. Noticing how shocked he was, Anita Mayberry began to talk animatedly about her son's illness and treatment. She spoke in a determinedly upbeat manner, as if she were describing an exciting adventure. "Luke's already had his second bone marrow transplant!" she announced triumphantly.

"I used to be a lot sicker," Luke himself commented, listening to his mother's explanation with interest, even with some pride. "I have to go the hospital a lot, but I'm not afraid. The doctors and nurses are all my friends." When he looked up, his baseball cap slipped, exposing his bald head. Lesley shot an anguished glance at Jim as she replaced the cap. But Luke wanted them to see his head, and he lifted his cap to show that chemotherapy takes your hair away temporarily. He used the word "temporarily" frequently; he understood almost everything about his illness, except that it was terminal.

"Jim, look what gleaming eyes Luke has!" Lesley exclaimed.

But Jim was watching Lesley's eyes: they were gleaming with joyful love as Luke's smile grew wide enough to reveal his small, white, even teeth. Jim tried to remember the last time that Lesley had looked at him with that kind of fervour. "You're absolutely besotted with that kid," he said accusingly when they got back to their apartment. Without responding, Lesley went to the bathroom to have a shower.

'I'm jealous of a dying boy,' Jim reflected, sitting down on a chair and pulling his fingers mechanically, one after the other, stopping abruptly when he realized what he was doing.

Lesley reappeared wrapped in a white bathrobe with "Gulf Views" embroidered on it in blue and stepped to the balcony, with her back to her husband.

"I hope I wouldn't have got so upset if the boy had another name," Jim said by way of apology. "I was worried that he's reminding you of our Luke."

Lesley wished she could tell him that every toddler reminded her of their Luke. "Would you feel less sorry for the boy if he was called Jeremy?" she asked. (Jeremy Norton was the Executive Chairman who had sacked Jim the previous evening.)

"Of course not. Poor kid. I'm glad you could make him laugh."

"It's amazing, isn't it? No matter how sick a child is, you can still make him laugh."

"He likes you – he senses that you love him," he sighed.

"Did you notice how Luke's parents hate each other?"

she asked. "Not having a child isn't the worst thing that can happen to you."

He hoped she meant it. During the night he clung to her as if afraid she would leave him. They ended up at the opposite edges of the king-sized bed. He was the first to wake, feeling the chill of the morning air. Jim drew her towards the middle. He hugged her and she smiled, but then pushed him away.

"Oh dear, we can't," she exclaimed. "I promised to have breakfast with Luke. I can't disappoint him." She gave him a strong kiss and leapt out of bed.

"What about disappointing me?" asked Jim, but by then she was gone.

Later, as he sat by the pool, pulling his fingers, his body hidden in a bathrobe, watching Lesley helping Luke to draw a heron on the back of a menu from the beach bar, he convinced himself that the most important person in her life had always been the child. Every time he heard Lesley laughing, his mind went into a spin, collecting all the evidence of his guilt.

No doubt Lesley would have spent more time with him if she had realized how despondent he was. But whenever she said "I promised Luke", or "I can't disappoint Luke" and left, Jim remained silent, not wishing to appear jealous of a dying child.

Lesley hoped that the sea air, the balmy weather and the peace would help her husband get over the shock of his dismissal, but after more than two weeks' rest, he had such a sense of ill-being that he longed for death.

3. COMET CLAUDINA

*Comets are the most spectacular
of the small bodies in the solar system. When
they pass near the Earth, they can be seen drifting
slowly from night to night among the stars.*
WILLIAM K. HARTMANN

In the evening before the fateful night of January 12, 2007, the Taylors were having dinner with some of the other guests in the terrace restaurant of Gulf Views. The electric lights embedded in pebble glass columns were superfluous. The early darkness of the winter evening was dispelled by Comet Argüelles, popularly known as Comet Claudina. Comets are named after the individuals who discover them, and this "fragment from the formation of our galaxy" had been discovered two years earlier, in 2005, by the amateur Mexican astronomer Claudina Argüelles.

Comets are flying ice. Pulled and thrown by the sun's gravity, travelling in an elongated elliptical orbit, they loop around the sun and rebound into distant space, just as a ball thrown on the ground bounces back into the air. The comet's surface is frozen far more solidly than anything on Earth. In distant space a comet is only an invisible iceball; it becomes what the ancient Greeks called a "long-haired star" when it enters the inner solar system and is caught in the solar wind - a radioactive gas which pours forth from the sun at the speed of several hundred kilometres per second and at a temperature of one million degrees. As extreme heat melts the surface of the ice, it releases glowing gases, bits of rock, and cosmic dust which are embedded in the ice and trail the comet in a stream of vibrating white light. For some unknown reason, possibly because of some unidentified compound in the ice, Claudina's flowing hair had the colour of fire.

It also had a unique orbit which brought it closer to Earth than any other comet in recorded history. It became visible to the naked eye during the evening in the summer. The vibrating flow of light in the sky which makes comets so thrilling to watch appeared at first as small as the flame of a matchstick, but it had grown bigger and brighter every night, and by 12/01/07 it was a flaming torch brightening the sky of the northern hemisphere. This out-of-this-world spectacle, the like of which none of the guests had ever seen or expected to see again, was the main topic of conversation. It had been in the news items for weeks, and was talked about everywhere. Academic researchers have established that there was no reference to a fire or orange-coloured 'long-haired star' anywhere, not even on the inner walls of the Pyramids or in folk epics predating the written word. This meant that Comet Claudina's previous appearance in our skies must have been before the beginning of recorded history, possibly hundreds of thousands of years earlier. One columnist commented that Claudina last flew across our skies, "when people were still monkeys." Claudina was 125 kilometers in diameter, over a hundred times larger than most comets - and large comets hover near the farther reaches of the sun's gravitational reach, which is roughly a million light years in every direction.

The comings and goings of comets can give us a sense of our place in time. Nearby comets swarming between the orbits of Neptune and Pluto may pass within sighting distance twice in a hundred years; those farther away may take much longer to reappear. Kohoutek's Comet, which acquired naked-eye visibility in 1973, is due back in about 72,000 years. *Seventy-two thousand years* makes you think. The last ice age was only forty thousand years ago, a long enough stretch of time for Arctic bears to change their brown fur to white and wipe out almost all traces of the human race. What is our future then? Can our endangered species survive for 72,000 years longer? What is the lifespan of humanity? Who will be around in seventy-two thousand years to watch a long-haired star streak across our sky? Until the appearance of Claudina, the brightest comet on record was the Daylight Comet of 1910, which is due to pass the Earth again in four million years.

The flaming torch in the sky affected everybody. They all felt that they had something important to say - except James Taylor, who sat beside his wife as if he wasn't there.

A rich dentist from New York, who clearly had the luxury of time to read and think, quoted the Astronomer Royal, Sir Martin Ryle: "Everything is comprehensible about the universe, except its size."

Anita Mayberry, Luke's tall, intense mother, wearing a bindi on her forehead and a blue silk sari, leaned forward to rouse the ex-executive from his gloomy silence. She used her standard conversational gambit. "James," she asked, fixing her demanding eyes on him, "if you could live your life all over again, what would you do differently?"

"Everything," he burst out. "Everything!"

The couples around the table, all middle-aged or worse, laughed appreciatively. They knew the feeling. Lesley squeezed her husband's hand to let him know that she knew what he meant. She didn't understand either - she thought he meant the child. He meant everything.

"James, if you would do everything differently," Anita Mayberry persisted, "do you mean you wouldn't marry Lesley?"

"Jim had nothing to do with our marriage, that was me," Lesley cut in with protective haste.

Her remark set off another ripple of laughter. They could laugh all the more easily because they were in no danger. Space centres around the world had confirmed that Comet Claudina would pass nearer to Earth than other known comets, but still at a safe distance. The conversation reverted to space - to comets and planets. There are over two billion suns just in our galaxy, and a new planet is discovered every other week, so wasn't it possible that there were other life-supporting planets like our own circling one of those suns? While the rest of the company exchanged their guesses, James Taylor sank back into himself. He had been watching Comet Claudina from his office window in London (when he still had an office), wishing that there was another Earth they could go to, but he was no longer interested - he had resolved to leave the universe during the night.

Tossing and turning in bed, he tried to imagine what it would be like to drown. He worried about the pain. Could he stand it? How long would it take? Five minutes? More? When would he stop feeling anything? Would he be conscious when the water filled his lungs? Tossing and turning, Jim twisted so violently that the whole bed shook and he got scared that he had wakened his wife. He froze and listened. She turned around and said a few indistinct words in an urgent voice, talking to someone in her dream. He waited for a while, until her breathing signalled that she was fast asleep again.

He remembered tossing and turning in bed when he was a child. "I can't sleep!" he would shout, and his mother would run upstairs to stroke his back. Or they would read together. Little Jack Horner sat in a corner. Little Miss Muffet sat on a tuffet.

The chief defect of Henry King
was chewing little bits of string.

It came to him then, a moment of absolute bliss: he saw his mother's cheerful round face and her loving brown eyes; he felt her smooth olive skin, her soft tickling hair as she leaned over to kiss him. And how good her thin, crispy Hungarian pancakes tasted! They melted in his mouth. He stood beside her at the stove and ate them as fast as she could make them. The plate she put them on was always empty.

Tossing and turning, he was amazed that he could remember the long-forgotten address of their first home back in Toronto: 38 Sanford Avenue. He hadn't thought of the place for years and now he had a vivid image of the three-story brick house, with its wooden porch. What fun he had, running up and down the stairs from the basement to the attic, and then down to the basement again, up and down, up and down, his heart filled with triumphant joy - until he fell so hard that he screamed his heart out against the pain. The deep cut on his forehead required four stitches and his mother dressed the wound every day, soothing him with kisses and hugs.

Tossing and turning, he wondered how old he was when he believed he could walk on water. Four? Five? His name was still Jim Kleermaker and he didn't worry then about the agony of drowning. They lived next to a family from the Dominican Republic who had a boy called Jesus. Jesus could kick a ball with perfect aim: he never once missed the cat. He used to come over to their house to play and eat. Jim's mother was fond of the boy but she liked her son better. "You're more like Jesus than that little devil!" she said, picking Jim up and hugging him with a passion. Of all the Bible stories his mother had told him, Jim liked best the one about Jesus Christ walking on the lake and calming the waves. It was just the kind of thing he would have loved to do. He asked his Dominican friend to go for a run with him on Lake Ontario.

"I mean your name being Jesus and everything."

"Did Jesus walk on water?" asked Jesus. "Oh, yeah, I heard about that. Nah, I don' wanna get my shoes wet."

Jim decided to do it on his own. Why not, if he was more like Jesus than his friend? One Sunday afternoon the family went for a walk along the lakeshore. His parents had him in the middle holding his hands, but when a sudden squall whipped up the water, he broke free and ran toward the lake, flinging his arms wide. "Be quiet, be quiet!" he shouted at the wind and the waves. He strained himself so hard to force the elements to listen that he grew dizzy and fell.

His father raised him and shook him violently to bring him to his senses. "What was that all about? What? You wanted to calm the lake?! You wanted to walk on water?!" His father, who hated anything fanciful, hit him so hard that his head rang. His mother wasn't quick enough to ward off the blow, but she kicked his father on the shin. She always gave Jim heart.

Stroking the scar on his forehead, the ex-executive was happy for a while, thinking of his childhood, but then he remembered the rest of his life.

4. A BROKEN VOW

O, where are you going? Stay with me here!
Were the vows you swore deceiving, deceiving?
No, I promised to love you dear,
But I must be leaving.
W.H. AUDEN

His mind poisoned with regrets, he got out of bed to die. The sliding glass door to the balcony had been left open to let in the sea air and, as he wore nothing to bed, it felt pleasantly cool on his skin. The sound of the waves lapping upon the shore covered the slight noise he made. Once he put on his glasses, he could see everything clearly by the light of the comet. His watch showed 2:35. He wondered whether he could slip out of the hotel unnoticed. Surely by now everybody was asleep?

He was tempted to take a last look at Lesley but didn't dare to risk it. They had been married for over thirty years and were so close that they could wake each other with their eyes. Lesley was particularly susceptible; she had such wide-awake skin, she could feel his gaze on her arms. Not quite ready to leave her, he stood on the cool tiled floor, staring at the edge of the bed and listening to her breathing. He pictured her half-waking in the morning, reaching out for him, then sitting up, looking around, calling his name, assuming he was in the bathroom. They were used to waking up together, so she would miss him, look for him all over the apartment, phone the reception desk.

Would his body be washed ashore by then? How would they tell her? No, that was no way to end their marriage. Lesley was a loving wife, she deserved better.

How would she cope, having to arrange his funeral in a strange place? Poor girl. To whom could she turn? Neither of them had any close relatives left. They were both in their fifties and couldn't count on anybody else. If only they had children! The thought twisted the dagger of guilt in his heart: Lesley had no children to help her. Tears welled up in his eyes as he brooded on how desolate she would be when they told her that they had found his corpse. But it didn't occur to him to spare her the grief and go back to bed.

There was a rustle of sheets and the sound of her turning around. Did she sense that he was up? Holding his breath, he tiptoed out of the bedroom without glancing in her direction.

He walked across the dark hallway without bumping into anything. She would cry for a while, he decided, taking a deep breath, but sooner or later she would remember the child - that would stop her mourning for him.

Was it day or night?

An explosion in space in the early hours of January 12th lit up the Northern hemisphere: an asteroid crossed the path of Comet Claudina and the collision, its impact multiplied by the immense force of galactic speed, vaporized the asteroid. A huge mass of frozen gases the size of the Alps broke off the comet's main body and, caught in the solar wind, exploded. Those in northern countries who were lucky enough to be awake during the early hours of 12/01/07 no doubt remember night turning into day. Though the window was only a narrow slit in the wall, Jim Taylor's bathroom was suddenly flooded with piercing light, revealing his bloated body in the full-length mirror with appalling clarity. 'There's no way she could still love me, it's just obstinacy', he thought, as he struggled into his swimming trunks, stretching the elasticised waistband to get it around his belly. The prospect of all that loathsome fat being burnt when he was cremated quite pleased him.

5. WHO DO YOU THINK YOU ARE?

*Foreigners should be recognized as an emerging
new nation. They already outnumber most nations and
they are growing faster than the population of China.
They should have a seat on the UN Security Council.*
ADAM BARDI

Jim Taylor's maternal grandparents, Adam and Elizabeth Bardi, born in Hungary, were stars in the world of classical music. Some readers may be familiar with Elizabeth Bardi's CDs of the Haydn violin concertos with the Chicago Symphony Orchestra, recently reissued by Virgin Classics. Adam Bardi's recordings of the cello concertos of the classic repertoire with the Berlin Philharmonic have never been out of circulation, though his most popular CD to this day is his *Suites for Solo Cello* by J.S. Bach.

This great musician's hobby was theorizing. His pamphlet, *The Nation of Foreigners*, published by the University of Toronto Press, can be found in the sociology section of university libraries. He argued that "people who have left their country of origin and their mother tongue share many common characteristics which are as strong as any other national bonds. Regardless of whence they came or in whichever new country and new language they settle, they share a common consciousness as foreigners. They are outsiders, they don't really know where they belong, yet they are at the centre of historic changes, involved in everything." As he wrote in his preface, he "wanted to boost the consciousness and pride of the new nation which will be the biggest nation of the 21st century, outstripping the population of China and India."

Bardi's ideas were inspired by his own life. Like many prominent musicians, he and his wife moved from one big city to another, from one country to another. Both Bardis were invited to join the Berlin Philharmonic, but those were still the Cold War years, there was still an East Berlin and a West Berlin, and that summer a war between the Soviet Union and the West seemed a real possibility, so the couple decided to take up the offer of professorships from the Royal Conservatory of Music in Toronto. They thought that it would be safer for their daughter to grow up on the other side of the Atlantic. Besides, Bardi firmly believed that the ideal city had a population of around a million and anything bigger "was a tiresome mess". Toronto's inhabitants had numbered only about a million at the time. The Bardis continued to perform and record with various orchestras in America and back in Europe, but they also played with the Toronto Symphony Orchestra every season. They were appreciated in Toronto, they had enthusiastic fans there and the city remained their base for the last fifteen years of their lives.

Their daughter was a teenager when they came to Canada. She trained to be a concert pianist but, like many gifted children of successful and famous artists, she panicked at the thought that she could never measure up to her parents and, just as she was about to enrol at the Royal Conservatory, she decided to study English Literature and Philosophy at the University of Toronto, where she met Jim's father at a Varsity ball.

Ten years earlier, Pieter Kleermaker had come to Canada with his parents from The Hague. The surprise discovery that they had both emigrated to Canada on the same ship called the *Ascania* (even if years apart) was the spark of joy that made their dance special. Unfortunately, apart from crossing the Atlantic on the same boat they had very little else in common. Ilona had grown up in homes filled with music, literature and ideas; Pieter Kleermaker's home, unusually for the Netherlands, had no books or music, nor did he miss them. Ilona was educated, intelligent and affectionate - three graces which rarely come together. Pieter Kleermaker, a few years older and studying for his PhD in pharmacology, was educated but neither intelligent nor affectionate. A tall, narrow-shouldered man with pale skin and pale eyes, he liked to look at people with a grave expression, preserving his self-satisfied silence until he could think of a cutting remark. Once the high tide of desire had receded, Ilona realized that his pomposity wasn't a boyish mannerism but a mask of cold stupidity. It was an all too common feminine destiny: by the time she got to know him they were married and she was pregnant.

Jim learned early in life that his parents didn't get along. When Ilona got angry she hissed abuse at her husband in Hungarian, which drove Pieter wild. "What does that mean?" he shouted. "Speak English!" Then he started to abuse her in Dutch.

His father's parents owned a pharmacy in Vancouver. The Kleermakers had planned to fly to Toronto to see their newborn grandchild, but by the time they actually arrived Jim was old enough to run to meet them. When his Dutch grandmother came through the door, he rushed towards her to be hugged and loved, but Mrs Kleermaker raised her arm to keep him back. "Wait until I take off my coat!" she said sternly. This was the only thing Jim could remember about the Kleermakers' visit from the distant shores of the Pacific, and he never saw them again.

He was about nine, in his fourth year in school, when he began nagging his mother that he wanted to have a Canadian name. "No way!" declared his father. Ilona, who was usually quite an accommodating wife, couldn't bear to see her son unhappy and insisted, unwisely, that the boy should be able to change his name. In the end the pharmacist got tired of hearing about it, and agreed that the boy could have the English equivalent of his name. "He's more your son than mine anyway," he said resentfully, feeling less of a father.

The boy's name was legally changed from James Kleermaker to James Taylor. From an early age Jim was determined to be a Canadian. In spite of his adored grandfather's insistence that foreigners would be the biggest nation on Earth in the 21st Century, Jim was glad he wasn't a foreigner. Born in Toronto, he took great pride in being the only member of his entire family who was a native Canadian. Throughout his childhood and teenage years, his whole world was his native city. Having no intention of ending up like his grandparents and his parents living in a country a long way from their native land, he developed a strong sense of himself as a Canadian from Toronto. He didn't think much about it, but his country's red maple leaf flag flapping in the wind always cheered him.

6. A PRIVILDEGED CHILDHOOD

When I was younger it was plain to me
I must make something of myself.
WILLIAM CARLOS WILLIAMS

Little Jamie had a privileged childhood: his mother quit her job when he was born.

"The trouble with Ilona is that it takes too little to make her happy," said her father, who thought that she should get a divorce, but she wouldn't. The young couple's incompatibility may be summed up by Peter Kleermaker's frequent complaint against his wife: "Ilona, you're too emotional about your feelings!"

Ilona coped as best as she could. She coped by not brooding. As some people collect grievances, she collected moments of joy. She counted her blessings - her piano, her records, her books, her husband's occasional good moods and, above all, her son's company. Although the deposit on their home (fifty percent of the value of the house) was paid for by Ilona's parents, Kleermaker resented that she was staying at home with their son instead of going back to work. Little Jamie, following his mother around, heard it all. She stood at the kitchen stove, stirring the pot as his father shouted at her that she should go back to work and start earning some money.

"I won't leave Jamie with strangers," she said casually, yet her voice had steel in it.

Since Jamie was the only person with whom she could be emotional about her feelings, she passed on to him all her enthusiasms. When she fell in love with a piece of music or a poem, she would share it with Jamie. He was not yet five when they played four-handers together on the piano. She recited poems usually when doing some boring domestic task. She stood on a stepladder in the kitchen, stretching to put some dishes on a high shelf, then looked down at him and raised her eyebrows to signal playtime. "Altogether elsewhere," she intoned,

Altogether elsewhere, vast
herds of reindeer move across
miles and miles of golden moss,
silently and very fast.

They soon recited Auden's stanza together, travelling on rhymes to another world, saying "very fast" very fast.

When Jamie was old enough to go to school, the boy stunned his teachers by being able to read, write and spell more or less correctly and saying things like *stately pleasure dome* or *fortissimo*. At home mother and son had a riot talking, playing and singing together - except in the evenings and at weekends, when Jamie's father was at home and they had to be quiet. One of Jamie's first perceptions was that his father loved television and his mother loved him.

His grandfather had ordered a small cello specially

made for Jamie's seventh birthday by the Brazilian master, Antonio Picado. The boy was thrilled with the instrument and declared that he was going to transport people to another world with his music.

"The kid who wants to walk on water," commented the pharmacist, who happened to overhear him. His son's vainglorious notions got on his nerves and he never missed an opportunity to cut him down to size.

"There is nothing wrong with trying to walk on water, provided you learn to swim first," his wife said cuttingly. "Jim has ambition and imagination, that's what's bothering you. But *a man's reach should exceed his grasp, or what's a heaven for?*"

"I know, I know," said the father sullenly.

Adam Bardi thought that his grandson had talent and paid for his teachers. He had high hopes for Jim as a cellist, both on account of his skills and his total recall. Classical music requires prodigious memory. Great conductors and soloists have every note of whole symphonies and concertos in their heads, which is the equivalent of knowing several Shakespeare plays by heart, word for word. Adam Bardi played cello concertos without the aid of a score. In our own day both Daniel Barenboim and Adam Fischer are famous for conducting immense amounts of music from memory: all of Beethoven's symphonies and the whole of Wagner's Ring Cycle respectively. The solo player of an instrument has to know at least his own part by heart, and be sufficiently familiar with the rest to blend in with the others. Jim gave his first concert at the age of fourteen at his school, playing Vivaldi cello concertos with the school orchestra, without the aid of scores, enthralling an audience of teachers, students, parents and relatives. This school concert was the last occasion that his grandfather felt triumphant. His wife succumbed to motor neuron disease and it killed them both. He died four months after her.

Ilona didn't want her parents to be cremated. She bought a family plot in Mount Pleasant cemetery and had both of them buried in wooden caskets so that they would become part of the soil, and live again in the sapling silver linden tree planted above their grave. Jim visited the grave with his mother every week when it didn't rain or snow. They exchanged their memories of the couple and sometimes they laughed, scandalizing other visitors to the cemetery.

Since Ilona was the Bardis' only child and heir, she became rich. Both Elizabeth and Adam Bardi came from once wealthy families in Hungary, and their fortunes were their instruments. Most of what they earned Adam Bardi invested in insurance policies (a habit Jim was to follow in later life) which paid for a four-story mansion on Douglas Drive in Rosedale – an inner city enclave of winding streets, huge ancient trees, little parks and handsome old houses. Before they moved into the mansion on Douglas Drive, Ilona enlarged and modernized the kitchen, and had the top floor turned into a separate apartment for her son. Jim was sixteen at the time, and among all his friends he alone had his own apartment. The ancient elm and maple trees in the garden were higher than the house, and he loved to wake during the green months. As soon as he opened his eyes he was greeted by the shadows of leaves swaying on his whitewashed bedroom walls, cheering him with their silent dance; if their swaying had the same rhythm as the music he had been studying, he could hear the orchestra in his head. The heart of the place was a big music room with his cello and his mother's piano. The walls there were lined with fibreglass to keep out the noise, and the fibreglass was overlaid with cypress, which is one of the best woods to improve acoustics and is used in concert halls around the world. He practised for hours every day, alone or with his mother at the piano. At times they gave concerts for friends. Jim was 17 when he won a scholarship to the Royal Conservatory.

Elizabeth Bardi's violin from the 1710s, made by the great Italian violin-maker of Cremona, Giuseppe Antonio Guarneri, was auctioned at Sotheby's in New York, fetching more than the last Stradivari they had sold. The pharmacist felt insulted that her parents didn't even mention him in their will and felt belittled by her inheritance. For the sake of domestic peace, Ilona bought him a large drug store on Dunford Avenue with the proceeds. In spite of this multi-million dollar gift, he was still resentful. Ilona, apart from the Steinway piano and her books, didn't have a strong emotional relationship with money or possessions and made him joint owner of all they had, including the convenience store next to the drugstore, which she turned into a bookshop, naming it ONLY GOOD BOOKS. By then Jim was old enough to have girlfriends and she went back to work as a bookseller. She stocked her shop mainly with classics in English, French, Chinese, Spanish, Italian, Hungarian, Greek, Portuguese, German, and half-a-dozen other languages, wishing to serve the whole of Metro Toronto's literate population.

Jim lived in music. Protected from the struggles and anxieties about survival which drain the strength and spirit of so many young artists, he was only nineteen when became the cellist of the Hart House trio and gave a triumphant performance in Schubert's Piano Trio in E flat. Afterwards he declared at home that he would be the principal cellist of the Toronto Symphony Orchestra in a few years' time.

"You're full of big dreams," Kleermaker commented, "but they'll never amount to anything."

Whenever Ilona saw Jim pale and angry, she knew why, even if she hadn't heard what went on before. "Never mind your father, he's jealous," she said. "We're a team and he hates that he isn't part of it." She kissed him on the forehead, then stepped back to look at him. She was proud of his big forehead which confirmed her faith in his genius. "You'll be just as great a musician as your grandfather, or even better - I know it." His glorious future shone from her eyes.

The upward curve of Jim's destiny broke one cold, sunless November morning.

7. ONE OF DEATH'S DOORS

I know death hath ten thousand several doors.
WEBSTER

Jim's father had an appointment with their accountant and his mother came over from the bookshop to help out. When an addict started a row at the prescription counter, Ilona walked over to quieten things down. She confirmed that they weren't allowed to give out amphetamines without a doctor's prescription and suggested to the man that the he should see his doctor first – or, if he was from out of town, he should go to the emergency ward of the Toronto General. Given advice instead of what he asked for, the enraged addict pulled a gun from his coat pocket and shot her in the face at close range.

That morning Jim had been rehearsing with the Hart House Quintet, and he took the streetcar to meet his mother. They had planned to visit his grandparents' graves, but when he arrived Ilona's corpse had already been driven away by the ambulance. The bookshop was closed and the pharmacy was in chaos. The police on the scene couldn't tell him anything. Jim could cope with his grandparents' death, because he had always known that they would go before him, but he could not imagine that his mother was dead. He could not accept that he would never see her again. The policewoman handling enquiries at the station knew nothing about her and a sergeant who did know refused to say where the body had been taken.

"There's no need - your father has already identified the body."

"I have a right to see my mother!"

"Well, go and see the captain," said the sergeant.

Jim was sent here and there and argued with several reluctant officials to no effect. "You have no right to keep us apart!" he screamed. The captain didn't think it was safe to let him go anywhere on his own, and a police car drove him to the morgue. There he was stopped again. The manager warned him that no one had attended to the body since it had been brought in– it was a busy day – but Jim wouldn't listen. He practically fought his way into the huge cold room where corpses were kept. When, finally, the elderly attendant, wearing a rubber apron, pulled out the refrigerated steel box, Jim felt almost relieved that he could be near his mother. All he could see at first was her hair soaked in blood and mixed with bits of her brain. The head was splintered bones, raw flesh; her eyes blood-soaked little balls. When he noticed her pearls attached to her woundless ears he collapsed on the tiled floor.

The attendant grabbed the inert body under the arms and dragged him out, grumbling, "He wouldn't listen. He asked for it."

Jim suffered the worst kind of grief: losing his mother, he lost faith in himself. He tried to raise his spirits by putting his grandfather's cello next to his mother's piano and playing solo pieces for her as if she were still there. She wasn't and he felt his playing wasn't any good. He wondered whether he would turn out like her - talented, but not good enough to be a professional. Her absence made him feel death in his bones. He took a sleeping pill every night. It made no difference. He kept dozing off and was startled awake, tossing about restlessly.

One night he fell into sleep and his mother stood beside him. She was wearing her familiar light blue summer dress. They stood on a crowded platform in the subway, waiting for the train. She was so lively and cheerful; he forgot that she was dead. They were happy, going somewhere together. When the train came, she smiled at him. He stepped forward to make room for her, assuming she would be right at his back so that nobody could get between them. When he looked back she wasn't there. Alarmed, he stood on tiptoe to look around over people's heads: he couldn't see her. Where had she gone? He ran along the platform, pushing people aside, searching for her face, her figure, her familiar way of walking, her blue dress, but everybody in the crowd was a stranger. 'Perhaps she had to go to the washroom,' he thought. Stirred by hope, he ran about desperately searching for a washroom. There were no washrooms in the station. Where could she have gone? He was frightened; he couldn't understand. How could she have disappeared? How could she suddenly leave him without a word? He got angry; he wanted to tell her off. She was too old, too intelligent to play hide-and-seek with him. He was so mad at her that he woke up.

He leaped out of bed to go downstairs to make sure that she was back in the house – then fell back on the bed, feeling sick of life.

8. BETRAYALS

We should smile,
And stop our weeping.
KURT VONNEGUT

Ilona's parents had never stopped saying that they had moved to Canada, away from the deadly dangers of Cold War Europe, so that she could be safe. She often felt like screaming when she has heard them repeating over and over again that she would have a long and peaceful life. Their faith in her safety was getting on her nerves, but just the same it made a deep impression on her. She had never thought of dying - certainly not as a young healthy woman – and didn't bother to make a will. In Anglo-Saxon law children do not automatically inherit from their parents, which explains all the news stories about fortunes left to cats. Ilona's husband was joint owner of all they had, and as the surviving partner, he inherited everything. Transferring full ownership to his name, he became the sole proprietor of the drugstore, the bookstore, the shares and bank accounts, as well as the Rosedale mansion with the a garden and the double garage. It wasn't fair to his son, but what did it matter? After his death, the boy would inherit everything.

Kleermaker turned his late wife's bookstore into an extension of his pharmacy and made it one of the city's biggest drugstores. Jim owned nothing, except his grandfather's cello. Kleermaker mourned his wife by studying himself in the mirror every time he went to the bathroom. His lips had grown thinner with the years, and he twisted and squeezed them to give himself more of a mouth. He tilted his head back to smooth out the wrinkles on his neck and the loose flesh on his jaw. There wasn't a skin cream in his drugstore that he hadn't tried. When there were no prescriptions to prepare and no customers to watch in the drug store, the well-off widower let his avid, pale eyes rest on the unattached girls in his staff, none of whom was likely to torment a man with poetry or classical music. Wondering which one would welcome a rise in her pay, he compared their breasts and backsides and settled on a bosomy nineteen-year-old bottle-blonde at the perfume counter. During a quiet period, risking a charge of sexual harassment, he bravely squeezed her buttocks. She pretended not to notice. He squeezed her harder to make sure she didn't mind. She didn't seem to mind, and he soon began groping her regularly in the stockroom, growing besotted with her freshness, the smell of her young body, her soft flesh, her passive silent malleability. After a couple of weeks or so she licked his earlobes, which he took for a promise of submission and exciting sex. She let her thin-lipped employer rub himself against her and even moved a little herself to help him along - then she pushed him away with a sigh.

"Oh, we could never be happy!"

His happiness interrupted, Kleermaker gaped at her with a pained expression. "What do you mean?" He was stunned to hear that Penny was still a virgin, believed in God and didn't believe in sex outside marriage. As he was trying to digest the idea of marriage she declared that she couldn't marry him.

"Why not?"

"Husband and wife should be equals," she wailed in a low voice.

"We are, Penny, we are," he said feverishly, drawing her back to warm himself with the heat of her body. "I believe in equality, believe me."

She shook herself free. "We're not the same sort of people. You're rich and I'm poor. I'd feel like a slave. You should find a girl who has her own money."

However, she let him take her out to dinner.

The house in Rosedale was large enough for father and son to live a long way from each other, but they usually had breakfast together in the big kitchen on the ground floor. Jim's mother had put in a large deal table and comfortable chairs, making it as good a place for talking as for eating. They discussed what to do with the stock of Ilona's bookstore, and Jim suggested giving most of it to the Central Public Library on Yonge Street which could never have enough foreign-language books, as the old Anglo-Saxon Canadian city was turning into a new Babylon. Jim had no idea that he got nothing of his mother's share of their properties, and the pharmacist saw no reason to enlighten him. Nor did he mention his dinners with Penny; it was none of the boy's business.

Instead he urged Jim to change the cello for an electric guitar and try to be a pop star. "All this cello business was the dream of your grandfather and your mother, but they're dead, you don't have to worry about disappointing them, you can think of yourself and forget your Bachs."

"They've just renewed my scholarship for next year. They don't finance many students to study there. Getting in isn't easy, you know, even if you pay."

"What if they gave it to you only because your grandparents taught there?"

Jim knew that his father enjoyed nothing so much as putting him down, and he shouldn't pay any attention to his malicious remarks, but it was still a blow. All his teachers had told him, at one time or another, that they admired his grandparents. Was it possible that he was nothing much on his own? "My teachers think I have real talent," he said with fake courage.

"I know, I know."

"Last night I got the loudest *bravos*! for the Boccherini Quintet."

"I know, I know. You go to classes for years, you lock yourself up with your cello at the top of the house, you practise day and night, your teachers are happy, and when you graduate you find that the girl at the checkout counter earns as much as you do. Provided, *provided* you're lucky enough get a job."

"There are orchestras all over the country, all over the continent, who employ musicians who graduated from our Conservatory. There are some who went to play in Europe. I know one who is with the Berlin Philharmonic."

"All that boring noise is just garbage from the old days of kings and emperors," Kleermaker said dismissively. Having become independently wealthy, he had acquired the serene conviction that he was right about everything. "I never hear that crazy music on the radio."

"I'm sure you never tried to look for it."

"Jim, among the thousands of young fools who've graduated from your Conservatory, how many have a steady job?"

"The best do."

"The best? That's it? The best? Jim, listen. Listen to your father. Any business where you have to be the best or you're dead is not a business. It's not a profession or a career, it's a hobby."

As they couldn't see eye-to-eye about anything, their morning talks became ever more impersonal. Each talked about what interested him about the previous day, which was profoundly boring to the other, but they made an effort to appear to be listening, thinking, 'After all, he's my father'; 'After all, he's my son.'

The boredom of his breakfasts with his son only heightened the importance of the widower's dinners with Penny. He drove her to expensive restaurants and they spent happy hours discussing food, celebrity news, their favourite television programmes, cars, clothes, houses. He certainly couldn't have had such enjoyable conversations with his late wife or her son who stuck up their noses at everything that interested normal people. Penny let the besotted pharmacist feel her in the car, but whenever he wanted to go further she pushed him away, telling him that he should marry a rich girl who was his equal. The infatuated widower wanted to marry her, but she couldn't overcome her misgivings about the huge financial gap between them.

It took Kleermaker a few months to face up to the only possible solution: he made her his partner, transferring half-ownership of the drugstore and the Rosedale mansion to her name – the transfer was to be completed the day they got married. She preserved her virginity for their wedding night, but once the date was set for the blessing of their union in Rosedale United Church, she gave him, without his asking, a blow job. It prompted the pharmacist to make a will, leaving her his entire estate if they were still together when he died. He had some qualms about disinheriting his son, but he wanted to be sure that he would have Penny until his last breath.

On a day when the snow melted a little, Kleermaker banished boredom from the breakfast table in the kitchen by breaking the news of Penny and the wedding. "Come to Rosedale United Church tomorrow at noon," he told Jim, "and we'll bring her home after the ceremony."

The prospect of another woman moving into his mother's house was such a shock that Jim couldn't utter a word. He pretended he didn't hear, and got up from the table to fetch some ice-cream. Their refrigerator was his mother's idea – she was the first person Jim knew who had thought of it. In their old house she had often been annoyed at having to unpack half the refrigerator to find out what was at the back of the shelves. There was always some food she had overlooked and had to be thrown out. For the enlarged kitchen in the Rosedale house, she had ordered a new refrigerator built to her own specifications: three times as wide as the standard models and half the depth. She could see everything she had as soon as she opened the doors.

"She should have patented her fridge," Jim said gloomily, coming back to the table with a carton of Ben & Jerry's vanilla ice-cream. "You should have had the decency to wait a while longer."

"Wait?! I'm not young enough to wait, Jim, did you think of that? How about 'three cheers, Dad, congratulations!' It doesn't happen every day that a teenage beauty falls in love with a guy pushing fifty."

Jim felt lucky that he had inherited his mother's looks, not his father's. "She loves you?" he asked, trying to suppress his incredulity.

The bridegroom drew himself up triumphantly in the chair. "Absolutely. She loves me like your mother never did. And you know why? I'll tell you why. Because we're equals, that's why." He raised his eyebrows with a significant air. "Jim, my boy, in love you must have equality."

"Good for you."

"You should be overjoyed that your father has found happiness again."

"Well, be happy.... but don't put her into mother's bed. Get a new bed."

"We bought that bed just last year. Why go to unnecessary expense?"

"I'd rather burn the house down, than let you screw another woman in her bed," Jim said with murder in his voice.

"Don't get excited. I'd no idea you'd feel so strongly about it. I'll buy one and have it delivered today. But you come to the wedding and act nice."

That night Jim was shopping with his mother. She told him that he should put the box of chocolate cake back on the shelf. Her voice was full of love, and he obeyed, leaning forwards to put the cake back on the shelf, but when he turned back, expecting her to be pleased, she wasn't there. 'Not again!' he thought. He remembered how she had had left him on the subway platform, and went in frantic search of her. Why was she playing such stupid games? "Mother, you're too intelligent to play hide-and-seek at your age," he muttered.

Jim slept in his T-shirt and it was soaking wet when he woke. He had a bath, attended the wedding and congratulated the couple afterwards - only to find that Penny tossed her head with an injured look whenever their eyes met.

"What's eating her?" Jim asked his father when she went upstairs to change from her wedding dress.

"You shouldn't have threatened trouble if I put her in your mother's bed."

"I said nothing to her. You only told me about her existence yesterday. I had never set eyes on her. I was talking to you."

"Well, I got a new bed, just as I promised," the pharmacist said lamely.

Whenever Jim was in the house, he would spend his time on the top floor. Most nights he was tormented by his nightmares and woke in the morning dead tired. He was the soloist in Dvorák's cello concerto at Hart House and afterwards the applause struck him as forced. What if they didn't renew his scholarship? He lost hope that he would ever improve.

9. BETRAYALS (CONT'D)

And yet, and yet - was this still his father?
KAFKA

With a belated snowstorm on the other side of the thick windows in April, Jim was sitting in his Swedish armchair, reading the score of C.P.E Bach's cello concerto in B flat, when he was surprised by his father. It was the first time Kleermaker had climbed up to the fourth floor. Out of breath from his climb, he sat down.

"Has something happened?" asked Jim.

His father waved away the question. "You go on doing whatever you're doing, Jim. I'll just sit here for a while, catch my breath, and look around. I've never been up here, you know."

"Mother designed it all," Jim said. He went back to the music and was so absorbed by the score that he quite forgot that his father was there.

The pharmacist rested for a while, then got up and went around inspecting his son's lair, turning on all the lights. "Look at this place!" he exclaimed, surprised at how classy and elegant the apartment was. "It's no wonder you don't worry about earning a living. This is a comfort zone, Jim, not the home of a young man who has to make his way in the world. Your mother spoiled you rotten. I've been spoiling you rotten. We should have asked you to contribute to the electricity bill, to the heating, to the stuff in the fridge. That might have made you more practical."

Kleermaker's talk drove away the music and Jim put down the score book. "Do you want me to contribute to the running costs of the house?"

"No, it's too late for that."

"What do you mean?"

Kleermaker sat down again and announced, with the air of a man who wants to get over an unpleasant business as soon as possible. "You make Penny feel awkward and miserable," he said hurriedly. "She doesn't want to live with a stepson who's two years older than she is. She wants you to move out."

It struck Jim as so absurd that he wasn't alarmed. "I hope you told her that this house was bought by your first wife. Mother gave me the top floor and there isn't a thing Penny can do about it."

"It isn't in your name."

"What difference does it make? You know it's mine."

"She's shy, you upset her."

"All right," Jim sighed. "I promise I'll never go to the kitchen downstairs. I have my own kitchen, my own bathroom – she'll never have to see me. That ought to satisfy her."

"She meets you on the stairs."

"Hardly ever."

"She always has to be fully dressed, never knowing when

she'll bump into you. You go out, you come back. You come and go three or four times a day."

"This is my home, for God's sake."

"You had a girl here the other night. Penny doesn't believe in sex outside marriage."

However little affection there was between the two, however often they had insulted each other, they were still family and it got dark by the time Jim understood that his father wanted him to leave. "Dad, I have nowhere to go," he pleaded.

Relieved that Jim didn't start shouting, which was his main worry, the pharmacist softened a little. "Believe me, Jim; I didn't want it to turn out this way. It's your mother's fault. She had no practical sense whatsoever. This joint ownership was her idea; she wanted to compensate me because your grandparents didn't leave me anything. She should have put the top floor in your name before splitting everything else with me. It's her fault. You'd be the legal owner of the apartment and Penny couldn't torment me about it. Your grandfather was smart, thank God - all I had to do was to tell Penny that the old man willed his cello directly to you and she didn't mention it again."

"You're my father."

This opened the floodgates of Kleermaker's own grievances. "You don't even bear my name!" he cried, leaping to his feet. "You don't show me any respect – you're hardly ever polite..."

"I'm sorry."

Seeing his son cowed, his father calmed down. "Well, let's not fight," he said complacently, patting Jim on the back. "As long as you had a comfortable home which cost you nothing, you would have gone on wasting the rest of your life with Bach or whoever. And what for? I saw a lot of musicians around your grandparents – not one of them had a decent car. Not even your grandfather, for all his fame."

"He left a fortune to mother, at any rate."

The pharmacist began to feel his cheeks and jaw. It was a newly acquired nervous habit of his: he was constantly checking whether he needed a shave. "Well, if you think I'm taking your inheritance, talk to a lawyer, but my advice is, stop worrying about your imaginary grievances and grab the chance I'm giving you. Having to leave your comfort zone will do wonders for you, believe me. It'll help you to give up this unprofitable classical shit, so you can find something more rewarding to do before it's too late. I'm connecting you to the real world – no father could do more for you."

"Does Penny want my furniture too?" Jim asked coldly. "I guess it isn't in my name either."

"Don't get paranoid, Jim, don't get paranoid. Poor Penny has no qualifications, she's full of insecurities, she needs to compensate, but she doesn't want your furniture or your records or your books. She understands that what's yours is yours. You can even take your mother's books. 'They are his mother's things, let him have them,' she said. She's a good girl."

"Fine. So I can have my mother's Steinway."

Kleermaker opened his eyes wide, losing his levity. "Well, that's something else. Penny wants to learn to play the piano. She's passionate about it. She saw some old man playing the piano on television and she thinks she could play better.

She's younger; she could hit those keys harder."

"Jesus!"

"Of course, you don't have to leave right away," his father went on hurriedly. "We don't want to send you out into the snowstorm. Penny knows that you need time to find a place, to organize yourself. Besides, I'm not leaving you destitute. Judging by what we got for your grandmother's violin, your granddad's cello must be worth a packet."

"I'll never sell it."

"Well, it's up to you. In the meantime, I'm always here to help you. If you really need something, you won't have to sue me for it. Just don't ask me when Penny can hear you. I'm your father, Jim, I'll always help you on the sly... and not just with cash!" he added, brightening up again. "If you need advice you know where to find me."

"Don't worry, Dad, I'll leave tomorrow. I don't want to crowd your stairs."

The father felt his jaw and cheeks again. "Right now you're upset, it's natural. But in the end you'll thank me for this, I'm sure."

Jim packed all night and left next morning before Penny emerged from their bedroom. His father gave him a handful of hundred dollar bills and let him have his mother's Lincoln Continental. Jim filled the passenger seats and the big boot, and drove to a storage place. When he came back, the pharmacist's Buick was gone, but Penny's smart new Volkswagen was still in the driveway. Using his own keys, Jim collected his hi-fi set. It was heavy. Carrying it down the stairs, he had to stop to catch his breath. The speakers required another climb. He could hear Penny slamming doors, but they didn't run into each other. He made several trips, leaving his clothes for last. When he came back to collect them, he couldn't get into the house. The locks had been changed.

Locked out of his home, Jim continued to go to classes at the Conservatory for a while and earned money busking in the subway and playing solo pieces in restaurants. He spent the nights at friends' homes, getting up early so that he wouldn't be in the way of his hosts, but soon got sick of never having a good night's sleep, of being a guest, a burden. To become good at anything is not a part-time job. He went to the conservatory for tutoring, practised on his own, earned some sort of living and fell into a state of permanent exhaustion.

Why was he killing himself? For what? In his nightmares his mother continued to play games with him. They travelled together, they went to concerts together, and then suddenly she wasn't there. When he woke he thought of death. Would he live long enough to become the musician his grandfather and his mother had hoped for? In the state he was in, he felt he would die young. He chucked it all in - the classes, the busking - and took a regular paid job. The lines his mother had often quoted kept going through his mind:

As long as the world is so vile,
I'll be merciful to myself.

Decades later in Florida, the guilt of giving up what gave meaning to his life helped him to get out bed to drown himself, but at the age of twenty-one it made perfect sense. He wanted some rest and he wanted his own home.

He was given a job by the father of a friend in whose house he was welcome to sleep over, as long as he didn't abuse the privilege. George Robson had all the records of Jim's grandparents and felt sorry for the young man disinherited by the father's young wife. The founder of Continental Office Supplies, George Robson, is still remembered in the trade as the first to add PCs to his stock of typewriters, ink, paper, and office furniture. He thought that Jim was the most intelligent of his son's friends and offered him the job of running his shop on a temporary basis. He meant to keep Jim only until he found the right person, but as it turned out, Jim proved to be the right person. He took to computers and running the company as easily as breathing.

"I can't believe that you had no previous experience in business," Mr. Robson told him.

"Why?"

"You've a head for details."

"Well, I trained as a musician."

Like his grandfather, he was also good at maths, understood computer software and could "play" the PCs. It was a doddle compared to performing a piece of music just right. By June he was manager on a permanent basis with a good salary and had an apartment on the top floor of a house on Waverley Road in the Beaches.

It had a small bathroom and kitchen and a huge single room with a thick glass window covering almost the whole wall facing Lake Ontario. The immense sheet of water spreading to the edge of the horizon was practically part of the room. From late afternoon till sunset, the weekend sailors were out in force every day: their boats criss-crossed the lake and their sails fluttered over the silvery field of water like butterflies. Girls who came to see the handsome young bachelor, offering to cook dinner for him, were enthralled by the view and the cello that stood against the wall beside the music stand. They asked him to play and stayed for the night.

A violinist who ran into Jim in the street asked him why he had dropped out of the Conservatory.

"I want to enjoy life before I'm too old for it," Jim replied defiantly, which is how the young betray their childhood dreams.

10. A CASUAL AFFAIR

One more swivel of my head and you are there!
LESLEY FERGUSON

"If you must meet young men, and I suppose you must, you should stick to art galleries and concert halls," Lesley's father said while driving her to the airport. "Anyone you meet there won't be an absolute ignoramus and is less likely to rape you than someone you'd meet in a bar. If you are lucky, he could be an intelligent boy who brushes his teeth."

Michael Ferguson, a lecturer in English Literature at Glasgow University, a red-haired, freckled Scotsman, loved his daughter for many loving reasons, but also because she was the living proof of the strength of his genes. Lesley Ferguson had red hair and freckled skin, in spite of her mother's olive complexion, passed on by her grandmother from Calcutta who married an officer of the Scots Guards in the days of the British Empire. Lesley's dark eyes, so unusual in a redhead, were the only jewels of her Indian inheritance. Having graduated from her father's university with a first-class degree in English, she was going to start teaching at Carlyle Grammar School in London in the autumn. (In the early 1970s grammar schools were still quite common and graduates didn't need a separate teaching qualification.) Before having to report at the school, Lesley was to spend the month of August in Canada, visiting distant relatives. In love with Shakespeare, great poets and with music, a member of the Glasgow Phoenix Choir, she was thrilled by ideas and all the arts, and had nothing in common with her second cousins in Toronto who lived in a nice big house in Don Mills with three television sets and no books except cookbooks and a book on cats. Lesley hated their mindless lives and could stand it only for a couple of days. She moved to a room at the YWCA in downtown Toronto and took a job as a waitress in a nearby Swiss Chalet restaurant. Looking forward to exciting encounters, she visited the Ontario Art Gallery and the great collection of Chinese art in the Royal Ontario Museum and kept her eyes open even in cafés, but none of the men who tried to pick her up was a reader. Noticing in the *Globe and Mail* that the Casadesus Trio was playing at Massey Hall with the Toronto Symphony Orchestra, she went to the concert.

Jim was also there. He thought of his job as a temporary break from music, not a decisive change of profession. Most days he still played a little and he would never miss a chance to hear great musicians. The Casadesus Trio were playing Mozart's Concerto for Three Pianos, which put the young people in an ardent mood even before they set eyes on each other. Lesley sat two seats to Jim's left in the row ahead of him. From the moment he noticed the redhead, her delicate profile and long, slender neck, his hearing became keener and the sounds acquired greater depth. Feeling a strange sensation on the back of her neck, Lesley kept twisting it until, turning her head, she saw him. Struck by his handsome, expressive face, her dark eyes pierced him with a flash of intense light. She turned away in the next instant but they kept stealing glances at each other while the musicians on the stage sounded all the chords of their hearts. Most of the audience was transformed by the music: whatever they felt, they now felt it more deeply.

"Wasn't it great," Jim said loudly to no one in particular as they were filing out of their rows during the intermission.

"Yes, wasn't it," Lesley echoed.

They were through the first hurdle - they were talking. They talked about the Casadesus Trio: father, mother and son. A few years later, Jean Casadesus, the son, was killed on his way to give a concert in Sudbury, the northern Ontario mining town, when his car skidded on ice. Subsequently the father, Robert Casadesus, died of cancer. Having lost her husband and son, Gaby Casadesus lived out her life teaching and giving solo performances. However, at the time of their Toronto concert the tragic trio had a sunny life. "Imagine what it must be like to spend your life making magnificent music with your family," said Jim as they stood in the foyer. "I used to play sonatas with my mother at home. Her parents were both professional musicians and I never knew a happier couple."

"What instrument do you play?" she asked, fascinated by his fine strong hands hovering about her.

"The cello."

"I used to sing in a choir," she volunteered. "Once I sang in *The Messiah*."

She wore a pale apricot cotton dress with shoestring straps, and Jim gesticulated a lot so that he could touch the soft, creamy freckled skin of her bare shoulders and arms, as if by accident, to avoid arousing opposition. But what opposition? She wished she could grab him by his thick, dark, curly hair and nuzzle him. He asked where the lilt in her voice came from, and she told him that she came from Scotland, from Glasgow. He praised her dark eyes, which got her talking about her Indian grandmother. She was going to Vancouver soon to meet her Indian relatives there, returning to Toronto only to take the plane to Glasgow, then to London. It was at the back of their minds from the start that whatever happened, it would be brief, and they abandoned themselves to each other all the more freely. He knew there wouldn't be enough time to get bored; she knew there wouldn't be enough time to be hurt.

They stood in the crowded foyer with less than a foot between them and as their blood speeded up, they watched its ebb and flow on each other's faces. Alert, their nerves drawn, they were like cats smelling fish, twisting this way and that way, with widening eyes and flaring nostrils, smelling happiness.

Jim offered to drive her down to the lakeshore, to see the moon on the lake. 'Oh, God, let him be bright!' she prayed, as she got into his car.

"Slowly, silently now the moon - Walks the night in her silver shoon," recited Jim as he started the car. *"This way and that, she peers and sees - Silver fruit upon silver trees,"* Lesley continued. They recited the whole Walter de la Mare poem they both had learned at school, each speaking a rhyming

couplet, then the other taking up the next two lines.

"My father likes to recite Swinburne," Lesley said afterwards, when they stopped laughing.

Jim stepped on the brake to avoid a collision. "I don't know much about Swinburne, but a few lines stuck in my mind. *When the hounds of spring are on winter's traces*... I came upon it during one winter, wishing it was spring. I still remember a few lines, I hope. Let's see...

> *For winter's rains and ruins are over,*
> *and all the season of snows and sins...*
> *and in green underwood and clover*
> *blossom by blossom the spring begins."*

This was serious. Had he told her that he owned half of Toronto, she would have been less impressed. If he could quote a poet whose name she had just mentioned, he had to have a vocabulary a lot richer than Basic English. He had to be more than intelligent, he had to be brilliant. He had to have a soul. He had to be one out of millions. She nearly told him that she used to write poems herself. Instead she quoted more Swinburne. Aware that they must be the only people on the road who used poems to sound each other out, they had another high: they shared what set them apart from the others.

Jim's small, neat, clean apartment confirmed all he had told her and all she had hoped for. The cello case with his chair for playing stood in the corner of the living room. Sheet music, scores, records, books covered the walls from floor to ceiling. There was a hi-fi set with speakers, but no television. He led her to the window and they watched the moon's silvery river on the water, swallowed up in the distance by dark waves. When Jim lifted her hair and kissed the back of her neck, she slipped away and settled herself in his Swedish steel-and-leather armchair, asking him to play for her. He played a melody from the Mozart concerto they had just heard. When the cello was put aside, she drew his story from him - his mother's death, the father's remarriage, the loss of his inheritance, and the new wife's insistence that he should leave his mother's house. It is the turning point for most beginners in love:

> ...I did speak of some distressful stroke
> That my youth suffer'd.

Lesley saw the wound in his eyes and longed to heal him. "You know, I was born on the twenty-first of March. My father says that I'll bring spring to everybody's life," she said, burrowing her fingers into his thick, dark, silky hair with a confident smile. She freed him of his nightmares, and she never took the train to Vancouver to meet her relatives and see the Pacific shoreline, with its snow-capped mountains running down to the dark blue sea.

All through August Lesley felt she was the most beautiful woman in the world. She was no longer unhappy about her small breasts. Her mother, a gynecologist, had assured her repeatedly that her breasts were fine. "They're pure lactic glands, with no fatty tissue; that's sexy. When you give birth, you'll have so much milk, you'll nurse the whole ward." But Lesley didn't trust her mother's expertise until Jim went crazy about her breasts. He could almost fit them inside his mouth – one after the other - and loved to massage them with his lips and tongue. And he was thrilled by her erect nipples. It took him no time to persuade her that her mother knew what she was talking about.

In August, thanks to the wide window-wall to the lake, the sun stayed on Jim's bed all afternoon, and it was there that they explored and exhausted each other. They were lying naked on the large crumpled bed facing the open window, when she mentioned that her mother was a gynecologist. "She knows a lot."

Jim was drawing circles around her belly button with his index finger. "Tell me."

"She says that the breasts need exercise just as much as the rest of the body, and next to breastfeeding your baby, the best thing is a lover who sucks your breasts. It improves the blood flow, tones up the tissues, and stimulates the hormones. A woman who has her breasts sucked regularly is unlikely to get breast cancer." She laughed triumphantly like someone who had one less thing to worry about. "And she says the best medicine is preventive medicine."

"If that's the case, we'd better make sure we've done all that's required," Jim said, leaning over to mouth her erect nipples. They ran the whole gamut of bodily pleasures, and he seldom gave her any rest until he fell asleep. She lay beside him and waited for him to wake up. One evening, propped up on her elbow to see her sleeping lover better, she had the sudden urge - for the first time in years – to write a poem. She made it up in her head and next day surprised Jim with a written version.

They were each other's inspiration. Lesley asked him to

play every day, and she was such a rapt audience that she gave him back his confidence. He decided to start saving so that he would have enough to pay the rent even if he quit his job. "It's less than a year since I left the Conservatory, perhaps they would allow me to come back," he told her. "They might even restore my scholarship."

A week before Lesley was supposed to be flying back to Britain, she noticed that her breasts were a little swollen and tingling. 'Could I be pregnant?' she wondered. Her period was overdue. She took a sample of her urine to the drugstore near the restaurant where she worked and they promised her the result for noon the next day, Saturday. Jim's apartment on Waverley Road in East Toronto was nearly an hour's distance by streetcar and bus, and as she worked until midnight, she slept in her room at the YWCA. She stayed there on nights when she worked late and used it to store her things that Jim had no space for.

The result of the test made their whole future crystal clear to her: they were meant for each other. She had always been prepared, except on their unexpected first night, but he had kept withdrawing in time, flooding her belly well above her crotch - and yet, in spite of all their precautions, she got pregnant. It was a sign: it was time for them to settle down. She was almost twenty-one and he was nearly twenty-two. Once she gave birth, she planned to make peace between Jim and his father, convinced that the baby would more than counteract the evil influence of the second wife. She took it for granted that sex couldn't mean a lot to a man of fifty, and that he would much prefer a grandchild he could play with to a mean, young wife. Jim would go back to the Conservatory, financed by his father, and she would be a mother instead of a teacher. She would teach her own child.

She hadn't said anything to Jim beforehand, but as soon as she got the result of the test, she took a taxi straight from the drugstore to Waverley Road. Even so, she arrived hours later than expected. Worse, Jim assumed that she would be flying out of his life in six days. She had no chance to say anything: he began kissing, nibbling and undressing her as soon as she stepped through the door, with the passion of a hungry man who wanted to have his fill before they took the food away. She didn't mind. What better way was there to celebrate?

"I was late because the pharmacy was late," Lesley explained when she finally had a chance to speak. "Yesterday I gave them my pee for testing, and I got the result just before I took the taxi to get here. I'm pregnant." She smiled triumphantly, expecting his cry of joy and a big hug that would take her breath away.

Perhaps if she had told him the news as soon as she arrived, before he had a chance to tear off her clothes, while he was still full of sap and hard courage, he might not have been so frightened of losing his freedom, the love of hundreds of women.

11. HYSTERIA

Beloved, we are always in the wrong,
handling so clumsily our stupid lives...
W.H. AUDEN

Hamlet speaks of his mind's eye, but there is also the mind's ear. All Lesley said was that she was pregnant, but what Jim heard was that his carefree days were over. Nothing new, nothing exciting, nothing unexpected would ever happen to him again. They had been resting, stretched out naked on the bed holding hands, facing the open window, letting the sun and the warm breeze from the lake dry the sweat from their bodies. Jim was breathing in and out, hoping that he had misheard.

"It must have happened the first night," she said snuggling up to him, with a belated tremor of pleasure running through her body. "Isn't it wonderful?"

Now there could be no doubt. He lay prostrate on the bed as before, but he was no longer resting: he couldn't move.

Surprised by his silence, she drew away to search his face. "What's wrong?"

What was wrong? He was having the greatest summer of his life, he couldn't believe his luck, and now it had all turned into a disaster. He had just started to save so that he could go back to music, and now there was going to be someone else he would have to support - a small noisy creature howling for food and attention day and night. That very morning in the supermarket he had been assaulted by the screeching sound of a bundle of rage screaming and wailing in a pram. The prospect of a howling fiend making his home uninhabitable filled him with horror. "We were getting along so well," he said mournfully, with a sigh that could have blown away a heap of leaves. "Everything was so perfect!"

"I thought so too,'" she said, seized by fear.

"This place isn't big enough even for two. Even now, we couldn't manage without your room at the YWCA. We don't have room for your two suitcases and we have room for a child? Where would you put a baby?"

"On my breasts," she answered defiantly.

"Think of the size of the bathroom. The kitchen."

"We could move. The baby could change everything."

"Yes, he could drive me crazy. I'm sorry, Les, I'm just not ready for a screaming baby."

"It would be a peaceful, quiet child, I can feel it."

"You start teaching in London next month."

She began to shiver in spite of the heat. Jim was lying next to her, but he sounded as if he were running away. Leaning over the edge of the bed, she drew up the top sheet from the floor to cover herself. "You told me you wished I wouldn't leave."

"I still do, but your return ticket says you're leaving in six days."

"Well, I guess I'd better hurry then, I mustn't miss my plane," she said, trying to sound sarcastic, but she couldn't stop shivering. Her mother thought she was too smart to have unprotected sex. How could she tell her? And how could she start teaching with a growing belly? And what could she do with a baby on her own? She made an effort to stop her teeth chattering, to sound casual, and twisted her neck as if getting rid of some muscle strain. "I really would like to know what it is that you don't like about me."

"Les, I love everything about you, you're perfect!" Jim said his voice full of misery.

"We might get married," she suggested in a small brave voice.

Jim jumped out of bed and started to dress in front of the window, pretending to watch the boats on the lake, with his back to her - scared that if he looked at her, she could make him do whatever she wanted. "I never said I wanted to marry you."

"You said you loved me."

"That's not the same thing."

"Who cares about getting married? We could live together. You were complaining that you had no family."

"I didn't mean children!" He remained resolutely at the window, facing the lake, denying her with his back. He loved her, yes, but how often had he been in love? In the end he got bored every time. Lesley was perfect, but the world was full of perfect girls! He had already promised to call Abby in September. Abby was a bassoon player and for years they had necked in the dark corners and empty rooms of the Conservatory. He had had too many erections for Abby to leave her out.

"Don't you want children?"

"I want to have lots of children – well, actually, two would be enough – but for God's sake, give me some time. Let me have some fun."

"What do you mean? Aren't we having fun?"

"You're only my eleventh girl friend," he blurted out. He was so distressed, he almost expected her to sympathise. It wasn't even a dozen.

She got out of his odious bed. "You resent that your father isn't a father to you but you don't want to be a father to your own child."

Jim could hear her opening and shutting drawers, but kept his eyes on the lake. "I've tried to be careful," he said sheepishly.

"The only time I wasn't prepared was the evening we met. I didn't expect anything to happen. I didn't foresee that I'd fall for an irresponsible selfish jerk who wouldn't withdraw in time."

"You kissed me first."

She picked up the bound scores of Haydn's cello concertos – a large, heavy book - and threw it at his back. "You can stare out of that window for the rest of your life, as far as I'm concerned. I never want to see you again!"

The sharp pain finally made Jim turn and he was shocked to see that Lesley was shaking so much that it seemed she might break her long fragile neck. She bent down trying to fasten her sandals but didn't have control over her hands. Jim rushed to fasten the straps for her. "I'm sorry, Les. I love you, I love you." He raised and hugged her. "Forgive me. I didn't mean to upset you. We're in this together."

"Oh, God!" She felt as if she had woken from a nightmare and let herself go in his arms; he could feel her heart beating hard against his chest.

"We're just talking, thinking aloud, discussing how to get out of this fix," he said affectionately, relieved that they were all right again. "What do you think? An abortion would be the best solution, wouldn't it?"

Lesley pulled back her head as if he had hit her and pushed him away with such force that he fell on the floor. The freckles on her face stood out against the pallor of her skin. "Just wait," she said in an unearthly voice, "just wait until you're sick. Nobody in the whole wide world will give a damn about you!"

As Jim got up, nursing his elbow, she watched him as if he had turned into a toad. Stung by her revulsion and contempt, he straightened up. "How do I know it's mine?"

She was out of the apartment before he could grab her.

"You know I didn't mean it!" he shouted after her, running down the stairs. When he stepped out to the street, he could see only the back of a taxi: it turned the corner and disappeared. "It was only angry talk," he protested, as if she could still hear him. "You can't just run out on me like that." Massaging his elbow, he went back to the house, arguing with her all the way up the stairs. "I won't be bullied. An embryo is not a child."

Back in the apartment, the unmade bed grabbed his eyes. The mattress still had the hollow of their bodies. The wet spots drying on the crumpled white sheet rekindled the intense sensation of her belly throbbing against his. How she had clung to him! He longed to hold her and turned around to drive to the YWCA and fetch her, but then stopped. He was afraid she would misunderstand. 'She'd think I want to settle down,' he reflected. 'It's much better to let her unwind on her own, and come back when she is in a more reasonable frame of mind.' Deceived by the memory of her joy in his arms, he felt certain she would soon be back. All he had to do was wait.

12. THE MEANING OF DISTANCE

...She sent her memory,
more strong than ten thousand ships of war.
SIR WALTER RALEIGH

It was hard work, waiting. He waited for hours with dwindling hope and crumbling pride. He didn't drink, he ate. He devoured half a dozen cans of unheated spaghetti in tomato sauce. Counting the girls who had given him their phone numbers, he used his fork to draw a strand of spaghetti to the edge of the plate for each girl. The more strands of spaghetti he moved, the lonelier he felt. In the end he fell asleep at the kitchen table.

After a while he slid off the chair and bumped his head on the kitchen floor. It woke him up. Getting to his feet, he walked about the apartment, rubbing his temples as he tried to figure out what was going on. All her clothes were gone from the cupboard, except the pale apricot cotton dress she wore when they met at the Casadesus concert. "This is my number one dress now," she had said, "I fell in love with you in that dress. I'll always wear it on special occasions." And she meant it. She must be coming back. Or was she discarding her lovely dress because she hated him?

In the bathroom he could find no traces of any of her toiletries. They both used her bottle of lavender, so that they would smell the same – but the bottle was no longer there. Their toothbrushes had stood beside each other in the same tumbler and they had used whichever came to hand. Now her toothbrush was gone. Staring at his lonely toothbrush in the tumbler, he felt all alone in the world.

The drawer in which she kept her underwear had only two packs of photos which obliging strangers had taken of them on the beach and in restaurants. Tempted to take a look, he got lost in the photos. Reminded of their happiness, he was happy – until he realized that all the photos were there, and all the negatives. His heart froze. Did she want to forget their summer? Was she trying to wipe any trace of him from her mind? The next drawer gave him hope: her return ticket to Glasgow was still there. She couldn't leave without her ticket; he still had days to put things right.

There was also a lined page torn out of a notebook with her handwriting. After love's labour in the afternoon, he tended to drop off to sleep while they were still skin-to-skin and she used to steal away from the bed without waking him, but often when he woke she was sitting at the edge of the bed watching him and they kissed with their eyes. It had to be on one of those occasions that she had made up her poem. She had written it on the lined page, in her clear round letters drawn with a blue ballpoint pen.

Still as a new-born, curled in the dawn of his days,

My love lies sleeping, all life's battles banished
For a little time. Another world
Claims your meandering spirit. Am I there?
Dare I touch your hand, scatter your dreams
To be with you? It is a separate joy
To watch and not to kiss and kiss again
Those soundless lips, to rein in my tongue
From whispering in unhearing ears, 'I love you!'
Sleep on, my love, and I shall be content
To tend my vigil, taking comfort from the gentle swell
Of your breath, waiting and waiting
For one flicker of your lashes to announce
That we are one once more in one world.

He had read it when she had first shown him, but now read it over several times, with shame and growing conviction that no girl had ever loved him so much and no girl ever would. He drove to the YWCA while it was still dark.

The caretaker of the YWCA, an enormous Jamaican woman, couldn't sleep but was lying in bed and endured the ringing and banging for some time, hoping that whoever was making all that frantic noise would get tired and go away. But the ringing didn't stop. She raised her heavy body from the bed with a groan, put on her pink chenille housecoat, shuffled to the entrance, unbolted the door and opened it halfway, breathing heavily from the effort. Squeezing the pain in her thigh that had kept her awake, she asked the young man whether he knew what time it was.

"I know and I'm sorry. Could you please wake up Miss Ferguson, it's urgent."

"She gone. She fly home last night."

"I mean the Lesley Ferguson from Glasgow. The Scottish

girl."

"She fly home."

"She couldn't have flown anywhere, I have her return ticket," Jim retorted, but even as he said it he remembered that her passport wasn't in the drawer.

"You is her boyfriend? You promise to drive her to the airport? She sit by this door on one of her suitcases. I tell her she must be uncomfortable, I have an armchair in the back room, she say no, her boyfriend might come. She wait and wait and take a taxi in the end. She say she sick of Canada."

Jim turned without thanking her for her bad news and ran to his car.

"Hey, mister!" she called after him. "Your manners!"

Jim started the car and pressed his foot down on the pedal. At dawn on Sunday, downtown Toronto seemed like a ghost town in the semi-darkness. The buildings were silent, nothing was moving. The traffic lights kept changing eerily on the deserted streets as he drove, gripping the wheel. If only he had gone to the YWCA while she was still waiting for him. Now they had the whole Atlantic Ocean between them. Though just then distance didn't matter. Remembering her wounded eyes, the sensation of her heart beating violently against his chest, he shot through a red light and was hit by a *Globe and Mail* truck speeding across an intersection on green. The truck hit the Lincoln Continental sideways, just a few inches in front of the windscreen on the driver's side. Those few inches made the difference between life and death. Had the truck hit the Lincoln Continental behind the windscreen, pushing the car door into Jim's body, he would have been crushed beyond repair. But the truck smashed only the front wing and bonnet, spun the car around and deposited it on the sidewalk.

The garage would take two weeks to fix his car; the hospital let Jim go by noon. The X-rays showed that nothing was actually broken. His cracked ribs were taped, his cuts and bruises cleaned and covered. Shaken and dizzy, he ached all over, but the doctor gave him some pills and assured him that he would heal.

Reaching home, Jim dialled the Bell Canada operator for the Glasgow number that would be on his next bill. (Lesley had phoned her parents from his place several times.) He longed to hear her voice, to make peace. "Lesley's in Toronto," her father said. "You might reach her at the YWCA, or you could leave a message at her friend's place. His name is Jim Taylor. I'll get his number for you, wait a second."

Jim looked at his watch: it was past one o'clock in the afternoon. They were five or six hours ahead of him in Glasgow, so it had to be early evening there. Clearly Lesley hadn't gone home, and her parents knew nothing. Doodling on a piece of paper, Jim wondered what he could say to the father. 'I knocked up your daughter and we had a fight. She should be with you by now. When you see her, would you mind sending her back to Toronto?' When the father came back on the line to tell him how he could reach Lesley's boyfriend, Jim stopped drawing circles, wrote down his own name and number, thanked Professor Ferguson profusely and replaced the receiver.

Next morning he went to work. Continental Office Supplies, which became a chain of stores, was the first in Canada to make PCs the main feature of their Christmas sales, and Jim was in charge of all the preparations, including training sales staff how to use computers and how to explain them to customers. He was surprised how easily he himself mastered PCs, but teaching others drained him. At the time computers were new even for the young and many of the salesmen weren't interested. Poor Les, Jim thought, did she have any idea what was involved in teaching? By the time he left the office late in the afternoon he had a huge headache. With his car in the garage for repair, he walked several miles to get home, hoping to clear his head and relax. It seemed that the babies of Toronto conspired to mock Jim. All the little fiends whose prams rolled by within his hearing were amazingly contented and good-natured. None of them cried.

Reaching his street, he passed a Chinese couple who were just unpacking their car. They lived only a few houses farther up from him, they knew each other by sight, and the wife called out to Jim. "Look, Jasmine likes you."

Jasmine, about a year old, had impossibly black hair and eyes. They left her standing on her own feet for a moment and she started out toward Jim with unsteady steps, smiling and waving her tiny fat hands at him. The father laughed as he picked her up. "It seems Jasmine would like to play with you." He went ahead, carrying his daughter, leaving his wife to lock the car and bring the groceries. Jim jumped to take her shopping bags, but she said they were light. He didn't insist. He didn't want her to think that he wanted to play with Jasmine. He would have his own child to play with.

The memory of Lesley's look of revulsion and contempt for suggesting that she should abort their baby filled him with loving pride. His chest and his cracked ribs from the car crash were still sore, but with an involuntary gesture he massaged his elbow, which had been hurt when Lesley had pushed him to the floor. 'What a strong character,' he thought, 'she's going to be a great mother.' Looking at the date on his watch, Jim saw that Lesley would be home even according to her original return ticket, so he called the Glasgow number again. Her mother picked up the phone. She thought that even if this Jim and her daughter had broken up, he should have a chance to talk to her. She told Jim that Lesley had flown to London and was staying with two other girls in her cousin's house in St. John's Wood. She gave Jim their phone number. 'I'll tell her that I was in the wrong but I've paid for it,' he decided. 'I nearly got killed, my car's a wreck, and my insurance is going up. That should soften her a little.' When he called Lesley he got the answering machine. Conscious that her housemates were likely to hear him, and reluctant to share his feelings with strangers, he did his best to sound cool. "This is for Lesley from Jim. Hi. You left your apricot dress behind. And some photographs. Call me with your address and I'll send them back. I'd also love us to have a chat. Don't worry about the cost. Just reverse the charges. Here's my number: double zero, one, four-one-six, four-six-one, twenty seven, twenty three. Cheers."

Lesley didn't call back. He called every day and was greeted by the answering machine.

13. GIRLS TALKING

They talked secrets late into the night.
BRIGID BROPHY

Lesley's cousin, Kate Rome, a bouncy woman with lots of bursting laughs in her, the deputy manager of one of London's grand hotels, shared her heavily mortgaged house and the costs with two other girls and Lesley. They were sitting on the leather sofa in the living room, occasionally getting up to go to the bathroom or to the kitchen for a bite or to fill up their glasses with red wine, and were discussing Jim's messages. Kate had been arguing that Lesley left Toronto in too much of a hurry. "Probably Jim was frightened by the idea of having to grow up. Many men are like that. They'd like to stay kids forever and they don't want competition from another baby. You should have given him time to get used to the idea of fatherhood."

The French windows were facing their garden and Lesley stared unseeingly at the ash tree, illuminated by the lights from the room. She remembered sitting on her big suitcase in the YWCA's hallway, waiting for Jim, convinced that he wouldn't let her leave Toronto. "I gave him forever to change his mind," she said bleakly.

Kate sipped her drink thoughtfully. "Perhaps he needed even longer. He still wants to talk to you."

"Yes, he wants me to get rid of his child. He hates babies crying. But how could a baby let you know if something is wrong if she can't cry?"

"He wouldn't have called if he didn't care for you," Kate persisted. "Talk to him – it costs nothing. He told you to reverse the charges."

"I did talk to him. He wants to have more girlfriends before settling down."

"Kate, you have priority as a relative, so I've kept my peace so far," interjected Jackie, a husky-voiced brunette from New York, a Columbia graduate in economics and a trainee in the city. "I don't think you should badger her to have anything more to do with that guy."

Kate ignored Jackie's remark and turned to her cousin. "Why wouldn't you talk to Jim? I don't get it. Who knows, he might have had a change of heart. What if he's willing to move to England?"

Lesley's hurt was still the most real thing for her. "Once I told him that I was pregnant, he turned into a monster. He said all sorts of abominable things. Anyway, he'd never leave Canada. It's quite funny, considering his background, but he's an old-fashioned Canadian nationalist."

"Would you go back to Toronto if he asks you? You said you liked the city."

Margaret, a tall, placid Indian girl who was studying medicine, urged Lesley to think. "Whether you make up with this Jim or not, my advice is you should wait until you know him better before committing yourself to a long-term relationship, let alone having his baby."

Even Kate agreed with that. Their most profound experience of men was disappointment and they wanted to protect Lesley from grief.

Lesley sucked in her lips and pressed them tightly together. She had bitten her lips since early childhood, whenever readying herself for a fight. "I'll have the baby, but I won't have anything more to do with him."

"Are you going to start your first job with a growing belly?"

"Why not? I wouldn't be the first."

"Grammar schools demand a lot from teachers," Margaret said. "If you're due in April, you'll be absent during the preparation for the exams."

Jackie came back from the kitchen with another glass of cheap Burgundy which she held up to take command of the conversation. "Girls, girls!" As they all looked at her, she continued with a serious face. "As you probably know, Manhattan's a big rock, infested with cockroaches. Cockroaches are a big annoyance to everybody. They're disgusting. So we had to learn how to get rid of them. Do you know how to get rid of cockroaches?"

"How?"

Jackie burst out laughing. "You ask them for commitment."

It was a new joke for Londoners and they smiled, except for Lesley. She winced and decided she didn't like Jackie. Jackie went on to tell them about her latest affair. She lent her credit card to her boyfriend so that he could pay his parking fine on time, without having to pay more. He paid the fine and handed back her card with thanks, without mentioning that he had also bought a pair of gold cufflinks, a pair of crocodile skin shoes, an Omega watch and a camera. "When I got the statement and saw that he had spent over £1800 on my card, I asked him when he would pay me back. I asked him very sweetly when we were in his bed, but the bastard was shocked. He claimed I gave him my card for the day as a gift. I didn't spell it out that he could use it *only* to pay the fine. He was so shocked that I wanted him to return what I had given him as a gift that he asked me to dress and leave. He didn't want to have anything more to do with me. How is that for brass? Failing to use the word *only* is costing me a small fortune. He's a currency trader, works in the same building, and still nods when he sees me in the elevator, as if I were some very distant acquaintance whose name he can't quite remember. We were together for months."

"Do you nod back?" asked Kate.

"No, I don't. He's a thief. And he earns a lot more than I do."

This cautionary tale increased the girls' concern for Lesley. Although Kate had tried to persuade Lesley to make up with Jim, she now swung to Jackie's opinion and they all turned against him. Listening to their hostile comments Lesley realized that none of them had any idea how handsome Jim was and how happy they had been.

"Lesley, you have to make a choice right now and stick to it," Margaret said. "A: you keep the baby. B: you give it up for adoption."

Lesley sprang up from the sofa. "How can you imagine that I would give up my child and spend the rest of my life wondering what she was doing? You're all so morbid."

Margaret had already learned to be patient with patients. "Well, then your only option is option C. You get rid of it. The point is that you have to decide right away. It's not two weeks since you discovered that you are pregnant. At this stage the embryo's unlikely to feel anything. But the later you leave it, the more problematic it is, both for you and the embryo."

"What if you give birth and then you meet the right guy?" asked Kate. "Most men would be put off by another man's child. Being a young single mother with a demanding job would be hard. I can't think of anything which would limit your life-choices so much. And in twenty years' time you'll be an aging forty-one-year-old. If you hadn't left Toronto in such a hurry, you could at least have found out whether he's willing to pay child support."

'Kate's right,' thought Lesley despairingly. 'Even when everything goes wrong, I should be able to reason.' She didn't mind Kate because she felt that Kate wanted the best for her. But she wished Jackie would shut up; her condescending voice grated on her nerves.

Jackie meant to be helpful, but it was impossible for her to forget that she was super-smart and Lesley was a girl who still had a lot to learn. "I don't think that you need to agonize about your predicament. Just relax and have another glass of wine. Abortion isn't a big deal. But having a child without a father is a career-breaker."

Kate agreed. "Jackie makes sense. Some women have a couple of abortions and then go on to have children when everything's just right."

Lesley got up and started walking back and forth in the room to calm herself. "I'll have my child and we'll manage. Stop, stop, you're just upsetting me."

It seemed that the girls couldn't stop talking even if they wanted to. They weren't immune to men's charms and they discussed Lesley's predicament as a problem they, too, might face one day. They were calling up stories of other girls who found themselves unexpectedly pregnant, and they kept interrupting each other, if only to repeat themselves. What silenced them was the ringing of the phone, and they waited for the answering machine to kick in.

Jim sounded angry. "Really, Lesley. You should take the trouble to return my calls. If you reversed the charges, it wouldn't cost you anything. Goodbye."

The girls looked at Lesley expectantly. She sat down again but said nothing.

"Well, he clearly has a temper," Jackie commented. "This guy kicked you in the stomach. The question is whether you want him to kick you again."

'You're unhappy, so you don't believe I can be happy either,' Lesley thought.

"Trust me," Jackie said with the passionate conviction of personal experience. "Guys never improve, they only get worse. Shits never turn into tiramisu. And remember..." She paused and her face became quiet solemn. She looked at each of her roommates, to make sure that they were listening. "Orgasms are lovely, but they're not the source of wisdom."

Lesley's freckles grew bright red. "Isn't there anything on television you want to watch? I'll be all right. I'll have my

92

child and we'll manage."

She used up her courage by thinking about all the difficulties she would have to overcome. Her reason said she should have an abortion, but she liked the feeling of the new life growing inside her and was reluctant to do anything. It was always the next day that she would decide. She was often tempted to call Jim, but she was afraid to trust him again and then find herself betrayed and abandoned.

14. THE APRICOT DRESS

She hath resolved and judged thee long ago.
SIR WALTER RALEIGH

Jim's first waking thought was that Lesley hadn't called back. "If you don't love me, I don't love you," he muttered aloud even before he opened his eyes. She hadn't called him back for over a week. He wasn't going to run after a woman who didn't want him. Angry pride sprang him out of bed and he opened the window to let in the fresh air.

There wasn't a cloud in the sky. It was a bright-blue, warm mid-September morning, a Saturday and the sailboats were crowding the lake. He watched the familiar spectacle as they crisscrossed the water. He had been watching them with Lesley, her head resting on his shoulder. Well, that was past history. He thought of Abby.

"I thought you would never call." Abby was surprised and delighted. "I'd love to come."

Jim wished Lesley had listened in and heard how welcome his phone calls were to another girl.

"It'll be a new experience, seeing you in your home," she said. "Do you realize that so far the only places we've ever

94

been near each other were nooks and crannies? All we had were snatched seconds."

"Minutes."

"My dear Jim, we've never had anything out of each other but frustration. I was in constant fear of someone opening the door on us."

"That's why you must come. You simply must see my fantastic front door."

"What's so fantastic about it?"

"That door has three locks and we can lock them all. There's a bell, but hardly anybody ever rings and if somebody does, we don't have to hear it."

Abby promised to come by in a few hours with her bassoon and asked him to find some good sheet music that they could play together.

As he replaced the receiver, Jim was cheered by the excitement in Abby's voice. He spent the morning looking for a Vivaldi concerto for two cellos. (The scores for the cello are the same as for bassoons.) Once he found a likely piece, it struck him that he had been thinking only of Abby's skills as a bassoon player and not of her skills as a kisser. 'Abby's gorgeous, I invited her, and I'm not keen,' he thought with amazement. He tried to recall his lust when he pressed his fingers into her flesh, but it made him long all the more for Lesley's small buttocks he could fit into his hands. But what was the use? Lesley had gone, Abby was on her way and he was not going to give up sex at the age of twenty-two.

When he opened the door, he greeted Abby with a cheery welcome, helped her off with her coat, hugged her and they kissed, but they were both relieved that they planned to play music first. Abby was a brilliant musician and Vivaldi gave them a chance to get used to each other again. Eventually they ended up on the bed playing their own music with their bodies. There were moments when Jim felt he would forget Lesley in no time. But when Abby left, the prospect of life without feeling Lesley's absence seemed to him worse than missing her. He would rather be miserable than forget her. The friendly affair with Abby lasted about a month. He thought every day of Lesley's amused smile as she watched him devouring three pieces of stuffed pepper and a dozen fresh Hungarian pancakes without any filling in Coffee Mill. He could almost hear her teasing voice. "If it wasn't for your extraordinary metabolism, you'd weigh two hundred pounds, instead of being slim and handsome." Dwelling on her loving flattery he felt more alive, but felt worse.

When he managed to pull himself together and started phoning her again, he could never get past the answering machine. One evening in the last week of October, when he was preparing for the Christmas display of computers, he worked past midnight in the office. Getting home, he thought of calling Lesley, but remembering that at one a.m. it would be only six in the morning in London, he decided to call in the afternoon. If he hadn't worried about calling too early, he might have talked to Lesley before she left for the abortion clinic.

It was only after coming out of the anaesthetic at the clinic that Lesley knew for certain that she shouldn't have done it. A nurse, who was there only because she needed a job, helped her to put on her overcoat and was spiteful enough to risk being fired to whisper into her ear: "It would have been a strong, healthy boy."

Lesley felt so low that when she got home she called her mother and told her everything.

Dr. Martha Ferguson was outraged. "I don't believe it, I don't believe it! I can't believe that I have an idiot for a daughter. I'm a gynaecologist. Surely your mother was the ideal person to ask for advice? I'll never forgive you for not consulting me."

"I didn't consult you because I knew you would want me to keep the baby."

'You're damn right,' her mother thought. The poor child had reason on her side. She was tempted to ask her how many weeks she had been pregnant, as in her experience girls with late abortions had fewer chances to give birth successfully later. But why worry her when it was too late? "Well," she sighed, "there's no point in grieving about it now. Let's not tell your father."

It was a ghastly experience, but it was over. Lesley felt relieved. There was nothing more to decide, all she had to do was forget it.

The phone rang. Jim had hardly said a few words to the answering machine when Lesley picked up the receiver. She didn't mind talking to him now: he couldn't hurt her any more.

"How are you, Les?" he asked.

"I'm fine," she said dryly.

"Are your friends listening?"

"It's Saturday night. They're out for the evening. I'm alone in the house." She sounded depressed, miserable and Jim's heart swelled with triumphant happiness: she missed him. "I wish I was there and I could just drop by," he said.

"I'm glad you're far away."

"Don't be mad at me, Les. Just give me your address and I'll send the ticket. I'll get us an apartment right here in the Beaches. With a big kitchen, a big bathroom, a room for the kid, and with the same fantastic view. Remember, you loved the lake. It'll be nice for the kid too, running up and down the boardwalk."

"That's typical macho talk. This is my first teaching job – I've prepared for it for years, I just started – and you expect me to throw it away and rush to you at the other end of the world on your say-so. You don't even ask. You just assume I would throw away all my studies, leave my job, my parents, my country, and fly to Toronto on your say-so. Did you ever consider how much you're asking me to give up? I'm sure not. You don't really care how I feel."

"I couldn't ask you how you felt about anything, because I could never talk to you. That's why I left messages."

"I can't imagine why you bothered."

"I bothered because you never called me back."

"And you didn't know how I felt?"

The hate in her voice was piercing; he had to take a deep breath to recover enough to speak. "All right, Les, you're upset, I'm upset, but you know I didn't want us to break up."

"You certainly fooled me."

"I'm sorry, I was stupid. And I'm sorry you left your apricot dress behind."

"Why?"

"You were wearing that dress when we first met. If you

had it with you, you might remember that we fell in love."

"Give it to Oxfam."

It occurred to Jim that her hostility might be just a symptom of her condition. "Do you feel the baby kicking?" he asked, his voice losing its edge. "Or is it too early for that?"

"It's none of your business. You didn't want a child."

"Are you all right?"

"Why shouldn't I be all right?" she asked belligerently.

"You sound awful. Do you feel weak?"

"Yes, I do. We talked long enough. I want to lie down."

"Can you have morning sickness in the evening?"

She sounded annoyed. "What morning sickness? Why should I have morning sickness?"

"What do you mean?"

"I did what you wanted."

Jim was speechless with horror. How could she have done it?

15. VENTURING ABROAD

It had become more important to him than his livelihood or his career, he could not rest until he knew where it would end.
SEBASTIAN FAULKS

The snow leopards of the Himalayas roam the barren mountains where they were born rather than descend a few thousand feet into the fertile jungle teeming with easy prey. They are tied to their native slopes with an instinct stronger than hunger. Like a snow leopard, Jim was bound to his home ground. He had no intention of becoming a foreigner who didn't belong anywhere. It was as a Canadian from Toronto that he knew who he was – or where he was, whichever street he happened to be on. All the family he loved was here: his mother and her parents were buried in Mount Pleasant Cemetery; now they were natives too, part of the soil. Here were his roots. The world was full of refugees: he was proud of being born in a country where it was possible to stay put. He assumed that he would see the world one day in the vague future, but he hadn't yet got around to applying for a passport. He could no more imagine abandoning his native land than moving to another planet.

Nevertheless, he spent Sunday going through his

possessions. What were the things he had to pack, the things he couldn't live without even for a short while? On Monday morning he went to the passport office. There was a problem: the name on his birth certificate was James Kleermaker, while his driving licence and all his other documents identified him as James Taylor. They had to find the registration of his change of name at the age of nine. It was almost noon when he got to work. The salesmen from Hamilton and Kitchener had been waiting for him; he was supposed to teach them about the use of PCs.

"So you finally showed up," observed his boss with heavy disapproval. George Robson, the middle-aged owner of the chain, with thin brown hair, wide forehead and alert blue eyes, took work very seriously, he even dressed for it. He was wearing a light rust-coloured summer jacket with leather elbow patches; a cupboard in his office was full of such working jackets for every season. "The salesmen have been waiting for you since early morning, wasting their time and my money." When Jim told him that he was quitting, Robson's face turned red with anger. "Are you angling for a raise?"

"You pay me well, Mr. Robson, I like it here, but I have to go to London."

"Why? Do you think you'll get a better job in London?"

Canadians, citizens of the British Commonwealth, used to have the same rights in Great Britain as those who had been born there and Jim might have hoped to get a better job in London, but he shook his head. "No, it isn't that."

"Then what is it?" Robson asked, getting impatient. "What's in London that we don't have here?"

"The girl I want to marry."

"Why don't you ask her to come here?"

"She's a teacher and she can't leave until the end of the school year."

"Well then, she certainly can wait until after the Christmas sales," Robson said firmly. "If you're going to get married, you'll need every cent. You're due a bonus for the year. And then there's the separate bonus for the Christmas sales. I'm sure your intended will appreciate this and she'll wait until I find somebody who understands computers."

"She isn't keen on me."

"Who isn't keen on you?"

"The girl I want to marry."

Robson closed his eyes for a moment, thinking of his own incomprehensible son. "Then why are you going?"

"I'll try to change her mind before she forgets me."

"What nonsense!"

"I'll bring her back to Toronto," Jim added hastily. "I'll back as soon as possible."

Robson tried to reason with Jim, wanted him to think it over, but in the end he grew weary. "So how much longer can I count on you?"

"I'll be here today – I'll leave the files in order, and I'll help those two salesmen as much as I can – but this has to be my last day. I need to get the documents to get my passport, I'll have to move out of the apartment I'm renting, sell my car..."

"If you leave today, don't expect to work for me again," Robson interrupted him. "And don't count on getting any money you think we might owe you."

"I'm leaving without notice, so that's fine. You've helped

me when I needed it most, and I'm grateful."

"Well, it'll teach me not to take in stray dogs," Robson sighed, dismissing him with a wave of his hand.

Before going to the airport, Jim went to Mount Pleasant Cemetery to say goodbye to the only family he had. He stood by their graves, occasionally touching the bark of the silver linden tree, as if his mother and grandparents were still alive and they were having a conversation. Like many affectionate families, they had been in the habit of touching each other frequently, even when discussing the most prosaic subjects, to express their constant love.

A young gardener at the cemetery, Roberto, had agreed to watch the graves, to keep them free of cigarette butts and other rubbish, to buy his mother's favourite flowers, a bunch of white lilies, and replace them as soon as they withered. Jim paid him in advance for a year, and Roberto gave Jim his address and phone number so they could keep in touch.

On a bright September evening he boarded a propeller plane at Toronto's Malton Airport for London. His two trunks in the cargo hold were filled mostly with sheet music, full scores, records and books which were no longer available and couldn't be easily replaced. Each trunk bore a large sticker of the maple-leaf flag. Jim didn't want to part from his grandfather's cello, and as the airline wouldn't accept it as hand luggage, he had to buy a full priced ticket for it, made out to "Mr. Cello." The plane wasn't full and Jim travelled comfortably with Mr. Cello, even in tourist class. They had a whole row by the window to themselves. The precious instrument was covered with Lesley's apricot dress and its bulky case, too, was adorned with a sticker of the maple-leaf flag. Mr. Cello and Jim had open return tickets valid for a year, but he hoped to bring Lesley back to Canada much sooner. As the plane took off, he repeated to himself his new mantra: 'She hates me now, but she won't hate me for long.'

Jim's prejudices about English weather were confirmed on arrival. He lost the clear night-blue sky with dawn breaking at the edge of the horizon as soon as the plane descended into the clouds and landed at Heathrow. There wasn't a sliver of blue above, just a giant blanket of dirty clouds. 'Our children will be better off living in Toronto,' he thought.

Truths are constantly forgotten and rediscovered, which is why history is not a straight downward slide to hell, but a rollercoaster. At the time the whole world believed that the strongest bond between nations was language, not geography. The immigration official, detecting Jim's Canadian accent, hardly looked at his passport.

Jim left his trunks in storage at the airport. It was still possible to leave one's baggage behind; travellers hadn't yet started carrying bombs in their suitcases. Taking the bus to London, Jim carried only his cello and deposited it at a bed & breakfast place near Victoria Station, then walked to Hortensia Road off the King's Road to get the numbness of the night flight out of his muscles. By 8.30 in the morning, he was standing on the pavement opposite Carlyle Grammar School trying to spot Lesley among the hurrying passers-by - mostly students - intent on reaching school before the bell rang. He recognized her from the way she walked as soon as she turned into street. As she got nearer, the sight of her grim face filled him with joy. She missed him!

"Hi, Les."

Halted by surprise, Lesley shook her head, as if wishing to rid herself of an apparition, and walked on. Jim followed her, talking quickly, telling her that he had quit his job, had given up his apartment, sold his massive hi-fi set, the Swedish armchair she liked, the Lincoln Continental. He had sold pretty well everything that could be turned into money for the plane fare to see her. "And I asked more than a dozen passers-by on the way to the school," he added, his voice trailing off, as she didn't respond. She ignored him as people ignore beggars to whom they have already given more than they could afford.

"Let's have dinner, Les," Jim suggested, "and let's get married."

Quickening her steps, she hurried ahead and went through the school gates before he could catch up. He watched her walk through the gravel courtyard and disappear into the building. Jim spent hours standing at the gate and was still there when she came out and headed for the bus stop. He kept in step with her, and lowered his voice. "We'll put it right. The new baby will be strong and healthy. It won't be an accident. I'll give it my all."

They were both listening to their own hearts beating as they walked silently side by side. The bus came to a halt just as they got there. Jim moved aside to let her go first. She stepped on the bus, but then suddenly stepped back on the pavement and turned toward him with alarm. "Did you sell your cello too?!"

Jim's face lit up and they made peace with their eyes.

They were in love: each felt guilty and each felt the other was innocent.

16. LUKE (CONT'D)

Nothing unites two hearts so much
as the pleasure of crying together.
ROUSSEAU

Having lost and found each other, they rented a tiny apartment on the Fulham Road, near Lesley's school. She continued teaching and Jim earned money by busking in Underground stations. Paradise is being young, in love and in the same bed, letting go without any restraint or tiresome precautions. They longed for their child. "Love, you're giving me the most fantastic birthday present," was the way she told him that she was pregnant again. It would be difficult to say which was greater, their joy or their relief. They fell in love with their baby while he was still in the womb. Their GP sent Lesley to St Mary's Paddington where she became one of the first patients for the testing of a new diagnostic device, an ultrasound scanner. Jim went with her and they were led to a windowless white room with the scanner, a television screen and an examination table. Lesley lay down, opened her blouse, pushed down her trousers and a nurse spread Vaseline over her belly. Jim felt uneasy about the male technician but there was nothing he could do about it. As the scanner was turned on and the overhead light dimmed several doctors and nurses came into the room, curious to see how this new equipment worked.

The live broadcast from inside Lesley's womb made Jim feverish. Looking into the mysterious cauldron of human existence, and thinking that he was seeing what he himself must have been like before he was born, he had the humbling sensation of being a link in the infinite chain of generations. Lesley had this sense in her veins, but it was new to Jim. Awed, elated, he gaped at the fantastic creature on the screen. It looked like an alien in its own space capsule: its head was almost as big as the rest of its tiny body. The foetus was only twelve weeks old, but the doctors could already tell that it was perfectly normal and healthy and would be a boy. Jim expected it to be inert in the foetal position, but it was actually waving its arms about and - most amazing - seemed to be doing a somersault. The plucky creature was showing off for them, doing exercises, getting ready for life. Once the numbing shock of the first moments wore off, Lesley gave a squeal of joy. Unable to restrain himself, Jim welcomed his offspring, shouting, "Hello, hello!" The men laughed; the women found nothing odd about his greeting.

As the triumphant couple were leaving the hospital, they decided to name the boy Luke after Lesley's Scottish grandfather. Now all Jim needed was a regular salary. His father, who was convinced that Jim had been wasting his time with classical music, no doubt would have been shocked if he knew that Jim got a good job thanks to Johann Sebastian Bach. A Microsoft executive from Seattle visiting London, a keen amateur oboe player, heard Jim playing one of Bach's suites in the Charing Cross underground labyrinth and stopped to listen. Impressed, he invited his fellow amateur for a coffee and they had a talk. Having seen a fair pile of coins in Jim's cello case but only a couple of small notes, the executive got him a job at Microsoft's London office which had just opened but was growing rapidly. Jim acquired a steady income with good prospects of promotion.

In the evenings, while Lesley sat at the table preparing for the next day's classes or correcting students' essays, Jim played Bach, Boccherini, Haydn and Mozart tunes, hoping his son was listening in the womb, growing brighter and more musical. He had read reports that some hospitals in the USA and Canada fed eighteenth-century music into maternity wards on the assumption that it stimulates the growth of intelligence. The couple married at Fulham Town Hall before Lesley's figure changed much.

Jim felt a stranger at his own wedding. The Registrar's office was crowded with Lesley's family. The door couldn't be closed because her relatives filled the waiting room as well. Twenty-four Fergusons came from Glasgow by plane or car: her parents, her aunts, her uncles and her cousins – plus wives, husbands, boyfriends, girlfriends. One uncle flew in from Dublin. There were also five Fergusons who worked in London and they didn't want to miss her wedding either. Kate was her bridesmaid. Jim's best man was his colleague at Microsoft, Jeremy Norton, whom he hardly knew. His mother, his maternal grandparents were dead, his father had locked him out – he had no family. The Fergusons embraced him, but his grim face didn't register their smiles and good wishes. The Ferguson tribe was alarmed. They thought that

Jim was regretting the marriage even before going through with it. They didn't want their Lesley to marry a guy who didn't seem to be keen on her. The parents were bombarded with questioning looks. Someone was heard to whisper in an undertone: "She still could stop it, it isn't too late." Lesley alone understood. She leaned over to whisper into Jim's ear: "Luke's here for you."

Her parents gave the crowd a wedding feast by renting an Italian restaurant, and under the table Lesley brought Jim's hand to her belly, to remind him that he, too, had a family.

Born in his sixth month, the baby was put in intensive care. The doctors allowed the parents to touch him. Jim held his hand and Lesley held his eyes: their eyes locked and she tried to infuse in him the will to live. Luke survived for nearly two days, forty-two hours.

After Luke's death Lesley's mother was seized by the kind of parental anxiety that drives grownup children to despair. "He'll go back to Canada," she kept saying, trying to prepare her daughter for the worst. "It's the best thing that could happen to you, believe me. You're still young; you'll find a better man in no time." Jim wanted to go back to Canada, but not alone. Lesley's first year at the school was ending and, as they were preparing dinner in their kitchen, looking at the brick wall across from the kitchen window, Jim suggested it was just the right time to leave. "Moving back to Canada would shake us up a bit," he said. "What do you think? We'd have an apartment in the Beaches and eat our pesto pasta looking at the sparkling lake. That would beat the view of the brick wall."

"You said there's more great music here," she said defensively. "I get pregnant so easily, I'm bound to get pregnant again soon. Let's stay until I give birth. I want my parents to see their grandchild before we disappear to the other side of the Atlantic."

Jim tried to persuade her that she would be happier by the lake, but in the wake of Luke's death, he had no heart to persist. "I only wish I hadn't paid for those expensive return tickets," he complained and called the Mount Pleasant gardener, Roberto, telling him that he was sending more money and warning him that their return had been delayed till "next year". Next year Lesley got pregnant again, but the embryo miscarried. The loss, the pain, the guilt bound them together. They clung to each other as shipwrecked people cling to a wooden plank on the wide sea. Some eighteen months later she got pregnant again and they agreed that they would return to Toronto after the baby was born and Lesley's parents had seen their grandchild. She miscarried in the fifth month and lost a great deal of blood. They often felt like one body, but their union had no living proof. Lesley conceived nothing but despair.

Millions would go mad with grief if they weren't saved by their daily tasks. Lesley had a teacher's overload of preparing her lessons, teaching, attending meetings, correcting essays, writing reports. She had two more miscarriages. Jim buried himself in computer software, which he found easy to understand and play with. Building software is not unlike playing chess; there are so many combinations to think of that there is no room left in the brain to think of anything else. Work was escape. At the computer for 10-12 hours day, he developed into a brilliant programmer and was promoted repeatedly. Yet in spite of his success at work and his rising salary, he felt unsettled and rootless and kept sending money to the gardener of Mount Pleasant Cemetery, with a note saying that they would be back next year.

17. LADY MARGARET

...and there begins my sadness.
ORLANDO

Jeremy Norton was the best man at Jim's wedding. They were both in their early twenties and they were both beginners at Microsoft. They had been riding the same lifts for weeks, but they actually started to speak to each other when they happened to share a table at lunch-time in the crowded *Star of India* restaurant on the ground floor of the building. Jim liked to listen and Norton liked to talk and they got into the habit of lunching together fairly regularly. Well-born, well-connected and penniless, Jeremy Norton had to work for a living. Tall and handsome, he was one of those large, burly men who are always ready to laugh – way back then he could laugh even at himself. Jim invited him to be best man at his wedding and afterwards invited him to dinner at their home. Subsequently Norton invited the Taylors to dinner at a restaurant, but this remained their only social contact. Perhaps Jeremy Norton was put off by Lesley's critical eyes. (She said that she had never found it so hard to be friendly to anybody.) But the two men got along fine at the *Star of*

India.

All this was so long ago that people could still smoke everywhere. Norton smoked in the restaurant even between courses, but he always turned his head away when he blew out the poison. His parents had invested in the insurance business through Lloyd's and had seen worldwide floods sweep away their fortune. They completed their financial ruin by sending their son to Eton, where he picked up many contacts which he continued to cultivate assiduously, playing tennis and riding horses with the rich. When he was a child, his parents owned a racehorse and they took him to the races. The horse was long gone but he continued to go to Ascot every year and at times bet and won. When he lost, he borrowed several hundred pounds from Jim. He always paid back the loans and swore that he would return the favour one way or another. He never asked his old schoolfellows for money, nor would they have given him any, but they invited him to their parties "to help to fill the room", as he himself put it. He was looking for a beautiful girl attractive enough to screw even if she were poor - except that she had to be rich. And if she "ran the course" in bed, he intended to marry her. He felt free to pour out his mind to Jim, because he didn't think that the Canadian would ever meet anybody from his social circles. There was no danger that Jim would ever show up in a race box. Whatever he said to Jim, it could never reach anybody who mattered. They were lunchtime friends.

One day, over the remnants of a curry, Norton announced that he had run into a possible victim at Ascot. "She's an aristocrat, and she's rich," he added, lighting a cigar and blowing the smoke toward the ceiling. "She's as tall as I am – I hate to bend down to girls. She probably feels the same about bending down to small men. She's difficult, but we're the right height for each other."

"Difficult" was too weak a word for Lady Margaret. She grew up on the ducal estate, where servants and deferential tenant farmers treated her with respect bordering on reverence. Even elderly people called her *Lady Margaret* and children fell silent with envy when they learned who she was. By the time her father put her on her first pony, she had absorbed the conviction that she was superior to practically everybody outside her own family. "They don't even have a village named after them" was the sort of disdainful remark she had overheard as a child. It was as if there were only a few thousand able-bodied people in the country and the rest were cripples. They were human beings, to be sure, the same sort of human beings as any duke or earl, often brighter and better persons - except that, well, they were cripples. And even if all this hadn't turned her head, she would have acquired her sense of superiority from her brothers and sisters: all six children were convinced that they took after their father, the Duke, and slightly looked down on their mother, the daughter of a Permanent Under-Secretary of the Treasury, but still a person who had to earn his living - middle-class, middle-class. Little Lady Margaret knew that she was made of finer flesh. On her father's side she had a 14th century ancestor who was beheaded for siding with the unsuccessful claimant to the throne, and a 15th century ancestor who got an earldom for siding with the right one. A lane, a row, a street, a crescent, a road, a square in London, a town and a whole region of England were named after her family and it never occurred to her to doubt that she was a superior person, entitled to more consideration and fairer treatment than most people - which left her with a permanent sense of injustice, for consideration and fairness are in short supply in this world, even for the daughters of dukes.

Life itself was unfair to her. She was thrown by her pony when she was only four. Her shoulder bone and her ribs healed, but she grew fatter, no matter how she starved herself. "A lot of beautiful women are quite heavy, my darling," her mother said. "A lovely face, flawless skin, a husky voice, lively eyes – that's what beauty is and you have all that. Your voice alone will take you anywhere." Or she would say, "This is just puppy fat, you'll outgrow it". But how would her mother know, she was only middle-class. In the end, the middle-class Duchess turned out to be right. Lady Margaret had grown into a stunning beauty with a shapely, slender figure and she only had to say "yes" to have all the sex she wanted. Yet life still was not what it ought to have been. Men were the worst: they were either rotten lovers or too pleased with themselves, and in either case they were childish. It would have been middle-class hypocrisy to pretend otherwise. None of them could take the least bit of honesty or truth, and she took pleasure in giving it to them in spades. There are women who can make men feel like gods; Lady Margaret could make them feel like worms.

She had mellowed a bit by the time she started an affair with Norton. "She must be in her forties, but you wouldn't

116

know it," Norton boasted. "Any model would envy her long, slim legs, and when you feel her soft white skin or her breasts, she could tell you she's twenty-something and you would believe her. But she's desperate – desperate to find a man who is worthy of her. She thinks nothing of flying thousands of miles for a ball or a dinner party." He lit a cigarette, filled his lungs with smoke, held it in for a few seconds with obvious pleasure and blew it out sideways before going on.

"It's stressful to be a Duke's daughter, Jim, it's terribly stressful," he said, grinning. He had a big head and a wide mouth, and when he grinned it was a big grin. "Just think of it. The boys she played tennis with are ambassadors now, CEOs of big companies or heads of government departments. One became a cabinet minister – a recent one was a famous Hollywood actor. And these are just the highfliers I've heard about. There must have been others, but they didn't marry her either. She's been playing, riding, dining, dancing and fucking with important men for more than twenty years. She sees their names in the papers – they get married, they get divorced, they re-marry, but it's always somebody else - a PA or a nurse or something like that. It's never her."

"Poor woman," Jim commented. "She pays a high price for her ego."

"Jim, your wife's miscarriage made you sentimental. She is not a woman to feel sorry for."

"But why wouldn't anybody marry her?"

"She would love to know why not! I tell her why not, but she doesn't believe me. She's the bossiest woman I've ever met. I wouldn't mind marrying her, though," he confessed.

"She's almost twenty years ahead of me, but the age difference could be a plus – it would make it easier for me to handle her."

"Have you proposed?"

"There's no point. I'm not anybody *important*. Hardly an hour goes by without her using the word. It's very important for her to be important - it's essential. If she can't be married to an important man, then what's the point of having ancestors who were characters in Shakespeare's plays? What's the use of seeing her name on maps? Some of the most valuable real estate in the world is named after her family. I guess things like that would unhinge most women."

In spite of Norton's scepticism about his chances, they finally got married. Norton regretted marrying her right after the wedding. Jim heard about it in the Star of India as soon as Norton came back from his honeymoon.

"The wedding ceremony was long and boring, and as soon as we got into the Bentley, I lit up. And you know what she did? She took the cigarette from my hand and threw it out of the car." He lit a cigarette defiantly and took a deep puff. "She told me she couldn't stand the smoke. We'd been together for more than a year, Jim. I smoked forty a day, I smoked even in bed - certainly every time after screwing - and she never once objected to it. Not once. After the wedding she tells me that she's allergic to tobacco smoke." He stubbed his cigarette into the ashtray with such force that it crumbled to bits. "If she had breathed a single word against my smoking while I was still a bachelor, I'd never have married her. At the reception she watched me like a hawk. And then, think of the long plane ride. Once we got to the island, she allowed me to smoke outside our cottage. But that didn't last long. She started complaining that she couldn't stand the smell of tobacco on my skin. We spent most of our time in the open air. She might have tasted sea salt on me, but not cigarettes. When I told her off for talking nonsense, she replied that it was my mouth that stank, and she mentioned my skin because she didn't want to hurt my feelings."

Norton fell silent as the waiter appeared, bringing their *lamb tikka passanda*. Once they were alone again, Norton picked up his knife and fork and sighed. "If I couldn't cry on your shoulder, Jim, I'd explode."

"So are you going to leave her?"

Lowering his eyes to his plate, Norton fell to thinking. "Ask me that when you've waved away a fortune," he said after a long silence. "She tries to compensate, I have to grant her that," he added with almost a smile. He took a cigarette from his pack, looked at it and dropped it into the ashtray without lighting it. "Giving up smoking is pure hell, Jim, pure hell."

"You'll live longer."

"Well, there is that," sighed Norton.

He was suffering the torments of withdrawal and never ceased to complain about it –until he disappeared, like someone who was run over or won the jackpot on the lottery. Rumour had it that that he had retired with his wife to her house on the ducal estate. Or that they had gone on a tour of China or the Philippines, or both. They were back in London when shares of the biggest UK computer company went into free fall. The new government had cancelled the launching of a National Identity Card, inflicting a loss of five billion pounds worth of business on Quantum Systems, which had the contract to produce the software. The crisis at this business giant gave an opportunity to Lady Margaret. As she hadn't been able to find an important man for herself, she decided to create one. She bought her husband enough *QS* shares to make him the largest individual shareholder in the company and secure him a seat on the board.

QS outsourced to Microsoft the job of salvaging some of the discarded ID software for a new program integrating child protection services. The task fell to Jim. The reshaped program passed muster and QS was able to resell it to the government for eighteen million. As a board member of QS, Jeremy Norton wrote to Jim congratulating him on his work, adding "You're the top software man in this country. I hope we'll be a team one day."

"If this ever leads to anything," Jim said to Lesley, "I'll owe it to Lady Margaret whom I've never met and who has probably never heard of me."

18. HOMECOMING

Everybody is always in the process of becoming somebody else.
LEWIS H. LAPHAM

You turn your head and a decade is gone. Jim was genuinely surprised that they were still in London. The return tickets to Toronto for Jim and Mr. Cello, had expired after a year, his passport after five years, but he had renewed his Canadian passport to be ready to leave at the first convenient moment. Every year, however, their return to Canada had to be postponed for one reason or another. They had season tickets to concerts, plays, the opera, they had grown fond of London - the grand squares, the great orchestras, the parks, but Jim had never ceased missing his hometown. While listening to Handel in the Albert Hall, he was seized by a sudden desire to be in Hart House, the auditorium of his teenage success, where he played Boccherini and Schubert. They visited the Victoria and Albert Museum several times, but when a tourist thrilled by a Chinese vase expressed her admiration in a loud voice, Jim couldn't resist telling her that the Chinese collection in the Royal Ontario Museum was richer and had far more amazing pieces.

Divided between two countries, two continents, their minds were made up by the medical report, based on countless medical tests and scans, which confirmed that Lesley would never conceive naturally. The British government also gave them a push. It abolished most of the grammar schools which could select students according to their aptitude and ability; Carlyle Grammar ceased to exist and Lesley lost her job. They decided to return to Toronto during Jim's summer holiday to find out whether he could find a job in his hometown.

"Is it just a visit or are you coming home?" asked the immigration officer looking at Jim's Canadian passport.

The word *home* sounded so good that Jim felt certain that everything would work out. "Yes, yes," he said cheerfully, "I'm coming home with my wife."

They took a taxi to the city and drove along Lakeshore Boulevard, but the only thing that was familiar was the lake. As the taxi turned up Avenue Road Jim felt younger when he saw the familiar grand old buildings which hadn't changed since his childhood. They checked into the Park Plaza Hotel and hurried to see his family's graves before Mount Pleasant Cemetery closed. Jim had been sending the money regularly to the gardener Roberto to look after the graves and was relieved that, even though he hadn't warned Roberto of their coming, there were fresh bunches of lilies in the stone vases. There were asters and dahlias on his grandparents' graves from admirers. Jim wished they knew that their CDs were still selling. The silver linden tree had grown. He fancied that his mother and her parents, all transformed, fed the tree through its roots with their flesh and bones and cells, and now lived in the tree. He stroked the silvery bark of the trunk, feeling that they were in touch. Seeing that he was moved, Lesley put her arm around him. Afterwards, back in the hotel, they got into bed and clung to each other skin-to-skin for a long time.

His old friends were surprised and embarrassed when he called. They were too busy that evening and also the next day, but wanted to know where they were staying. Jim was disappointed and Lesley suggested they should go to Coffee Mill. They had Hungarian pancakes and the next day they wandered about the city. Jim saw enough familiar places to reassure him that he hadn't dreamed his past, but many buildings he remembered had disappeared without a trace. A few times he got lost.

"Don't you know how you get to Massey Hall from here?" asked Lesley, surprised. "You used to play there."

Jim looked around and read the street sign over and over again. "Let's take a taxi," he sighed.

The friends he had called alerted other friends and left messages for them at the hotel. There was a reunion dinner, but they talked across the abyss of too many years. In a way Lesley got along with them better, for the very reason that they had never been close. In the morning Jim went with Lesley to the Beaches and they sat on a bench where they could have the same view as from Jim's old flat. They watched the boats criss-crossing the lake, just as they had a decade earlier, their sails fluttering over the sparkling water like butterflies. But the city at their backs wasn't the city where Jim had grown up. Toronto had changed so much that he felt like a stranger. He made a few calls to find out what work he could have if they moved back. It was clear that he would have to start over again from scratch.

Before taking a taxi to the airport, they walked to Rosedale. Jim wanted Lesley to see, at least from the outside, his mother's house. He pointed at the top-floor windows where he had given recitals with his mother. Yet he wasn't as moved as he had expected; he had a keen sense that the house no longer had anything to do with him. They went around to the back to peek into the garden over the hedge and saw his father sitting on a garden chair, leaning forward intently as if watching a cricket hopping in the grass. He looked shockingly old. Penny had ballooned up and was circling his chair, talking in an angry voice. They couldn't make out the words, only the sound of rage. Her face was distorted as she shook her fist at the air.

"It doesn't look like she got much joy out of the Steinway," Lesley whispered. Jim felt sorry for his father, but Penny was there. They slipped away from the hedges unnoticed.

"It seems I'll never get pregnant again, so I was thinking that we should apply to adopt a baby," Lesley said on the flight back to London. "What do you say?"

"Agreed. And if we're staying in London and start a family we might as well settle properly. I'm going to apply for British citizenship. I'm sure I'll fit in better. I won't be an outsider."

It was one of those occasions when Jim realized that something wasn't true only after he had said it. He had become a stranger in Toronto and he knew in his bones that he would remain as much a stranger in London as he had ever been.

"Grandfather would be pleased," he sighed. "I've become a foreigner, too."

19. FEELING LUCKY

We have been such as draw
The losing straw.
ROBERT GRAVES

On their return the Taylors found themselves more at home in London than they had expected. Lesley found work at a nearby comprehensive in Fulham. The Head teacher, impressed by the letter of recommendation from the abolished Carlyle Grammar School, appointed her Head of English. Jim was lucky as well. The search engine he had built for Microsoft a year earlier became a worldwide hit and his big bonus came through just days before their return.

They looked for a bigger apartment where they could settle down for good, and they saw one they couldn't afford. It was in an Edwardian block, built at the end of the 19th century when high ceilings and big rooms were standard. The manager of the block, Mr. Wheeler, led them through a living room, four bedrooms, two large bathrooms, a utility room and a huge kitchen.

"That's the kitchen we need!" Lesley exclaimed.

They couldn't buy the place, only rent it. Jim loved all the space, but didn't want to say anything until he heard the price of the rent. The apartment was on the second floor and the French windows of three of the bedrooms overlooked a large garden of tree-shaded lawns and flowerbeds. Jim joined his wife looking at the garden. It was like his mother's garden in Rosedale but much bigger. One of the trees grew high enough to be at eye-level. It was a moment from his childhood: he could watch the shadows of the leaves dancing in the breeze on his bedroom wall as soon as he opened his eyes, and try to match some music that went with the dance of the leaves. In any place Jim had ever lived the most important thing for him was the view, but he said nothing. Lesley couldn't contain her enthusiasm.

"Beautiful," she kept saying, "beautiful."

The rent was staggering.

Jim grimaced. "It's very nice, but we don't really need quite so big a place, Mr. Wheeler. A room less would do for us. Don't you have anything smaller?"

The manager was a well-built, well-dressed man with a wide-face and a small smile. "I'm sorry, but this is the only one free at the moment," he said with flashing eyes. His attempt to look regretful failed miserably.

Jim tore himself from the window and was ready to leave. "Well, thanks for showing it to us."

Lesley didn't move. "This is heaven," she said. "There's all the space in the world to run around. It would be a crime not to have children here."

The manager cast a quick look at Lesley's figure, wondering whether she was pregnant. "I'd say about a third of the tenants are couples with young children."

Lesley's voice was full of joy. "You can hear them shrieking, running to that tree trunk."

"That mulberry tree is four-hundred-years old," the manager said with a touch of pride. "It's from the time of James I, when all this was still open country. The king wanted people to plant mulberry trees for silkworms. He planned to reduce Britain's dependence on Chinese imports and kick-start a home-grown silk industry. That ancient tree was ready to fall and had to be cut down, but it wouldn't quit. Its thick trunk grew again sideways and, and as you can see, sprouted new branches."

It was a sunny afternoon and the garden was full of children. Lesley watched them running in flocks to look at the thick trunk which was no higher than they were. They jumped up and down to touch the growing branches, then ran away in great hurry, shrieking, and then raced back to the tree and ran away again.

"They do this every day when it isn't raining," commented the manager. "And they're safe."

The garden was surrounded on all sides by the four wings of the block. The openings to the streets were protected by wrought-iron railings and gates with Banham locks and video cameras trained on all the gates, and someone was always watching the monitors in the porter's office.

Jim agreed to rent the apartment, even though he knew it meant that they would be short of money for the rest of their lives.

Their decision to settle in London, followed swiftly by Jim's bonus and her new job as Head of English in a nearby comprehensive – and finding the ideal apartment for bringing up children –all these things struck Lesley as good omens. At weekends at home she wore nothing but a T-shirt to tempt him. The sight of her bare bottom was one of the profoundest joys of his life and he could never resist it. She would dress only after they had enjoyed themselves, and as she didn't get pregnant, she decided to have another fertility treatment.

"Jim, our luck has changed," she told him. "I can feel it, let's give it another try."

"You start teaching in less than three weeks," Jim objected. He still had nightmares about her last miscarriage.

Her gynaecologist mother, her GP, the consultant, all tried to dissuade her, warning that, in view of her previous miscarriages - all of them accompanied by profuse bleeding - another miscarriage might be dangerous. They also explained to her the gloomy statistics of the higher rate of mortality and illness in IVF children, but she wouldn't listen. She felt lucky and insisted on having another fertility treatment.

"I don't understand," her mother commiserated with the consultant gynaecologist, Michael Snider. "Lesley was a bright and intelligent girl who has grown into a bright, intelligent woman. It's hard for me to accept that my daughter believes in omens. It doesn't make any sense."

"Lesley may be intelligent, but she wants a baby badly," replied Mr. Snider. "Everybody is superstitious Dr. Ferguson."

"I'm not."

"Do you play the lottery, Dr Ferguson?"

"Most certainly not."

"You have your superstitions just the same, believe me. Everybody does. I had an interesting encounter this summer.

I attended a conference on cervical cancer in Florence. At dinner I was seated beside a distinguished gynaecologist, a professor at Harvard among other things, and we had a pleasant conversation about art when she suddenly asked me, quite earnestly, '*What is your sign?*'"

"Did she believe in astrology?"

"I guess we all half-believe something stupid," replied the consultant.

They carried on discussing the pros and cons of Lesley's case and, as in most consultations, they ended up clarifying all the good reasons for doing one thing or its exact opposite.

Lesley had her way. Jim gave his sperm and Mr. Snider and his team went ahead with the IVF treatment. They dilated Lesley's cervix and scraped her womb; they X-rayed her fallopian tubes and blasted them with air. They stuck hypodermic needles into her ovaries. They removed her eggs, put them in a test tube with Jim's sperm and implanted them in her womb. She got pregnant just as she started to teach again. The embryo was developing normally, her breasts were swelling, and everybody expected a safe birth.

"I'll be fine and the baby will be fine," she said primly whenever she was asked, delighted to be proven right.

The bonus almost covered the expense of furnishing their new home, and Jim paid the last bills with his credit card. When not at the school or in the hospital, Lesley directed the workmen, paying special attention to the baby's room. The fitted carpet there was the softest and thickest pure wool available. Everything was in soft colours and soft textures. She bought a pram, a changing table, a bouncy chair, a cot, a playpen, and a whole menagerie of animals, adding to the ones they had bought for Luke and which she had kept for just such an occasion: there was a teddy bear, a panda, a plush rabbit, a woolly lamb, a tiger and a pink velvet pig that went "oink" if you pressed it.

Just a few days before the Christmas break, Lesley was having breakfast when suddenly her waters broke. She miscarried with "a catastrophic loss of blood" while still at home, and only the promptness of the paramedics in the ambulance taking her to the hospital saved her life. Mr. Snider decided to keep her under observation for several days and wanted to see both her and her husband before discharging her. "We fear that another miscarriage would be life-threatening," he told them. "I blame myself for allowing you to go ahead with the treatment. We'd certainly not put your life at risk again, Mrs. Taylor. We can't count on the ambulance bringing you to us in time. Here's a copy of my letter that was posted to you."

"We shouldn't complain," Lesley said on the way home in the car. "There have to be some couples without children. The world cannot support a billion more people in every decade."

"Right, right."

Putting his arm around her shoulders, Jim drove with one hand. 'Let the police stop us,' he thought, 'it might help to distract her.'

When they went to bed they lay in the dark, holding hands.

"I have hundreds of children at school."

"You have more children than any mother," Jim assured her.

They went to sleep holding hands but later, as they turned, she curled into herself. Each winter night was the same. Hugging still felt good, it evoked affection and comfort, but after a while they rolled apart. They touched each other without desire, overworking their facial muscles as they forced themselves to smile.

The spring brought some respite. The ancient chairman of Quantum Systems reluctantly retired by dying, and Jeremy Norton, the best man at Jim's wedding, already a member of the board and the largest single shareholder on the strength of the shares that Lady Margaret had bought for him, was elected Chairman and Chief Executive. Quantum Systems, better known by its logo *QS* printed on all its products, was the UK's most profitable software company, the main provider of software to government departments, health authorities, educational authorities, local councils and other public bodies. A few weeks after taking charge, the new Chairman gave a call to his old lunchtime friend. "Jim, when can you come by?"

It was a call to the big time.

20. EXECUTIVE FRIENDSHIP

All rising to great place is by a winding stair.
FRANCIS BACON

QS Tower, the company's headquarters south of the Thames, was a featureless 24-storey block built during the architectural disaster years of unadorned concrete. Behind the drab and ugly facade, the interior of the building was agreeable imitation marble, corporate cool. Jim was greeted at the main entrance by a young brunette with a slim figure and a prominent bust who introduced herself as "Janice, Mr. Norton's PA" and she led him to a lift bank. "Here we are on the executive floor," she announced when they reached the 21st floor, leading the way.

They still had a long way to go before reaching Norton's study which (behind padded doors) was quiet and enormous.

"I see it's a long walk to the top, Jeremy," said Jim by way of greeting. He was determined to preserve the tone they had used with each other when they were both nobodies.

Norton laughed, rose from behind his large mahogany desk, came forward with his huge strides and patted Jim's upper arms. "Welcome, Jim, welcome," he said, gesturing towards a small leather sofa shaped in almost a full circle. "I see you have grown some grey hair. Aren't you too young to have grey strands?"

"Jeremy, aren't you too young for those bald spots?"

Norton laughed and they both sat down. They had a friendly chat, bringing each other up to date, asking about each other's wives.

"How is Lesley?" Norton asked.

"She's fine, thanks. How's Lady Margaret?"

In the middle of some chit-chat, Norton suddenly interrupted himself. "Well, Jim, how would you like to work for me?" he asked briskly.

The importance of the question could be gauged by the hospitality. Before Jim could respond, a side door opened and a waiter with the *QS* logo sewn on the lapel of his white jacket rolled in a low, round, oak table. The table, covered with a damask cloth, was laden with caviar, pâté, slices of toast and a chilled bottle of Pol Roger. The waiter soundlessly opened the champagne, filled their glasses and withdrew.

"I'm surrounded by nerds and they are all new acquaintances," Norton went on, once they were alone again. "Let's face it – I'm only an accountant and they could lead me by the nose without my noticing it. I need a guy who knows everything there is to know about software and can invent what is still needed."

"Jeremy, there are at least half a dozen people like that in London."

"You're too modest, that's the Canadian in you," Norton retorted, and got up to pat him on the back, and not too gently either. "I need a friend I can rely on, a friend I can relax with, a friend I can talk things over with at lunch. I need somebody in charge who knows more about software than anybody else in this building. And everybody I consult tells me that you qualify."

"I understand the company also has a President."

Norton laughed. "My predecessor was so worried about his age, that he also gave himself the title President. He was Chairman, President, Chief Executive. I guess he thought in his senile way that if he had three titles Death would be confused and wouldn't know where to find him. I inherited all three positions. But basically you'd run the company. The Financial Officer and I would continue to look after the accounts, our real estate portfolio, but you'd be in charge of everything else. You'd be Senior Vice-President of *QS* and also join the Board. I know you're valued highly at Microsoft but they don't really pay you well, and this job comes with a seven figure starting salary and bonuses."

'With a job like that I could save enough money in a couple of years to retire and get back to music,' Jim reflected.

Mistaking Jim's silence for reluctance, Norton was shocked. "You mustn't pretend Jim that you get that kind of offer daily," he said, flaring up. "This is one of the best jobs in London and I'd have expected you to jump up and down with joy."

"I'll jump, I'll jump, if we can come to an agreement."

"Well, let's finish off this snack and then discuss it."

"You're the boss, you set the schedule."

They ate everything on the table brought in by the waiter; they discussed everything, they drank champagne and agreed on the main points which Norton dictated to

Janice on the intercom. She printed it and brought it in for them to sign.

"I already got rid of the idiot who was in charge of software," Norton said. "You can move in as soon as you can leave Microsoft."

"Did you ask for a million a year?" asked Lesley incredulously when Jim reported to her in the evening.

"No, I simply accepted it. The figure came from Norton."

"I hope nobody at the school will hear about it. We earn less than that in a lifetime. Do you really think your work is worth that much?"

"If I refused, I wouldn't have got the job. I haven't seen the books, but judging by Norton's offer, he must be getting at least three or four times that much. Bosses overpay their underlings as a kind of justification for paying themselves a lot more. I don't see how I could have asked for less than he offered me. It would have been like my saying 'you're robbing the company'. Anyway, our rent won't be a problem and I can save enough in a couple of years to be able to quit and get back to music."

It took nearly a month before Jim could leave Microsoft. When he returned to *QS* Tower, Janice led him to his domain. Ranking behind the Chairman and the Finance Director, Jim was to have the third biggest suite of offices on the executive floor to accommodate him and his assistants. His study was almost as big as Norton's, with a bathroom and a wardrobe attached. "Of course you'll have a chance to refurbish your rooms if you don't like what you find; we have a budget for that," she said. There was a stack of newspapers on his desk, all folded at the relevant page of Business News. The photos and the articles about his appointment as Senior Vice-President of *QS* reminded him that he used to dream about being praised on the Arts Pages. It was too late for him now. He hadn't practised regularly to be a professional, but quitting after a couple of years, he could probably find a grammar school where he could teach the cello, and once he had more practice, join a good amateur orchestra.

The glass wall ran the full length of the room and offered a vast expanse of the sky and the city below. He was higher than any nearby building, and when he sat down on his swivel chair behind the mahogany desk he had a breathtaking vista of Somerset House by the Thames and the dome of St. Paul's. He ran his eyes over his huge study, thought of his fantastic salary and bonuses and he, too, felt lucky, convinced that life was going his way.

Leaving the building, he felt confident he would be able to break the ice at home. The day was unusually warm and sunny; the parks were full of flowers and lovers. When he got home Lesley hugged him, she even laughed, but nothing else happened. They still had the cold of winter in their bones. When they were in bed for the night and Jim tried to stroke her to rouse both of them, she stopped his hand. "Please don't. You don't have to. We've had such great times. I don't feel cheated."

At *QS* Tower the new Senior Vice-President remained an enigmatic figure. Many people commented on his gloomy demeanour both inside and outside the company.

"He acts as if he'd lost his job instead of climbing to the top of the tree in no time."

"It's fake humility."

"He looks gloomy because too many people hate him."

"Why would they hate him?"

"Why, he got ahead of them."

No one guessed that the handsome 32-year-old Senior Vice-President feared that he had become impotent and expected his wife to leave him.

21. REMEDIES

Fourteen centuries have learned
From charred remains, that what took place
When Alexandria's library burned
Brain-damaged the human race.
TED HUGHES

Jim slept restlessly. Whenever he woke, he reached out to touch Lesley, to assure himself that she was still there. One night she wasn't and he flung his arm across her part of the bed so that he would know when she came back from the bathroom, and went back to sleep. Later when he turned again and moved his arm without hindrance, he woke with a start. He tried to guess how much time had passed. Five minutes? An hour? The faint glow of a crescent moon shone through the French windows; he could see that she wasn't anywhere in the room. He listened for noises. A deadly silence filled the apartment. So she was gone, she had left him after all. To avoid a scene, she had left while he was asleep. Who could blame her? He would certainly not oppose her if she wanted a divorce. She could start a new life and wouldn't have to subsist on her teacher's pay either. She could afford to be choosy while looking for another man who wouldn't remind her of all the useless pain. He recalled stories about executive wives who took fortunes in alimony.

Considering his income now, she could sue him for quite a bit of money. And why not? She had more than earned it, he wouldn't fight her.

The next moment, he despised himself for thinking that she had left him for the alimony. He had told her what he was earning, but doubted that she would remember the figure. She had an amazing memory for everything except money. She was the most foolishly, maddeningly generous person he had ever met. A busker's delight. Even when they had lived mostly on an overdraft, she had to give and give and give. He remembered how furious he was when she gave their bus fare to a beggar and they had to walk for miles. Picturing her dancing walk, the way she laughed at him and tickled his penis through his trousers to stop him complaining, he was seized by a suffocating loneliness.

The deadly silence was broken by a sudden explosion - a noise from her study. Was she just leaving? He leaped out of bed, reached the next room with a bound and stopped in the open doorway. Lesley, wearing her favorite old blue flannel dressing-gown and fleecy slippers, was sitting at the desk where she corrected her students' essays. She evidently hadn't heard him. Her red hair fell forward and half-covered the page; she was writing with manic speed. Her farewell note!

When Lesley woke up crying for the children she would never have, other reasons for misery crowded into her mind. (We only have to think of one, the rest come by themselves). The government had cut subsidies for library funding, and she remembered the education minister's defence of the cuts. He had claimed that "literacy was important for our economy, but we have entered a new era in which people learn mostly from images, from TV, films, videos; today the visual media are the main means of learning and communication." Her sudden loathing for the man dried up her tears. She felt an education minister ought to know that reading is about more than being able to hold down a job. She got out of bed, put on her dressing-gown, went into her room and sat down at her desk to write down the ideas that were racing through her brain. Unlike most people, she did not unload her unhappiness on her nearest and dearest, but on the government.

Using an almost empty exercise book, she wrote down whatever came into her head. She compared the minister to those cocky students who assumed that they were smarter than their teacher, because they were up-to-date visual people, while she, a book person, was just a relic.

"They feel sorry for me, as if they were flying about in jets and I was stuck in an oxcart. Of course the assumption that we acquire the most up-to-date knowledge from images is an attractive one, especially as watching television requires no mental effort, but what we learn mainly from images is what even an intelligent dog or a crow might pick up: animal knowledge, feelings without much thought. That may be quite a lot but it isn't enough to create a civilized human being or a functioning society. There are good films and television programmes, but a daily diet of several hours watching a screen shrinks the brain. One of the deadliest consequences of a daily overdose of films and videos is that the visual media are limited in the number of words they can use, so they reduce the number of words in common usage, and thereby reduce our ability to think. It is impossible to think without words. You can only think what you have a word for. You can

only say what you have a word for. There's not a lot you can think and say with a meagre vocabulary...

"... Our mind needs exercise just as much as our body. Watching a man entering a room on the screen, we see the man and we see the room, our brain doesn't have to do anything. By contrast, when we read that a man enters a room, even if the scene is minutely described, we have to imagine both the man and the room. To keep our brains fit, we have to perform mental gymnastics; we have to exercise our imagination."

She was so pleased with this that she started quietly humming to herself. It came to her, as she was writing, that attacking the library cuts might serve as an introduction to a book about the way she taught. She didn't follow some prearranged schedule of recommended books; she would pick one to read and discuss to suit the students' mood. She timed Kafka's *Metamorphosis* for an outbreak of acne in class. If the students were in good spirits and the sun shone, she brought out love poetry. She had already filled a dozen or so pages when Jim came in. Stepping into the room to confront her, he was as pale as the wall.

"What on earth are you doing?" he asked hoarsely.

She went on writing for a moment, and then looked up with a glint in her eyes. "I couldn't sleep, so I thought I might as well get up and see whether I could write a book."

Jim sank into a chair to breathe, belatedly realizing that she couldn't possibly have meant to leave him in her dressing-gown and lambskin slippers.

Lesley assumed that he was still struggling with sleep. "Did I wake you?"

"No, no, never mind. Read me what you wrote, please."

"Are you sure?"

"Don't be coy, get on with it."

Persuaded that he was really interested, she let out a delighted little laugh that wiped the lines off her face. Still puffy under her eyes from crying, she began reading from the notebook: "The written word can never be surpassed by any other medium, because only words can communicate thoughts precisely..."

Jim listened to her cheerful voice. He didn't care what she had written, as long as she didn't leave him. Lesley's sixth sense, developed in the classroom, told her that his mind was wandering. She held up her index finger and gave him a commanding look "Pay attention, you're not listening."

"I am listening," Jim lied. 'She's going to be a mother after all, nursing her brainchild,' he thought.

"Wait, here's the most important bit!" Too excited to sit still, she got up and carried on reading aloud, her words accompanied by bolts from her eyes.

People talk mindlessly about mindless passion, but the mind is the source of lust as of all else. As she moved about, stirred by the force of her arguments, leaning against a bookshelf, perching on the edge of the desk, her dressing-gown slid apart. Her cotton nightgown came down only to the level of her crotch. Her voice became husky and she kept laughing, bringing back the memory of their happy days, waking him from head to foot. Surprised and relieved that he wasn't impotent, he felt a sudden urge to reach out, to stroke the insides of her smooth thighs and feel her warm centre. He resisted the impulse, deciding that she would take it as a criticism of her writing.

"Are you listening?" she asked suspiciously.

"I'm all ears!" he exclaimed, all eyes.

"Is this all too obvious?"

"It's important," Jim said.

When they went to bed Lesley, pleased by what she had written and his attentive listening, seduced him before he could seduce her. It was their first time since her last miscarriage.

They hadn't slept much that night, but she still got up early to write. The flow of her pen made her juices flow and she wrote a poem before rushing off to school:

> *The Well*
> *All our generous cells in love are fused,*
> *Yet still return, renewed with more to give,*
> *Like water surging from earth's deepest well.*
> *When all seems spent, our reason will insist*
> *There is no more to give, the season's dry.*
> *But seasons have their order and their end,*
> *Dying and yielding in their timely suite.*
> *Nor time nor system will our love observe,*
> *But make its own sweet nonsense laws from all*
> *Exchange of touch and look and magic sound*
> *Of the beloved voice. There is one law:*
> *The more we love, my love, the more we love.*

She went back to her book in the evening, describing how she got parents involved in getting the students to learn poetry by heart, and gave a new twist to an old saying: *"The family that recites poems together stays together."*

Balzac, the Shakespeare of the novel, once complained that many of his books were never written because he had spent too much of himself in women's arms. He wrote too many books to make his complaint convincing, but even if he could have written more if he had been less keen on women, it only proves that Balzac was a male. Lesley did her most inspired writing after a couple of orgasms and read to Jim what she had written. She felt she was doing something that mattered and had more energy than ever. And however late they went to bed, they went to sleep still later.

Her friend, the maths teacher, who read the typescript and liked it, tried to warn her that nobody would be interested in an idea book by a teacher nobody had ever heard of. "Let me quote you Stendhal," he said, "the habit of thinking clearly and not being content with empty words is a crime in anyone who is not considered important; all sound reasoning gives offence".

Lesley shrugged off all sceptical remarks. In the heat of writing the book, she couldn't imagine anybody not liking it.

They didn't go on holiday that summer. It was Jim's first year at *QS* as Senior Vice-President and he was still trying to come to grips with managing a corporation. Lesley finished her book and sent off copies to several agents and publishers. Social services promised to come and assess them as adoptive parents.

"Will you love the baby as our own?" she asked.

"They might give us twins."

"The main thing is we should love them even when they cry."

"Right, right."

The bedroom that Lesley fitted out for the baby before her last miscarriage had remained untouched. The teddy bear, the plush rabbit, the woolly lamb, the tiger, and the pink velvet pig that went "oink" - the whole soft menagerie waited for the child with more patience than Lesley. She daydreamed about a motherless baby longing for her to be its mother. She conceived the little stranger on waves of tenderness in Jim's arms. They would have a child to love and bring up.

It is the story of many lives: old wounds heal, new wounds open.

22. TONY ROSS

...useless, utterly disgusting, destitute of any
talent, the incarnation of unbounded vanity -
that special vanity of a complete nonentity.
DOSTOEVSKY

It feels good to lift a heavy bag for a child or someone weak and old. There is an increased sense of self-worth in helping the helpless and there are those whose helping instinct is so highly developed that helping others becomes their vocation. Multitudes in the world owe their peace of mind, their ability to cope with the cruel vagaries of their existence, their very lives, to the doctors, nurses, health visitors, social workers and other carers who were there when they were needed. Unfortunately, Tony Ross was not one of them. Driven by the urge to lord it over others and the lust to spread misery, he was the kind of character who gives a bad name to any profession.

Short and thin, with a narrow head, Tony Ross had a week's growth of beard and wore his hair in a ponytail to declare his solidarity with the underprivileged members of society. As his hairstyle suggested, he was a character from the 1970s who somehow had survived into the 1980s. When he passed people living in doorways, he had the warm pleasurable sensation of kinship with the downtrodden. He himself had a deep sense of deprivation: he had two degrees, a BA in sociology and an MA in social work, yet he was only a social worker in one of London's outer boroughs instead of a Member of Parliament. As far as he knew (and he had a total lack of self-knowledge) he was devoting his life to helping the underprivileged.

Yet somehow the underprivileged who had the misfortune to encounter him in his official capacity fared no better than the privileged. The last family he had ruined were the Reillys, who lived on welfare. When Ross visited them to check whether Mr. Reilly had the right to claim unemployment benefit, the ignorant labourer and his wife were so incensed by his contemptuous manner that they responded with obscenities. The would-be Member of Parliament could not be insulted with impunity. He promptly obtained a court order which empowered the council to take the Reillys' two boys into care. At the secret hearing, Ross did not dispute that the Reillys were caring and loving parents (their neighbours, their GP and their priest all testified to that) but, as he regretfully explained, "the Department had to step in because the parents could not provide an intellectually stimulating environment for their children".

Beware of officials who avoid using the pronoun *I*.

Whenever Ross interfered to wreak havoc, he didn't speak of himself, it was the Department which grew legs and stepped in."The Department" and "we" were the words he forged into a shield, filling him with an exhilarating sense of invulnerability. Whatever he said or did, it had nothing to do with him personally - it was the Department. The worst of it was that his disclaimers were half-true: the Department approved most of his proposals. It is the same story from town halls to the United Nations: meetings held to provide a critical review of any proposal are blunted by the give-and-take of committee work. ("I approve your proposal, you approve mine.") To be sure, most of the social workers were decent and conscientious people who objected to breaking up the Reilly family, but they hadn't persisted. What if the father with the low IQ ended up breaking his son's bones? They had vivid memories of social workers who were abused by the media and almost lost their jobs because they left children with parents who murdered them. They were damned if they did and damned if they didn't - a predicament which discouraged all but the foolhardy from exposing themselves by advocating any action too strongly. Ross was different: he had enough fire in him to be fearless. He was the wolf of the department and the good sheep couldn't bleat down his howl. A mixture of fear, inertia, office politics and the class solidarity of salaried officials, magistrates included, gave Ross the power to tear two little boys aged three and five from their caring and loving parents for the sake of their intellectual development. At the time family courts were still secret and crimes flourish in secret courts.

At first this fine example of justice and council care was ignored by the media; there are just too many rotten boroughs to write about. The destruction of the Reilly family acquired news value only when Kate Greenall, a high-profile journalist with *The Daily Mail*, was contacted by Tony Ross's estranged wife, who claimed that one Saturday, getting home from her weekly shopping, she came upon her husband humping the neighbour's daughter on the sofa in the living room, while their baby girl and the cat sat on the floor watching them. "Is such a man a fit person to judge other people?" asked the enraged Mrs. Ross.

The answer was a resounding yes from the head of the department, the mysterious Ms Dunnett - mysterious because nobody could fathom how such a woman ever rose to be the head of a council's social services. Tony Ross was her favourite and she did her best to defend him. She declined "to adjudicate a family quarrel", and argued that she had to evaluate Mr. Ross on the basis of his work. She declared that "Mr. Ross has the best academic qualification in the department, and has always sought to achieve the highest professional standards within the framework set by the Department of Health." She confirmed her good opinion of Ross when the plight of the Reillys and Mrs. Ross's complaints were aired on BBC *Newsnight*. Tony Ross's own appearance on the programme inspired disgust in millions.

That was the end of public scrutiny of Ross and his misdeeds. Once an outrage is publicly exposed, people assume that something is being done about it and stop being concerned. Ms Dunnett, with the complacency of unchecked authority, did nothing. Unluckily, the Taylors missed all the news about Tony Ross, both *Newsnight* and the article and they also missed meeting Kate Greenall, who lived in the same apartment complex. The large four-winged block had more than six hundred inhabitants and they coalesced into a community, much like a small village. Mothers, chatting away boredom, became friends while watching their children running around. Eventually all the tenants met in the garden. If the Taylors had gone to the garden more frequently, they would have met Kate Greenall and would have learned about Ross's earlier exploits. When trusting parents of a pregnant sixteen year-old called social services for help, Ms Dunnett sent Ross to visit them, and he decided that the girl was emotionally and mentally unstable. You might have thought it was normal for a thoughtless teenager to be unstable when she finds herself expecting, but Ross, with the council's regular psychiatrist, who knew on which side his bread was buttered and always backed the department, went to Court to seek a judgment against the teenager. Winning a Court order, he went back to the family to inform the girl that her child would be taken away from her as soon as she gave birth. According to the girl's parents, she wanted the baby so badly that Ross's threat put her into premature labour. She died and her child was stillborn. Describing Tony Ross, Kate Greenall quoted from Coriolanus:

> *There is no more mercy in him than*
> *there is milk in a male tiger...*

It was only after Ross visited the Taylors that Lesley finally heard about Kate Greenall's article and learned that the Greenalls were neighbours and lived in the same apartment block. She invited them to dinner, and told them about Ross's visit. Her story broke the ice; the dinner was a success and they became friends.

"We should have read Kate's article and I should have contacted you before confronting that creep," sighed Lesley.

"You should keep up with the news when you have anything to do with officials," said Kate. "I could have told you that Ross managed to transfer to our own borough with Ms Dunnett's glowing recommendation and with the help of his degrees."

"We'd need thousands of King Solomons to make the right decisions about parents," commented John Greenall, the journalist's husband, himself a social worker. "This job should be mainly for retired people whose egos have settled down. The job requires intelligence and life-experience, not degrees."

"Anyway," Kate said, "if you had known that Ross might be the one coming to see you, Jim could have taken a tranquilizer and you would have been all right."

It was on a rainy November evening that Tony Ross rang their bell. He arrived in a wet coat and a bad mood. He had nothing but bad moods since his wife had thrown him out of the house. She had also kept their car, and as he couldn't find a reasonably priced one-room flat any nearer than Crouch End, he had to spend nearly two hours travelling by bus and Underground between northeast and southwest London every working day. And now even his evening was taken! The Taylors were at home only after six. What did they want a child for, when they were free only in the evenings and at weekends? To make his life unbearable, he stepped into fresh dogshit on the way. He began cursing loudly and several passers-by looked at him with surprise, wondering whether he was drunk or mad. What did they know about the stressful life of a lowly civil servant! Every other day someone addressed him with fear and respect, confirming his sense of superiority. He could help people with their problems or make them worse, but he didn't earn enough to buy a car. And how many times he had to step in dogshit, if only metaphorically speaking! The muck mocked him, whether it stuck to his shoes or was put to his nose. If there were courts to judge people's characters, a clever lawyer could put up a plausible defence for the poor man's touchiness, his morbid malevolence: "Members of the Jury, power and low income are a maddening combination."

As Ross was scraping the soles of his shoes against the kerb, it started to rain. Naturally, his wife had kept all their umbrellas.

As Lesley opened the door for him, Ross didn't waste time on wishing her good evening. "Tony Ross from the council," he said curtly, still in the grip of resentful anger about the umbrellas, the rain and the dogshit. Walking straight past Lesley, he hurried down the long hallway with his hands in his coat pockets, dripping water on the parquet floor. His narrow head, his stubble beard, his dripping coat and ponytail, his boorish manner, his youth, affected Lesley's judgment and she made the mistake of reprimanding him in her teacher's voice.

"Could we spare the floor, please?"

Ross was stung by her tone, so utterly devoid of any respect, of any desire to please him. 'She's putting me down!' he raged in his mind, raising his head and staring at the ceiling. 'She saw that fucking programme. She thinks it means something. She thinks she can insult me and I'm still going to give her a child.'

As he stood silent and immobile, like a dripping statue, Lesley began to feel sorry for him; she thought of Helen, the social worker who organized the care for her ailing aunt. "Let me take your coat, I'll hang it up in the bathroom," she suggested in the friendlier tone of a welcoming hostess.

Having had a tantrum in his head, he calmed down sufficiently to assume his official self. He looked at Lesley and shook his head reproachfully, swinging his ponytail, sprinkling more drops on the parquet. "I got wet on my way here to help you, but I don't see how we can approve of you as adoptive parents," he said, sounding almost sorrowful. "How could you give loving care to a child if you're fussy about your floor? Children are messy, you know."

'Of course we don't mind the wet floor, Mr. Ross, I don't know what made me mention it, I apologise. Please, by all means, drip all over the place' would have been the correct response, but instead of begging his forgiveness, the Taylors looked at him with silent amazement which couldn't possibly have been mistaken for an apology. He resented it and added it to his other resentments. In fact he got a tremendous kick out of building up his resentments and then discharging them. As a child he had enjoyed directing his pee not into the urinal but at the boy standing next to him in the school lavatory, and whenever he used some bushes in the open air he never failed to direct his flow at a bird, a dog or a bug, if nothing bigger was around. Such boyish pranks became second nature to him, and he still enjoyed giving a shower to cats, dogs and people, aiming the stream of his temper at them.

He took the size of the flat - and he hadn't yet seen the

end of it - as a putdown. "I see you're a privileged couple, a child growing up here would have very little idea of how most people live," he observed tersely. There was a Nicholas Herdon canvas on the wall. Ross didn't know anything about art, but Herdon's striking colours and shapes made him think that it was an expensive original - which was another put down, another insult. "But it's a very nice roomy place, of course," he added, all of a sudden sounding quite appreciative as he spied a crumpled carpet and smoothed it out with his feet, passing on unobtrusively the remains of the dogshit from his shoes. He was so adroit about it that the Taylors, a few steps away, didn't realise what he was doing until after he had left. 'You worry about your parquet floor,' he thought, 'now you can worry about your carpets too. And you can't complain either: I picked up some dirt on the street and didn't notice. It can happen to anybody.' Delighted with the success of his footwork, Ross went into the room prepared for the baby. Drawn to the menagerie in the cot, he picked up the pink velvet pig and squeezed it several times to make it squeal, then threw it back with a dismissive shrug, as if to say that he had heard piglets squeal better.

A dog is obeyed in office and Tony Ross knew it.

"I assume neither of you has a criminal record?" he said in an offhand manner, without looking at them, as he moved into the sitting room. Finally taking off his wet coat, he threw it on the blue velvet sofa and settled himself in an easy chair, indicating with a gesture that they might sit down as well. An uninformed onlooker might have thought he was at home and the Taylors were the visitors.

The couple remained standing and said nothing, but their faces spoke for them. Ross, caressing his stubble beard, went on to ask them a whole series of questions which he deployed to make them squirm. "Please don't take any of this personally," he said, pursing his lips and waving his hand dismissively. "These are standard questions. People have so many different lifestyles these days that I have to ask everybody. Do you have a lover, Mrs. Taylor, who might come to the house and confuse the child? Of course not. I didn't think you would. How about you Mr. Taylor? Do you have problems with alcohol? Drugs? How much money do you earn? Are you prone to violent behaviour? Have either of you ever tested positive for sexually transmitted diseases?"

Assuming the gravity of a judge, he was thrilled by the sight of the couple trying to pretend that they didn't mind. They probably had two cars, but he could make them sweat.

"I take it you can't have children of your own," Ross remarked with a fine blend of derision and condescension.

Jim fielded that one. "That's correct."

"And why is that?" Ross asked sympathetically. "Do you have a low sperm count, Mr. Taylor?"

Jim took a deep breath, smiled and swallowed hard. He wanted to get over the formalities once and for all. People swallow a lot of bile to save time.

"I had several miscarriages," said Lesley.

"You must appreciate that we have to check up on all applicants," Ross said unctuously. "Society can't entrust children to just anybody."

Having had years of battle-training in the classroom, Lesley could cope with Tony Ross, but Jim, a high-ranking executive, had grown unused to insolence.

"Mr. Ross," he asked, "don't you think you're overdoing this?"

"The department paid you the compliment of sending one of its best qualified people," Ross went on reproachfully, just in case they were tempted to feel intellectually superior because of all their books, the Herdon painting and CDs with German names. "I have a BA in sociology and a Master's in social work."

"That's wonderful," said Lesley.

Jim bent his head to hide his face.

Ross's eyes flashed in triumph. He had cowed them. Rising from the chair he spread his arms with the expansive magnanimity of a winner. "It's a common problem these days, low sperm count in males. It's all the chemicals in our food. But I'm sorry, I'm afraid I'm getting too personal. I shouldn't probe that *deeply*." He shook his head, sprinkling drops of regret with his ponytail.

The Taylors hoped that this would be the end of it and he would go, but he was having so much fun. They were in his power: they needed his report.

"Let me see the rest of the flat," he said firmly, and went ahead without waiting for them to show the way. In Lesley's study he turned over a few pages of the typescript of *Literature in the Classroom* that lay on the desk, pursing his lips, unimpressed. Jim's cello lay in its case by her desk and Ross kicked it nearer to the wall. "A child could trip over it and injure himself," he commented.

The cords of the cello inside the case made an eerie noise. Jim rushed to check the impact of the kick. "I hope you didn't damage it," he said in a peaceful voice, but the effort used up what was left of his forbearance. He was still busy examining his cello when Ross moved on to their bedroom.

By this time Ross was quite beside himself. He pressed down their mattress with both hands, testing the springs with a knowing smile. "We must ascertain that you could provide the right environment for the child," he explained and looked around, searching for something specific, something that would compensate him for the dogshit and the rain. His eyes came to rest on the cupboards and drawers.

It was a kind of mental rape that froze Lesley. As Jim came into the room Ross had his hands in her drawer, fingering a pair of her white silk panties. They fell from his hand as Jim grabbed his neck and threw him against the wall. Jim felt such relief hitting him that he hit him again, thumping him on the nose.

"Don't, Jim, don't," Lesley cried, "don't!"

"We don't entrust children to violent people," Ross sputtered.

Jim gripped Ross's shoulders and pushed him out of the room. At first Ross let himself be pushed, but in the long hallway he twisted himself free from Jim's grip and turned around, his eyes burning with sudden courage and determination. Blood trickling from his nose, he raised his arms, clenched his fists, ready to fight to the death. "I won't go without my coat," he said fiercely.

"I'll get it," said Lesley and rushed back to the living room. Jim stepped aside to wait for her.

"All this violence and aggression will be stored on our

national database," Ross seethed. Lesley came back with his coat and he grabbed it. "If you ever give birth," he said ominously, "the department will take the child from you as soon as it's born."

Once Ross was out of the door Lesley ran to the bedroom, pulled out the drawer with her underwear, carried it to the backroom and emptied its whole contents into the garbage bag. Emotionally drained, they both ended up slumped on the living room sofa, breathing hard.

"What did we do to deserve this?" Jim said bitterly, but immediately regretted it as he caught Lesley's look.

23. AFTERSHOCKS

The disturbance may consist of a single shock
lasting a few seconds, or of a series of shocks,
which may continue for days or weeks.
FUNK & WAGNALLS

Nobody wanted Lesley's book, neither publishers nor agents. Her self-addressed envelopes thudded through the letter slot like relentless blows. The returned typescripts had a printed card stuck to the title page, thanking her for her submission, but saying that her proposal was not for them. She hadn't sent a proposal but a finished book. Was it possible that they hadn't even glanced at it? One London agent, though, liked it sufficiently to write her a personal note. "Your ideas are sound and interesting, but ideas sell poorly," wrote Christina Bolt. "Publishers wouldn't even look at a book like this unless it was by a well-known academic or a celebrity. Considering that nobody knows you, I think we would be wasting our time trying to sell it. If nobody knows you, they think you're a nobody. If you became famous for any reason, even as a newsreader, we might give it a try. In the meantime, why don't you write me a romance?"

Lesley crumpled up the letter before she started out for school. She was on playground duty that day and during one of the breaks she had to rescue Pete, a timid, contemplative twelve-year-old with protruding teeth who asked "why?" all the time. She was fond of Pete; his eyes were like her Luke's. Small for his age, Pete had a permanently trusting look in spite of being bullied and baited by most kids. A bulky classmate of his, Cecil (son of the chairman of the school governors, who thought that he could get away with anything), amused himself by pushing Pete to the ground. When Pete got up, Cecil pushed him again. Pete fell and started crying. Lesley rushed to the boys and just caught Cecil's arm as he was about to push Pete to the ground again. Cecil, annoyed, kicked Lesley in the shin.

She snapped and slapped the boy.

"You have no right to hit me," screamed the kid and kicked her with greater force.

The second kick, worse than the first, hurt. Lesley had been teaching at a tough comprehensive for nearly two years and had been quite proud that she had always managed to keep her cool. Now the shame of failing helped to restore her presence of mind. She simply held out her arm to keep the boy from kicking her. It was too late: Lesley was suspended for slapping a defenceless child. She had to face a disciplinary panel and was dismissed. The incident was reported in the papers, illustrated by her photograph, and she was widely condemned in the media for her unprofessional conduct. It wasn't the kind of fame the agent had in mind to help to find a publisher for her first book. Who would be interested in a violent teacher's book about teaching children anything?

There was no way they could adopt a child, not even through private channels; the evidence showed that both of them were prone to violence.

Lesley had neither child nor book. She had burned the rejected typescripts except for one copy which she hid in the backroom, not to be reminded of it.

24. ARE HUMANS RAW MATERIAL?

A language becomes ugly and inaccurate
because our thoughts are foolish, but
the slovenliness of our language makes
it easier for us to have foolish thoughts.
ORWELL

Lesley had lost her job for slapping a child and she had no teaching degree, but the Head Teacher of one of the remaining grammar schools in Southwest London took her on for a three-month trial period on the basis of her first class degree in English Literature from Glasgow. At the end of three months he called her into his study. "The best judges of your teaching skills are your students," he told her. "They are full of enthusiasm for your lessons. Clearly, you have the gift of empathy; you can connect to your students. You're able to transmit your knowledge and your deep love of your subject. Your students respect you and they are eager to learn. I'd say you're qualified. These qualities are worth more than any teaching qualifications. Welcome to Edward Gibbon School." Once more Lesley had hundreds of students to make up for not having children of her own.

As Jim would have preferred to be a cello teacher in a secondary school than a senior Vice-President at *QS*, they tried to save most of his salary. Lesley paid for the food and his considerably higher income covered standard bills such as rent, electricity and outings for concerts, the opera, theatres or restaurants – and most of it was put in the bank to be saved for the day Jim could quit business without reducing their living standard. He was ready to quit when the property market crashed.

In the last financial year *QS* still had a turnover of two billion, although the new government's cancellation of the identity card scheme remained a continuing drag. The loss of this business, that had already earned the company five billions, meant the end to a flow of profits which could have gone on forever, with thousands of newborns and new arrivals every day and each requiring an ID card. As the new man in charge, Norton had been eager to prove that he was more than Lady Margaret's husband and moved into the property market during a period of easy credit and a real estate boom. *QS* had bought office blocks and commercial properties in several major cities with borrowed billions. He planned to offload its property portfolio when prices rose even higher. He counted on doubling the value of the company in a few months. However, he had to hang on to them for years rather than months in hope of making the kind of profits he envisaged, and in the end he waited too long. In wake of the crash the properties were worth half as much as *QS* had paid for them. The banks threatened to call in their loans unless the company refinanced. The management could think of nothing but to propose a twenty percent wage cut and a wage freeze. Representatives of the work force refused and threatened to strike. The biggest and most successful UK computer company was on the brink of bankruptcy.

Jim had nothing to do with the real estate speculation, and he thought of quitting sooner than he had planned, but he couldn't see himself as a rat leaving a sinking ship. He argued at the extraordinary meeting of board members and senior executives that they should agree to cut their own remunerations by the same twenty percent and freeze it at that level, just like the employees, until *QS* was free of debt. Fearing disaster, they agreed and Jim was charged with drafting a statement about the management's commitment to sharing the burden of the cuts. The statement was posted in the form of an individual letter to each employee and people kept quoting from it. *QS* Tower was buzzing with "we are all in this together", a phrase that Prime Minister David Cameron made infamous many years later, at the time of another crisis.

Jim was appointed head of the team negotiating with the unions. He suggested to Norton that they should start by announcing that they would restore the Department of Human Resources to its original name, Personnel. He had discussed it with Lesley the previous evening and could be eloquent on the subject. "Coal and oil, gas, stones you quarry, water - these are resources, raw materials, they don't have feelings and they don't suffer whatever you do to them. It's bad English to use the same word for people. It's a mean word invented by the mean-spirited who think of others only as a source of income. People are not things to be depleted and thrown away. I'd like to start negotiations by mentioning that we're going to restore the department's original name, Personnel, as a small symbolic sign of a new era."

Norton shrugged. "Jim, what's human resources? It's such a common expression it no longer means anything. None of those people would understand what you're going on about. But if you think it'll make a few poor buggers feel better to be considered persons rather than resources then do it. Just be sure to tell them that it's the chairman who insists on it."

"Of course," said Jim.

The Head of the Department of Human Resources, Virginia Cunningham, who had been appointed by the dead chairman, rushed to Norton as soon as she heard about this interference with her authority. "People are more difficult to manage if they think of themselves as more than a resource," she protested.

Norton didn't want to antagonize her but didn't want to disclaim credit for the new name either. "It's all in Jim's hands. He's in charge of negotiations with the unions. Talk to him."

Virginia Cunningham had been the dead chairman's darling and hated Jim since the day he had joined *QS* and replaced her as the second most important executive. Believing that she owed her position mainly to her efforts to warm the late chairman's shrivelling carcass (God knows, it was hard work), she was consumed by anxiety about the loss of her power and possibly her job. She would never forgive Jim for her sleepless nights. The change of her department's name confirmed her worst fears. She went to see Jim to complain that she wasn't consulted and argued the danger of chaos if employees thought too highly of themselves.

Jim wasn't impressed by her arguments. "Do you want

people to be humble?"

"I want them to be manageable."

"I'm sorry, Virginia, but I began to negotiate on the basis that we don't equate our people with inanimate objects."

"Jim, do you really want to waste money on door signs and stationery? I don't think it's wise to change our business cards. I don't cherish the idea of changing my business card and it's my department."

"I should have consulted you, but it's too late," said Jim, stabbing her in the stomach. That was how it felt: a knife thrust.

She would bleed for years.

The new agreement, voted for by the vast majority of employees, included a wage reduction of twenty percent as well as the freezing of the reduced wages until *QS* cleared its debts, "in return for a guarantee of life-time employment, barring gross negligence or criminality." The guarantee was legally binding even if *QS* was sold or restructured; it became null and void only if the company went bankrupt. The media praised the resolution of the conflict, the willingness of both parties to make concessions and sacrifices and several government ministers echoed the media - a significant boost when *QS* depended on public bodies for business. The banks extended their loans and Jeremy Norton learned that he would be knighted.

"Jim, I congratulate myself on signing you up," the future Sir Jeremy told him. "I knew I needed an old friend who'd look out for me."

"I think I secured the livelihood of over twenty thousand people," Jim boasted to Lesley at home. "Not bad for a foreigner, is it?"

"Didn't you say the company has fewer than ten thousand employees?" she asked, surprised.

"I'm including the families, the grandparents as well as the children. Counting all the dependents, there must be more than twenty thousand of them. I feel like patting myself on the back."

"You can't do it – I'll do it for you," said Lesley, hugging him. "I'm proud of you." She liked to praise him; it made him happy.

It was just as well that his wife praised Jim at home, because he received no more compliments from his boss. Once the danger of bankruptcy receded, Sir Jeremy began to think that Jim had played a dirty trick on him, talking him into giving up twenty percent of his salary and bonuses without there being any need for it. That was half a million a year, a sufficiently big loss to make a man feel resentful. He resented it all the more as he couldn't very well complain since he had been knighted for his sacrifice.

The person who convinced the chairman that there had been no need for the executives to give up any of their benefits was Virginia Cunningham. "I hate to say this, but I think Jim was in too much of a hurry," she said. "All we would have needed to do was to hold off the banks for a week. That's all we would have needed, another week. The country's flooded with software engineers looking for work. We could have browbeaten them."

A lawyer by training, still in her twenties, Virginia

Cunningham was a short, thin woman with too wide a mouth for her narrow face, framed by wiry brown hair cut at the jaw line. Her habitual expression suggested that she had just been insulted by somebody. Her expressive green eyes shone with resentment or darted about. She reminded Jim of a weasel, but she could also look the picture of amazement and admiration whenever she looked at a man who could do her some good. She had no sex appeal, but she had the appeal of a devotee. She hung on Sir Jeremy's every word with a look that said *now I understand!* Her eyes, her face displayed a wide variety of amazements - the way she leaned forward or bent backward raising her head, as if hit by his powerful ideas - her very body language convinced Norton that he was speaking pure wisdom. And the more she admired him, the more he believed her. She became a tiresome rival to Jim. When Jim talked to Norton about something that he didn't like or didn't quite follow, he stopped listening, thinking *'talk away, talk away, you have already talked me out of millions!'*

He appointed Virginia Cunningham head of the legal department.

Virginia Cunningham was the most gifted sycophant, but there were others too. As Chairman and Chief Executive of a gold-plated company, Jeremy Norton could bestow many gifts at no cost to himself and, with considerable help from the people around him, discovered that he was a great man. It didn't make him any happier. A naturally jovial character, he laughed less rather than more. In keeping with his importance, his whole bearing had changed. Now and then, quite unexpectedly, even when he was lunching with

Jim in private, his large face became suffused with so much dignity and turned so rigid that one might have thought that he was having his picture taken. *'Hey, Jeremy, I'm not a photographer!'* Jim felt tempted to tell him, but Norton could no longer take a joke about himself.

"I can hardly talk to him anymore, he's so grand," Jim complained to Lesley one evening as they were discussing their day in the kitchen. "He suspects that I think I'm smarter." Preparing dinner at home was a fun habit from their younger days.

"Well, you *are* smarter."

"We'd be better off if he was smarter. When the chairman and the chief executive are the same person, the rest of the staff might as well be brain dead."

"Remember, I took a dislike to him the very first time I saw him," Lesley said with some satisfaction. "There was something creepy about a grown man tarting himself up with a diamond watch."

"It was his wife's present."

"Yes, you kept making excuses for him."

"He was brighter when he was younger."

"Anyway, it was bright of him to marry Lady Margaret. I doubt if he would have got far without her shares and the seat on the board."

"He complains about his wife even when his mouth is full. He says I have no idea what a harridan she is. He can't understand what possessed him to marry her."

"Greed and base ambition," Lesley said promptly. "I could have told him that."

"No, you couldn't."

"More's the pity."

"Actually he tends to forget that he owes his wealth to her. The other day he told me that he couldn't think of divorcing her because she would take half of everything he has."

"I suppose he feels he earned it all by giving up smoking," Lesley commented.

The first visible rift between the Chairman and his Senior Vice-President occurred in the lift bays of *QS* Tower. Sir Jeremy felt increasingly uncomfortable in close proximity to his lowly employees, even for the time it took him to ascend from the underground garage to his office and descend back to the garage, and he ordered alterations to the lift bays. One lift in each bay was converted into an exclusive executive lift. The call buttons were replaced by card slots and the key-cards were issued only to executives and their staff. These special key-cards proved to be quite popular on the 21st floor, not only with receptionists and personal assistants but also with their bosses as an extra trinket of distinction and authority. Jim, who saw himself as a failed cellist rather than a corporate big shot, continued to use the same lift as ordinary mortals.

Norton was annoyed when he first heard about it. When his deputy lowered himself to mixing with ordinary employees he felt his own authority was compromised. "You take this equality nonsense too seriously," he commented wryly when they next met.

"I like to be friendly with the people I work with."

"You don't work with them, they work for you."

"We're a team."

Norton made a belittling grimace. "You're still a musician; you'll never be a business leader, never."

"Do you want me to quit?" Jim asked, with the bravado of a man who was half-wishing just that.

Norton pointed a warning finger at him, his diamond watch flashing. "Don't be funny! Make sure that you clear our debts."

The Chairman and his deputy had a complex love-hate relationship, common enough in offices. Norton didn't know anything about software (nor did he want to) and it made his life a lot easier to leave Jim running *QS* without having to worry about the details. He needed Jim and didn't wish to antagonize him beyond a certain point. They fought, but they stopped short of drawing blood. Norton was fond of Jim as his own creation, having raised this Canadian outsider to dizzying heights, but he resented Jim for behaving as if they were equals. There were times when Norton remembered that he owed his knighthood to Jim's bright ideas, but couldn't forgive him for never addressing him as "Sir Jeremy". And he hated Jim every time he looked at his bank statements and saw the twenty percent reductions. And when he put his losses out of his mind and relaxed a bit, Virginia Cunningham managed to remind him.

Virginia Cunningham had found many ways to discredit Jim in Norton's eyes, yet she couldn't quite cut the bond which the two men had formed in their younger days. When they started at Microsoft Jim was a safe confidant, because Norton moved in higher social circles and Jim couldn't gossip to anyone who mattered. They were lunchtime friends. In time, though, unburdening himself to Jim without restraint became both a habit and a release he couldn't do without - especially as Lady Margaret was getting more and more impossible. Jim did cost him millions, but Sir Jeremy needed a friend to whom he could complain about his wife.

25. THREE MANTRAS

...my bit of inward peace, where I am at one with myself.
D.H. LAWRENCE

You turn your head and a decade is gone. You try to understand how it happened, and that's another decade.

Jim's horizons had been raised by music and literature, he was familiar with noble thoughts, he believed that he was born for something more than making money and spent his life making money. He had intended to quit for years, but never got around to doing it. In time he came to believe that he could make a greater difference running a great corporation than teaching music in a secondary school. Just the same, he felt truly himself only at home. The last two decades as Senior Vice-President of QS could be summed up by three mantras. To summon the strength to go to the office in the morning he kept telling himself

'I can help a lot of people if I get on with it.'

He still enjoyed designing software, but most of his time was spent with supervision and management. Since he was in charge of everybody connected with the research, development, sale and maintenance of software, more than half of *QS* employees took direction from him or his deputies. Answerable for the competence of all those involved, he had to approve the hiring and (what he hated most) the firing of people. The *QS* factory in Glasgow employed around two thousand workers producing ordinary laptops for schools and specially-built computers adjusted to individual software. Jim had nothing to do with the factory, but even those who didn't work directly for him depended for their livelihood on the success of what he and his people were doing. As he bore ultimate responsibility to ensure that each program performed the functions the purchasing authority needed it for, he had to know the requirements in detail and was involved in pre-sale negotiations as well. Having lost several projects to competitors, he learned the intricate if dispiriting ways of finding out how much he had to offer officials to win the contracts for *QS*. He had a free hand to spend on 'promotion' and simply added the kickback to the price. They were defrauding the taxpayer, but if he refused to take part, he knew that his competitors would be more than happy to take his place, costing the taxpayers just as much, if not more. His mantra had grown longer, as he chanted it in his mind:

> *'I can help a lot of people if I get on with it
> and swallow my scruples.'*

When the bribe had to be big, he had another mantra:

> *'If I don't do this, someone else will.'*

'What would my mother say if she could see me now?' Jim wondered gloomily when he was congratulated on winning a new government contract worth millions. He didn't tell Lesley about such triumphs, knowing that she would have been just as disappointed as his mother. *QS* salesmen began to bid for software projects from the European Commission and once there was interest, Jim invited the officials from Brussels to ascertain exactly what they required. In seven years *QS* cleared all its debts. The reduction of wages and the wage freeze had become bad memories. Jim's own salary and bonuses rose into seven figures and he often wished he had the strength of character to quit.

The outward relationship between the Chairman and his Senior Vice-President remained the same, in spite of their many inner resentments and disagreements. Jim was the only one who could openly disagree with the Chairman, as Norton had many reasons to trust his loyalty. The records showed the Chairman and CEO had been ignorant of Jim's methods in securing contracts, so Norton knew that if the bribes came to light, Jim would be the one who would be charged.

Jim often chilled out by standing at the glass wall that ran the full length of his study. He let his eyes wonder over the grand old city – and the vast expanse of sky. In the winter when it got dark early he loved to look at the stars, wondering whether people were watching the Earth from some distant globe. He installed a Sky-Watcher Explorer telescope to see more. Yet star gazer as he was, the arrest of a ministry official for taking bribes gave Jim such a scare that the sensational discovery of Comet Claudina made no impression on him at all. He forgot it as soon as he heard about it. He even ignored the view. The arrested official had given *QS* a software project worth nearly twenty million pounds and Jim expected to be arrested himself.

For weeks he missed a heart-beat when the phone or the doorbell rang. However, it was a recent case of corruption that tripped up the official and the *QS* software program, which worked flawlessly, was above suspicion. It was a close call, and in the euphoria of relief, Jim decided that he would finally buy the flat they had been renting as well as the neighbouring flat which came up for sale at the same time. Hardly more than eighteen months before he walked into the Bay of Mexico to drown himself, he felt a sudden need for more space. Hiring Polish builders to transform the two apartments into one, he had them build a replica of the music room in his mother's house, the walls coated with fibreglass overlaid with cypress wood. His cello faced the French windows overlooking the trees and shrubs in the garden. Playing steadied his nerves.

In spite of his seven-figure salary, Jim had relatively little cash to deposit for their enlarged home. He had paid his taxes and Lesley had persuaded him to give fifteen percent of the remainder to charity. He had savings, but he had been saving as his grandfather had done, regularly upping his payments to his life insurance policy. Withdrawing money from his policy would have been more costly than taking out a big mortgage.

26. THE PRINCESS AND THE MAID

She flew into a rage beyond imagination.
THOUSAND AND ONE NIGHTS

The two apartments Jim had bought were hideously expensive because their block was in the richest borough in the whole United Kingdom. From the kitchen window of the extra apartment, which became their enlarged kitchen, they overlooked the garden gate of Prince Jaalver's London residence on the other side of a quiet cul-de-sac. They knew little and cared less about their illustrious neighbour, but Prince Jaalver was a daily subject of conversation among refugees from Saudi Arabia - Muslims who wouldn't accept that beheadings and crucifixions had anything to do with their religion and believed in the equality of the sexes and all kinds of freedoms. Their women faced the world without hiding their faces and they thanked Allah every day for helping them to flee their country ruled by Prince Jaalver's family. They described the Prince in a leaflet as "a blood-thirsty monster who grew fat on oil and wouldn't share a single drop of it." This was clearly an exaggeration, motivated by personal hatred. They all had relatives left behind who were beheaded or died under torture. Being Minister of the Interior, it was the Prince's job to get rid of people whose minds were poisoned by Western music or ideas like democracy and who openly denounced the stoning of adulteresses and other religious practices. Prince Jaalver spent most of his time back in the kingdom, hard at work keeping a lid on people. There was a failed attempt to murder him and the perpetrators were caught. The Prince, far from being "a blood-thirsty monster", refused the invitation of his security people to watch the torture and execution of his would-be assassins. In London the Prince was a liberal who wore Savile Row suits and talked and laughed with Christians and Jews, leaving his deeply held religious convictions at home. Whatever else can be said about him, not even his fiercest critics could deny that he enjoyed an interesting life.

His first wife, Princess Latifa, wasn't allowed to share any of it. She learned of the assassination attempt only months later and when she did, the Prince did not wish to strain her mind with the complexities of politics and simply told her that it was a group of Jews and Christians who had tried to blow him up. Princess Latifa's whole world, her prison and her fiefdom, was her home, and it wasn't even the first deformative experience of her life. She came to London whenever her husband married a new wife or took a new concubine - usually once a year - and stayed for several months. She was a tiny woman in her thirties with a narrow face which had grown unattractive and she disliked to be stared at. When she ventured forth she always wore a black silk chador which covered her from head to toe. The chauffeur drove her in the white Rolls-Royce to Harrod's where she usually found something which seemed to be worth buying. Once she had bought the thing, she no longer cared for it. Unloved, bored, unhappy, the Princess blamed her unhappiness on her Filipina maid who arrived to serve her only a few days before they flew to London. Maria Santos, a poor farmer's wife with five children, had never been outside the Philippines and had no idea what a lowly creature she was. She was a Christian servant dog yet she didn't lower her eyes and at times looked the Princess full in the face as if they were equals. She didn't know her place.

Princess Lafita instructed her gently without beating; she tried to help her to find her own level by ordering her to place her plate on the kitchen floor and eat crouching down. If the Princess was angry, she kicked over the plate and the maid had to scrape her food from the floor if she didn't want to go hungry. Food was the Princess's medium of instruction and correction, the sacred embodiment of her power, and it was guarded in the house more jealously than gold or precious stones. Jewels were scattered about on top of dressing tables and in open drawers, but the refrigerators had locks. Only the Princess had the keys. The Prince had his own refrigerator stocked with snacks and fine French wines in his part of the house. (Drinking alcohol in secret was private apostasy and Allah the Merciful winked at it.) But in Princess Latifa's fiefdom no one - in theory not even the cooks - could eat a single morsel that was not gifted to them by the gracious hands of the Princess. After the family had their meals, the cooks appeared with their plates and stood in line with the rest of the servants, awaiting her bounty. The Princess wielded the ladle judiciously, giving each servant as much as he or she merited that day. On days when the Prince happened to be in London, he remained at the table and watched with a bored expression this ritual confirmation of the fact that members of the household were sustained among the living only by the grace and favour of the Princess.

For weeks Maria Santos's plate received the contents of the Princess's ladle on the kitchen floor. The Princess was confident that eventually the slave would learn to be respectful. But no, she got worse, she grew insolent. She had the temerity to stop the Prince in the corridor when he dropped by with his attendants for a brief visit to London to buy armoured cars. The Prince was in a hurry but she stood in his way and complained.

The Prince stroked his fat cheeks, and then raised the palm of his hand to command silence. "You must never address me again," he said firmly. "If you have any complaints, speak to the Princess. You belong to Princess Latifa."

"But I can't eat from the floor, your Highness, it gives me cramps."

The Prince grimaced with annoyance and walked on. One of his flunkies pushed the maid against the wall. "Didn't you hear His Highness tell you that you must not address him!" he snapped, glaring down at her before rushing after the Prince. The Prince allowed his wives to abuse their servants for the same reason some parents let their children torture the cat - he wanted to be left alone. As he saw it, he was obeying Islamic teaching: the household was the wife's domain. Practice corrupts all ideals.

Complaining to the Prince, Maria Santos practically asked to be kicked and beaten. This was hard on the poor Princess; chastising the maid hurt her delicate feet and arms.

There was a permanent staff of six in the Jaalver residence: the housekeeper, the butler, the cook, the chauffeur, a housemaid and a bodyguard. The Princess had no trouble with them, they were not ignorant Asiatics, they knew their place and they served her reverently with bent backs and downcast eyes, demonstrating at all times an awareness of their inferiority and her exalted station. *They* knew better than to look her in the face. But hardly a day went by without her personal maid forgetting to lower her eyes and bow. It was galling and the Princess didn't spare herself in punishing her. The creature had no rights. Having entered the United Kingdom on a visitor's visa as Princess Latifa's domestic, she would be deported back to the Philippines if she left her employment. Just the same, many servants in the same situation ran away from their masters and lived in Britain illegally, and every time the Princess beat Maria she worried about her running away. She confiscated her passport, stopped paying her wages to make sure she had no money to escape and gave orders that she was not to leave the house.

One Sunday morning the Princess, happening to look out of the window, saw Maria walking down the street with the cook. "Stop her, stop her!" she screamed. When the butler and chauffeur brought back the maid, she slapped the maid's face, accusing her of trying to steal a fortune.

"I just wanted to go to church," Maria protested.

"It's true, Your Highness," said the cook, deciding to do something right on a Sunday.

"You insult me?" the Princess cried, rounding on the cook. "You insult the Prophet?" But then she suddenly stopped, remembering her husband's warning that Christianity was still legal in Britain. "You can go to church, I can't stop you," she said to the cook, "but this thief is not going out."

"I'm not a thief," Maria objected in a low voice.

Nothing had been stolen, but the Princess counted the commission she had paid to the employment agency in Manila and Maria's airfares. Maria would have robbed her of all that investment if she had managed to escape. As punishment for going out of the house, she was given no food that day, not even on the kitchen floor.

As the Princess was drifting off to sleep at night, she was roused by the sudden fear that Maria had broken the refrigerator lock and was stuffing herself with stolen food. She leaped out of bed and ran down to the kitchen. The lock seemed untouched, but what if Maria got hold of an extra key, stole some food and was eating it in her room? Determined to catch her red-handed, Princess Latifa tiptoed down to the basement and put her ear to the maid's door, listening for sounds of chewing or lip-smacking. Instead, she heard the kind of sounds she herself tried to make on the rare occasions when her husband lay with her. 'Why is she pretending?' wondered the Princess. 'Is there a man in there?'

Maria Santos was alone in her room, but her loneliness spread beyond the room, beyond the house, beyond

183

continents and oceans. Apart from her jailers, there wasn't a single person for thousands of miles who even knew that she existed. There was no one she could talk to; her family and friends lived in another world. Why had she let her husband talk her into signing up to work in the Middle East? Why did she have to suffer if she received no money to send home? How could she be in far-away England, at the mercy of a stupid, vicious woman?

Lying in bed in the dark, convulsed with regret, resentment and bitter incomprehension, she felt that her last hour had come. Her loneliness, her helplessness, her tears were choking her. She wanted to breathe, she wanted to escape, and her mind raced back into her children's arms. She thought of her three-year-old, laughing as he patted her. Recovering a little, she tried to hum a song and hugged herself to feel less lonely. How her husband had hugged and caressed her before they had children. Memories of her youth came flooding back as she caressed her breasts and her *higo*. Pleasure made her forget her prison: she was the most beautiful girl in the village, running along the river-bank, chased by two boys who kept calling after her, "Maria, Maria!"

When Princess Latifa opened the door of the basement room and switched on the light, Maria's hand froze under the blanket, but it was too late; her body went on shaking.

"Stop, stop!" Princess Latifa shrieked as she rushed to the bed and grabbed the blanket. They had a tug of war with the blanket, which Maria won: she was stronger. The Princess clenched her fists and began pummelling the Filipina over the head. The slave hadn't eaten, she should have been hungry and miserable, but she was enjoying herself on the sly. "Why aren't you hungry?" she demanded, pummelling her. "Answer, answer!"

Maria raised her arms to protect her head.

"Answer, answer!"

"I'm not hungry."

"What were you doing?!" the Princess raged tirelessly, raining blows on the maid. "Answer, answer!"

"You didn't let me go to church," came the sullen reply.

Princess Latifa spent a terrible night. She had a horror of unnatural practices. Her family, which had originally come from North Africa still observed the old traditions. She had her clitoris cut off when she was a child, and she learned to be grateful for it. She was proud of her purified body, free of the ugly little growth that made other women susceptible to animal lust. She had more refined sensual thrills, derived from her French perfume, created especially for her. She always put a dab of the scent behind her ears and in the hollow of her neck before wrapping herself in her chador and setting out to shop, with the bodyguard in her wake. Her heart beat faster when she saw a man's nose come alive and sniff the air as she passed him. The absence of mad excitement, a touch of thrill at a distance - restraint! - All these made her feel superior to English princesses. As for the servants, Princess Latifa did not associate them with joy, not even with animal pleasure. The image of the shameless woman shaking under the blanket sent waves of disgust through her, startling her awake every time she dozed off. She felt defiled, insulted, robbed of her authority. Next morning she kicked Maria, but the maid didn't scream and kept her eyes to the ground.

The Princess didn't know what to do with herself. Kicking the Filipina gave her no relief. She escaped to her bedroom, where she dabbed her unique perfume in the hollow of her neck, on the inside of her wrists, behind her ears and wrapped herself in her finest chador, spraying it with a cloud of the divine scent. Fully dressed, covering everything that she didn't like, she rushed to the full-length mirror, excited by the thought that nothing could be seen of her except her deep, sparkling eyes, which reflected her inner beauty, the purity of her soul. Just at that vulnerable moment of self-adoration, there was a slight movement at the edge of the mirror and she caught sight of her Filipina maid watching her from behind the half-open door with a mocking smile.

The Princess went berserk. Shrieking with fury, she pulled off one of her stiletto-heeled shoes and tried to pierce the Filipina's eyes, but the woman covered her eyes, so the Princess hit the top of her head, then stabbed her cheek repeatedly with great force, until the stiletto cut through the flesh and cracked a tooth, bloodying the maid's whole face before she broke free and locked herself in a bathroom. Maria Santos spent the whole night there, growing delirious. When she finally came out of the bathroom in the morning, the poor woman was such a shocking sight that the servants didn't have the heart to stop her as she staggered out of the house through the garden gate.

The Filipina managed only a short distance and collapsed. The quiet cul-de-sac had very little traffic and she lay unconscious on the pavement, baked by the sun.

Lesley noticed the bloodied and apparently lifeless figure while preparing breakfast; she called Jim who called 999 and they both went down to the street. They were the first to stop by the body and the Filipina's ravaged face – the white of her teeth showing through the bloody baked holes in her cheek – was such a shock that his mind switched. He was back in the cold morgue in Toronto confronted by his mother's blasted head in the steel box with her earrings in her unwounded ears. When the police arrived, Jim tried to follow the Filipina into the ambulance to the hospital to learn how serious her condition was. He had already one foot on the step when the paramedic stopped him.

"Do you have a connection to the injured woman?"

"Yes!" said Lesley in a strong voice, pushing Jim forward.

27. THE OATH

If angry, count to ten; if very angry, swear.
MARK TWAIN

It was winter again and the rain turned to sleet, as expected. But unexpectedly, without any warning, the world turned honest. It was a disaster. A high-ranking civil servant was arrested in a dawn raid, followed a few days later by a whole series of dawn arrests which had the untoward consequence of afflicting all officials with scruples. There were fewer and fewer public software projects and even shoddy deals had to be spread impartially among the various applicants. *QS* salesmen were busy, but most of the new orders were coming from banks and factories, and private companies paid as little as possible. Profits were disappearing at an alarming rate and Jim's life was getting more difficult just as he was hitting fifty-four.

One mid-February morning when Jim came in to work, he found half a dozen of his staff crowding around the desk of his PA, Ellie Wade. He overheard her saying, "Don't worry, Jim will protect his people."

They all looked at him with an expression of anxiety and

hope.

"What's this all about?" he asked.

"They say our jobs will be shipped to Malaysia," she said.

"Well, let's make sure it won't happen," said Jim. "Go back to work."

He went into his study and Ellie Wade followed him with a file which she placed on his desk. "Today's mail and emails and the replies I drafted for you."

"You're a treasure, Ellie."

He often praised her to his wife as well. Jim had to make corrections to very few of her drafts before he could sign them and reckoned that she saved him at least an hour every day. He had originally picked her from the secretarial pool because her mother was a Canadian from Toronto and she seemed to be full of energy in spite of being ungainly and overweight. She turned out to be also intelligent, competent and reliable – lucid on every subject except her looks. She refused to wear glasses because they spoilt her face. She had been working for Jim for more than two decades and he had never seen any sign of a boyfriend. When her father got sick and could no longer look after himself, she brought him to London and her private life consisted of caring for him.

"And her father is back in hospital," Jim reported to Lesley one evening. "In her place I would be bitter and miserable. I don't understand how she can she be so content."

"She enjoys being useful."

On that mid-February morning Ellie looked grim and remained standing in front of Jim's desk, confronting him with her pallid winter face. With all the things wrong in her life, at least she had a good job and now that, too, was under threat. The whites of her pale grey eyes, already pink under the contact lenses, were turning a deeper shade of pink. "They say you'll be taking on a young assistant," she said accusingly.

"Nobody told you that, Ellie. Relax. You were here during the years of famine, you agreed to the cut of your wages and a wage freeze in return for a guarantee of lifetime employment. The company is legally committed to keep you."

Elli made a face of disbelief. "There's a rumour that only people in their twenties will be kept. The rest of us will be sacked."

"I just heard you saying that I look after my people."

"It's my job to talk you up, but I don't see how you could prevent it."

Jim sighed. "Ellie, how long have we been working together?"

"Twenty-two years at the end of next September."

"Then what the hell are you worrying about?"

"You might prefer to have somebody younger around."

"How old are you?" Jim asked.

"Thirty-nine...forty-one." She spoke with such apprehension that she looked much older.

"I'm fifty-five. If you were a day younger, you'd make me feel too old to work. How's your father?"

"He's back in hospital."

"I'm sorry. That's tough on both of you. You want to have some time off?"

"No, thanks. I want to work as long as the job lasts."

"Well, I hope he'll be better soon and you can tell him that as long as I'm here your job's safe."

"Thank you, Jim." She left with a smile, but rushed back a minute later, more scared than ever. "Jim, what did you mean, *as long as you are here?* Are you thinking of quitting?"

Jim complained with a grimace. "Ellie, please. Let's work."

"Sorry," she said and disappeared.

In spite of Jim's confident assurances to Ellie, her fears alarmed him. *QS* was the only technological giant which still manufactured its hardware and software in the UK – and the only reason for this was the guarantee of lifetime employment which Jim had negotiated to avert bankruptcy. As they had been solvent for years, several executives and members of the board blamed Jim for saddling the company with such an absurd commitment and they had little sympathy for his argument that cutting *QS* into two and sacking thousands would breach their legally binding commitments to the workforce.

Ellie marched back into his study with forceful steps and placed a sealed bulky envelope on his desk. "I just got this from Sir Jeremy's PA," she said with grim satisfaction. "I never give you misleading information, Jim."

The envelope was marked "for the eyes of your principal only", but clearly it had been read by all the PAs and secretaries. It was a report by the management consultancy firm Opportunities, which recommended that at least half the workforce in the UK should be sacked and set out the advantages of moving production to Malaysia where people were cheaper and there were no labour laws to speak of.

The Taylors were having dinner in the kitchen, eating

healthy according to Lesley's recipe: sea bass with broccoli and lettuce. After her miscarriages she had let her husband enjoy food as much as he wanted, but she became alarmed by how heavy he had become and reduced her cooking to steamed vegetables and fish.

"Surely nothing will come of it," said Lesley. "Norton can't make four thousand people redundant just like that."

"Our profits are steadily shrinking," Jim said, "we're down to 5.2 percent."

"What does this 5.2 percent amount to?"

"Seven hundred and forty."

She was so surprised she choked and had a coughing fit. "That's less than your salary," she said, when she could talk again. "Seven hundred and forty thousand?"

"No, no. Millions. Seven-hundred and forty million."

"You sounded so gloomy I thought the company was going bust."

"Well, it's a possibility. We have enough projects in hand to do as well as we've been doing only for another year. I'll have to drum up more business. A decade ago I was still young and had some good ideas..."

"Don't talk like that," she interrupted him, annoyed. "You're not old."

"I have some good ideas. I shouldn't let them go to waste. I'm particularly keen on a software lock which would protect your computer not just from viruses, but from constant updates, which seem to be based on the notion that people have nothing better to do than explore new programs. I've also done some work on a tablet..."

Too upset to listen, Lesley interrupted him again. "I can't

get over it. After all your costs, the raw material, the factory, that huge building, your *QS* tower, with all its bills, taxes, you still had a clear profit of seven hundred and forty million. And that bastard is still thinking of quitting the country for more dosh?"

Jim wished he could tell her that these profits depended on the bribes he had paid and the arrests of a few officials made them all more circumspect. "We have some new obstacles," he finally said.

"What do you mean?"

He didn't want to upset her and didn't want her to think less of him. "We're in a worse place than we used to be."

"That doesn't mean anything."

"Well, if you're really interested in the details..." He took a deep breath, emptied his glass of water and told her about the bribes. He told her everything.

"Poor Jim," she sighed and pushed her plate away.

"I'm sorry. I should have kept my mouth shut", Jim said, but even as he said it, he was glad that he no longer had secrets from her and at least at home he wouldn't have to watch what he was saying.

"So how many more hundred millions do you need?" Lesley asked, trying to keep her distress out of her voice. "When is it enough?"

"It's never enough," said Jim. "That's the system."

They had tickets to Covent Garden to see *Rossini's La Cenerentola* for the following night, but Jim had no time for music now and Lesley took their journalist neighbour Kate Greenall instead. Jim had less than two weeks to prepare for the board meeting which was to decide whether or not the company should split into two. When Lesley went to bed, Jim was still in the office and when she woke, Jim was already at his computer at home. Worried about his health, Lesley begged him to slow down. He wouldn't listen.

"I'll be damned if I let our jobs go to Malaysia," Jim swore every time Lesley tried to talk sense to him. "I risked jail to keep them here."

28. WE DIDN'T MAKE THE WORLD

In every act there is a final choice
in spite of all complexities
between the silence and the voice.
GEORGE JONAS

According to the rules of *QS*'s corporate governance, all major decisions were made at the joint meeting of senior executives and members of the board. They sat at a long rectangular table in the windowless boardroom on the 21st floor of *QS* Tower, breathing processed air. Emphasizing the importance of their deliberations, the table was an exact copy of the 10 Downing Street cabinet table used by the government to decide how to govern the country. Senior *QS* executives and members of the board were to decide whether there were sufficient opportunities for growth to continue to manufacture their hardware and software in the UK, or accept the report of the management consultants and cut costs significantly by moving production to Malaysia. On the table on front of them lay everything they could possibly need to do their reflective best. Each had a tall glass and two bottles of mineral water (one carbonated, one plain), a stack of relevant written reports and a shiny new *QS* embossed leather bound notebook with a *QS* Crystalline pen to jot down ideas during their discussion.

Janice, Norton's PA, sat in a corner at a separate small table transcribing every word on a computer with a sound recorder which provided vocal evidence of what was said. Visual evidence was provided by CCTV cameras placed high up on the walls of the room.

Unknown to all except Vitek Rattan, the Finance Director and Virginia Cunningham, head of the legal department, Norton had already made the decision for them. When their meeting started at 10 am London time, it was 5 pm in Kuala Lumpur and builders in the industrial suburb were near the end of their working day erecting a replica of the *QS* plant in Glasgow. The meeting was to sanction, albeit belatedly, what had been going on for months. Reversing the dates later would be child's play.

The Chairman sat midway at one side of the rectangular table and, six feet four inches tall, towered over the group even in a sitting position. Everybody owed his appointment to him and he had no worries about the outcome. Non-executive board members – a museum director and the head of a charity among them - were the least of his concerns. He had picked them for their ignorance of the computer business and they received a five figure sum for attending a few meetings a year. They didn't even try to understand what was being discussed. What did they know about the issues? What did they care? They regarded their well-paid presence as one of the perks due to people who had other important jobs. They invariably voted with the Chairman. Among the active members of the board who received six figure remunerations, there were two bankers and an MP who asked questions and required plausible answers for form's sake. Norton's only problem was his Senior Vice-President who knew most about the company but had the guarantees given to the workforce on his brain. Norton opened the meeting by praising him. "I think we should formally thank Jim for adding forty million to the order books since our last meeting."

"Hear, hear!" was followed by smiles and nods by way of homage.

This was Jim's only hope: he had worked hard to produce credible grounds to argue that they were doing too well to split the company between two continents. He outlined several current projects which could generate billions in sales receipts. "My team prepared detailed reports about all the projects which are nearing completion," he concluded. "I'm sure you've read them, but in case you want to refresh your memory and ask questions about any of them, it's in one of the files in front of you."

The mention of billions and comfortable profit margins would have meant bigger bonuses and higher remunerations and it galvanized many around the table. None of them had read any of the reports but now they reached for Jim's file and cast searching looks at its pages, trying to spot a Caribbean cottage or a ski chalet among the graphics, the drawings, the mathematical calculations, the incomprehensible scientific reviews, the sales projections.

Seeing how tempted they were, Jim made his main point. "All these projects would be jeopardized by halving the number of UK employees, as the management consultants suggested."

Norton frowned.

Virginia Cunningham, alive as she had always been to the expressions on the Chairman's face, was quick to translate his frown into words. She had improved with age, especially her clothes. Dressed by a couturier, her wiry hair softened by a celebrity hair dresser, she was strikingly elegant and her eyes had lost their angry glint and shone with forgiveness rather than resentment and malice. As the company's director of legal affairs, she had an additional career as a lecturer for various worthy societies as well as being a guest on radio and television chat shows, speaking eloquently on the need for the feminine perspective in the nation's boardrooms. It enhanced her effectiveness as the Chairman's most slavish sycophant.

"Jim," she said kindly, "I read the file and I must say it does credit to your team. I'm certain that some of those projects you referred to will be successful and eventually find their own niche. But they are too small to sustain a big corporation like ours."

"I don't think you can say at this stage that any of these projects is small."

"My dear Jim," she sighed, her patronizing voice morphing into a speaking-to-an-idiot tone, "all those projects of yours are oddities and we are mainstream."

"My dear Virginia," Jim replied adopting her speaking-to-an-idiot voice, "I appreciate that this is alien territory for you, but in the realm of thought, there is no such thing as mainstream."

"You don't think much of women's intelligence, do you?" she said with a forgiving smile, deftly turning Jim's personal criticism into an attack on womankind. She wished that he would make a pass at her so that she could destroy him.

The enmity between the Senior Vice-President and the head of the legal department was well known and it didn't stop the curious asking Jim about the new products, while the MP doubted that making thousands redundant and a likely lawsuit with the unions would improve the company's chances to win new orders from government departments, quangos and other public bodies which were their main customers.

"We didn't make the world," Norton declared abruptly.

The cacophony of voices was suddenly cut short, replaced by absolute silence as the executives and the board members looked at the Chairman expectantly, eager to learn what he wanted.

"We didn't make the world," Norton repeated.

Having heard him twice, the executives were blown over by the Chairman's profound wisdom. They emitted appreciative grunts and guffaws. As sure as hell they didn't make the world. It was God's truth.

"Of course I share Jim's desire to help our own people," Norton went on, "but there's so much competition, we have to cut costs. Our products are great, but they are still considerably cheaper to manufacture abroad, and these days Malaysia is cheaper than China."

The silence deepened as the participants were steeling themselves to speak eloquently in favour of moving.

"Yes, there is a lot at stake," said the Head of Distribution with heavy approval. "We have to be profitable."

"We must use our heads," Norton said in a commanding tone.

There was a ripple of approval. They agreed that they must use their heads.

"We didn't make the world," Jim countered, "but we signed agreements with our employees. Breaching them would bring on walk-outs, strikes and expensive lawsuits which would tie up the company in litigation for years, costing more than we could gain by moving."

"Jim," Virginia Cunningham said graciously. "I think you can safely leave the legal issues to the legal department. We are in difficulties and that negates our guarantees. We will get rid of people quickly and cheaply."

"I heard you lectured audiences that companies should be family friendly."

She blushed defiantly. "Jim, we all know that you have a kind heart, no need to make an issue of it. Anyone made redundant will get unemployment and child benefits. We pay enough taxes. Let the state look after them."

"When you sack good people, you lose the ones who could look after you."

"We have to consider our investors," commented Malcolm Lester, a director of a High Street bank, a grey-haired man with pink puffy cheeks that spoke of too many power lunches and exquisite bottles of wine.

"The employees whose jobs you want to give away," Jim told him, "are investors in the company."

The banker opened his eyes wide. "Where did they get the money?"

"They've invested their salary cuts and their whole

working lives in *QS*."

"I see," said the banker. "It sounds good, but it makes no economic sense."

"Whatever we decide, it is going to be controversial," said Norton quickly. "My preferred option is to move production to Malaysia, but we must keep an open mind. We must be certain we haven't overlooked a single aspect of the issue. This is why it's essential that everybody should have his say. I urge you to speak up, to share your thoughts."

In the past, executives and members of the board who had taken the Chairman's curiosity about their thoughts seriously lost their jobs and board members whose opinions differed from the Chairman's were not reappointed and lost easy money. The survivors were not about to disagree with him. Even if the executive was reduced in numbers, they had a chance to go on for a while, but if they annoyed Norton, they would be out in a couple of months.

Jim's arguments, with some tentative support from the MP and the merchant banker, made no headway against the rest, who enthused about the excellent choice of Malaysia as if it were a delicious meal, peppering their observations with "we must use our heads," and "we didn't make the world." They didn't need their fancy notebooks; they could echo the Chairman without jotting down reminders. The only person using his leather bound notebook was Jim. He was drawing guns.

"So we all agree, with only Jim dissenting, that Kuala Lumpur would make the most economic sense," the Chairman concluded. "Just the same, Jim made the most important point," he went on, surprising everybody. "The process of dividing the company will take months and during this time we could be ruined. Walk-outs, strikes and lawsuits are real threats. We can't ignore all that."

Jim heaved an inner sigh of relief; he hadn't lost yet.

29. THE FRONT LINE

Life carries us through all our humdrum days, but there always comes a moment when we have to carry it.
CAMUS

News in offices travels faster than the speed of light. The air in *QS* Tower was poisoned by fear. Like gas from broken pipes, anxiety seeped along the phone lines and through doors suddenly flung open.

"Did you hear?!"

An article in *The Times* property section the following morning noted that Goldman Sachs had bought the lower 14 floors of the 24-floor *QS* Tower. There was no need to issue a scary notice to the staff about unavoidable redundancies. As the space shrank, so would the number of employees.

Ellie stormed into Jim's study with the newspaper in her hand. "You must have known about this, Mr. Taylor, and you didn't tell me."

When Jim realized what it was about, he grew so pale that she rushed to pour him a glass of water. He downed it as if he were dying of thirst.

"No, you're too decent to have kept me in the dark," she added quietly.

His deputy, George Nicholson, the only Oxford graduate in the company, called him on Skype with news from Glasgow. When workers came to the *QS* plant in the morning they were told that the plant was closed, that they should collect their things and go home. They would be contacted later about compensation, severance pay and the help they would be offered to find a new job. The workers were angry about not getting any warning, but only one of them was bitter enough to break a machine. A security guard, a girl, tried to prevent him from causing damage. The engineer hit her and the girl broke his arm. What caused as much sensation as the engineer's broken arm was that the security guard belonged to the infamous Asbo Girls, a gang formed on a Glasgow sink estate whose members had all been convicted of mugging and other violent crimes. Dedicated parole officers and social workers had managed to turn these violent young criminals into useful members of society who formed a legitimate security company and broke arms only in the performance of their duties. Their company was called SAFE, but they were tough and they were rough and continued to be known as The Asbo Girls.

"Jim, how come you didn't know that the plant would close?" asked Nicholson. "You're the second man in the company. It's incredible. You and Sir Jeremy are supposed to be close friends."

"Clearly we're not."

Seething with silent rage, Jim got up from his chair and went to confront Norton and resign. Hurrying along the corridor, he felt liberated, doing what he should have done ages ago. Another hour and he wouldn't have to see Norton again. Or Virginia Cunningham. He felt younger with every step. Suddenly, as if he had been struck, he stopped. He remembered that he still owed two million four hundred thousand on their home. They couldn't afford to keep up the payments if he resigned. 'We didn't need to buy the apartment, let alone enlarge it,' he thought. 'Lesley didn't care.' He took a deep breath to move his legs and reached Norton's offices at a much slower pace. He had a mortgage, he wasn't a free man.

Janice, Norton's PA and girlfriend, knew that Norton expected trouble, and when the Senior Vice-President came in she stood up and greeted him with apprehensive solicitude. "Good morning, Mr. Taylor. Please go ahead; I'm sure I don't have to announce you."

Jim went through, ignoring her.

"A friend when I need him!" the Chairman exclaimed, rising from behind his shiny mahogany desk from the other end of the vast room, stepping forward with his huge strides and wide smile to clasp Jim by the shoulders. "I was just about to send for you," he said, squeezing Jim's arms and holding onto him with a firm grasp.

Grim-faced, Jim stared at him without a word.

Norton let his arms drop and pointed towards the long curved leather sofa. "Sit down Jim, please, sit down."

Jim remained standing.

"How is Lesley?" Norton asked, ignoring Jim's angry silence. "I envy you your wife. You're a lucky man." He went on talking and smiling, praising Lesley as if nothing had happened which required an explanation. Not getting any response, he gave Jim a worried look. "Why are you standing?"

Jim, swallowing his fear of losing their home, willed himself to say that he was resigning "with immediate effect."

Norton raised his head to stretch his wrinkled neck and began massaging it, emitting sounds as if he were clearing his throat. "Er... you can't do that Jim. Please sit down, let's talk."

Jim remained standing.

"You're sore because I didn't involve you in the sale of floor space, but how could I? Look at it from my point of view. You were so keen on those guarantees and you're so excitable, I couldn't risk this getting out before we confronted employees with a *fait accompli.*"

"Perfect. You don't trust me – we don't trust each other I should say, so it's a good time for me to go."

"You're unfair, Jim." He shook his head sorrowfully. "Terribly unfair. It's not like you at all. It was your idea. All I did was act on your advice. If we had gone about this the normal way, there would have been strikes and lawsuits, restraining orders, paralyzing the company before we could move as far as the next street. That was your argument and I listened."

"I'd been arguing that we should honour our commitments."

Norton stretched his wrinkled neck again and massaged it a little more, avoiding eye contact. "I know you have a lot on your plate, Jim, and I know you hate this kind of thing and I hate to inflict it on you, but I've no choice. We have only six months to clear people from the lower fourteen floors and you're the best man to do it."

Jim was so surprised he sat down.

'He sits down, he won't quit,' thought Norton, feeling in charge again. "The management consultants will do most of the work, but you'll have to look over their shoulders."

Having sat down, Jim wasn't ready to get up and walk out. "Do you mean Opportunities? Those consultants have quite a history."

"That's right, they're sharp, and they're smart."

"They're the smart guys who don't make anybody redundant. They *non-retain* surplus people, they *negatively employ* them, *excess* them, *deselect* them. They spread a lot of happiness."

"You're having fun, Jim, but it's unfair. Not all those awkward terms were their inventions. Besides, you're talking about the Stone Age, when people expected to work for the same company all their lives. You couldn't sack them without some waffle. It's different these days. Next week we'll open a new and improved version of our Glasgow plant on an industrial estate on the outskirts of Kuala Lumpur. It was the consultants who arranged the whole thing. Anyway, they won't be able to sack anybody without your approval. Who is dispensable? Who is indispensable? We can't leave these questions in the hands of outsiders. You'll have the final say. You're ideal for this. You know hundreds of them by name. You know how they perform. You know who the best are and who the losers are. At one time or another you've travelled with every one of them in the lifts." He raised his eyebrows and his index finger. "Remember, this is not just about sacking people. It's just as important to identify those we have to retain. Production moves to Kuala Lumpur, but our customers are here, the brain work has to be done here. You can make sure we'll keep the best software engineers, the best computer technicians, the best service engineers – in short the best."

Jim remembered people smiling at him in the lift, and how good they made him feel. The memory beamed him up into a world of goodwill and comradeship. "The ones we have are the best we can find," he said when he could focus on Norton again. "And most of them have contracts which I helped to negotiate - contracts which granted them job security. And now you want me to betray them?"

The Chairman looked down from his great height on his Vice-President sitting on the sofa. "Are you telling me that life is unfair?" he asked pityingly.

"No, I'm telling you that we are unfair."

"Jim, we didn't make the world." Standing on the deep blue pattern of an antique Persian carpet, with his hands clasped behind his back, he began rocking on the balls of his feet and recited the lines:

> *"Some are born to sweet delight.*
> *Some are born to endless night...-*

"I know some poetry, too, old friend," he added with the flicker of a triumphant smile. He had learned the lines from his brother-in-law, the Duke, and he spoke them with feeling and conviction. They were precious to him: they contained the wisdom of the ages and, besides, they were the only lines of poetry he knew.

"You'll still have strikes, lawsuits. You're screwing people and they won't take it lying down."

"Ah, you still believe in the divine spirit. It's all those cello solos in your head. Actually, I don't think there will be much of an appetite for a fight. We'll be able to utilize people much better when they're scared. Those who hope to keep their jobs won't want to annoy the management. Quite the reverse. They'll work twice as hard to prove we need them. It's already happening. You can sack half the workforce and get the same results. Basically we should keep the young ones and sack all the buggers over fifty."

Jim's mouth dried up and his heart hit his rib cage. He was over fifty. "Over fifty is experience," he said in a hoarse voice. When his heartbeat returned to normal, he remembered that Norton was the same age.

The Chairman pursed his lips. "Experience, you say? That may be, that may be. But the over fifties have less energy, they get higher wages and they're sick of work."

"Are you speaking of yourself, Jeremy?" Jim asked. He no longer had the courage to repeat that he was resigning, but if Norton took offence and fired him – why, then it was out of his hands.

Sir Jeremy reddened and grew dignified. "I don't think your frivolous tone is appropriate." He retreated behind his desk and sat down on his high-backed chair covered in red velvet which could have passed for a throne.

'We'll sell the apartment and move to a smaller place,' Jim thought, trying to prepare his soul for giving up their palatial home. He couldn't quite imagine life without all that space, especially his music room. Yet he couldn't imagine giving in either. "Tearing up people's lives is a job for Virginia, not for me," he said.

"Virginia has the right spirit, but she doesn't know much about the business," Norton declared dismissively.

'So ass-licking doesn't take you all the way,' Jim reflected with some satisfaction.

"This is an unpleasant business, Jim, and I don't blame you for hesitating, but," he raised his eyebrows and his index finger, "if you won't do this, someone else will."

The echo of his own mantra sapped Jim's resistance. It occurred to him that if he was in charge, he could keep the people who needed their jobs the most. Dozens were brilliant, but they were all competent. He could protect families with small children.

"Perhaps you were right and I've made the wrong decision," Norton went on to assure his old friend that they were on the same side. "But at this stage the only thing we can do is to carry on. Do you want somebody else to pick the losers? There's nobody who could judge the staff as well as you can. If the wrong choices are made, the company won't be profitable enough to survive. They could all lose their jobs if you're squeamish. Besides, they like you; you're popular. They'll take it better from you than from anybody else."

Jim spat out the name. "Giles Orbiton."

The Chairman's blue eyes clouded with suspicion. "What about him?"

"You just mentioned losers. Twice a year Giles Orbiton gives you a policy paper cobbled together from the *Financial Times* and the *Wall Street Journal*. Nobody reads it, not even you, and he's paid a hundred thousand a year for it."

"What's your point?" Norton asked irritably.

"It's news when he shows up. That's another thing – he takes up a whole office and I have a couple of brilliant mathematicians, imaginative software creators, who have to share a room. He even has a secretary. You simply cannot lay off thousands and keep Giles Orbiton."

"I don't see why not," Norton said, casting an involuntary glance at the Constable which had a whole wall to itself: majestic trees and a spring half-buried in the grass. Lady Margaret had placed the painting in his office to bestow on her husband the inherited glory of the rich. "Giles isn't one of them. Surely the buggers can see the difference?"

"They see the difference and it isn't in Giles Orbiton's favour."

Seeing that this wasn't an argument he could win, Norton relaxed his shoulders. "I can't do anything about it," he sighed. "I can't go against Margaret. Giles is useless and the family can't think of doing anything else with him."

"There's no way I could look people in the eye and sack them while this parasite's in the building. They'd be right to spit in my face."

Norton shook his head gloomily. "I could never convince Margaret. You know what she's like. In fact she's bossier than in her youth. Her looks are gone, her body has gone to pieces. Being headstrong and impossible are the only things left from her beauty years, so she's worse than ever. She won't change her ways." He shook his head. "I'm sorry Jim, but I'll have to let you go – unless...?" The unfinished sentence was accompanied by a suggestive smile.

Jim heaved himself to his feet. His despairing air alerted Norton that it was decision time. He was trying to think who could replace Jim in getting orders worth millions. He didn't have to think about it for long. "I'll make a deal with you, Jim," he proposed. "I'll get rid of Giles and you clear me fourteen floors. Is it a deal?"

"It's a start," said Jim, growing bolder. "If I take this on, I don't want a repeat of what happened in Glasgow. I won't have anybody's arm broken. I won't have loyal workers frogmarched out of the building. Why subject them to such indignities?"

"But Jim, people are watched everywhere. Security is in the background unless it's needed."

"I'd rather see a few machines broken than anybody's spirit. You must also think of our wizards you want to keep. Do you think they'll do their best for you if you humiliated their friends and colleagues? One day you may treat them the same way. They can build viruses into our programs, wiping out the company."

Norton brushed aside Jim's objection with a wave of his arm. "You underestimate the power of fear."

Jim steeled himself once again for the loss of his home. "This is a job for Virginia, not for me."

The Chairman, CEO and President of *QS* rose from his chair with a threatening look, but in the end he agreed not to bring the Asbo girls to London. "I trust this is all," he added resentfully.

"I think we should also increase redundancy payments beyond the minimum requirement. Think of the media, Jeremy, the publicity. You don't want the company to stink."

This new piece of impertinence brought Norton forward from behind his desk again. "You should have left your cello at home," he thundered, sorely tempted to crush Jim. After another argument, he agreed only to an extra week's salary for every year.

Jim, having risked his home for more than a couple of hours, felt gutted and gave in about everything else.

Once again, Norton became an amiable old friend and grabbed Jim by the shoulders. "I knew you'd rise to the challenge. It takes courage to kick ass, it takes character and you've got it."

Back in his own office Jim walked to his wall-length window. Past five in the evening, it was already dark and he was staring at the shining stars in the clear winter sky. He longed to be free and live on another planet. The comet's distant pulsating light among the stars never failed to cheer him. It appeared bigger and brighter – nearer – than the evening before. Bending down to his *Sky Watcher Explorer,* he aimed the telescope at Comet Claudina to take a closer look. The flickering, living light rid him of his depression. He went back to work and resolved to save the jobs of every employee with small children by marking them indispensable. As he left late in the evening he saw Giles Orbiton in the elevator, carrying boxes and looking daggers at him.

'So the parasite is kicked out; it'll make everybody feel better.' Jim thought. 'Even that is something. I'm helping by not quitting.' Still, he couldn't quite convince himself that he did the right thing.

When Jamie was a little boy, still called Kleermaker, his father took him to the movies and he found himself in a battle on an island. After the guns fell silent, American soldiers in the trench watched the sun sink into the sea, listening to the groans of a wounded comrade lying beyond their trenches. "Go and bring him back," said the sergeant when it got dark. Two soldiers crawled out of the trench with a stretcher, but before they could reach the wounded man the Japanese machine guns opened up and the rescuers stopped crawling. Jamie saw their dead faces turned towards the sky. "All right, let's give it another try," grunted the sergeant. "I'll go myself." He asked for a volunteer to go with him, but nobody volunteered to climb out of the trench. They were all afraid.

Jamie wasn't afraid. He would rather risk his life than leave the poor helpless soldier at the mercy of the enemy. He climbed on his folding seat and shouted as loudly as he could so that the sergeant on the screen would hear him. "I'll go with you!" His father hit him over the head and he crashed down on his seat, but the joyful pride in his bravery had rooted itself in his heart. There are not many moments in our lives that tell us what kind of characters we are; peacetime existence confronts us with few life-or-death choices. Perhaps this was why Jim still remembered the imaginary heroism of his childhood. He admired people who would rather be killed than act like shits. All his life he had assumed that there were things he would not do, no matter what. Now, driving home, he felt he was crouching at the bottom of the trench with the other cowards. But then it is easier to risk one's life, even for real, than to risk a large office with a great view, a grand apartment and a yearly income of millions.

30. WHO SHOULD SUFFER?

The mass and majesty of this world
That carries weight and always weighs the same
Lay in the hands of others; they were small
And could not hope for help, and no help came.
W. H. AUDEN

Jim was mobbed wherever he went in the building. Most executives were disliked for their arrogance; they took too much pride in giving orders, they kept their distance. No one counted on their goodwill. But most employees assumed that Jim was on their side, even those who didn't know anything else about him except that he took the ordinary lifts like the rest of the staff.

One day in the lift, crowded with employees arriving for work, Dominic Malone, a software engineer (whom Jim had hired a couple of years earlier), turned to Jim. "Do you remember me, Mr. Taylor?"

"Of course, Mr. Malone."

"Am I for the chop, Mr. Taylor? I would just like to know."

"We would all like to know that," a woman called out. Her remark was greeted with laughter which had more bitterness than cheer in it.

Dominic Malone hadn't been with the company long enough to have his job protected, and Jim didn't remember whether Malone was on the list of employees with small children; nor could he let on that this was a consideration and scare employees without a family. "Nothing's been decided yet. Mr. Malone," Jim lied. "By the way, how are the children?"

The man looked disconcerted. "I have no children." He gave Jim a worried look, but it was his floor and he had to push his way out. As Dominic Malone left the lift he turned his head with a pleading face and waved. Jim had no option but to respond with a lying smile.

He found it increasingly difficult to move about in the building. Even those he didn't know him blinked, squinted and their mouths twitched in strange ways by way of greeting. One day in the corridor of Sales and Marketing, a pretty girl who could have been his daughter brushed against him, then apologised with a tempting smile and blew him a kiss. Old colleagues waylaid him to ask how Lesley was and when could they have lunch. It became unbearable and he asked Ellie for a key-card for the executive lifts.

Jim was hiding out in his office as much as possible, usually in the company of Charles Lacey, the team leader from the firm of management consultants. Lacey had already prepared a list of parents with small children and also a list of employees who had been long enough with the company to have legally binding guarantees of lifetime employment. However, their number had shrunk considerably in three decades. Over fifteen hundred of them had retired, died, or left the company of their own volition and dozens had been fired. Honouring the contracts with older employees still with *QS*, who were to be retained, as well as parents of little children – and holding on to all outstanding employees, there still remained two thousand people whom Jim had to get rid of. To be fair, he could rely only on their performance records.

One day Lacey was with Jim, as they were waiting for a computer printout. The most striking thing about Charles Lacey was his hair – wavy and jet black; he also had a jet-black beard that covered his cheeks right up to his cheekbones. Jim had no idea what his face looked like. However, he was impeccably combed and groomed; he had an electric shaver that kept his beard exactly one inch long. Lacey was a chubby, cheerful young man smelling of eau de cologne, who laughed and joked through it all. Jim had never encountered anyone like him: he didn't know who his father was. His mother, a real estate agent in Boston, didn't know who his father was either. "She never set eyes on him, she got me at a sperm bank," Lacey told Jim. "All she knows is that he was a university student, wanking off into a tube," he explained, laughing at Jim's amazement.

"Surely the tube had a name on it?"

"No way. The students wanked for pocket money, they didn't want to be sued for child support. I don't mind. It gives me curiosity value. Whenever I mention it to a girl, she wants to know more about me and I get a date. But actually there are lots of us. Am I the first one you've ever seen?" he asked, smiling. "Watch it, Mr. Taylor, watch it! You're out of touch; you'll be next for the chop!" Lacey had impeccably tight-lipped office manners, but having discovered that the Vice-President preferred bantering to boredom, he risked the odd joke at his expense when no one else was around.

"Have you ever heard of Oedipus?" Jim asked him, gloomily.

"Is that a new software?" Lacey asked. He had a master's degree in business administration, the science which excludes knowing anything else.

"It could be a computer virus, I guess. But I was thinking of a young Greek. He didn't know his parents and killed a stranger who turned out to be his father. You're going from one business to the other, crossing people off the payroll, and for all you know one of the men you ruin might be your dad."

Lacey's eyes flashed. "You're making my work real fun, Mr. Taylor."

For the first time since being turned out of his home, Jim thought of his father almost with affection. At least he had known the man, he could picture him. He was inclined to think that Lacey's origins must have something to do with his cheerful way of wrecking people's lives. Except that Lacey's colleagues, children of real fathers, coming from regular homes, seemed to be just as unaffected by the misery around them. Perhaps it was their youth. The eight members of the Opportunities team were all young, like doctors on cancer wards. Firing people was a young man's business.

Jim approved of the sacking of thirty employees every day.

The mass firings created a great deal of hostility and Norton directed all the fear, all the bitterness, all the loathing, toward his lunchtime friend. Anyone who attempted to appeal to the Chairman for redress was told by Janice Walker that Sir Jeremy could not interfere, that the Senior Vice-President had been given full authority by the board to oversee the process and deal with contentious issues. Dominic Malone told everybody that he was made redundant because he had drawn attention to himself, addressing the Senior Vice-President in the lift. The air began to thin around Jim. People no longer crowded around him in the corridors - they kept out of his way, afraid to remind him of their existence. One day two harried-looking women bolted through a fire-escape door when they saw him.

Most executives who have reached the peak of authority will be familiar with Jim's predicament: people feared and hated him for being in charge of all the pain but he himself felt powerless, impotent. He began to eat seriously, taking to food as other people take to drink, eating whole cheesecakes at one go. He began to sleep with his watch on and woke up every half hour or so to check the time. Whenever he got up to go to the bathroom he went on to the kitchen to raid the fridge, ignoring the plates of raw carrots and celery and the bowl of apples that Lesley had put out for him.

The first couple of hundred employees who were laid off could leave the building at their leisure; take time to have a last talk with their colleagues, without being harassed by anyone. Winning this concession perhaps meant more to Jim than to the victims. Not for long, though. The first employee who responded actively to her dismissal was one of the switchboard operators who had been replaced by an automated system that played recorded commercials for *QS* products while customers waited on line. ("It's their time or our money.") A widow in her forties who was rarely seen without a thick paperback, Antonia Smith saved herself from a nervous breakdown by pouring coffee into various computers and printers during her lunch break. She did it quite surreptitiously, armed with nothing more conspicuous than a Styrofoam cup. It wasn't noticed, or rather, no one admitted to noticing it, until after she had left. She inspired others who were leaving the place for good, and they poured their farewell latte with sugar and crème into as many pieces of machinery as they could without making any noise.

John Howe, a burly delivery man, put up more of a show. He invited his mates for a farewell drink, including the foreman who had picked him for redundancy, assuring them that he "didn't give a fuck". He wasn't going to look for another job either. If businesses hoped to prosper by making everybody unemployed so nobody would have money to buy anything, well, that was fine with him. He looked forward to collecting benefit and watching DVDs. After a jolly time in the pub he came back to the storeroom to collect his things and started smashing up some forty thousand pounds worth of computers and hard drives before the others managed to restrain him.

Jim had to fly to a meeting in Brussels, but his mobile kept ringing with bad news all day. One of the calls was from Norton. "So you were worried about hurting their feelings!" he bellowed. "You didn't want to humiliate them. I should charge you for all the damage." He sounded almost pleased.

Next morning Jim found six strange women waiting for him

in Ellie's room wearing identical grey trouser-suits. They were the Asbo Girls from Glasgow with closed cropped hair, wide unresponsive faces and fixed smiles.

Jim hated them on sight. "What are you doing here?"

"We're the Exit Attendants," replied the heftiest of the group in a deep voice, resonant with professional pride.

Charles Lacey bustled into the room to apologize. "I'm sorry, Mr. Taylor, maybe I should have phoned you last night but I knew you just got home from the airport, I didn't want to bother you in the evening..." He explained that the Exit Attendants worked in pairs. "They'll get people out of the building in no time at all. Without any damage to equipment. Without the disappearance of a single file. And being young ladies, they make the whole process less antagonistic."

"I was under the impression that I'm in charge and I didn't ask for anybody."

"Mr. Norton told me you might object, but..." Lacey raised his hands in a gesture of helplessness.

"All right, Mr. Lacey, but put them somewhere else," Jim said in a rasping voice. "Let them wait in your room. I don't want to see them every time my door is opened."

"As you wish, Mr. Taylor - you're in charge."

The Asbo Girls listened impassively, their eyes as blank as ever, as if the dispute had nothing to do with them. They were moved to a room farther from Jim's study, but they chilled the whole building with their frozen eyes and frozen smiles. The employees called them the Angels of Death. Those whom they approached knew that whatever they had done, whatever they felt, whatever they would have liked to say, counted for absolutely nothing.

That night Jim was halfway through a family-sized carton of vanilla ice-cream when Lesley came into the kitchen looking sleepy and cross. Without a word, she took the carton from Jim, replaced the lid and put it back in the freezer. Then she walked over to where he was sitting and kissed the bald patch on the top of his head. "Come back to bed."

He looked at his watch and got up from the table. They went back to bed and she placed his hand on her bottom. Feeling her bottom always calmed him or made him horny. Either way he would end up getting a little sleep.

31. SHAME

What their foes liked to do was done, their shame
Was all the worse could wish, they lost their pride
And died as men before their bodies died.
W.H. AUDEN

The basement of *QS* Tower served as the underground garage and the base of the lift shafts and all the machinery, pipes, wires, cables and everything that was necessary for servicing the 24-storey-high structure above. It was owned jointly by *QS* and Goldman Sachs. The ground floor and the foyer at the centre of the three hundred and fifty metre wide building were also jointly owned. Over five thousand *QS* programmers, engineers, technicians and sales teams worked on the next fourteen floors owned by the bank, and Jim had to empty those floors for the new owner. Employees involved in the core activities of *QS* either had to be moved to the remaining eight floors on the top or made redundant. The management consultants produced a plan of "streamlining"- basically sacking more than half the people and making the lucky ones work more than twice as hard. The management consultants in the building, headed by the youngish Charles Lacey, proposed to abolish the jobs of the deputy directors of all departments, as well as their staff.

Their work added to the tasks of the remaining executives and their assistants, whose numbers and office space were also cut in half. He argued that it was essential, for the sake of staff morale, to make cuts at management level as well, including both in Norton's office and his own. Jim had the authority to alter the proposals, but without reducing the total number redundancies, so he approved.

Norton cursed Jim under his breath but didn't object. As for eight of Jim's own people (out of sixteen with whom he had worked well for years), he told each of them personally that they had lost their jobs, but also handed them a letter which assured them of extra financial help to restart their careers. He had arranged with Accounts that the one million pound bonus due to him personally for a big software deal with the EU, which he had been negotiating, would be paid directly to his staff. It was the kind of selfish generosity that characterizes millions who give money to charities; it freed Jim from worrying too much about those whom he couldn't protect.

Emptied offices on the Executive Floor were given over to the Department of Customer Relations. Those who stayed with Jim kept their rooms, as he kept his own study, with his great views of the Dome of St. Paul's, the city, the Thames and, with his telescope, the sky. He worked late trying to decide who needed their jobs most and who could be sacked.

Some choices were easy. A few incompetents, thieves and shirkers who had somehow managed to stick to the company were identified by the new scrutiny of the records and Jim approved their dismissal without agonizing. There was a minority of individuals who were so outstandingly brilliant that they were indispensable and had to be retained at all costs. He also automatically honoured the guarantees of life-time employment to survivors from the old days. The stressful part of the job was to sack people who had done nothing to deserve it. He felt he was committing a gross injustice whenever he approved people's redundancy on the basis of miniscule differences in their performance records.

One of the easiest choices for sacking seemed to be Pierre Beckford. A tall, handsome man in his early thirties, one of the best line managers of the sales force. During his five years with Quantum, Jim had never seen him walking at a leisurely pace: he always seemed to know where he was going, his blue eyes blazing, his dark brown hair bouncing with every brisk step. He had all the attributes for survival: he was clever, competent and energetic. His wife was the daughter of a multimillionaire barrister. They had an eight-year-old daughter and a big expensive house on the edge of Hampstead Heath and he always wore Savile Row suits with Jermyn Street shirts and ties. His wife had recently given him a state-of-the-art Mercedes for his birthday. Jim asked to see him just before lunch.

Beckford's mother was French from Marseilles and he had the imprint of eons of sunlight on his skin. He had a straight nose and surprisingly blue eyes; everything about him exuded health, money and pride. He took his dismissal without flinching, leaning back comfortably in the chair with his long legs crossed. Impeccably dressed, he was cool, self-possessed, almost bored. "You don't have to explain it to me, Mr Taylor. You have to cut costs, you've got to be competitive," Beckford said in the slightly impatient voice of someone who didn't like wasting his time listening to what he already knew. "It's self-evident."

Jim thanked him with a sigh of relief. "Well, you're admirably level-headed about this, Pierre. I must say I kind of hoped you would be. You struck me as somebody who could cope with reverses."

"We should have downsized years ago," Beckford said firmly.

"I was against the idea, but I can't tell you, Pierre, how much I appreciate your attitude. I'm really grateful." He offered young Beckford retraining counselling, but Beckford was interested only if the counsellors knew about "first class positions". Jim, who regretted ever more keenly that he hadn't stuck to his cello, suggested that Beckford was still young enough to start life all over again.

"What do you mean, Mr Taylor?"

"Well, what did you want to be when you were a teenager?"

"The chief executive of a multinational," came the prompt reply.

"Why don't you go into business for yourself?" asked Jim, thinking of Beckford's rich father-in-law. "If you're your own boss, nobody can lay you off."

A superior smile flickered over Beckford's face. "The future is in managing companies, not owning them. You can set your own salary."

"Well, I wish I could do more..."

Every inch the future CEO, Beckford thrust his lower lip forward dismissively. "It's not your problem. I don't see my job as an entitlement. I can't imagine any corporate entity owing anyone a career."

"Pierre, I've come across very few people as understanding as you are."

The paragon of corporate wisdom suddenly uncrossed his legs, leaned forward and flashed a smile. "But why me?"

Jim threw up his arms and growled with disappointment. "Everybody asks that."

Beckford's eyes were burning, but he still managed to sound polite. "Well, you're not laying off all the line managers, so really... actually..." His voice trailed off and became indistinct as he struggled to gain control of himself. "I just want to learn from my mistakes," he finally managed to say in a clear, calm voice.

Jim listened shamefacedly. "Pierre, I have no criticism of your work," he sighed. "To tell you the truth, I thought of you because it seemed that among all the people at your level you are best equipped to make a new start."

Beckford's Adam's apple jumped forward as he swallowed. "Well, that's the liberal ethos: the strong are discriminated against. However, it's your privilege."

Jim gave him one of his most glowing letters of recommendation and called Ellie in to retype it when Beckford wanted him to add that he had never been a nine-to-five man, often worked late without being asked, and didn't drink or smoke.

As Beckford was reading the retyped letter, his personal assistant phoned to say that his wife and daughter were waiting for him in his office. Beckford leaped up from his chair with a look of horror. He had forgotten that this was "take your kids to work day" at her school and his wife, who didn't work outside the home, was going to bring Melinda to her father's office. They were just in time to see him sacked.

"Didn't you tell your wife what's going on here?" Jim snapped, losing his temper. He hadn't planned to humiliate anybody in front of his family. "This is no place for an eight-year-old girl, when half of the workforce is being laid off."

"I didn't think I could be... well... well... anyway... " Beckford fell silent again, as if too tired to speak, but then resentment against his wife revived him a little. "She's always asking me when I'm going to be promoted."

"Well, couldn't you make up some excuse? Why didn't you tell her that taking the child to the National Gallery would do her more good? Who knows, great paintings might have inspired her to be an artist. Life's tough whatever you do, so she might as well be an artist. If she has any talent, that is. Or you could have suggested the Science Museum... the Planetarium."

"Alison wanted to bring her here. She wants Melinda to be an executive."

Apparently the whole family had executiveship on the brain.

Two Asbo Girls were waiting for Beckford in Ellie's room. Jim told them to stay there: he was going to accompany Mr. Beckford himself. The women nodded assent but followed them just the same.

Alison Beckford, a leggy blonde with frizzy hair, was waiting for them with a look of absolute hate in her eyes. Beckford's assistant was already packing and crying with two other Asbo Girls standing over her. Melinda, a chubby fair-haired little girl dressed in a smart navy outfit and shiny patent leather shoes, stood still beside her mother, her huge blue eyes full of alarm and curiosity. Beckford greeted his family with a curt "hello" and asked his assistant whether she had an empty carrier bag, but then immediately corrected himself with a lopsided grin. "I'm sorry, June. It's force of habit. You don't have to do anything for me."

Sniffling, June handed over a plastic bag from Sainsbury's.

Beckford's wife looked daggers at her husband. "Where's the briefcase I bought for you?"

"I left it in the car," said Beckford with a nervous twitch. He picked up the photo from his desk and showed it to his daughter. "You see, Melinda, Daddy had your picture right in front of him." Putting the photo into the Sainsbury's bag, he began to collect his personal belongings from the drawers, attempting to hum a tune, now and then stopping to throw a forced smile toward the child. "Well, this is the office world, Melinda, look around! Do you like it? Would you like to work in this room?"

Too stressed to split his attention, Jim ignored the weeping assistant and concentrated on Alison Beckford, telling her that her husband was leadership material who would quickly find a position worthy of him. She stared at him coldly without a flicker of expression. Jim turned to the little girl to compliment her on her outfit. Taking her cue from her mother, Melinda compressed her lips and looked back at him unsmiling.

One of the Asbo Girls grabbed a leather-bound file from Beckford's hand. "That's mine!" shouted Beckford, and tried to wrest it from the woman. His daughter came to his aid with a piercing shriek that distracted the attacker. Beckford took his file back and opened it to show them: it held his car papers. "Come on, June, let's all have lunch somewhere," he said to his ex-PA as they left.

Jim watched them from the open doorway, worried about the little girl, whose shrill scream still rang in his ears. But as they were walking down the corridor, with four implacable women at their heels, he heard Melinda remark in a normal voice, "Daddy, I thought you worked here."

32. A PAIR OF HANDS

Let me sit heavy on thy soul tomorrow!
THE GHOST OF YOUNG PRINCE EDWARD

After the Beckfords left, Jim was too shaken to do anything but eat and went to a nearby Italian restaurant for lunch. He had a salad for starters and devoured, in quick succession, a *cottoletta Milanese* with rice and hot pickles, a medium rare steak with French fries and potato salad and rounded off his meal, ignoring the peculiar looks of the waitress, with a dozen cream puffs, six filled with chocolate, six with vanilla custard, popping them into his mouth with avidity and passion, digging his grave with his teeth. Bloated and slightly dizzy, he was ready to get back to his office to sack people and take their hate.

His deputy, Nicholson, had already been waiting for him in the study, pacing up and down. He stopped to face him. "What about fairness, Jim?" Nicholson demanded. "What about some pretence of solidarity?" Taciturn by nature and quietly proud of his "British reserve", he was behaving like an Italian, waving his arms, his lean furrowed face flushed with indignation. "What about some sense of shame? Some sense that we're all in this together?"

Jim walked to his desk and sank into his chair. How had Nicholson learned that his job was gone? Had Charles Lacey talked?

"I don't blame you for being upset, George. I can't put a shine on this." George had been working for him for eighteen years. He knew the man's whole family. Lesley knew them, too. She had the Nicholsons for dinner a couple of times a year. The first time was so long ago that the two Nicholson girls were young enough to make a mess at the table. Anne Nicholson, a vivacious, pretty woman, worked for Oxfam for a token salary. The two couples often ran into each other at concerts. The last time the Nicholsons had come to dinner, Jim had played Vivaldi and Boccherini for them. Now their girls were at university, probably costing more than ever.

"This is not England, we're not a nation, a happy breed of men. We are dogs in a kennel and its dog-eat-dog time!"

Nicholson went on raving, but Jim's ears were buzzing with his own misery. Jim wanted Nicholson to be the very last to be made redundant. But if he already knew, why wait?

"I'm glad you have some notion of my predicament, George," he said with a sigh which turned into a belch.

Nicholson tossed a copy of the *Evening Standard* in front of Jim. Jim glanced at the headline.

Chairman of Software Giant gets an extra 2.5 million while thousands lose their jobs

At the time, only a few years earlier, this was still a shocking headline and Nicholson banged his fist on Jim's desk. "Does he have no shame? What are we going to tell people now?"

'How will you talk when you learn that you, too, lost your job?' Jim thought gloomily, belching. He knew he could wait another couple of weeks, but realized that he couldn't face Nicholson's rage again. "I have to tell you that the jobs of all the deputy directors are being abolished," he said quickly.

There was an oppressive silence.

"You can't tell me that, Jim," Nicholson said quietly, stroking his hand. After a while he began to pull his fingers from their sockets with all his strength, his face becoming distorted with the effort.

Like other musicians, Jim noticed hands more than most people and he had never looked at his deputy's hands without being impressed by the width of his palms, the length of his fingers. They reminded him of his mother, interrupting herself at the piano, exclaiming, "If only my fingers were longer." Nicholson, who wouldn't have had difficulty covering two octaves with a slight flick of his wrists, was pulling his fingers with increasing violence, cracking the joints. Galvanised by guilt, Jim invited the Nicholsons to dinner to decide what they should do.

"No, thanks. You've spoiled the taste of Lesley's cooking."

"She doesn't know about it, George. I haven't told her. She'll be devastated when she finds out."

"So you were ashamed to tell her," he said, giving another wrenching pull to his index finger.

'Stop mangling your hands before you do yourself some harm,' Jim wanted tell him, but he felt awkward making a remark that might sound like criticism. He glanced at his watch instead.

"You're telling me I've lost my job and you're checking the time?"

"It's just a nervous tick, George, I'm not sleeping well."

"You're just obeying orders."

When Jim got home, he wanted to tell Lesley about his day, but she wouldn't listen.

"You have to do it, Jim. I realise that, but I don't want to hear about it," she protested, getting as upset as if he were having an affair and wanted to discuss it. "Just spare me the details, please. I can cope as long as I don't know."

In the middle of the night the phone rang. He woke up and looked at his watch: it was 3.02. He got out of bed and tried to reach the phone in the other room before Lesley woke up. A voice shrieked down the line, "You murderer!"

"Who is this?"

"Murderer, assassin! I hope you rot in hell."

Jim put back the receiver and listened for noise from the bedroom. There was none. Thank God, the phone hadn't wakened her. He went to the kitchen, closed the door after him quietly and checked the fridge. Lesley had thrown out the cake, the chocolate and the ice creams he had brought home, but there were eggs, milk, flour and soda water and he made Hungarian pancakes.

He wondered about the caller. Who was it? Was it Nicholson's wife? Was it Beckford's wife? Who hated him that much? Whoever it was, she was exaggerating, he thought. Sacking somebody is not quite the same as murder. He ate the pancakes while they were still crisp and warm, put the used dishes into the dishwasher, looked at his watch and tiptoed back to the bedroom, trying not to wake Lesley.

"Who was it?" she asked from her side of the bed in a wide awake voice.

"I'm sorry. Did the phone wake you?"

"I wasn't asleep."

Jim sighed. "Wrong number."

Ellie put the morning papers on his desk. The big event of the previous night, front-page news in all the papers, was Comet Claudina, which had become visible to the naked eye for the first time. However, the journalists were calling Quantum Systems about a small item on one of the inside pages. Pierre Beckford had driven down to the family cottage on the Isle of Wight and hanged himself. He was found in the garage, dangling from a beam, with one end of his daughter's skipping rope tied around his neck.

Jim spent the morning talking to the press and trying to phone the widow, who hung up on him each time, then went over to Norton's office. "We're not in the charity business," Norton exclaimed, raising his palms to stop Jim proposing assistance to the family.

"It's about the funeral."

Norton sighed. "There's so much publicity about the suicide, I guess we can't avoid paying for the funeral. Tell the widow that the company will pay."

"You'll have to tell her yourself. She won't talk to me."

"I'll steady her a little," said Norton confidently. "I see you're upset, but don't blame yourself." Jim's alarmingly pale face prompted Norton to rise from his chair to accompany him to the door. "Don't blame yourself; you are doing a great job, a great job. You must look at the bigger picture - this is just a micro-negative. Besides, Beckford may have killed himself because his wife was cheating on him. We'll never know." He slapped Jim on the back. "Don't let this depress you. In a couple of weeks' time you can sign a 285 million euro deal with Brussels. We've got to celebrate! Let's have lunch after the funeral."

Alison Beckford refused Norton's offer. She asked her father to pay for it.

33. THE WAKE

*A man should have the fine point of his soul
taken off to become fit for this world.*
KEATS

Most religions hold that suicide, throwing away God's gift of life, is the ultimate sin. However, ways are always found to get around ancient dogma with notions borrowed from criminal jurisprudence, such as *temporary insanity.* It was agreed that Pierre Beckford was not in his right mind when he hanged himself and could be buried with pomp and ceremony. People passing the Brompton Oratory would have been justified in assuming that there was a High Mass for an important public figure: the great classical columns of the Church's neo-baroque façade were draped in black cloth. It was a sunny morning in early November with a clear blue sky and the mourners swelled into a crowd on the steps as they stopped to exchange greetings in spite of the cold. Most employees and ex-employees from *QS* Tower had never even heard of him before his suicide, yet they came to honour him in this Catholic place of worship regardless of their race, colour or creed, if any. The poor young father could never have imagined that he could draw such a big crowd. He didn't make it to chief executive, but in death he became an eloquent ghost of a disappearing working community. Jim attempted to offer his condolences to Beckford's widow and daughter, but the widow ignored him and Melinda compressed her lips and stared at him with her father's clear blue eyes. He caught many hate-filled looks, some from brave individuals still with the company.

Norton wasn't there but asked Jim to meet him afterwards. They lunched in one of the chairman's private clubs. The white damask napkins and tablecloths, the heavy silver cutlery, the wood-panelled walls graced with framed prints of birds and famous horses, the largely male clientele, recalling the traditional separation of the sexes, gave the place a stately, old-fashioned English atmosphere. The absence of the deafening chatter that plagues overcrowded fashionable restaurants enhanced the air of exclusiveness: all the tables were occupied but there was room enough between them to allow the guests to talk to each other without having to raise their voices.

"What happened?" Norton asked.

"A lot of our people were there."

"Was there any trouble?"

Jim didn't answer.

They sat at their regular corner table having cold cherry soup. Norton used to swish the tasty concoction around the big bowl of his mouth with visible pleasure before swallowing it. This time, judging by his morose expression, the cherry soup might as well have been dishwater.

Jim thought that Norton, too, felt bad about Beckford.

Putting down his spoon, Norton picked up his white damask napkin, patted his lips with a dispirited air and, resting his pale grey eyes on the noble face of a racehorse on the wood-panelled wall behind Jim. "There are worse things in life than death," he said remorsefully. "I married a crazed old woman."

Ideally Jim would have liked to throttle the man, but he only sighed.

"You can't imagine what it is like," Norton went on complaining. "I'm a bull pawing the ground; I need a woman twelve years younger, not twelve years older. Oh, God, what I'd give for a young wife!" he exclaimed in a whisper. He was a bull, but he was a sad bull. "You wouldn't believe what happened last night."

Through all this, Jim was looking down at his plate. Slowly and carefully, he spooned up the last of the cooked cherries one by one and swallowed them. He knew now that he was in for another session of Norton parading his double vision of himself as a great man and as the helpless victim of his cantankerous wife. Lady Margaret was always tired, she never wanted to go anywhere, she refused to take hormone pills and was as dry as the sands of the desert. "Last night topped it all."

"What happened?" asked Jim, rolling a bread crumb into a ball in an effort to show some interest, accidentally knocking his soup bowl over.

Charles, their distinguished grey-haired waiter standing some distance away and observing them through his gold-rimmed glasses, waved to his assistants and the two boys hurried to the table: one collected the plates, the other changed the tablecloth so swiftly that it looked like a conjuring trick.

Norton was impatient to go on complaining, but, since the young waiters were hovering around them, he asked about Lesley instead.

"She's upset."

When the waiters left, Charles stepped forward, cast a critical look at the table, filled their glasses with effervescent Malvern water, made a bow and withdrew.

"Lesley's upset about the suicide."

Norton nodded several times, growing more sombre with each nod. "It's tough. I appreciate that. But she doesn't understand much about economics, does she?"

"She can't quite see suicide as good economics."

"It's awkward for you, I can see that," Norton said. "You feel responsible."

"Don't you?" asked Jim.

Norton didn't seem to hear. "You're a lucky man, Jim. Your wife doesn't torment you. What does she say?"

"She doesn't say anything, but she blames me."

"That's nothing compared to Margaret. I didn't think she could still surprise me, but she's inexhaustible;" he went on, his voice growing resonant with feeling, now that he was talking about something that touched him deeply. "You know, she never wants to go anywhere. She manages to throw out most of the invitations that come to the house before I see them. All she wants to do is sit at home and talk on the phone. Our phone bills should be in the Guinness Book of Records. You mention any kind of get-together and she looks at you as if you were mud. You'd think she'd never been to a party in her life."

Charles brought their baked sea-bass. Jim attacked his plate and ate and ate.

Watching Jim stuffing himself like a starving man, Norton shook his head disapprovingly, but went on with his story.

"A couple of weeks ago my brother-in-law invited us to dinner and to my great surprise she accepted. I was pleased; there are always some useful people at the Duke's dinner. She took two hours to get dressed, mainly because she kept moaning that she could not leave the house until she had a face-lift. I managed to prevail and finally we were at the door. We were actually ready to get into the car. Then she turned around and went back to the house." Norton leaned back from the table and raised his arms in renewed disbelief.

"Jim, I couldn't believe it. I just couldn't. She went upstairs to her room. Can you believe that? I went after her, shouting, 'What happened? What's wrong now? Let's go.' She wouldn't. She had changed her mind. I asked her, 'Would you mind telling me why?'" Norton leaned closer to Jim. "Do you know what she said? Can you imagine?"

"No."

"She said, 'I already know too many people. One of them has to die before I meet anybody new.' Quote, unquote." Norton bent his large head and raised his eyebrows for emphasis. "What do you think of that?"

"You lead a dog's life, Jeremy."

The Chairman's laments lasted through the main course. Jim kept up a steady flow of sympathetic noises, sickened by his own baseness. This was not the way to bury that poor young man.

Charles wheeled their coffee and dessert to the table.

"Ah, our *ghalaktoboureko!*" Norton exclaimed loudly, displaying his ability to pronounce the name of the fine crispy pastry with custard and syrup. Having unburdened himself, he became quite jovial, ready to enjoy the little pleasures of life. "I'll have the smallest piece, Charles. This is a sad day, we shouldn't gorge ourselves," he added sententiously.

Jim took three pieces.

Norton leaned forward to pat his friend's arm. "I see you're getting bigger suits, Jim."

They were on excellent terms; Jim's loathing of the Chairman didn't change that. He allowed his hatred to show only in the privacy of his home.

Charles, their elderly waiter who had served them for decades, thought they were the best of friends.

34. THE ART OF MODERN CALUMNY

Calumny is a light breeze,
it glides into people's ears,
penetrates their brains
and stuns them with horror.
CESARE STERBINI

There were thirty-five suicides in France when French Telecom made thousands of workers redundant. In London James Taylor got rid of more than four thousand employees with only one suicide. Members of the *QS* Board were impressed. Their respect for the Senior Vice-President increased when they learned that he kept program makers and engineers in constant training and they had up-to-date skills to handle new technologies. As a result of his training programme, he could honour the guarantees of life-time employment to older staff without slowing down the company.

Jim's on-going negotiations with the EU for a €285 million deal for new software was a powerful reminder that, before his arrival, the company had not gained a single penny from the vast riches of the EU. Most key figures in *QS* would have liked to replace Norton with Jim, but only three of them felt this so strongly that they wanted to do something about it: Ms Woodward, the head of a pension fund and the only woman on the *QS* Board, the MP and the merchant banker, Paul Lybovitz.

None of them was ready to challenge Sir Jeremy openly, for Norton could have dropped them from the Board, but they agreed that they should discuss the problem. They met at Ms Woodward's home for dinner. An attractive woman in her fifties, she had the figure of a solid column, heavy but not displeasing, unobtrusive breasts, but no visible signs of belly or behind, which drew eyes to her clear open face and high forehead suggesting intelligence and a righteous spirit. Her maid served the dinner. She spoke little but listened attentively, an ideal hostess, making her guests feel at home. The MP was particularly keen on Jim's becoming chairman because Jim had prevailed in honouring the guarantees to the workforce. Lawsuits from sacked employees would have brought to light the politician's involvement with a company which took jobs from British workers and shipped them to the Far East; he feared that it could jeopardize his chances of re-election. The merchant banker, Paul Lybovitz, joined them because he liked the idea of a program protecting his computer from constant updates. The conspirators agreed that that it made no sense to have the most capable man in the company as number two. They invited Sir Jeremy to lunch at the Savoy and praised him highly for splitting *QS* between the UK and Malaysia, and praised him for picking Jim as his deputy who performed beyond expectations.

Paul Lybovitz hadn't become a multimillionaire merchant banker without a strong attachment to easy money, such as he was receiving from Norton for lending his name to the *QS* board. He meant to stay on the right side of the Chairman and started out like the others. "As we all know, Jeremy, you know how to pick your assistants. Getting the right people around you is the most important qualification of a chairman. Clearly, you're a born leader."

He stopped and let the others do their flattery, but listening to them he got bored. In fact, whenever he was depressed, he had the depressing thought that his professional life was a dreary routine. Inspired by boredom, the fear of boredom, he took the expensive risk of plain speaking. He didn't frequent casinos, but now craved the thrill of a gamble. "Anyway," he interrupted the politician, "we think it would be great if you named Jim your successor. Jim clearly knows what he is doing and has a good rapport with his creative staff. Besides, it would help *QS* if the next Chair and CEO would be a software man whenever you feel like easing your own workload. You could revive the dormant title of President, and as President still have the last word on policy."

The MP was quick to protest. "No, no, Paul's wrong. You must remain at the helm. It would be a disaster if you quit. We only thought you might reward Jim with some extra responsibility for his good work."

Ms Woodward nodded to indicate that this was also her view.

"I can't tell you how pleased I am that you appreciate Jim's work," said Sir Jeremy. He beamed his pleasure at each of them in turn, wondering which of the two-faced bastards had alerted the *Evening Standard* to his 2.5 million pay rise before it had to be disclosed. The threat to his powers completely altered his view of his old friend: he had nursed a viper in his bosom.

"Jim was my find," he told them. "I spotted his potential while he was wasting away at Microsoft and promoted him to his present job as soon as I took over. He's hampered by his background, though," he added.

"Why, was he a slum kid?" asked Ms Woodward with some concern.

Norton shook head. "No, no. You may not know this, but his grandfather was a famous cellist. Jim gave me some of his CDs. I understand you can still buy them on the internet. Jim himself plays the cello and he's quite good at it."

"I had no idea, it's fascinating," commented Lybovitz, who went to concerts and the opera. "What was his grandfather's name?"

"Adam somebody. A foreign name, but not German."

"A cellist whose first name was Adam..." Lybovitz wondered aloud. "That must be Adam Bardi."

"It's possible," said Norton. "The name sounds familiar."

The merchant banker was delighted that he got the name right. "I have one of Adam Bardi's CDs. I don't see this as a negative background."

Norton sighed. "You wouldn't think so, but it is. Jim's heart isn't really in business. Profit is the last thing he thinks about. As you know, he was against moving production to Malaysia – and he was against sacking employees."

"He handled it well enough, though," commented Ms Woodward. "One suicide, instead of dozens."

"That's the upside. The downside is that he refused to employ extra security guards. He thought people's self-respect was more important than a few pieces of equipment.

But the buggers who got their notices destroyed computers, tablets, printers, copiers, software programs and electronic communication tools before I could put a stop to it. The damage from Jim's romantic, artistic notions is estimated at nearly four hundred thousand pounds." He didn't lie, just multiplied the truth. "I called in a group of tough female security guards from Glasgow to protect our properties. Nothing significant has been broken since - maybe a few glasses and plates in the staff buffet."

"Well, Jim was certainly wrong not getting extra security," said Lybowitz, losing some of his enthusiasm for Jim.

"You can recover your loss through the Courts," commented Ms Woodward.

"I take good care not to," Norton replied. "Any publicity would give people ideas and result in more destruction. I'm sure we're not the only company which suffers its losses in silence and for the same reason."

"Jim's €285 million deal from the EU will more than make up for the loss," said the MP. "I understand it'll be concluded any day now."

"Our profit – just on this deal alone," Norton explained, "will be at least fifteen million more because we'll manufacture the software in Kuala Lumpur instead of Glasgow."

"The loss of jobs here, I'm sure, will cost the Treasury at least fifteen million," said the MP, lapsing into thinking about the country.

Norton raised his eyebrows. "You don't really mean that, Bob."

The MP beat a hasty retreat. He rubbed shoulders with

dozens of multimillionaires and it was driving him crazy that he wasn't rich. He needed that hundred and twenty thousand a year extra from Norton. "I'm simply saying that that's what people think who don't understand the global economy."

"Anyway," the Chairman went on briskly, "you wanted to discuss Jim and I can tell you he's a better man than you think. I can't help admiring him. One of their neighbours is a Saudi family. The Taylors found their Filipina maid unconscious on the street. She was beaten so badly by her Princess that she required surgery; they had to reconstruct her face. The Foreign Office stopped prosecution, citing diplomatic immunity, and the Princess was spirited out of the country."

"Oil," sighed Paul Lybovitz.

"Yes, but Jim financed a private prosecution on the Filipina's behalf and the High Court granted her half a million to compensate her for her injuries and her unpaid wages with interest. The maid is now back in the Philippines with her children and has the money to take care of them."

"I'm proud of our Courts," Ms Woodward said, straightening her back. "The government can play politics, but our courts uphold the law and protect the defenceless."

"Give credit to Jim, too," said Norton. "Without him nothing would have happened. It must have cost him more than a hundred thousand to finance the Filipina's case – the Saudis put up a strong legal team. How many people do you know who give half a hundred thousand to help to get justice for someone they don't even know?"

"Very, very few," commented Ms Woodward. "I can tell

you that sixty percent of the donations our charity receives is under a thousand, thirty percent is under five thousand, and none is above twenty thousand."

Norton raised his eyebrows for emphasis. "Exactly. That's my point. I'm not proud of it, but I must admit Jim's a braver man than I am. I wouldn't have had the guts to risk our Saudi contract. My spirit doesn't rise above the bottom line."

"Well, we must have a moral bottom line as well," Ms Woodward said with a tinge of disapproval, to put Norton right.

"Do we have a contract with the Saudis?" asked the investment banker alarmed.

Norton nodded. "We did have a contract about to be signed. Of course, Jim tried to keep his involvement secret, but the Saudis found out about it, and cancelled."

There was a long silence. They did not even move.

The investment banker finally spoke up, sounding a note of misery. "How much business have we lost?"

"Come on, I wouldn't have done it, but we must agree that there must be times when we put principles, decency ahead of business."

"But how much have we lost?"

"I don't want to upset you, let's wait to the end of financial year and see how much we can recover from other deals. You can't blame Jim for being a decent and generous man," Norton said unctuously. "I mention this only to show you how inconceivable it is that Jim would have done anything nasty and I am doing everything I can to defend him against a phoney claim of sexual harassment."

This was a surprise to all three. What claim of sexual

harassment? Who was the woman? What did she say?

"Please don't be alarmed, don't be alarmed." Norton hastened to reassure them. "It's nothing serious. We're not talking about rape. It would be nothing except that we live in this atmosphere of political correctness."

"The woman could be lying of course," commented Ms Woodward.

Norton raised his index finger to agree. "A valid point. But even if there's some truth in her complaint, we shouldn't let it ruin the career of a brilliant and decent man. As my brother-in-law says, a horse has four legs and still stumbles, but that's no reason to put it down. Anyway, so far I've been successful in persuading the woman victim not to make a formal complaint either to *QS* or to the police. I reminded her that false accusations can land her in jail."

"We're still in the dark," objected Ms Woodward. "What is her claim? What is the evidence? Give us some details."

Norton hadn't yet invented any details, but it didn't faze him. "I'm trying to hush this up, so right now I don't want to say anything more about it."

Ms Woodward wasn't so easily put off. The possibility of a sexual harassment claim clearly upset her, especially if it was unjustified. "I understand the Taylors have a good marriage."

Norton emphatically agreed. "Yes, it's an exemplary union. Still, when they were younger, they were found unfit to adopt a child. I'm sure it was a misunderstanding. In a few decades we all collect black marks we don't deserve. I'm sure Jim mentioned this to you and explained what it was all about."

"No, we haven't talked to Jim, we wanted to talk to you first," the merchant banker protested.

"Well, you should certainly talk to Jim," Norton said, satisfied that they would never support him for anything.

35. SAYING GOODBYE

Come, come, dispatch;-
'tis bootless to exclaim.
LOVEL

Promotion was the last thing on Jim's mind. Having had very little sleep for months, he felt close to collapse and longed to get away from it all, to have a bit of a life with Lesley, without having to jump out of bed in the morning and run. Business was relatively quiet and he decided to take three weeks off. The company owed him five. Norton agreed and pencilled in the celebration of the Brussels deal for the last Friday of January.

Before he could rest, Jim worked hard to make sure that the office would run smoothly during his absence. As it got dark early and he worked late, he could see Comet Claudina from his desk every evening, hanging like a votive lamp over the mighty dome of St Paul's.

On the 24th he gave a little lunch party for his personal staff, wished them all a Merry Christmas and Happy New Year, handed each a present chosen by Lesley, and sent them home at 1:30 pm to give them some time to shop. Ellie, whose father had died the previous week, stayed behind for last-minute instructions. "I'm glad you'll be in charge here for three weeks. It will help to take your mind off your father's death," he told her. He spent the rest of the afternoon on his own with the files, checking that nothing had been overlooked. After leaving some further instructions for Ellie, he left his office with a great sigh of relief. He felt that the worst part of his business career was over.

At about 8:30 pm he stood in the corridor waiting for the lift to take him down to the garage, wondering whether he should have bought a plane ticket for his cello. He was just about to step into the lift when Janice Walker came running along the corridor. Sir Jeremy wanted to see him for a moment. "He wants to say goodbye to you," she said, out of breath.

'He must have forgotten that we've already said goodbye,' Jim thought and followed Janice, stifling a yawn.

Norton came out from behind his desk to greet him with a wide, reproachful smile, holding out both his arms. "Jim, Jim, you wouldn't have gone off like that without saying goodbye, would you?" He motioned to Jim to sit down, then immediately turned away and started walking about the room.

Glancing at his watch, Jim dropped down on the couch. "I thought we said goodbye this morning and I'll be back before you leave for your winter break."

Norton smoothed his eyebrows with his index finger. "Didn't you get my letter?"

"What letter?"

"Where are you going for your holiday?"

"Lesley's booked us into a hotel in Florida; on a little

island off the Gulf Coast. All the flights to Barbados were full, so she decided we should try some place we've never been to. It's called Magdalena Island."

"Not really!" exclaimed Norton with joyful surprise. "Great minds think alike. We were on Magdalena last March. Margaret's sister has a place there. It's a small island with a few private homes and one hotel right on the beach."

"Do you know anything about the hotel?"

"Some friends of ours stayed there, it must be all right. You'll love it."

"Jeremy, what's that letter you were talking about?"

"Wait, let me tell you about the island first," Norton went on, enthusing about Jim's holiday. "You'll have a mile of white sand right in front of your hotel. You can have long walks with Lesley. I envy you for your wife. You won't have to be ashamed of her, she still has a terrific figure. I'd gladly exchange places with you. *You* don't have a wife who's crossed her legs for good. Or do you? You don't tell me your secrets, Jim, you keep your old friend at a distance. Anyway, those Gulf islands are ideal. Thanks to the causeways, you have all the advantages of the mainland - same-day delivery of vegetables, newspapers, everything. But you're on an island just the same - no through traffic – everything's clean and quiet. It's just the place for you to get back into shape, to ready yourself for new challenges."

"What new challenges? What's this all about?" Jim asked with restrained impatience, unable to fathom why Norton would write him a letter.

"Well, I don't understand," Norton said, scowling. "Janice was supposed to hand my letter to Ellie hours ago.

Which of the girls should we blame? But you were having a party, weren't you? I guess in the hubbub the letter was overlooked."

"Jeremy, what is this all about?"

Avoiding eye-contact, Norton went on talking and walking in circles. "As you often said, staff morale is important. As you know yourself, you're not exactly popular these days. They blame you for the suicide. Janice overheard the staff talking about you. Some woman said she wished you were dead and nobody objected. As you're always telling me, staff morale is important. Team spirit. We have to be a happy family. Anyway, I wrote to say how much I regret the way things have turned out..." He spread his hands in a gesture of helplessness. "There's nothing I can do about it. We have to let you go."

Jim's heart hit his ribs. "You mean I'm being sacked?" It was a redundant question, but it's difficult to think clearly when you lose your job.

Norton replied with a gesture of regret.

After a while Jim's heartbeat slowed down to normal, which surprised him. He was calm, detached. He had the curious sensation of being outside his own body, watching himself listening to Norton. He remembered George Nicholson mangling his hands and it struck him that his former deputy might easily have dislocated all his fingers without noticing.

"And one of the non-executive directors," Norton went on, "got the whole board upset when somebody told him that you and your wife were found unfit to adopt a child. That was years ago, wasn't it? I'd forgotten all about it myself. I don't know how they dig up these things. Anyway, they feel that our senior executives should have moral standing in the community..."

Jim heard himself arguing, trying to persuade Norton to change his mind, then suddenly stopped. 'Why do I humiliate myself?' he wondered. 'Do I want to work for him? Do I want to work with Virginia Cunningham?' He remembered commiserating with Norton about his problems with his old wife, right after Pierre Beckford's funeral and was overcome with self-disgust. 'No wonder I became a pariah,' he thought.

"What's wrong?" asked Norton, alarmed by Jim's sudden silence, worried that Jim would start a fight and try to unseat him with his allies on the Board. "Jim, you need a complete change to get back into shape," he pleaded. "You've let yourself go."

"I'm all right, I'm fine."

"Good Lord, of course you are!" Norton seconded vigorously. "All you need is a good rest. Fresh air and exercise. Plenty of exercise. After three weeks on Magdalena Island you'll be so fit, companies will be beating down your door. I'm sure you'll end up with a better job. Maybe with IBM." He reached out towards Jim with both hands. "We're still friends. Incidentally, about your company car. You'll need it to drive to the airport tomorrow. Leave it in parking; Janice will have it picked up."

Jim knew that he was expected to say thanks but couldn't bring himself to do it. "What about my assistants?" he asked, as if he didn't know.

"They were given their notices as they left the building."

"Ellie Wade is very efficient. Not many people are as

capable as she is."

"She's been with you too long. She couldn't adapt to a new boss."

"You know that her father just died?"

Norton raised his eyebrows. "What's that got to do with anything? Jim, we're not in the charity business."

Jim was followed back to his office by Janice and Douglas Jackman, the security guard. "I feel really bad about your goin', Mr. Taylor," said the security guard, with a defiant look at the Chairman's woman.

Janice watched Jim closely as he cleared his desk. "You should give me your cards and keys," she said sharply.

Jim dropped them on the desk which was no longer his, and asked Jackman to carry the telescope to his car.

"Of course, Mr. Taylor, sir," the guard said defiantly.

Before leaving, Jim stepped to the glass wall for a last look at the view. While Janice gave regular warning coughs to hurry him on, he gazed at the reflections on the river, and the pulsating glow of the comet. It was much brighter than the day before. He wondered how many Earths there might be among the billions of planets circling billions of suns, and was moved by the thought that people might be speculating about the same thing millions of light years away.

Behind him Janice kept coughing impatiently. As Jackman was carrying the telescope, she was forced to turn off the lights herself.

Lesley took the news in her stride. "I'm glad you're not working for that bastard anymore."

"He told me I need a holiday - have a good rest before

taking on new challenges," Jim said grimly.

"I'm sorry I didn't let you buy me jewellery. Now we could sell it and pay off the mortgage."

Jim was trying to pull his fingers from their sockets. "I only wish I hadn't caved in back in February."

She was thinking the same thing. "Don't torment yourself about it. We still have the insurance policy. We could cash it in."

"I'm not going to do that. We'll need that money when we're really old." He stopped pulling his fingers and went to the phone to call Nicholson.

"Hi, George, it's Jim."

"Who?" Nicholson asked with venom in his voice.

"I just wanted to find out how you are doing. How's the family?"

"It's none of your business."

"Do you have any problem with your hands?"

"Why are you calling me after all these months? Do you have a job for me?"

"I'm afraid not. I got the sack too."

"Good. That's the best news I've heard for ages."

"I thought you'd be pleased."

"There's still justice in the world. You betrayed people for nothing," Nicholson said and slammed down the phone.

Jim called Ellie Wade to reassure her that as soon they got back from Florida and he got a new job, she'll be his PA as before.

Ellie was delighted. "Oh, Jim, I'm so pleased you called. I realized that they wouldn't have sacked me if you were still in place. But I've faith in you and I know I'll work for you again."

Listening to her cheery encouragement, Jim knew that it would never happen. "Well, I'm glad you're not worried," he said. "See you when we got back from Florida." He put down the phone, walked to the French windows and looked at the garden veiled in darkness. He thought of Pierre Beckford tying his daughter's skipping rope around his neck and wondered whether there was a rope in the apartment.

Lesley hugged him from behind and kissed the back of his neck. "Come on, Jim, let's eat."

She unearthed a cartoon of ice cream, gave it to him with a spoon, and made a sandwich for herself. "Nothing would surprise me about Norton," she said," but I didn't think he was a sadist,."

"Norton isn't a sadist, he's just saving money. Sacking me before the EU contract is signed, he saved on severance pay. He'll have to pay for a year less."

"What about your bonus on the last EU contract?"

"It isn't signed yet, so Norton won't have to pay me a bonus. I promised that money to the staff and now they won't get it."

The Taylors could not afford a luxury holiday in Florida, but their first-class air tickets and the hotel had already been paid.

"Norton's right, the revolting shit," Lesley said later in the evening as Jim got the suitcases out of the cupboard. "You might as well have a good rest before you start looking for another job. And we'll have fun just to spite him."

36. IF ONLY

The past can turn into the present.
OTTHONITE PROVERB

A man of fifty-six has many reasons for wanting to drown himself and Jim had plenty of time to think of them during their three weeks on Magdalena Island. Hiding his bloated body in a fluffy bathrobe, he sat by the pool in a graveyard mood. 'If only I hadn't quit music,' he thought, racked with guilt. 'I wasn't as talented as grandfather and I could never have been so successful, but I'd be at least a member of a good orchestra somewhere and I wouldn't have done anything vile.' He had the gift of total recall which served him ill as he collected all the memories that accused him. He could see his mother's eyes shining with pleasure and pride as he played for her. He was relieved that she was dead. She would not understand. She would be ashamed.

Trying to pull his fingers from their sockets, he saw himself marching along the long corridor of the executive floor, ready to confront Norton with the firm intention of quitting with immediate effect. He hadn't quit and had sacked thousands. He had driven a young father to suicide.

And what had it gained him? He had gained two and a half stone, growing disgustingly fat.

Lesley was sitting at a nearby table at the pool bar with the dying boy. He was watching her but she no longer felt his eyes on her skin, although she was wearing a bikini. She didn't even glance at him. She ignored him. She forgot that he was there.

If only he hadn't been so scared when she got pregnant. What would have been so terrible about a crying baby? He wished that he could hear his own grandson crying, but what he heard, through the abyss of a lifetime, was his own voice asking Lesley, "Are you sure it's mine?" If only he had asked her to marry him instead. If only he hadn't insulted her she wouldn't have bolted. If only he had run after her while he could still catch her. If only he hadn't been vain and stupid, expecting her to make the first move. Didn't the concierge at the YWCA say that she had been sitting on her suitcase waiting for him? They could have made up right away. By now they would have grown-up children and Lesley would be playing with their own grandchild, instead with a dying stranger. If only he had applied for a passport as soon as she had flown back to Glasgow, it would still have been all right. He could have reached her before the abortion and she wouldn't have had her miscarriages. The words *if only* that can drive people mad lodged in his brain.

He thought of their second Luke, the plucky creature in Lesley's womb, waving and somersaulting, getting ready for life that was not to be.

Lesley drew a heron on the back of a pool bar menu and the living Luke burst into an eerie little laugh. She turned

261

towards Jim with a triumphant smile. He smiled back at her with a pleading look but she didn't see it; she had already turned back to Luke.

'That's all right, Les, I understand,' he thought, addressing her in his mind. 'The most important people to you will always be your sons who couldn't live.' He was no longer jealous. He had given up on her – he let her go.

'Die, die,' he kept telling himself every time he heard Luke's chilling little laugh. He was ready to die that very night, but the universe has a say in what happens to us.

37. A COSMIC HAPPENING

And who knows but the world may end tonight?
ROBERT BROWNING

In the early hours of December 1st, 2007 when the impact of the collision between Comet Claudina and the asteroid lit up Jim Taylor's bathroom and the Northern hemisphere, turning night into day, there was a less spectacular celestial event of equal significance for the characters of this story.

There was a spacecraft on the comet with a boy inside it. The boy had parked the vehicle on one of the comet's flat ice-fields to have a nap. The crash woke him up and at first he was as clueless as the people on Earth.

The comet's original path presented no danger, but on its new path Comet Claudina headed toward the 384,000 km gap between the Earth and the moon, within the gravitational pull of both planets . To avoid panic, official communiqués had stopped referring to Comet Claudina's size or density. The coldest region of the Earth is the South Pole where the sea is permanently frozen. The sunrays fall on ice that remains several kilometers thick all year around. And we are only about nine light minutes from the sun.

Large comets hovering from thousands to a million light years from the sun are correspondingly colder and more solid. Comet Claudina would have obliterated life as we know it, if it had hit the Earth.

The Harvard-Smithsonian Centre for Astrophysics issued a bulletin announcing that the comet would pass the Earth at slightly closer range than had been expected but there was no reason for alarm. The bulletin was broadcast on radio and television at regular intervals and, as the sky grew progressively brighter, it was amended to include the qualified assurance that the new orbit of the comet was "unlikely to have any adverse effects on Earth".

"Unlikely? You mean they don't know?!" was the cry heard in households all over the world, in dozens of languages.

To prevent mass hysteria, announcers appealed to the public to stay indoors and remain calm. Experts were summoned to pour their soothing wisdom on jangled nerves. Few were as reassuring as the authorities wished. "We can observe such small sections of space that anything we can see is no more likely to harm us than all the things we can't see," said one astronomer with disdainful coolness. "We see so little of the sky that if there is a disaster, more likely than not the first we'll know about it will be when we feel the impact and see the fireball over the horizon". Professor William K. Hartman of the University of Arizona was quoted as saying that "quite possibly it was a collision with this same comet which precipitated the last Ice Age 40,000 years ago."

If the comet locked into the Earth's gravitational field, the collision would ignite worldwide fires or else bring on a new Ice Age. Predictions were divided, as in Robert Frost's poem:

> *Some say the world will end in fire,*
> *some say in ice.*

Religious fanatics were ecstatic: their prophecy was coming true.

In spite of the broadcasts urging everybody to stay indoors, the streets filled with people. Perhaps they were just curious; perhaps they wanted to be part of the crowd. Whatever was happening, they didn't want to face it alone. There is nothing like a cosmic upheaval to remind us that we are related to each other. Local stations broadcast their respective national anthems. Somebody started a rumour on Facebook that it was a publicity stunt for a new disaster movie. A scaremonger posted a note announcing the meltdown of a nuclear power plant in Florida.

Magdalena Island was spared all the drama. Electronic signals were knocked out, all the phones were dead and the TV screens went dark. At Gulf Views the only person fully awake was Jim Taylor who was in no state to pay attention to the blinding light pouring through the hotel's glass surfaces. He was drained even of curiosity. In a hurry to drown - afraid of losing his nerve – he was shocked to find that all the exits were locked.

Teresa Ramos, the pregnant night-clerk dozing at the reception desk, was startled awake by the frantic punching of the desk bell in front of her.

"I want to go for a swim," complained the guest from Suite 206.

"I'm sorry, Mr. Taylor," Teresa said, suppressing a yawn. "We're locked up for the night."

"I want some fresh air."

"I suppose I could buzz you out to the garden." (Gulf Views had a large walled-in garden that separated the hotel building from the sand and the waves.) "You'd have to ring the bell when you want to come back."

"But I want to go for a swim."

Teresa became wide awake at the enormity of the request. "Oh, no, that's not possible, Mr. Taylor. Unless there's a fire, I'm not allowed to unlock the garden gate at night. It's our number one security requirement. We couldn't get insurance without it."

"What security? The beach is deserted at night."

"That's good for thieves. There are lots of them on the mainland."

"You have security guards at the bridgehead."

"The night guards are always asleep. The thieves could sneak past them and get on our beaches between the properties. You wouldn't like kids with knives sneaking into the garden, would you? And once they are in the garden they break a window, get into the rooms and rob the guests while they are sleeping. Not here, not yet, but there were cases like that in Florida, you know. The guests who woke up had their throats cut."

Gripping the two ends of the towel around his neck, the would-be suicide had endured the lecture with lowered head. Couldn't he die in peace? It seemed so simple.

"Are you OK, Mr. Taylor?"

Reminded that he must avoid arousing suspicion, Jim

Taylor raised his head and looked at her with what he thought was a winning smile. "It's such a beautiful night, Teresa, I just feel like going for a swim."

His sickly grimace confirmed her unease. "I offered to buzz you out to the garden. Have a little walk; it might help you to relax."

"I couldn't be more relaxed," he insisted in a shaky voice. "Buzz me out to the garden, and then buzz me out to the beach."

"The garden gate works with a key."

"Then give me the key."

"The water is freezing cold," she said carefully. "It's winter in Florida too, you know. You could catch pneumonia. And there is no lifeguard to watch out for you."

They went on arguing about the key to the garden gate, unaware that the world might come to an end at any moment. Teresa was profuse with excuses to put him off and he became more and more agitated. Flushing pink, he gave the two ends of his yellow bath towel another menacing pull. "I'm a guest here, not a prisoner."

"I know, but..."

"I wonder how much English you know!" he snapped at her.

Teresa's face tightened. 'You can drown for all I care,' she thought. Opening a drawer, she rummaged among the ballpoint pens, keys and paper clips. "Please don't lose it," she said in a fed-up voice, throwing a large brass key on the counter.

Having grabbed the key, Jim became hyper-polite. "When do you expect the baby, Teresa?" he asked solicitously, trying

267

to make up for his temper.

"I'll still be here when you come back," she replied, looking over his head, allowing herself to show that she was offended. "You must lock the garden gate from the outside when you go out and take care you don't lose the key."

"I'll keep it in the zip pocket of my swimming trunks," he assured her.

"If you lose the key, you'll be charged for replacing the lock."

"Of course, Teresa, of course. If my wife wakes up and calls the desk, would you be kind enough to tell her that I just went for a swim." He gave her a parting wave and walked jauntily across the cool marble floor, humming a cheerful tune. Not a man who would contemplate suicide. Absolutely not. To make sure Teresa would tell the police that he was in a happy frame of mind, he stopped and turned back toward the reception desk, confronting her with his bloated belly one more time, waving and smiling. He no longer cared if the young woman found him disgustingly fat and old.

Fat and old? That was the least of it.

At first only the instruments knew that the Earth was out of danger, escaping with the loss of some communication satellites. Passing nearer to the moon than the Earth, Comet Claudina lost another huge mass of ice which hit the moon, making it waver for an instant. The mass of frozen gasses blasted new craters and some of them exploded, melting into intense flames, while Comet Claudina sailed on, continuing its incomprehensible journey. Readers interested in the source of its unique fire-colour and other details will find them in scientific journals.

Space centers had been tracking the comet ever since its discovery by Claudina Argüelles and as the Comet's flight narrowed the distance, the telescopic radio photos and satellite photographs became clearer. The extraordinary presence of a spacecraft on the comet showed up on NASA screens as a dot. Just before the comet was to pass the Earth, the dot took off from the comet, veered toward the Earth, collided with a communication satellite and crashed into the Gulf of Mexico. This accident, which had far-reaching consequences, did not receive focused attention; it was lost in the thousands of space data observers tried to work their way through during the spectacular cosmic happening. The knocking out of the satellite was attributed to space debris.

But who could have paid attention to a dot when the Earth was showered with glowing gasses?

Distance cheats our vision. The comet's tail, which had seemed as small as the flickering light of a match, was in fact four million kilometres long. As it passed over the Earth, it showered the hemisphere with cosmic dust and glowing gases containing hydrogen, oxygen, carbon dioxide, methane, ammonia and a whole host of ions and organic molecules - the basic building-blocks of life which are scattered all over the universe. They dispersed in the air and settled on the ground. As it became gradually manifest, they caused a massive surge of new life which all but overwhelmed the world.

Creatures which were incubating on wet surfaces or lived in the water burst to life. There was a plague of mosquitoes, flies, spiders, beetles, frogs, cockroaches. Fish stocks recovered overnight. In the following days there was an explosion of premature births of people as well as animals. The cities were overrun by wolves, bears, rabbits, stray dogs and foxes. But it all began with joyful amazement: people were enthralled by the fire in the air.

This great fire didn't burn anybody, it didn't feel hot, it didn't change the temperature of the air: it was pure, clear, cool radiance. Touched by light that came from deep space, from the unfathomable past of billions of years, from the beginning of things, people felt soothed, elated. They had a sudden sense of the vastness of the universe, which no numbers can convey. It is a vastness that cannot even be imagined, but it can be felt. Those who were awake that night felt it. Breathing the rich air full of life-giving substances, they felt at one with the immense totality of matter and space. Even those who were unaware that life breaks through matter throughout the universe were infused with a joyful consciousness of a living cosmos. This was such an elemental, exhilarating feeling, such a profound gladness, that thousands suffering from chronic depression, minor ailments and even some forms of cancer were permanently cured by it.

Once Jim Taylor stepped out into the open air, he too was affected: the force of the light jolted him out of the stupor of despair. Never in his life had he seen such a bright night. The hotel garden's coconut palms with their giant, shining fronds duplicated themselves on the luminous lawn: their shadows were so dark, so dense, so sharply defined that they looked as real as the trees. He finally became aware that something magical was happening: all the birds were up, singing their three bars of music. The strange radiance alerted all his senses, lifted his spirits. 'She'll manage,' he thought, filled with confidence about his wife's future. 'She's tough, she's a fighter. She loves children, she'll go on teaching and she'll see that maths teacher every day. He's had his eye on her for years and he is a widower.'

Under the eerily bright night sky, Jim walked through the hotel garden between the palm trees and the sculpted bushes, following the shadow of his swollen belly. His conscience was clear: alive, he was no earthly use to his wife, but his death would make her a rich widow with her own spacious home in one of the safest parts of London. He was leaving her enough to pay off the mortgage, with plenty left over for whatever she wanted to do: he had a fully paid-up life insurance policy worth 3.5 million. The policy wasn't valid if he took his own life, but what was wrong with accidental drowning? Not knowing anything about the statistics on suicide, he assumed the insurance company would never suspect that he had drowned himself deliberately while holidaying on an island off the Gulf Coast of Florida.

As he stepped from the grass onto the cold sand in his bare feet, he started shivering. The ominous shadow of the big wings of a low flying pelican slid over him and chilled his heart. He felt that they were the wings of death. He took a deep breath, waited a little, then stretched himself and took another deep breath. He was ready. He stepped into the icy water and it prompted him to wade in and start swimming right away to warm up. A school of flying fish kept leaping into the air ahead of him and others were brushing against his heels. The crowded sea was transparent under the glowing sky; pelicans kept hitting the water and emerging with their prey in their beaks.

Jim swam for a long time, perhaps longer than an hour and he couldn't understand why he was still swimming. He wanted to stop moving and sink, but he drew a deep breath with every stroke and his arms and legs kept moving against his will. He had swum far out to sea to use up his strength. When he noticed shark fins in the distance, he turned back towards land, so that his body would wash up on the beach for the insurance. Beginning to tire after a while, he resolved to get a grip on himself, to dive way down like the pelicans and not come up. He took a last look at the living world – and it wouldn't let him go.

His mind on death, he had forgotten how amazing the world had become. The moon shone as brightly as the sun. The air was full of floating lights drifting toward the water. Magdalena Island appeared in brilliant daylight green, beckoning him to return with its gently swaying trees. The beach was a white phosphorescent ribbon with a fringe of shimmering froth; it didn't seem too far.

The one form of suicide that can be recommended without reservation is drowning, especially to good swimmers. It gives them time to change their minds, to see the hidden truths which reveal themselves only in extreme moments. He had the sudden tremendous insight that the differences between the lives of a night-watchman and a senior executive of a multinational were not all that significant and he could be perfectly happy even in a small apartment with low ceilings.

The night sky had a sun and the clouds were on fire.

The fog of misery lifted from his mind. Life was so full of surprises that anything could happen, even something good.

He remembered that he had left the garden gate ajar, with the key in the lock. They might suspect that he had forgotten the key because he was thinking of drowning himself. If Lesley didn't get the insurance money, he would have made her old age a misery. She would be poor, old and on her own. He swam with a purpose now, resolved to reach dry land, to reach his wife, to lose weight and start again.

2

1. THE DIFFICULTY OF DROWNING

O God, can I not save
One from the pitiless wave?
Is all that we see or seem
But a dream within a dream?
EDGAR ALLAN POE

The night sky had a sun, the clouds were aflame, spreading an eerie radiance. Swimming towards the white phosphorescent ribbon of the island's beach with its fringe of shimmering froth, towards the gently swaying trees beyond the beach beckoning him, Jim had nothing to do with death now. What mattered was to breathe and live, to save his wife from misery and save himself. Swimming towards a new start, every breath he drew filled his lungs with joy. He had been swimming well over an hour, his limbs were growing heavy, but he hardly needed to swim. The low, heavy waves carried him nearer to land and he relaxed a little to enjoy the sensation of being alive – and it was then that a sudden violent pain pierced his chest and his neck, twisted his muscles, his whole used-up body. He cried out, bit his tongue in panic and swallowed salt water with his blood. He thrashed about in agony for air, as long as he could. His limbs became rigid, turned into a dead weight and dragged him down. A wave took his glasses and the sea sucked him in. He had left wisdom too late.

"Help! Help!" cried a voice from somewhere.

The cry made his heart pound as if it were about to burst from his chest, pushing him to the surface. Was someone else drowning near him? Another suicide? He gasped for air, vomiting, spitting, determined to help, to do something useful before he died.

"Don't give up, I need you!"

The voice sounded next to his ear, giving him another shot of energy. He strained his eyes to look around. The sea was deserted. "Where are you?" he asked in a hoarse whisper, forcing the words past his bleeding tongue. There was no sign of anyone struggling near him. I'm beginning to hallucinate, that's the end, he thought, his mouth full of blood.

"I'm right under you. Just open your eyes and look!"

Somehow his eyelids obeyed and, managing to stay afloat, he peered into the transparent water. There was a carnival of fish down there and for an instant he was blinded by an explosion of sharp colours. Fish of all shapes and sizes crowded the water, sporting their bright scales. Clouds of tiny sparks, recently spawned, drifted about. Just beneath him he saw a dark creature sliding back and forth over a silvery surface. After a while he realized that the dark creature was his own shadow sliding over some round metal object on the seabed. Fish are hopeful creatures: they think everything is food or hides food or has some food attached to it and they leave nothing uninspected. But they would have nothing to do with the silvery object. When they came near it they made a sharp about-turn, like smart, well-trained soldiers on parade. What was it that the fish didn't like?

"Hey, baldy!" came the voice from the sea. "You wanted to help me, remember?"

The weight of exhaustion had lifted from his limbs; he could tread water and hear someone from the seabed, but in an act of mental self-defence, his mind blocked out what he couldn't understand. What struck him was that the voice was a boy's voice - light, high-pitched, insolent. "If you want me to help you," he said sternly, with some kind of pedagogical intent, "you had better mind your manners."

There came a prompt and humble apology. "I'm sorry, baldy; I didn't mean to hurt your feelings."

Jim thought that the voice came from the round object on the seafloor. Was it a new kind of submarine? He peered into the water, trying figure out what to make of it. The next sound he heard sounded like a cry of pain.

"Yay, yay!"

"What's wrong?"

"Yay, yay!"

"Are you hurt?" he asked.

"I'm alone and I'm bored!"

That made sense, but how could a kid be in a submarine all by himself?

The sound of extreme impatience bubbled up from the deep. "Could we please forget about submarines?"

"Then what is it?"

"Haven't you heard about fly-whirl disks? Or is that too advanced for you? OK, how about rockets for intergalactic flights?"

"I see you have a sense of humour."

"Do you think so?" The boy sounded pleased. "My Dad says I try too hard. But you're right," he added contritely, "rockets are a joke. Nobody uses them any more – I'd never have found this planet with any of those old machines. You're so far from everywhere! We use fly-whirl disks now. They move faster than light."

"Faster than light?"

"Much faster."

The ex-executive, who had interviewed hundreds of people, believed that every lie contains a truth. "I guess you watch a lot of movies."

"I would, but my Dad won't let me."

'What an imaginative liar!' Jim thought. He tried to remember what the speed of light was. How many light seconds to the sun?

"Your sun," the boy commented contemptuously. "It isn't on any sky map *I've* ever seen. I skip thousands of light years in less time than it takes you to turn around."

"So where did you come from in such a hurry?" Jim asked wryly.

"How about getting acquainted after you've got me out of here?"

The boy spoke English without any obvious accent, but it didn't sound quite right somehow. "Is English your second language?"

"I can send up a cord – strong enough to let you pull me to shore."

"Come on, tell me. Where are you from?"

"Why do you want to know?" came the plaintive reply. "I hate prying. You should respect my privacy."

"There's no way I'll pull you to shore unless you tell me where you come from," Jim said with the firmness of an immigration officer at a port of entry.

"It's too far; it wouldn't mean anything to you."

"Just tell me."

"You've never heard of the place."

Jim insisted.

The impatient juvenile finally gave in with a sigh. "Oh, all right. I'm from the Centre of the Universe."

"*The Centre of the Universe?*"

"You see," the boy exclaimed triumphantly, "I told you you'd never heard of it!"

Jim remembered Einstein saying that infinity is infinite in every direction. "Is there such a thing as the Centre of the Universe?" he asked.

"Just as I thought. What you don't know doesn't exist. It's the best planet ever, but its billions of light years from you."

Jim tried to bring the inveterate liar down to Earth. "How come you're stuck on the seabed?"

More bubbles of frustration ruffled the water. "That's another story. I was just cruising around, but then I got sleepy and parked on one of those chunks of ice that buzz around. I must have slept for a while, but then the ice shook and woke me up. I saw your blue planet and I thought I'd take a look at it before the ice hit you. I thought it might. But when I got here, some flying tube knocked against my disk and I crashed. I've never seen a planet with so much fucking junk floating around it."

Fucking junk? The gall of the kid trying to claim he was from another planet.

"Watch it, watch it!" The voice was both offended and scornful. "You're still alive, you know. A *bright* individual would have noticed it by now. And he would be grateful. He would show some respect."

Surely all this was happening inside his head? Jim focused his mind on his chest, his limbs; there were no cramps, no pain, nothing. His tongue was no longer bleeding. 'If the pain has gone, I must be near death,' he thought, beginning to suspect that his bloated body was floating in the water with just enough life in it for a dream. He remembered an article he had read about the brain scans of accident victims, which showed that even when the body was dead, the brain lived on for a little while: there were flashing lines on the scanner as electric impulses kept darting about the brain cells. Drowning was hallucinogenic and no doubt the excitement about the comet accounted for the drift of his hallucinations. Just the same, he wished he was hallucinating about something else. He disliked science fiction, little green men and absurd stories about creepy aliens. Kids' stuff for underdeveloped minds. What nonsense – a kid skipping thousands of light-years in seconds!

"You can believe it or not, I don't care."

"I'm not keen on belief, I prefer rational explanations."

"Oh, all right... if you really want to know... This isn't really my machine, it's my Dad's and he always buys the fastest model. He's crazy about speed."

Jim wished that his dying dream wouldn't be poisoned

with this nonsense. He wished he could think of Lesley and hear her calling him, but he was afraid that if he tried to clear his mind of the imaginary adolescent it would just go blank and he would never see or hear anything ever again. Even dreaming was living.

2. A JOYRIDER

I seemed to believe the boy, I didn't know why.
Something in me seemed to believe him - my
consciousness, you might say; but my reason didn't.
MARK TWAIN

Through the transparent water a long white cord wound itself to the surface. It was a mooring cable which the adolescent directed from inside the silver disk. At the bidding of the voice, Jim tied it around his waist. The buoyant cable felt as soft as silk and bent as easily as the cord around a Franciscan monk's robe. Jim started to swim, pulling the disk after him. In spite of its enormous size it weighed almost nothing. That, too, made sense: nothing had any weight in a dream.

"Every object submerged in water loses as much weight from its body as the weight of the water it displaces," said the juvenile from inside the disk with triumphant condescension. "Haven't you people figured that one out yet?"

"So you go to school."

"Not by choice."

"How old are you?"

"It depends on how you count time."

'He's going to tell me he's a zillion years old,' Jim thought.

"No way! I'm fourteen today. I thought I'd be somewhere nice and interesting on my birthday, but so far all I've seen is a lot of fish."

"Well, Happy Birthday!"

"Celebrating your birthday all by yourself at the bottom of the sea isn't much fun, I can tell you. I've been waiting for someone to come by for hours. I aged a lot down here."

The sea was rapidly filling up with fish; some brushed against Jim's skin. There was less and less room for him in the water. He had to struggle to make way for himself.

"Hey, I don't want to be rude or anything, but can't you pull a little faster? We could be on the beach by now if you'd get moving."

'And all these years I might have had a lively kid like that, keeping me on my toes,' Jim reflected. 'Maybe I wouldn't have got so fat and so old.'

"Don't you have any kids? Well, we can be friends, I don't mind... I'll call you Jim and you can call me Neb."

The mind always fastens on the least puzzling puzzle: Jim was bothered by the strange, unreal sound of the boy's name. Neb? Maybe it was a nickname, but what was it short for?

The voice flared up through the water with the belligerence of wounded pride. "There's nothing strange about Neb. It's a good name. It's a lot nicer than Jim. It's a lovely name."

"I was just wondering..."

"It's one of the best names there is."

"Fine."

"It's the best name in the universe!"

The subject of Neb's name being exhausted, Jim started worrying about something else: he hadn't told Neb his name.

"Didn't you notice that I can read what's in your head? I'm smart. If I manage to concentrate, I can read whatever anybody has on his mind."

"That's smart, no question."

"I'm pulling your leg - you don't have to be smart to read people's minds. Everybody can do that. You just look at their mindscreens."

"Their mindscreens?"

"Even my stupid little sister Eoz can do it. When she manages to concentrate, that is. My Dad says success is concentration, but it's hard to concentrate."

"If everybody can read everybody's mind, you've very little left to talk about."

"That's not true," Neb said defensively. "You can't read the mindscreens of your family. You have to listen to them if you want to know what's on their minds. They can lie to you, though. That's bad, but then you can lie to them! Ages ago our ancestors could read everybody's mind and stopped having sex and they were always fighting, wishing each other dead. Our species became practically extinct. So during eons of evolution we changed. We can't read the minds of our close relations, because it would destroy the family. It would be terrible for us kids."

"How come you speak English?"

"I wished it."

'That certainly beats language CDs,' Jim thought.

"Well, I listened to some broadcasts and wished to

understand them and I copied your vocabulary from your mindscreen. That was simple."

"You copied my vocabulary from my mindscreen?"

There was another big sigh from the deep: the boy had well-developed lungs, probably from sighing so much. "If you hadn't come along, I might have died of boredom. But get us to dry land and open the hatch. I can't open it from the inside." Though Neb hated prying, he told his secrets readily enough when he felt like it. "Dad saw me taking off and sealed the exit from me while I was still within his wishing range."

It was too much to take in. He wished that they could have a break. *"His wishing range?!"* he asked aloud.

"My Dad's wishes carry farther than most people's - and he wishes a lot of mean things. Seeing me close the hatch, he wished the exit mechanism to turn Neb-proof, which is what he calls making things resist me. I wasn't doing anything, I just wanted to take his toy for a spin."

"You mean you didn't want to go any farther than a light-year or two?"

"Yeah, but then I got carried away." Neb sighed again. "He's going to be furious. He likes getting mad at me. He hates me. He's crazy about my stupid little sister, but he hates me."

"But why would your father lock you inside this disk?"

"Now you can see how evil he is! He locked me in so I'll need him to get out. He likes people to need him. I guess he was afraid that if I could leave the disk on my own I would settle on some other planet and they'd never see me again. He wanted to make sure I'd come home. He never gives me any choice."

"Maybe he likes to have you around."

"It's not me he's worried about – it's this precious machine! He can't live without it. When Eoz and I are shouting at each other at home, he leaves the house, flies off and parks on some barren planet and reads. He has lots of books on board. He loves them. He loves a lot of things, but I'm only good to be shouted at. He screams at me. He never shouts at my sister. And he didn't think of this accident, did he? What chance did I have of landing on a live planet with intelligent beings who could help me? What if this was a dead star? I'd be locked up here forever. Yeah, sure, Dad says he loves me, of course. But as far as he's concerned, I could have died in this disk, going mad from solitude!" Neb shouted, overwhelmed by a vision of his tragic end.

Jim slowed down to catch his breath. The glowing gases evaporated, the clouds on fire turned into embers, even the sunlike fire on the moon began to fade. A huge grouper nearly knocked him over. In the distance he noticed the shadows of sharks. Some big fish struck his flabby belly and he decided he must be tired and would just tread water for a while.

"You're not tired," Neb insisted. "You're getting younger, you're strong. You were such an old wreck, I had to wish something about it if I wanted us to reach shore."

Getting younger? It was so obvious. At dinner Anita Mayberry had asked him what he would do if he could be young again, and now he dreamed it was true.

"Well, it takes time," Neb said defensively. "I could do it faster if I could touch you. Don't forget, I'm only a kid.

Wishing is work! And you're not a simple case, you know. The years really got to you, they're sticking to your bones. I have to concentrate hard to take them off."

'What if this juvenile with his big talk is a real person?' Jim wondered. 'I'm still old and fat, but children often pretend that they can do impossible things.'

"I said I'm a kid, I didn't say I'm a child!" protested Neb, deeply insulted. "Get going. You can do it, I promise. Pull, pull!"

3. AN OLD TALE REMEMBERED

*He felt that his whole past life had been
a nightmare, and his present life
was also a dream, but a pleasant one.*
VOLTAIRE

When Jim finally dragged the edge of the silver disk onto the sand, he noticed that his arms were the arms of a young man: lean, strong, sinewy. He didn't believe it, and then he did. The sea ran up the sand and wet his feet - then retreated - then came up again - so, too, his sceptical adult mind was flooded and emptied and flooded again by the credulous confidence of childhood, when anything was possible, even quelling the waves of Lake Ontario.

"Hey, hey, what about me? You can admire yourself after you let me out of here."

Jim slapped a mosquito which stung his neck. As the creature inside the disk kept clamouring to be let out, he remembered an old tale of three wishes.

"Three wishes?!" Neb groaned. "Oh, all right, all *right*, but be quick about it. I have to go home or my Dad will kill me. Don't forget, I've already granted you one wish."

"What do you mean?"

"You're younger."

"Oh, no, that was *your* wish. You wanted to make me strong enough to pull you to shore," Jim snapped. There was too much at stake for gratitude. He walked back into the water, half-circling the round spacecraft with a searching look. The great light had gone and the sun wasn't up yet, but it was almost daybreak and he could see that the disk was huge and quite high at its centre, with bits of white foam and seaweed on its strange shiny surface. He frowned and stepped back. The craft was another reminder of little green men, aliens who devoured people.

"Come on, I'm not an *insect!*" Neb wailed from inside.

"What do you look like?" Jim asked warily. "What does your head look like?"

"Head?" Neb sounded bewildered. "What's a head?"

Without a word, Jim tried to push the disk back into the sea.

"Hey! I was just kidding. Stop. It's a joke, a joke! I'm normal. I look exactly like you - I mean, like humans."

"Not bloody likely."

"Ages ago we used to have two heads but they disappeared during evolution. They weren't practical."

Jim leaned against the rim of the craft with both hands and tried to give it another hefty push to slide it back to the sea, but it wouldn't move an inch.

"Hey, can't you take a joke? I really do look like you. Only younger. And better looking."

Jim couldn't possibly move the huge craft, so he just turned his back on it and walked away, leaving the creature safely locked inside.

"*Everybody* in the universe looks like you or me!" Neb

shouted after him.

Jim came back.

"It's true. A head on top with a brain, not too big - one mouth, two eyes, two ears, a nose - a body, not too tall, two arms with hands at the end of them, two legs with feet and those little things between your legs – they're ideal! They are the best for survival. The universe has never come up with anything more useful. It's the winning shape. We have a book at home called that, *The Winning Shape*. It's about all the different races in the known galaxies, and they all look like us."

The winning shape. The phrase made Jim think of Lesley in her blue swimsuit. He had a sudden desire for her and laughed out loud. He hoped that he could slip back into bed without waking her and she would never find out that he had tried to kill himself. He walked back to the disk and swam to its centre sticking out of the water, and peered down through the transparent hatch. There was Neb looking up at him, waving. He seemed normal. All the same, before letting him out, Jim insisted on a precondition.

"Youth, three wishes, plus a precondition?! You call that fair?"

"Fairness has nothing to do with it. I have to be able to read your mind, to know whether I can trust you to keep your promises."

"Well, I told you I can't do everything."

"I want to be sure that you'll do your best."

"Reading mindscreens," the boy muttered. "That's not a precondition, that's an extra wish."

"I won't let you out until I can read your mindscreen."

Neb was no match for a business executive well versed in negotiation and eventually gave in. Jim opened the hatch and the creature from The Centre of the Universe climbed out of the disk. He had a long, narrow face and brown eyes, long, dark-blond eyelashes and thick dark-blond hair, with one wavy lock flopping down over his forehead. Everything about him seemed to be long except his nose. He had long, gangling arms and legs, a slender neck and long, slim fingers with well-shaped nails in need of a good scrubbing. Jim's heart skipped a beat when he saw that the boy had freckles like Lesley, only smaller ones - tiny pale-brown specks sprinkled like a sunburst across the bridge of his small nose.

"Here I am," said Neb, grinning. "Pretty scary, hey?" He stretched his limbs, glad to be out in the fresh air again, then went off to check his disk from the outside. He busied himself with some dents, then turned to Jim. "Okay, let's hear your wishes, let's get it over with," he said peremptorily, thinking how pleased his mum would be when he got home.

"I need some time to think."

"What about? Don't you know what you want?"

"I'm not sure."

"Are you stupid?"

Jim would not let himself be hurried. He retained the slow wisdom of a middle-aged man who had made all too many mistakes: he wouldn't trust the first idea that came into his head; he wasn't going to be hasty about anything. To Neb's great delight, he started choking. He had partial plates in place of his rear molars and the new set of teeth growing in his mouth had pushed them out - he had nearly swallowed them. He took out his fake teeth and threw them away. For quite some time he had assumed that he was awake and sane and all the things that could not possibly happen were actually happening, but he had always been interrupted by disbelief. Now he checked his bald spot again and touched thick curly hair. He put his hand on his chest: it was flat. He lowered his hand to his paunch. In the water, he still had it. Now it wasn't there. Neither were his swimming trunks. They had fallen down around his ankles. His stomach was perfectly flat; he had no extra weight. A mosquito stung his penis and Jim grabbed it and squeezed it to lessen the pain. The sting convinced him that he was awake.

The worst thing about life is that we can never go back; there is no way we can return to the past and unsay what we have said, undo what we have done. But as Jim stared down at his young body, the terrible weight of an irrevocably ruined life lifted from his mind. It was incomprehensible but true, as true as the first rays of the sun hitting the sky from below the horizon: he was alive, he was young. "Jesus Christ!" he exclaimed.

Neb stared at him in utter amazement. *"Jesus Christ?* Did you say *Jesus Christ?* You mean he was here too? Incredible!"

4. A SUSPICIOUS STRANGER

Of twenty year of age he was, I gesse.
CHAUCER

Walking back to Gulf Views on the deserted beach at dawn, holding onto his giant swimming trunks with one hand, Jim suddenly stopped, let go of the swimming trunks which fell from his slim body and looked down to admire his perfect figure. He patted his flat stomach with pleasure, then flexed his long delicate strong fingers and studied them. He used to have hands like that ages ago. Hearing the buzzing of a mosquito, he quickly pulled up his swimming trunks and hurried on; he wanted to get back to the hotel before his wife woke up. He was shocked to find the garden gate of *Gulf Views* wide open with the brass key in the lock. He was supposed to lock the gate from the outside and take the key with him. When they fished out his corpse, the insurance investigators should have found the brass key in the zip pocket of his swimming trunks. The key left in the gate lock could have aroused suspicion. Poor Lesley might not have got any money.

'It's lucky I didn't drown,' he thought, carefully locking

the gate from the inside. He walked up the path to the building, slapping the mosquitoes that landed on him. The sun was up and the sculpted bushes looked exactly like the day before, but he hardly heard any birds. Being up all night singing, they seemed to have overslept. Coming up against the revolving door, he gave it a push. It wouldn't turn. He remembered – it seemed now a lifetime ago – that Teresa had to buzz him out into the garden. He focused his mind on the metal frame and tapped it lightly, curious to see what would happen. The door swung open and he stepped into the lobby.

Dozing peacefully, Teresa Ramos, the pregnant night-clerk, was startled awake by the sharp, painful noise of the brass key hitting the bell on the desk. A young stranger, naked as far as she could see, was smiling at her from the other side of the desk. She had a twinge of fear; she was alone.

"Here's the key to the beach gate, Teresa," he said, dropping it on the desk. "Thanks. You see, I brought it back, just as I promised."

She eyed him, utterly perplexed. The lithe dark-haired young man's face looked vaguely familiar, but how did he know her name? She certainly didn't know his. The American Olympic fencing team was renting one of the big private houses on the island and she wondered whether the good-looking stranger might be one of them.

"Would you please give me a key-card? I forgot to bring one and I don't want to wake up my wife."

"What apartment?"

"Our apartment, Teresa. Surely you remember? Two-o-six."

Seeing her confusion, Jim realised that he must have become a stranger to the world. Why, he was a stranger even to himself! He had no idea what he looked like. Seized by curiosity, he turned away from the desk to search for a mirror, catching his outsize swimming trunks just before they fell. The opposite wall of the lobby was covered with big square mirrors fitted to each other like tiles. He came face to face with multiple images of himself at the age of twenty-two. Noticing the scar on his forehead, he remembered the stairs in their home in Toronto. How he screamed when he fell! He remembered his mother's hugs and kisses as she bandaged him. He studied his lean torso, his thick hair, his smooth skin, looked into his own bright eyes. He was a young man now, but conscious of being more than a young man. He was a young man now with the knowledge of his fifty-six years. This time around he would be wiser. The stranger's peculiar behaviour alarmed Teresa. Having turned his back on her abruptly, as if in a hurry, he went to the mirror wall and contemplated his image for what seemed like hours. Holding onto his swimming trunks, he raised his free hand, turned it back and forth, carefully examining and flexing it. Then switching hands to hold the swimming trunks, subjected the other hand to close examination. Only when the intruder seemed to be satisfied with both his hands, did he walk back to the desk.

"Swimming at night makes you look younger," he asserted firmly – all the more firmly as he was aware that it sounded absurd.

Teresa glanced at the key he had dropped on her desk. It

was the key with the shiny chipped head that she had given to James Taylor. How had this man got hold of it? She looked at him, narrowing her bright eyes. For all she knew he might have murdered the poor old man. "Sir, you're not registered at this hotel. I must ask you to leave, or I'll have to call the police."

"You can't place me because I have my hairpiece on," Jim lied helpfully. "I left it by the pool this afternoon and picked it up just now, on my way back from the beach. By the way, Teresa, I asked you to tell my wife I went for a swim."

Teresa's small oval face grew thinner from incomprehension.

"I wanted you to reassure her in case she phoned down, looking for me. Did she call you?" Jim was worried that Neb would be getting impatient waiting.

"Come on, Teresa, come on. Wake up! Give me another key-card to two-o-six."

Teresa eyed him with a stubborn expression. "But you're not Mr Taylor, you're *not* a bit like him!" Teresa burst out. "You're young and handsome and Mr Taylor is a fat bald old man."

Taking umbrage on behalf of his former self, Jim pointed an accusing finger at her. "Now I've got you! The other day when I complained that I felt old, you told me I didn't look a day over forty! You were serving at the pool bar and you had just given me a freshly-squeezed ortanique juice, remember? Did you or did you not tell me I didn't look a day over forty? And all the while you were thinking I was a fat old man! Teresa, you flatter the guests shamelessly, saying things you don't mean at all. What kind of role-model are you going to be for your child?" He held out his free hand

and snapped his fingers. "The card, please!"

Stricken, she handed over the key-card without a word.

"Don't worry, Teresa, you're not going crazy. This sort of thing comes with the last month of pregnancy," Jim assured her, waving goodbye. He walked across the lobby to the lift. The thought that he could start again with Lesley filled him with joy. Would they be able to have children now? He turned from the elevator, deciding to try the stairs, to test whether he would still find it difficult. It was so easy that he quite forgot that climbing the steps was a test of his strength. Thinking of the reflection of his young self in the mirror, he wondered whether Lesley would recognize him. And how would she take it? He hoped it wouldn't be too much of a shock.

Teresa leaned back in the swivel chair and rested her hands on her belly to remind herself of the only thing that mattered. The baby was kicking, everything was in order.

5. THE EYES OF LOVE

My love, we will go, we will go, I and you,
And away in the woods we will scatter the dew.
W. B. YEATS

Jim halted on the threshold of their bedroom. It was already daylight and beyond the transparent lace curtain which covered the open balcony door a cloud of mosquitoes was circling as if waiting to be let in. Lesley was breathing regularly, deliberately; her whole being was given over to sleep. What a first-class character she was! Whatever she did, she did it with total concentration, total commitment. To avoid making any noise, he bent down and didn't let go of his wet swimming trunks until they reached the floor. Carefully, he slipped into bed. Lesley stirred, sighed, turned towards him but went on sleeping, breathing evenly.

Jim raised himself on his left elbow and propped up his cheek to look at her. Like most people in their fifties still in love, he had acquired the habit of ignoring, and in time not even seeing, the signs of her ageing - but now he was looking at her with a young man's twenty-twenty vision. He had always imagined that, of the two of them, she was the stronger. Now he saw how vulnerable she was. All the blows had left their marks on her face. He remembered when he first noticed the crows' feet, puckering the skin at the corners of her eyes: it was during the weekend after her first miscarriage. Her whole life was on her face. Those lines grew deeper with every disaster.

With all his love in his fingers, Jim brushed the marks of crushed hopes and indignities from her face – the crows' feet, the frown marks, the wrinkles on her forehead and on her neck. The wrinkles disappeared. He stroked her slack jaw line and the slackness disappeared. The skin smoothed out, turning fresh and creamy with a scattering of freckles. Her jaw line became an unbroken curve. The only people who will know how he felt restoring the youth and beauty of her face, are those who have caressed a no-longer-young face, wishing that they could wipe away the traces of time and pain.

"Stop tickling me!" she said, still half asleep.

Jim promptly covered her eyes with the palm of his hand to protect her from the shock of seeing him. Lying down on his back, he freed his other hand to reach under the sheet to brush away the loose skin of her belly, the cellulite on her inner thighs. He stroked her crotch, her pussy, wishing away the dryness and restoring her hormones to start again the abundant flow of her juices. His free hand stroked its way up to her breasts, to make her nipples live again. Ever since the menopause, her nipples were more sensitive, but as kissing, fondling and sucking them had always been Jim's way of arousing her, she didn't want to remind him that her body had changed. Oestrogen pills replaced the hormones of her youth, she could flow and burst as profusely as ever, if not as often, and her nipples, when stimulated, started her juices flowing, but at first they hurt. "All right, my darling, have fun," she said, hoping that he was getting over his depression. She steeled herself for momentary pain when she felt his hand brushing against her breasts. The pain would melt into pleasurable sensations, trickles of enjoyment, the comfort of exchanging flesh, contentment that she was giving her husband relief and peace of mind. After nearly three weeks by the sea, though, she had the sun and the clean air in her blood and she wanted more than contentment.

Oh, God, she prayed, give him an erection!

His fingers moved back and forth over her body, fondling her in all the right places, to do away with any blemish he might have missed. She was impatient for the pain, wanted to get it over with and move on. But this time there was no soreness; her nipples sent lightning flashes through her body, heralding a storm of pleasure. Jim forgot about covering her eyes, but she closed them herself, as they coupled, horses and riders both, and galloped back to their youth - an impossible feat which is accomplished in millions of beds every night, even without the assistance of a hellion from outer space.

As the clouds inside her burst, Lesley opened her eyes and buried her fingers in his thick, dark curly hair. "Oh, my darling," she said, "to me you will always be young!"

6. GETTING REACQUAINTED

My wife received me with great surprise and joy.
SWIFT

The young man was still rooted in her body and she was combing his thick, dark curly hair with her fingers when the sound of a foghorn blasting into the room broke the spell and she became aware that his youthfulness was not a trick of the senses: he had real hair and no paunch. She turned her head to look for her bald, overweight Jim beside her. He wasn't there, but she still felt too fizzy, too dazed, too far beyond the bounds of ordinary experience to be alarmed. 'Oh well, it's done, it's time I had a fling, there's no point in getting hysterical about it,' she thought, as she twisted her bottom to ease out the lovely young stranger.

"Come on, Les, don't you recognize me?"

There was such a triumphant sparkle in his eyes that she couldn't help laughing. Panic struck when she tried to make sense of it. She pushed him away, sprang out of bed and, snatching up the sheet to cover herself, tried to run out of the room. Jim caught her, carried her to the bathroom and set her down in front of the full-length mirror. Lot's wife turned into a pillar of salt could not have been more rigid than the middle-aged teacher seeing herself as a young girl again.

"Don't worry, Les, you'll get used to it."

She must have heard him but she seemed to be petrified, unable to reply or to move. Jim felt that he could safely leave her and find out whether he could wear any of his clothes. Having secured a pair of huge underpants by knotting one of his ties around them, he went to the cupboard and tried on all the trousers he had brought from London. They all fell off. He took in the waistband of his thinnest cotton trousers with a safety pin and walked about the room triumphantly until the safety pin sprang open and dropped on the tile floor with a *ping*. His trousers fell down. So did his underwear. Jim picked up his underpants, at a loss what to do. Finally, hesitantly, not really knowing whether the power of his hands extended to clothes, he drew his hand around the elasticized waistband, wishing that it would fit. It immediately shrank to a perfect fit. Then he did the same with his trousers. He put on a blue polo shirt; it was so big, he was lost in it. Having had an overload of extraordinary experiences, he talked to his shirt. "So you think you can defy me, do you!" he muttered, and touched the shirt here and there until it shrank to the right size. As he started to shrink his shorts, he remembered Lesley and ran to the bathroom.

She was still standing in front of the mirror, clutching the sheet around her body with the same desperate frozen gesture as before, staring at her face from her student days. Jim saw he had forgotten her hair. It had thinned quite a bit and the grey roots were showing. She needed a new dye. "Remember," he asked, as he tousled her hair, "how much silkier, thicker, softer it used to be? Remember its glorious rich red? You don't even have to remember, just look at yourself in the mirror."

The transformation of her hair finally loosened Lesley's grip on the sheet and it slid to the tile floor. The curve of her back was like a drawn bow – her ass was small but striking. She was his BAC, the girl with brains, ass and class. "You look your best stark naked," he said approvingly.

Lesley didn't react. Who knows how long she would have stood at the mirror, motionless, speechless, if Jim hadn't bent down to squeeze and bite her buttocks. He could never resist bending down and squeezing and biting her when he found her dressing or undressing; the sight of her bare bottom was one of the profoundest joys of his life.

"Now I know it's you!" she exclaimed.

Jim stroked her all over with his fingers, his mouth and his voice. "I'll have you know, that you have the best possible shape for survival and pleasure. That's a fact. I got it from the horse's mouth – from a kid from the Center of the Universe. Your gorgeous shape is the winning shape everywhere in the universe!"

"You don't make sense."

"His name is Neb and he took his father's fly-whirl disk for a joyride, without permission." He told her everything that had happened, except the reason why he went swimming in the middle of the night.

She grew pensive. "So you can do whatever you want with your hands."

"Actually I didn't think of you when I made the wish – you have the perfect shape. I was thinking of the cello. I wanted to make up for all the years I wasted hardly practising."

"You played every week at least a couple of times."

"That's not really practising."

"Do you think we might have got our baby this morning?"

"If we didn't, we will."

They pressed against each other, skin to skin and she felt him harden again. How was it possible? Why, they had hardly finished making love. It was another little shock, a new awareness of their second youth. As they moved to the bed, Jim squeezed his fellow to make it thicker, longer and not so impatient.

Why didn't they go mad? How did they manage to keep their sanity after their sudden release from the gravity of time? They went mad on the bed, but that was lovers' madness. Although their hearing had become far more acute, they didn't hear the second blast of the foghorn, absorbed as they were in each other's bodies, so familiar, yet so new. Afterwards they lay on their backs, holding hands, their hearts filled with their radiant future.

"Now you can help Luke," Lesley said after a while.

Jim raised his hands to take another good look at them. He kept turning them around, flexing his fingers. "I'll try, I'll try..."

"What about your other two wishes?"

"You'll approve."

"I hope you didn't waste a wish on some stupid male thing like avenging yourself on Norton."

Jim became serious. "I have to think about that..."

"Just forget it."

"I want to figure out the best way to make the rest of his life a misery."

"You're a better man than that."

"I see this is going to be a battle between good and evil."

"Hate is evil."

"What are you talking about? You hate Norton yourself."

She laughed. "You're right! I'm so happy, I'd forgotten. What are your other two wishes?"

Jim's face became a big smile. "I told you you'll be pleased."

She sat up and rapped him on the chest. "All right, out with it! What did you ask for?"

He put his hands behind his head and looked up at the ceiling, savouring his triumph in advance. "I told Neb I'm a married man, I'd have to discuss my wishes with my wife."

She hugged him and the hugs and the kisses sent the world away. Once again there was no one else, nothing else but their bodies alight with sensations and desire. Another infernal wail, loud and persistent, made people on the beach clap their hands over their ears long before the Taylors heard anything.

"The sun is shining and somebody's blowing a foghorn?" Lesley asked.

"That must be Neb. I told him he'll have to wait until we make up our minds. I guess he's getting impatient."

She sat up. "Well, let's decide what we want to wish for."

"Let's just lie here for a while", Jim proposed.

Lesley fell back on the bed instantly.

No one observing the couple lying on the bed would have

guessed that they were living beyond the limits of human destiny. There were moments when they had an eerie sense of their new existence, but on the whole they took their rejuvenation very much in their stride. By and large people accept the most fantastic improvements in their fortunes as quite natural; miracles are always overdue.

"You said Neb had already been away from his home for months," she mused. "It's cruel to make him wait."

"He'd agree with you."

She leaped out of bed and grabbed a skirt from the closet. Her clothes needed no alterations: when she zipped up the skirt it fitted perfectly. "Jim, don't be so mean. Let's decide what we want and let him go", she said, reaching for a top to go with her skirt.

Jim rested his hand on her belly. "Before we even know if you're pregnant?"

She dropped her arms and looked thoughtful. "We have to find things that would tempt him to stay here for a while."

"What do we have on Earth that would interest a kid who can have everything he wishes?"

"Well, I certainly won't give him games and play-stations. Let's not introduce him to mindless thrills."

There was another angry blast. This time the sound of the foghorn was so loud that it cracked the sliding glass doors to the balcony.

Jim stretched his arms like a man who has had a good time, then sprang up from the bed. They looked out at the sea. The fly-whirl disk lay submerged over a hundred metres offshore, far beyond the few swimmers. Only the top of the hatch at the centre of the disk was showing, looking like a round glittering silver dinghy. Dazzled by the sun, they could hardly make out the boy who sat on the open hatch, scowling in their direction.

7. A DANGEROUS PLACE

*I saw nothing in this country that could invite me
to longer continuance, and began to think of returning home.*
SWIFT

Having waited for Jim long enough to get furious, Neb swam
ashore to find him and turn his life into hell. For Neb, hell
was embarrassment and he planned to make Jim knock
over glasses, drop food from his mouth, spill hot coffee on
his trousers, forget who he was talking to, piss his pants
in company. He intended to make Jim embarrassed out of
his mind until Jim hurried up and told him his remaining
wishes so he could go home.

Walking along the beach toward the hotel in his black
swimming trunks, Neb looked like any other tall, skinny,
blond teenager and passed as one of the crowd. He was
mildly curious about his fellow creatures, so familiar yet so
alien, but he read nothing on their mindscreens that could
tempt him to linger on Earth. Many were eyeing the bare
bodies around them, trying to guess how much money the
others made, or were adding up how much money they
themselves made or how much they were spending. There
were so many numbers, Neb thought the Earth was crowded

with mathematicians. And health experts. Sunbathers who were attracted to passing bodies were wondering what terrible sickness they might catch if they went to bed with them. Some of their mindscreens looked like pages from a medical encyclopaedia, introducing him to several dreaded Earth diseases. Some had replays of memory imprints: luxury cars at bargain prices raced through their heads, followed by girls washing their long hair. Still others thought of the comet that had skirted the Earth during the night and were worrying that the next one would hit them... but most of them had thoughts too pale, too confused to be read, and some had blank mindscreens.

Neb only wished his little sister Eoz was there running to keep up with him and chattering non-stop. He could have had fun listening to her stupid comments. Right now, he was certain, she was tormenting his parents, pestering them with questions, demanding to know when he would be coming home. He had no time to waste; he had to get the little brat off their backs.

He walked through the open gate into the hotel grounds, looked for Jim around the swimming pool, then raced on to the main building. As he went through the revolving door, he wished shorts and a T-shirt on himself in place of his swimming trunks and sandals on his bare feet. The garments materialized on him in a split-second while the door was still swinging. It was so neat, he was sorry in a way that no one noticed.

At the same time, the Taylors were on their way down to the lobby. With no one else in the lift, they could talk openly about their predicament. Lesley was worried that they looked too young. What could they say to people who knew them?

Jim remembered his trouble with Teresa. "Don't worry, they won't know who we are."

"That's not good either. How are we going to travel? We look much younger than our passport photos. We'll be lucky if they don't suspect us of murdering ourselves."

As they stepped out of the elevator, they nearly bumped into the hotel manager, a man with dark hair, a deep tan and watchful blue eyes. "Mrs. Taylor, you're looking terrific, I see Florida agrees with you!" he exclaimed.

"Very kind of you to say so, Mr Douglas," Lesley replied.

The manager stopped to chat, wishing her to feel appreciated. "How did you like the fireworks we arranged for you during the night?" he asked jokingly, but then, noticing the young man accompanying Mrs. Taylor, he looked puzzled for a moment and left them with a quick half-bow.

"As my poor mother used to say, half your worries never happen," commented Lesley just before Neb spotted Jim and started shouting.

"Jim, Jim, your willy is showing!"

Looking down, Jim saw his fly unzipping itself.

Elderly couples resting in the cool peace and quiet of the lobby, who had long since resigned themselves to the fact that young people were always doing something idiotic, didn't even look up from their glossy magazines. They raised their heads only when Jim let off a tremendous fart that bounced off the walls.

'That's the absolute limit,' thought Jim, quickening his steps to get to Neb and strangle him.

"Jim, you have AIDS!" Neb yelled triumphantly.

The elderly couples, afraid of catching it from the fart, heaved themselves up from their comfortable leather armchairs and fled, leaving their magazines behind.

Passing the desk in a white tennis outfit, the beautiful brunette whose disdainful look had crushed Jim the first day on the beach dropped her racquet as she turned to look at him. Other guests walking through the lobby demonstrated with their strained expressions how difficult it was to pretend that they hadn't heard. The clerk behind the reception desk glared at Jim with a face which said: *Go away and die!*

Jim grabbed Neb's arm and steered him into a corner. With his back to the others, he rearranged his trousers and looked straight into Neb's eyes to make sure he read his mindscreen. Neb glared back at him, just as determined. *I don't care, while I'm here you won't have a moment's peace!*

They might have come to blows if the manager with the watchful blue eyes had not materialized beside them and touched Jim's arm, asking whether they might have a word in private. By then he had figured out that Jim must be Mrs. Taylor's husband, and offered to cancel all their unpaid restaurant bills if they agreed to check out. He was full of apologies but it was an awkward situation and he had to consider the sensitivities of other guests.

"No problem," Jim said, surprising the hotel manager, who had expected a scene.

"Is the young man your friend?"

There was no possible way Jim could explain who Neb was. "Yes, the son of a friend from another island. Don't

313

worry, we'll clear out of the room right after lunch."

The manager's face clouded again.

Jim assured him that they wouldn't eat in the hotel.

"That's very considerate of you. Believe me, I'd much prefer to let you enjoy life in peace while you're well enough to...to..." His voice trailed off and he left him with a slight bow.

The young hellion sat down in one of the armchairs that his cry of AIDS had vacated. He was delighted with his prank until he became aware of the hostile thoughts flickering on the mindscreens around him. *How did he know? He must have it himself! Does he have boils under his T-shirt?* Neb was scandalized. His skin was perfect - he didn't have a single blemish on his body.

"Are you registered at the hotel, sir?" asked the massive security guard who came to tower over him, polite and threatening.

"I wouldn't dream of it."

"Then get up and walk."

Neb corrected him. "Get up and walk, *please!*"

"Jump, kid, or I'll help you," growled the guard in a whisper, working himself up to be mean and tough. He was about to do something violent but instead, perhaps for the first time in his adult life, his broad, coarse-featured face acquired the peaceful expression of utter helplessness. A wet spot appeared on his white cotton trousers and rapidly grew bigger and wetter.

Neb got up from his chair in a leisurely fashion, looked the guard up and down, wrinkled his nose and sauntered out into the fresh air.

The Taylors emerged from the building a couple of

minutes later. To Neb's immense disappointment, they were laughing and talking, though Jim grew grim-faced when he saw him. He wasn't looking forward to changing his clothes.

Stepping up to them to wish something more awful on Jim, Neb glanced at Lesley just as she was thinking, *What a handsome boy!* He relented instantly and, taking his first good look at her, was overcome by a curiously agreeable sensation. Lesley invited him to try some Earth food with them at the pizzeria in the yacht harbour, just a short walk away.

"All right, if it won't take long," the boy said grudgingly.

As they walked along the path behind the beach, the Taylors plied Neb with questions about the world he came from. He told them that Jesus Christ returned to The Centre of the Universe every year to preside over the hearings of their Supreme Court.

"I can't believe it!" Lesley exclaimed.

"First people think I have boils, and now you tell me I'm lying!" Neb protested, ready to walk away. "What sort of creatures are you?"

She tried to placate him. "I'm not saying you're lying... I'm just surprised."

"Why?"

"Christ only came here once and that was a long time ago." Jim explained.

"Was he a judge here too?"

"Well, not exactly. He was crucified."

"Crucified. What's that?"

Jim reluctantly described the shape of the wooden cross and the way they nailed Christ's hands and feet to the wood.

Horror stricken, the boy turned pale and stopped in his tracks. "And you're surprised that he hasn't been back?"

"That was the age of barbarism, nobody's crucified these days," Jim said lamely.

"I've had enough of this planet," Neb announced, holding up his hands, wanting to push them away. "Make your wishes, I'm leaving right now. You people are *dangerous.*"

8. CHANGING COLOUR

*And who knows but that even this prodigious
race of mortals might be equally overmatched
in some distant part of the world,
whereof we have yet no discovery?*
SWIFT

The Taylors had a hard time calming him down. Luckily, by then they were only a few steps from the harbour-front restaurant and, touching his arm, Lesley finally managed to coax him inside. They were seated by the glass wall overlooking the berths of the harbour. Having never known an adolescent boy who wasn't crazy about pizza, Lesley ordered a crispy-crust monster with extra cheese, sliced tomato, bacon, green pepper and pepperoni. As he was devouring the tasty exotic food, Neb felt less hostile, less impatient to leave. After being cooped up in the disk, hurtling through space in total solitude, millions of miles away from any living thing, he began to relax and enjoy sitting next to the lovely redhead, eating and talking.

They entertained the boy by listening to him. They asked him questions and he enjoyed telling them about his superior world. The Taylors were relieved to learn that mathematics and timekeeping were the same on the Centre of the Universe as on Earth, so they could understand what he was talking about.

"We are big," said Neb, straightening his back, so he could look down on them. "The Centre of the Universe is at least a thousand times bigger than the biggest planet around here." He explained that their planet was so huge and its gravity so powerful that everything within the radius of two light hours orbited around it, including its two suns.

"Two suns?" Jim and Lesley asked simultaneously.

"Two suns, yes," Neb said smugly, pleased that he had reduced the Taylors to such a state of stunned amazement that they didn't touch their plates. He himself stopped to savour another slice of the crispy-crust pizza. "As one of our suns sets, the other rises, so we have sixteen hours of daylight a day," he explained between two slices. "Teachers tell us that it is the abundance of light that develops our wishing power and enables us to live twice. We have two suns and two lives."

"Two lives?" Lesley and Jim asked in unison again.

"But having a second life is tricky," Neb admitted. "You can't wish to be young. Nobody can rejuvenate himself. You need someone who loves you enough or needs you enough to want you to be young again, that's the only way," Neb went on. "Those who are unloved and unwanted by everybody sink into old age and die in their first life. But even those who are needed and wanted can be rejuvenated only once. Two's the decisive number, the scope and limit of everything."

The Taylors' hearts gave an extra thump when Neb reminded them that their second youth was going to be their last.

"I just didn't want you to get your hopes up," said Neb.

"You can thank your lucky stars, Jim, that I could make you young at all, even though I don't love you."

"You needed me, that's just as good."

"Anyway, it's easier wishing here, your planet weighs so much less, its gravity is so much weaker."

Forgetting to eat, the couple were sufficiently stunned that Neb felt that he could stop bragging for a moment. "When our ancestors named our planet, they didn't realize how big the universe was. They thought that all the planets, all the suns were circling around us. We aren't dancing around anybody – we stay put, so they thought we're the Centre of the Universe. But at school they teach that there must be even bigger planets than our own, and eventually we're going to discover them."

"What do you call the Centre of the Universe in your language?" asked Lesley.

"*Otthon.*"

"And what are your people called?"

"We're the *Otthonites,*" Neb said, oozing pride.

"Do you have books on your spaceship?" she asked.

"Sure. Jim already knows that when my Dad can't stand the noise in the house, he whirls away and parks on a dead star to read. He has a whole library on board, but he's a prosecutor and most of his books are law books. Or serious books. Not much fun."

"Neb, darling, you must teach me your language!" exclaimed Lesley.

Neb was horrified. "I'm not staying that long!"

"I would love to read your father's books and make notes."

"No way, no way. I'll just finish this pizza, Jim can tell me his remaining wishes, and then I whirl home. I'll be out of your solar system in seconds."

'To think of what he can do just by wishing, and he's still a child,' Lesley thought, forgetting that Neb could read her mindscreen.

"Only people under twelve are children and they have no wishing power," the boy protested. "Wishing power grows with the body and doesn't amount to anything under the age of twelve. And even after that, only good students can wish for anything," he added, pointing at himself with his thumb.

"Your teachers must have an easy time of it," sighed Lesley.

"You're missing the point." Neb was playing proud but he was feeling prouder inside. "I can wish things. And that means you're talking to a brainy person who gets at least nine out of ten in every subject."

"That's magnificent, Neb."

Praise made him modest. "Actually it isn't all that difficult. Studying increases your mental powers."

"Neb darling, I'm dying to learn your language," Lesley begged.

"No way, no way!"

Just the same, he liked telling her things. He had never had such an eager and curious listener, apart from his Mum. Only he had less to tell his Mum and besides it was no fun trying to impress her, she already thought that he was perfect. The beautiful redhead was more of a challenge; she still had to be convinced that he was a great person. Putting down his knife and fork, he declared that he played all the instruments in the orchestra.

"*All* of them?" gasped Lesley. "You must be a genius."

"Yes, I am!" Neb raised his head and looked somewhere far away.

Seeing that Neb talked more readily to Lesley, Jim had sat back from the table, but now he couldn't resist leaning forward and getting involved in the conversation. "How can you even keep track of all the instruments?"

"It's easy."

The Taylors' admiration lessened when they heard that there were only four Otthonite instruments. They were similar, as far as they could make out, to the flute, the guitar, the trumpet and the drum. The flute was for sadness, the guitar for love and joy, the trumpet for triumph and exaltation, the drum for anger. Not wanting to hurt Neb's feelings, they said nothing, but he was disconcerted to read on their mindscreens that there were a lot more ways to make music on Earth.

He glared at them defiantly and announced that he could do things even without wishing. To demonstrate, he crossed his eyes and looked down at the tip of his nose. He was evidently proud of this performance, but thought nothing of his ability to change his pigmentation at will.

The subject came up as the restaurant filled up for lunch. The customers represented practically every skin colour imaginable. It was the same on Otthon: the Otthonites were born white, black, yellow, brown and all shades in between, just as on Earth, but they could change their colour if they really wanted to. The Taylors were incredulous but Neb found nothing remarkable about it and mentioned it only to make them understand what a preposterous creature his "stupid little sister" was. Most of them were happy in their skins and never changed them – Neb's parents were always the same colour – but there were people, like "my stupid little sister Eoz who has a mad desire to be loved by everybody."

Neb so enjoyed bad-mouthing Eoz, he stopped eating. "Eoz always changes her skin to the colour of the person she's talking to. She changes colour so frequently that one never knows where she is in a room. I have a hard time locating her at a party - she could be black, pinkish-white, tawny, golden or brown in quick succession."

Lesley was so incredulous, that she forgot to be on her guard. 'What an imaginative liar! *How can he invent such fanciful lies?'* she wondered.

Neb jumped up from the table. "All right, that does it. I'm just going to ask for the pizza recipe for my Mum and then I'm going home. Goodbye!"

"What about your promise?" Jim called after him, but the boy didn't turn around.

Lesley sighed. "It's difficult to deal with a person who can read your mind."

They hadn't eaten since the previous evening and devoured their cold scrambled eggs and toast. Afterwards Lesley felt nauseated but Jim, reverting to his old gluttonous habits, ordered a slice of hot apple pie with three scoops of vanilla ice-cream. He had cleared his plate by the time Neb came back with the recipe, grinning. "Scared you, didn't I?"

Lesley tried to apologize. "I'm sorry, darling, you mustn't mind me - but it's not easy for us. You're so different."

"I am not."

Though Neb considered his stupid little sister's behaviour unprincipled and vulgar, he himself was not above changing colour if he wanted to be liked. Sitting down, he brushed against the lovely redhead's bare arm. As their skins touched, he blushed crimson and his dark-blond hair and eyebrows turned red in an instant. Demonstrating the powers of a chameleon was not the way to persuade Lesley that they had a lot in common, but she was reassured all the same that he had reddened on her account.

"Look!"

A heavy Asian girl wearing a floral-print sleeveless shirt jumped up from her table and raised her round arm to point, shrieking with excitement. "Look at that! Look, look!"

A tall white yacht was coming in to dock right on the other side of the tinted glass wall.

Customers got up from their seats to find the best view. *The Challenger* had three antennae and two satellite dishes on top. There were seven crew-members on deck. Were there even more below? Except for old people who had outgrown reverence, everyone was deeply awed by the sight of such solid evidence of great wealth and some got up and went outside to take a closer look at the glittering luxury craft. The owner of the yacht stood on deck high above them, leaning against the gleaming brass rail; they only had to look up at him to see that he was from an alien world. A stunning young woman joined him.

The awe inspired by the couple from the yacht gave Neb an idea. "Jim, do you want to be rich?" he asked eagerly. "Do you want a boat like that? How about making it your second wish?"

"I'm in no hurry. I like having you around."

'Don't grow too fond of me. "

"I would have to be an idiot not to be able to make a fortune with my own hands," Jim said as he began to play with his paper napkin.

Neb looked at him scornfully. *"Your own hands!"*

Jim folded the napkin more or less into the size and shape of a dollar bill. Why not? His touch worked on bodies and even clothes. The napkin was thick and creased, so he got a new one, set it down on the table and ironed it out with his hand, concentrating on the mental image of a thousand-dollar bill. The paper became smoother but it was still a napkin.

Neb watched him with a mocking grin. "Money has its own magic, Jim, it resists all other magic. Don't you even know *that* much?"

The fabulous pair from the yacht walked with leisurely steps down the gangway and progressed toward the pizzeria.

The spectators gave way and followed them inside, their eyes burning with the kind of admiration which is sublimated envy. They paid no attention to the young couple who had been thirty years older the day before and the lanky red-haired teenager who had changed colour in an instant before their eyes. It just goes to show how difficult it is to know whom to gape at.

9. GUILT-FREE GLUTTONY

I eat when I'm at home. I eat when I go out.
I eat when I'm alone and when others are about.
MARIANNE EDWARDS

The yachtsman at the nearby table certainly knew something about the magic of money. In his youth, Ward Bunting had been the head of the Cornwall District Council, and managed, in a single year, to run up on his gold card, issued by the council, a million pounds in expenses for himself and his partner. Meals in smart restaurants with expensive wines, flowers, health spas, clothes – travels to the Caribbean, Thailand, China, Brazil, and luxury hotels everywhere. With a taste for the finer things in life, he also bought diamonds in Hong Kong. This was viewed as theft of public funds, and the UK is famous for dealing harshly with pubic officials who rob the state. Bunting lost his job and received only half a million pounds from the Council for the termination of his contract. He was quite resentful about it.

Bankers, who spend millions on tarting up their offices and make deals which ruin their shareholders and the national economy, never receive less than a couple of million in compensation when they're kicked out. Bunting felt the injustice done to him so keenly that he emigrated to California. Still in his twenties, tall and handsome, he had a break when a famous pop singer and sex symbol left a night club with him in a blaze of flashbulbs. The photo made the front pages of some newspapers and featured in every celebrity magazine. He appeared with the goddess in the media, walking in and out of places for the best part of a year. On the strength of these appearances, he joined the management of an investment fund. Actually, the singer was a cold fish compared to his secretary at the brokerage firm, but all the men he knew - and he knew mostly men who worked with money - envied him for this siren whose writhing near-naked body spread around the world on videos, inflaming multitudes. His business acquaintances pressed him very hard for some *inside* information. One curious bank executive, wanting details about the joys offered by the sex goddess, wished to trade secrets for secrets at a party. He told Bunting in the strictest confidence, in the deserted corner of a very large room, that financial institutions hardly ever granted multi-million dollar loans to individuals without a thank-you payment to the executives involved. The talkative banker added even more confidentially that he himself sometimes lent trusted friends millions without collateral in return for a personal cut of three percent of the total amount borrowed, and he had never had any cause to regret it. By way of thanks for this interesting information, Bunting shared his memories of his secretary, attributing her passionate performances to the famous singer. Later he borrowed ten million from his banker friend for a promising business venture. Having learned how to secure unsecured loans, the most elusive of all commercial blessings, he amassed over half a billion, left his wife (without divorcing her, to avoid splitting his fortune), bought a yacht and retired from business to enjoy life.

But there is danger in the magic of money. Living from the interest on his fortune, Ward Bunting had nothing to distract him seriously from the preservation of his body and the struggle to recapture the glory of his playboy years when girls were plentiful and he was brimful of testosterone. Even in his forties and early fifties, when he was not only rich but still quite good-looking, he attracted more women than he could handle. Some were driven into his arms by sheer curiosity: they wanted to find out how they compared with the famous singer. He had had three good decades and, as he saw it, he had become an all-round success in life because he was a *real* man. He was also unscrupulous, miserly, shrewd, mean, tough and wilful, but he believed all these virtues sprang from the same hardness as his pleasures. Convinced that his prick was the most special thing about him, he would not give up on it.

That meant young women, but according to a distant American relative who had the same surname, he didn't know how to pick them. William Bunting, an octogenarian, lived on the Bahamian island of Santa Catalina with a wife half his age whom he had acquired in his late fifties. Still hale and hearty at eighty-six, he attributed his perfect health to the fact that he had never let his young wife wear him out, reasoning that carefree comfort and luxury were the only joys he owed to the ex-ballerina who had married him for them. "Female satisfaction? Who cares? It's none of your business," he lectured his nephew. Ward Bunting, not quite seventy, spurned his uncle's out-dated philosophy. For the past fourteen months he had lived with Amanda Minton, a young divorcee. ("a life-threatening choice", according to his uncle.) Ms. Minton was a feminist with the kind of strong conviction that comes from a combination of received ideas and bitter personal experience. By the age of twenty-six she had learned everything that can be learned about male ingratitude and perfidy; a number of selfish young men had taught her how little they valued self-denial, devotion or love. No longer content to be *used*, she joined the exclusive group that A.A. Gill called "oceangoing whores". She attached herself to rich old men, without letting herself be bought. Or exploited. The clothes, the jewels, the yacht, the Lamborghini, the gold card weren't everything. She wouldn't lie with aging playboys just for the rich life, she wanted her orgasms too. And so did Bunting. He wanted her to love him not for his millions but for his prick. Ignoring his doctor's advice, he kept up with her by judiciously alternating between injecting his penis, taking blue pills and sniffing cocaine.

As they made their entrance to the Pizzeria Napolitana and took their seats at a table, they seemed a matched pair in spite of the difference in their ages. Both were tall, tanned, and both had dark hair, though his was scanty and hers was a magnificent, long, thick, glossy black mane that swayed around her slender neck and shoulders and framed her flawless oval face. They wore identical clothes: open-necked white muslin shirts and crisp white linen shorts. Both had the sort of elegance that comes from never wearing anything for more than a few hours. The cocaine sores inside Bunting's nose didn't show and both had the sleek, healthy look of people who spend most of their time in temperate climates and the fresh air. And both were slim, though evidently at a price: they ordered only salads and mineral water.

They were the centre of attention. Sipping her water and then looking thoughtfully at the glass as she replaced it on the table, Amanda enjoyed being stared at. Bunting, for his part, was watching the handsome young couple with the lanky teenager. They were only two empty tables away and he could hear them ordering dessert. The woman advised the lanky teenager to try all the flavours of *gelato*, while she decided on hot coffee and two scoops of *nocciola*. The young waitress with an exhausted face ignored the young man who was already halfway through his apple pie, and went off with the two orders.

Jim called her back. "Don't leave me out!"

"Well, I thought... another slice of apple pie with vanilla ice-cream?"

"No, no, let me look at the menu."

"Yessir." She came to stand beside him with pen and note-pad ready, straining to pay attention.

Having deprived himself of sweets ever since his first walk on the beach when he was still fat and old, Jim suddenly realized that being twenty-two meant that he could eat again. Whatever he wanted. To celebrate, he ordered a *Morte per Cioccolata.*

"One slice MPC," said the waitress, writing.

"No, no, no - a whole cake please," Jim corrected her.

The waitress gripped her pen and note-pad harder. "Excuse me?"

"I feel like a whole cake."

"To take away?"

"No, no - I feel like eating a whole cake right now."

"It's all chocolate."

"I know."

Stricken with anxiety, the overworked and underpaid waitress, a fair-haired woman with a head too big for her short body, looked like a trapped animal. The daughter of a single mother who had also earned her miserable living as a waitress, Mila Zomski's life was mostly pain. She resented her mother for aborting her other children, depriving her of brothers and sisters who might have loved her and cared about her. Poverty and unattractiveness are disadvantages which spirited women mitigate by a cheerful disposition that lends them charm, but Mila Zomski's permanently beaten look robbed her even of this defence against the indifference and casual cruelty meted out to people whose appearance and manner promise no joy to anyone. Now, after a half-night stand with a man who didn't even say goodbye - and a dressing-down from the manager when she arrived late for work in the morning – getting a customer who asked for a whole chocolate cake was the last straw.

'Another joker! Why does this always happen to me? He orders a whole cake and when I bring it he starts shouting, calls me stupid - the boss comes... Why didn't Mom abort me too!'

Shocked by her mindscreen, Jim smiled at her reassuringly

and slipped a handful of bills into her apron pocket. "I'm not a joker, I won't complain, I promise," he said. "It's just that I have a hankering for that cake."

Mila Zomski sighed with relief: customers who tipped didn't make scenes. "Yessir. Right away." (That evening, when she emptied her pocket and saw that Jim had given her hundred-dollar bills, she scared herself again, fearing that she would lose her job the next day for taking advantage of a customer's mistake. People who are down don't have to be kicked all that often; a few kicks are sufficient to teach them how to go on kicking themselves.)

The yachtsman, overhearing the conversation about a whole cake, became ravenous for something sweet and fulfilling and waited to feast his eyes on the *Morte per Cioccolata* more eagerly than Jim. When the cake arrived, all he could do was stare. The young man was devouring the three-layer chocolate cake with chocolate cream filling and chocolate icing, while the young woman and the teenager with him showed no sign of surprise or concern.

That rich, black-brown cake must have had some flour in it, certainly a pound of butter and a pound of sugar, eight eggs perhaps, but mostly it was pure chocolate, three thousand calories a bite. Jim savoured every mouthful. He could detect the difference between this cake and the cakes he had gorged on in the past when he was Senior Vice-President, which had always had a bitter aftertaste of guilt, a layer of awareness that he was doing something unwise, clogging his arteries, weakening his heart and stretching his stomach, that he was a man without will-power, his own worst enemy. But now, as the delicious chocolate melted in his mouth and trickled down his throat, there were no alien flavours of guilt in all that rich goodness, only the extra thrill of knowing that he could eat all the cakes in the world and they wouldn't make an ounce of difference. He could be a pig with impunity!

"Young man," Ward Bunting called across the empty tables in a shaky voice. His stomach heaved and burned with hunger, but he tried to sound amused and patronizing. "How often do you indulge yourself like that?"

Jim didn't know who Bunting was, but he read on his mindscreen curses against fate, the bitter thought that he could have hundreds of millions yet could not afford to touch anything with a four-figure calorie content. "I guess I'll have at least one more of these tonight," Jim said smugly.

Bunting's lean but somewhat wrinkled and jowly face registered this brutal remark with a nervous twitch. "How come it doesn't show? You look like you live on lettuce."

Jim patted his stomach with both hands. "I burn it up."

Seized by a surge of envy, Bunting couldn't breathe. Suddenly all the air was squeezed from his lungs and the restaurant turned dark around him. He jumped up from his chair, pounding his chest to fight whatever was squeezing him. "The bill!" he gasped, then collapsed on the tile floor.

Even before remembering that he might actually be able to help, Jim sprang to his feet. Shocked by the deathly blue of the prostrate man's face and wrinkled neck, he crouched down, tore open Bunting's shirt and began to massage his chest.

The young woman behind him was screaming hysterically. "Oh my God, oh my God!"

Working away on the motionless body, Jim wondered whether his taunt about the cake might have had anything to do with the man's heart attack.

"Should I call an ambulance?" the waitress asked eagerly, quite revived, assuming that Jim liked her.

Still not certain if his hands would do the trick, Jim ignored the question.

"Oh my God, oh my God!" the young woman wailed, beside herself with fright. "Oh God, don't let him die!"

Amanda Minton sounded as if she was having a nervous breakdown. When Bunting started to breathe, Jim glanced back to see whether he could help her. With strands of her long glossy black hair sticking to her tear-stained cheeks, she was down on the tiled floor, sitting on her heels, pounding her knees with her fists, sobbing and crying "Oh, my God, oh, my God!" But what Jim read on her mindscreen was: *Oh my God, he's going to die and he didn't change his will. Everything will go to that old bat!*

Jim let her go on grieving.

10. HOW MUCH IS LIFE WORTH?

Life is the only wealth.
PUSHKIN

Ward Bunting lay on the cream-coloured leather sofa in the stateroom of his yacht. The skipper and the two crewmen who had carried him on board on a stretcher stood near the door with an air of silent concern. Amanda Minton, who couldn't bear looking ugly, had disappeared for a moment to put her hair and face right. When she came back there were no signs of tears, but she paced the room restlessly, stopping every minute to ask: "Will he recover?"

Jim was bending over his patient and, as he moved his hands over the wrinkled forehead and mottled skull, the purple-blue tinge slowly faded away. The face lost its dead idiocy. Breathing regularly, Bunting was now asleep rather than unconscious. The sick man stirred and his blank mindscreen suddenly lit up: his consciousness woke into a nightmare. He was hanging on to the end of a long rope which was swinging in circles over an immense black void. There was the *zzzzoom-zzzzoom* of the circling rope. He kept thinking: *I can't let go, I can't let go!*

Jim rested the palm of his hand on Bunting's forehead. He groaned and opened his eyes.

"Ward, at last, at last!" Amanda Minton cried out and rushed to the sofa, pushing Jim aside.

Ghastly pale under his tan, not quite knowing whether he was dead or alive, Bunting stared at her without seeming to see her. But as his vacant pale blue eyes acquired the light of recognition, he turned his head to one side as if trying to avoid a sickening sight. "Go, go!" he said feebly.

She leaned closer to him so that he could smell her perfume and feel the warmth of her breasts on his chest and called him by her pet name for him in their hot moments. "Rooster, Rooster, it's *me*, Amanda, A-man-da!"

"Go away," Bunting groaned, turning his head from side to side to escape her.

She stood up and narrowed her eyes. She knew that it spoiled the perfect symmetry of her face but she had to do it, because otherwise she couldn't think. She tried to remember whether she had done anything to annoy him. But no, Ward had no cause to be mad at her: she hadn't even flirted with anybody for months. There was only one explanation: he had suffered a stroke and his brain was affected. She turned to the skipper and ordered him to call a helicopter ambulance. "Mr. Bunting has burst a blood vessel in his brain! Get him to hospital. Fast. There's no time to lose. Go on, get on the radio."

"There's no need," Jim said calmly, sitting down in one of the cream-leather armchairs and crossing his legs. The skipper and the crewmen looked from one to the other, not quite knowing which of the two they should obey. "Mr.

Bunting is perfectly all right," Jim assured them. "Take a look. His colour and his breathing are normal."

Amanda Minton turned on him with the contempt she reserved for people who didn't know their jobs. "But he's lost his memory."

"I don't think so."

"He doesn't recognize me."

"Go, go!" Bunting begged plaintively. He raised his hand to wave her away, and then, gaining strength, he shouted, "Get that bitch away from me!"

"Perhaps he does recognize you," Jim suggested.

Amanda Minton's eyes widened with surprise and there was a tremor around her lips; she wasn't used to being spoken to in such a manner. She looked around for help, but there was none. The crew were galvanized by the word *bitch!* This was serious: Bunting had to be obeyed. The skipper opened the door to speed Ms Minton's exit but, assuming that she would soon be back in favour, he didn't wish to make an enemy of her. Holding the door open, he sighed, gave a grimace of reluctant acquiescence and looked at her imploringly, as if to say: I disapprove but we must humour a sick man. The crewmen, who loathed her for treating them like dirt, could not contain their joy at her humiliation, temporary or not, and grinned openly, looking her in the face.

She crouched down by the sofa again, unable to believe that Bunting wouldn't want her near him. "Rooster, it's me, Amanda, Amanda!"

"Take her away, take her away!" Bunting sputtered, waving his hand.

The grinning crewmen stepped up to her. She stood up and turned to Jim, her face contorted with rage. "I hold you responsible for this!" she hissed with all the viciousness at her command. As one of the crewmen was about to grab her arm she shook her head, making her hair fly defiantly around her shoulders, and marched out. "And you'll all be fired!" they heard her saying on the gangway.

Jim almost felt sorry for her.

"Has she gone?" Bunting asked crossly, as the back of the sofa blocked his view.

"Yes, sir!" cheered the two crewmen.

"Good," said Bunting, but he was still testy, like a man who just had a profoundly disagreeable experience. "If I'm sick why wasn't I put to bed?" he demanded querulously.

"The doctor said there was no need," replied the skipper.

"You had a heart attack, but you're all right now," said Jim. "You can sit up if you want to."

Thinking himself very ill, Bunting made a cautious attempt to raise himself and was surprised to find that he could manage it. Then he shifted about in search of a comfortable position and, having dismissed the skipper and the crewmen, studied his torn Armani shirt with a frown for quite some time before looking up and saying sarcastically, "You're a doctor and you ate a whole chocolate cake?"

On a sudden inspiration, Jim decided to call himself an osteopath with specialist skills.

"I am of course very grateful to you for trying to help," Bunting said briskly. "Still, I ought to see a real doctor, I guess." Having recovered his wits, he began to wonder how much he should offer to pay.

Jim had a natural sympathy for the man whom he had brought back from the brink of death, that was reward enough, but reading on the yachtsman's mindscreen the sums Bunting was thinking of paying annoyed him. "How much are you worth?" he asked.

Bunting began fingering his torn shirt. "You ruined my shirt!" he grumbled.

Jim remembered the million pound bonus which he had promised to his staff who had been sacked and who would now get nothing. He thought of the thousands he had sacked. Why not get the whole business of money over with once and for all?

"That was an expensive shirt, made to measure," Bunting went on complaining. He was so obvious, it wasn't worth reading his mind.

"Come on, I asked you how much are you worth?"

"Why do you ask?" the yachtsman asked, alarmed.

Jim explained that the method he had used to revive him after the stroke could also be used to repair his heart and rejuvenate him.

Bunting cast a wary look at the young man but, not seeing him clearly enough and quite forgetting that he might be too weak to move, he got up to search for his glasses. His right eye was still strong enough to allow him to go about without them, but now he wanted to be sure that he wouldn't overlook anything. He found his glasses beside the television set, placed them firmly on the bridge of his nose and walked over to the young man to study his face. It looked normal, serious, confident - and the eyes were clear and bright. There were no signs of mental disorder.

"How could you possibly claim to make me younger?" Bunting asked suspiciously. "Osteopaths are serious professionals. You had better explain yourself."

"It's easier for me to do it than to explain it," said Jim, echoing others before him who had done amazing things. He stood up and passed his hand over Bunting's left cheek but then, seeing that Bunting was thinking *'What's that? That's nothing!',* he smacked him so hard that his glasses fell off. "Now look in the mirror."

With methodical deliberation, Bunting bent down to pick up his glasses, took a handkerchief from his pocket to polish them, pocketed his handkerchief, put on his glasses again, then walked to a wall mirror and stood in front of it for a long time. The left side of his face was transformed: his wrinkles were gone. The bags under his left eye and a large mole had disappeared. The flabbiness was gone. His cheekbone stood out once again. He turned to Jim, with two kinds of puzzled expression on his half-and-half face. "What did you do?"

"It's just a question of stimulating the nerves and muscles. It's reflexive osteopathy."

Bunting still looked puzzled, so Jim slapped him still harder on his left cheek. To make sure he understood, he hit him again several times. The pain made the "cure" convincing. There was no doubt; he looked younger on the left side of his face. He went back to the cream-coloured leather sofa, sat down and scratched his chest to help himself think. He wasn't worried about the process being painful, but the osteopath's interest in his total wealth was another matter. "You only fixed the left side of my face," he said sternly, in the sort of voice he used with the crewmen when they had washed only one side of the deck. "And my left eye is as bad as before!"

"You can have twenty-twenty vision for forty million."

"I'll stick to glasses."

"And you could be twenty years old if you want."

"You mean I can be a young man again?"

"Yes, for a million extra for every month."

"I can't afford it," Bunting replied promptly.

Jim sat down and crossed his legs. "As you wish. You still haven't told me how much you're worth."

Bunting suddenly looked miserable, even on the younger side of his face. His wide shoulders slumped; he actually shrank. No man who had three hundred and forty million in tax-free municipal government bonds and three hundred and ten million in other assets could have looked sadder or poorer. "I'm retired," he sighed. "I have to watch it."

"How much are you watching?"

Bunting made the mistake of reviewing his holdings in his mind and wondering what he should confess if it became absolutely necessary.

"Well, if you're worth 650 million plus change," Jim commented, "you can easily afford to pay a million for every month I take off your age."

The poor old man nearly had another stroke. "What are you talking about?" he gasped, putting his hand on his chest. Afraid to excite himself any further, he threw his head back to rest it on the back of the sofa and breathed quietly, waiting for his heart to slow down. When he recovered, he sat up straight. "I'm far poorer than you think, you can look at my tax returns if you don't believe me," he said in a slightly quavering voice. "I have never, never ever, said to you or to anybody else that I'm worth so much," he added with greater firmness.

"No, I said it."

Bunting continued to protest heatedly that he wasn't really a wealthy man, his boat and women were ruining him. He started to list his expenses in great detail and Jim waited for him to run down, thinking *'Once this is over I won't have to waste any more of my life on money.'* It was a powerful idea; even a cellist of the first rank might have been seduced by it.

"Even if you made me a teenager again," Bunting objected irritably, "I could be run over by a car the next day."

"Of course."

"I could be struck down by a fatal disease."

"True."

"I could be flying somewhere, and the plane could blow up in midair."

"You're in deadly danger all the time."

"So youth isn't solid value, is it?" Bunting asked, rather cleverly he thought. "We're talking about a perishable commodity."

"Perhaps I should put the left side of your face back as it was, you don't want to have two faces," Jim suggested, getting concerned about Lesley and Neb waiting for him in the pizzeria. If the boy got bored he would soon be performing another horrendous prank. He got up to leave.

"Wait!" The yachtsman grabbed Jim's arm with surprising

vigour for a seventy-year old. He promised the osteopath twenty million if he really got him perfect vision in both eyes.

Jim slapped him a few times and the yachtsman, stroking his burning cheeks, walked about looking here and there, testing how well he could see. He went to his desk and took out his insurance policy to check whether he could read the small print.

Finally satisfied, he wanted to be younger. He started negotiating, but Jim was anxious to leave and had no time for haggling. Defeated by the osteopath's impatience, Bunting agreed to pay the outrageous price of one million for every month.

"So do you want to be twenty?"

It took Bunting two seconds to multiply fifty by twelve. To be a young man of twenty again would cost him 600 million. He would be left with less than sixty million. Considering his outgoings, inflation, the depreciation of assets, he would end up living on the street. He had a vision of himself standing on a street corner, holding out a greasy hat for change. He shook his head despairingly. "I couldn't afford it." he sighed.

"So how young do you want to be?"

Bunting heaved a deep sigh and looked at Jim expectantly, hoping that he would relent and give him a discount.

Jim got up to leave and Bunting gave a cry of pain. "I'd have to sell my boat!"

"You're right," Jim agreed, "what's life without a yacht?"

In the end Bunting bought twenty five years off his age.

Beginning to feel more energetic as Jim slapped him about, Bunting had the happy thought of paying in instalments and stopping halfway through, then waiting to see whether the osteopath would sue. It was a common practice in business, but as delayed payments did not appeal to the other party he was forced to go to the computer. The internet transferred bonds and utility shares worth a fortune from the Cayman Islands to James and Lesley Taylor's joint account in London. No doubt in biblical times when the sea parted, the blind opened their eyes and the dead unwound their shrouds, sending a weighty fortune across the globe in a matter of minutes would have seemed the greater miracle.

As Bunting emerged from the stateroom, Amanda Minton threw her arms around him and hid her face in his chest, murmuring softly, "Oh, Rooster, you've recovered, I'm so glad, I'm so *happy*."

"It's Jim's new osteopathic treatment," Bunting said offhandedly, with a slight smile. She had often treated him offhandedly in the presence of the crew and he was pleased that the crew was watching her fawning over him.

Relieved that he hadn't pushed her away, she rubbed her crotch against him, displaying to the company her small firm behind wriggling under her tight white shorts. "I love you darling, I love you so much, let them hear it, let them see it, what does it matter, I adore you!"

The two crewmen who had made insolent faces at her watched the scene with sinking hearts, saying goodbye to their jobs. But after a minute or so Bunting disengaged himself and pushed her away with such force that she nearly fell.

Her pupils dilated, her mouth trembled, but she kept her

balance and her smile and kept saying, "Rooster, my darling Rooster". Her mindscreen read: *You worm, you rotten crook, you flabby prick, who are you to push me away? Your mouth stinks.*

She turned to Jim with a radiant smile, saying "I'll never be able to thank you enough, you saved Ward for me," while thinking: *It's all your fault, you bastard. I don't know how, but you set him against me. Well, I'm not such an airhead as you think, I'll see that you pay for it.*

Jim thanked her for her thanks.

11. SAVING GRACE

Alas, pitiable boy, if you could but escape your cruel fate!
VIRGIL

"What happened on the yacht?" Lesley asked Jim as they were walking back to the hotel.

"He's a young man now and we won't have to worry about the mortgage."

"That was really mean," Neb growled. "You asked me for something that allows you to get everything you want without having to use up your wishes."

"Of course, that's the idea."

"My parents are already in their second life. At this rate they'll be *dead* by the time I get home." Neb was thoroughly *pissed off* (no other expression quite conveys that kind of rebellious yet suppressed, downcast, impotent adolescent rage).

"No, no, Neb darling, no." Lesley said, feeling sorry for the boy. "Honestly. I promise you'll be able to go home soon. I won't let Jim keep you for long." Pleading for his patience with a look and a smile, she touched his arm, vaguely ashamed that she was flirting with him.

Neb made a face at her. "I'm glad you feel guilty about it, at least."

The hotel staff placed the Taylors' suitcases on a motorboat and Jim drove the boat himself, taking their luggage and their young friend with them to what looked like a round silver dinghy some hundred metres from shore. As none of the people on the beach swam out that far, there was no danger that anybody would see the submerged part of the disk. Jim brought the boat back to the hotel on his own, then swam out with a fast crawl stroke, eager to be on his way. Neb and Lesley were sitting on the silver rim, their feet dangling down into the water, waiting for him. Jim pulled himself up and sat down beside them to catch his breath. The sun was strong but pleasant; he was dry in a minute.

Neb suggested that Jim's second wish should be a trip on the fly-whirl disk to London. "It would be a unique experience for both of you. This fly-whirl disk could take you there in a few minutes. You'd never forget it."

"I'm not going to waste my second wish on travel," Jim protested. "We've return tickets to London."

"All right, I'll take you to London, and you can keep your wish," Neb said grudgingly, giving in to save time. He swung his legs inside the craft to get down to the controls.

"Poor Luke Mayberry!" Lesley suddenly exclaimed. "How could we have forgotten about him?!"

"Why didn't you remind me?" Jim said angrily, as husbands do.

"We must go and see him right away."

Neb aimed the disk toward a deserted spot on the beach,

muttering. "The couple with a thousand wishes."

"Hey, wait a minute!" Jim cried in alarm. "That wasn't a wish. I can easily swim back again."

"I'll take you back, its faster." said Neb with a martyred sigh. "Unfortunately I have to stick to you until you make up your minds."

"Neb, you have a good heart, you wouldn't want to..." Lesley started to say.

"I don't get it," Neb protested. "This planet is billions of light years from Otthon, and you don't look anything like my little sister, but you have exactly the same way of getting more and more out of every deal. Jesus!" He drove them near enough to land so that they could wade ashore. "Try to think of your second wish," he called after them. "And the third!"

The Mayberrys hadn't left their suite in the hotel all day. During the night Luke had wakened whimpering and when his mother went to him she found the skin of his skull shiny red and his eyes strangely dull. His whole body was burning. She gave him his pills with lemonade but he threw them up. His temperature was over a hundred. The hotel doctor was summoned and gave him an injection, after which he drifted in and out of sleep. His parents sat by his bedside, nodding off from time to time.

Although Anita Mayberry was usually good at controlling herself in front of the child, this time exhaustion and panic drove her wild. "I *hate* doctors!" she screamed at her husband, pounding the dressing table with her fist. "They lied. I'll kill them! They said we could count on a month. They lied, they lied. They don't know *anything*. They tricked

347

us."

Luke was quiet, scared, thinking that he had made his mother angry. He pleaded with his eyes, as if asking them to explain what he had done wrong.

His father bent over him and wiggled his ears, which usually made him smile or even laugh if he was feeling well enough, and asked: "Isn't Mummy funny when she screams like that?"

Chastened by her husband's reminder that their son was listening, Anita Mayberry pulled herself together in an instant and rushed to the bed. "Don't worry, love," she begged him, "we'll go back to England, and then we'll both be all right."

"But I *like* it here," Luke protested. His parched lips drooped at the corners and he started to cry, though he had no tears. "I like this place. I don't want to go away." They had to promise to stay before he would calm down and, when his mother sang to him, he fell asleep.

When he awoke an hour later he had only a slight fever, and he kept down the pills and the fruit salad his mother gave him. In the meantime his parents had packed, not knowing whether they should stay or go. They sat on chairs near the bed, their faces drained of all life but pain, which showed most when they tried to smile at Luke. No medieval sermon, nor Dante, nor Hieronymus Bosch, ever evoked such a hideous vision of hell as the torment of parents watching their child die.

Sensing that his mother and father were ready to break their promise and take him back to England, Luke began to whimper again. He wanted to get up and go out.

The Taylors found them at the deserted swimming pool. There was no one else around. The emaciated little boy and his parents who had the news of death on their faces had emptied the area. People hurried past Luke as though they didn't see him. Only when they were at a safe distance did they turn around to wave and smile. We love you, we feel for you, their smiles seemed to say, but we can't stand the horror of it.

Luke lay in a lounge chair, almost lost in the cushions, under the shade of a big umbrella, while his mother walked up and down behind him with her head bowed. Now and then she fixed her hate-filled eyes on her husband. *You murderer!*

Mayberry returned her poisoned look. *You stupid bitch!*

Jim looked away, he didn't want to read their mindscreens.

The Mayberrys greeted the young couple as strangers with a nod and a vague smile - except for Luke, whose pinched face lit up when he saw Lesley. His matchstick arms moved with excitement and he tried to get up to run to her, his face reddening with the effort, but then he fell back on the cushions.

"Hello, my little friend," said Lesley, crouching down by his chair so that their heads were at the same level.

What is leukaemia? Auschwitz. Huge eyes in a living skull which sometimes move, skin on bones. Lesley tried to smile at Luke, but she couldn't, she was so shocked by his overnight deterioration. She tried to excuse the dismay on her face by pointing towards the sudden clouds in the sky.

"It isn't a nice day, is it?"

"No," came the hardly audible sound from under the red-

and-white baseball cap.

"Are you still my friend?" she asked.

"I know you," Luke whispered, "I just don't know who you are."

The sight of the boy put Jim in a rage. He no longer believed in God but he hated Him. Didn't Christ say 'It is not the will of our Father who art in Heaven, that one of these little ones should perish'? He must remind Neb to write Christ a letter about it the next time the big man came to preside over the Otthon Supreme Court. Jim wondered what kind of waffling reply Neb would get.

"Of course, you're Lesley and Jim," Anita Mayberry said a little uncertainly, and rushed to Jim, grateful that he had not hurried past them like the others.

"Sorry, I didn't recognize either of you," Mayberry said. "You both look youngish today."

Anita looked at her husband with withering contempt, and turned back toward the Taylors. "He never recognises anybody," she said, her whole body shaking with bitterness and hatred.

Her absurd outburst froze the air for a moment. Mayberry raised his head as if he had noticed something in the distance. The strong, ruddy-faced man Jim had seen only the day before had a sickly pallor, as if he were at death's door himself. Lesley turned her head to look at the mother, trying to calm her with a smile. "We're leaving, we just stopped by to say goodbye to you and Luke."

Anita burst into tears. *If they only knew how little time he has left.*

"Don't worry, Anita, Luke will be all right," Jim told her

firmly.

"What do you mean? How can you tell?" she asked with such anxiety, pain and hope in her voice that for a moment Jim was paralysed by it.

"We were thinking of taking him back to England today," Mayberry whispered so that Luke wouldn't hear it.

Jim turned to Luke and crouched down beside him. The boy looked at him suspiciously without recognizing him, then turned his eyes towards Lesley, wondering why she had deserted him and let this strange man take her place.

Remembering Luke's remark about his illness when they had seen Luke on the beach for the first time, Jim quoted it back to him as he ran his fingers lightly over the boy's skull. "It's only temporary."

"It's not temporary," the little fellow said soundlessly, with terror in his huge eyes. Now he sensed that he was dying, he didn't want lies.

Jim began to caress his chest with a light circular motion, hardly touching his ribs, but Luke drew back. "It hurts," he whimpered.

"Please don't touch him, his skin is very sensitive." his mother protested. "How can you... I don't understand... a grown man... please leave him alone."

Jim ignored her and kept stroking Luke's body. As the boy twisted in his chair, crying, evidently in pain, she would have leaped on Jim like a raging lioness protecting her cub if Lesley had not restrained her.

"Let him be, for God's sake!" Lewis Mayberry burst out, lunging toward Jim.

Letting the mother go, Lesley stepped in front of the

father and grabbed him by the arms, immobilising him with surprise. He didn't understand. They seemed such a nice couple.

"He's not hurting him, believe me," Lesley pleaded.

The boy stopped whimpering and watched Jim's fingers brushing his arm. His parents stared at him, trying to guess what his silence meant.

Mayberry turned on his wife. "I told you we shouldn't bring him down here. I'm going to call the airline. You take him up to his bed."

"He wanted to see people. Why do you always want to deny him everything?"

"Not temporary!" Luke shouted in an amazingly strong voice and swung his thin leg, kicking Jim in the chest.

Never in his life had Jim felt such contentment. He had saved a life and felt he deserved to live. It was an emotional high that would save him from a life of ignoble ease. He stood up. "All right, Luke, you win!" he said, backing away and waving goodbye.

But Luke wouldn't let him get away with it: he ran after the Taylors, shouting, "Not temporary, not temporary!"

The parents watched, awestruck.

"Let's hurry," Jim said to Lesley in a low voice as they were going away. "I don't want to get back and find that Neb has gone."

Lesley wasn't worried. "He'll be waiting."

"What makes you so sure?"

"Don't worry, I know."

"How do you know? He's had enough time to get out of the solar system by now."

Lesley stopped. "Do you know what the most alien thing about Neb is?"

"All the things he can do, I suppose."

"No, no. Do you realise that in spite of all his complaining and making you fart and all that, it has never once occurred to him to break his word?"

"Well, that makes him an alien all right."

With the Taylors gone, Luke was running all over the place, splashing about in the pool and eating a huge lunch. Anita Mayberry told their bewildered fellow guests, who all came to look at the boy, that the young couple who worked the miracle were not the Taylors at all. The Taylors were much, much older. These two were reincarnations of Vishnu, the Preserver of Life, and his wife Lakshmi, the Goddess of Fortune.

12. A VOCATION

The greatest good that mortals know,
And all of heaven that we have below.
ADDISON

Even in coasting gear, the fly-whirl disk made the journey from Florida to London in a few minutes. In mid-January it was already dark at half-past four and everything was wet. It had been raining heavily. There was no one about in Holland Park and Neb landed on an empty spot. They took out their luggage; Neb took only his drum, and, closing the hatch, sank the machine into the ground and covered it up again. In the space age the shortest distance takes the longest time. It took longer to get a taxi and crawl through the traffic for a few blocks than it had taken them to cross the Atlantic.

When they entered the flat Lesley went ahead to switch on the lights and the central heating. "You'll have a lovely view of the garden," she said to Neb as she led him into the room, now furnished as a guest room, which they had never used since the cot, the playpen and the toy animals were moved out. "I hope you'll be happy here," she added, turning toward him with a strange smile.

The boy was shocked by her mindscreen.

"I'm not going to be your son. I already have a mother, thank you very much!" he protested angrily. "First of all, I'm not a kid, and second you're hardly older than me. There isn't that much difference between fourteen and twenty-one, you know. Besides..."

"I have fifty years of memories, Neb."

"Get rid of them, just tell Jim to ask me," Neb suggested crossly, almost certain that it wouldn't work this time either. "Jim, Jim," he shouted, "come here, we have your second wish."

"But I don't *want* to get rid of my memories."

Jim had gone straight to Lesley's study where he kept his cello, leaving her the task of looking after Neb. He was impatient to find out how well he could handle the bow and the strings. When he heard Neb calling him from the other room he got up and closed the door so that he could tune his grandfather's instrument in peace.

Annoyed that Jim didn't respond, Neb turned back to Lesley. "Don't even dream of keeping me here for more than a day."

"Come on, Neb, you can stand it for a little while. The Earth isn't such a terrible place."

"Not a terrible place?" Neb started stamping around and flailing his arms. "I don't understand how anyone can live on a planet where it's dark and cold all the time."

"It wasn't cold in Florida. Anyway, January is one of our darkest months. In a few weeks we'll have plenty of light here."

"A few *weeks*? I won't be here that long."

"You like pizza, you like ice cream. There's a lot of other

355

great food around that you should try. There is a very good French restaurant nearby; I thought we might go there for dinner tonight."

"You're trying to make me stay, but I'm not stupid," Neb growled, striding up and down the room. "I'll give you one more day and if I'm still here, I'll turn nasty. One more day and you'll wish you'd never seen me. That will be your second and third wish." He laughed triumphantly. "And you think you were lucky to meet me!" He lay down on the floor to laugh more comfortably, kicking his heels in the air and slapping his stomach with his hands so hard that Lesley exclaimed, "Watch it, you'll hurt yourself."

Neb sat up and pointed an accusing finger at her. "Just because you're the most beautiful woman in the universe, you think you can get around me. I'm not that stupid. "

He looked at her hard and she let out a big loud fart which stank so much that she twisted her nose in disgust.

Neb flopped down on the floor again to go on laughing and kicking his heels in the air. "The beauty farts, ha-ha-ha! The beauty farts, ha-ha-ha!"

"You're not that young, Neb, you should be ashamed of yourself."

"It was *you* who farted, ha-ha-ha!" He stopped laughing and sat up again. "Now you see what's in store for you tomorrow! Come to think of it, why should I wait until tomorrow?" He looked hard at her, blushed deeply, and her blouse fell off, then her skirt. She nearly tripped over her panties as she ran out, terrified that he would follow and rape her. Having hurriedly put on some clothes, she went to her study and closed the door behind her.

"Listen to this," Jim said as she came in, and lifted his bow.

"There's no time for that," Lesley whispered in a shaky voice. "Let's ask him for something and then let him go. He wished my clothes off just now. Next thing you know he's going to rape me. If he gets serious about it, we won't be able to stop him. You can't live with someone who can look at you and your clothes fall off. I want that fiend out of here. Tonight."

Jim sighed, wishing he could go on playing.

"If I'm not pregnant yet, I think we'll be able to manage," she added with an unconscious smile. She was too upset to think of their pleasures, but somehow her body remembered.

"All right, let's decide what we want," said Jim grimly, hating to be hurried about their future. As they were thinking, he picked up his bow again and started to play Bach's Suite Number 3 in C Major, the cello piece he knew best. At first he played in a desultory fashion, the way people play with worry beads when there is something weighing on their minds, but then he stopped and started again. He willed his hands to convey to the bow and the strings the surge of emotion that gripped him as he played the melody in his mind, and his hands obeyed him for long sections of the piece. Jim focussed on the notes of the music so absolutely that for a long time he didn't hear Neb beating, pounding and banging a drum two rooms away. Lesley's first impulse was to go and tell Neb to stop making that horrible noise, but she checked herself, afraid that he would undress her again. As Jim went on playing, the drum grew quieter. It still flared up sporadically; then it fell silent.

Lesley heard steps in the hall which stopped on the other

side of the door. 'Oh, God, what's he going to do now,' she thought with alarm as the door quietly opened and Neb came in. But one look at him dispelled her apprehension. His face was transfigured. He tiptoed to her to ask in a whisper: "What's that?" Getting used to the fact that he could read her thoughts, she just turned her head towards him: *This instrument is called a cello, and he's playing a suite composed by Johann Sebastian Bach.* Signalling that he got the message, Neb lay down on the floor, folded his arms behind his head, closed his eyes and breathed in the sound. Even after Jim had finished the piece he remained stretched out on the floor, apparently still listening with his eyes closed. "Johann Sebastian Bach..." he whispered reverently, without moving. A moment later, struck by a terrible thought, he leaped to his feet. "Did you crucify him too?!"

Seeing how music affected Neb, Lesley put on the CD of Handel's Ode for St. Cecilia's Day, and Neb lay down on the floor again to listen. When Felicity Lott hit the high C in the last aria and held it, he raised his arms as saints do in old paintings when the sky opens and an angel appears.

With a speed more extraordinary than the speed of his father's spacecraft, he grew up in an hour. He was not an adolescent any more, but a young man with a vocation: he had a burning desire to become a musician. They had nothing like Earth music on the Centre of the Universe and he had resolved to gather it all together and take it to his people.

After a few days getting his bearings, he settled down to study music in earnest. With many lies and false documents about his background, he enrolled as a special student at the

Royal College of Music under the name of Gary Clearwater from Cleveland, Ohio. He learned to read and write scores in the same way he had learned English: he mostly wished it. He even learned to play the piano by the same easy method, but he didn't play it all that well. It seemed that he could wish anything that could be learned, but he could not wish artistic achievement, which required stronger magic than wishing - it required the power of blood, sweat and tears. But he was ready for that, too. Native talent, concentration, perfect pitch, ambition and application carried him forward.

Lesley went back to teaching, telling her colleagues at school that she had a facelift in Florida, and as she wore the same clothes that she had worn before the Christmas holidays, she got away with the lie. Having discovered sex again at the age of twenty-one, she came to school every morning with a honeymoon face and talked to her pupils about the thrill of thinking and the joy of good books. Many of her students fell in love with her and some became readers for life.

A young man again and back in London where everything reminded him of his recent past, Jim's remorse and desire for revenge flared up like an illness; he was resolved to make amends and make Norton regret that he was ever born.

Neb's passion for music gained the Taylors time. They could get on with their lives, farting only for natural reasons.

13. DON'T SPURN A HELPING HAND

Don't spurn a helping hand, it may never be offered again.
OTTHONITE PROVERB

The three-storey Beckford house with big bay windows stood at the edge of Hampstead Heath. It was a cold January day. The wind cleared the sky for the sun which gave no heat but shone all the brighter. The silver Mercedes, which had marked Pierre Beckford as a man who could cope with losing his job more easily than most of the others, was parked in the driveway. The silvery surface beat back the light and hit Jim in the eye, reminding him that if it wasn't for that expensive car the poor fool would be alive and working. He felt ashamed that he had pretended to commiserate with Norton about his old wife after Beckford's funeral. 'I'll never again have to fake what I don't feel,' Jim thought. He walked up the few steps leading to the entrance of the Beckford house and rang the bell, hoping that the widow wouldn't recognize him. They had met only twice before: on the very day her husband was sacked when she had brought her daughter to *QS* Tower and at the funeral service in Brompton Oratory. But then Jim was a bloated, elderly man of fifty-six.

Now he was a slim young man and put his faith in his good looks.

Answering the bell, the elegant blonde opened the door and sized him up. "Yes?" she asked with a smile.

"Good morning Mrs Beckford," Jim said. "I used to be a colleague of your husband and I just wondered how you and Melinda are getting along. Is there anything that needs to be done? Anything I could do to help?"

As he spoke, her smile faded. She looked at him suspiciously. There was a flash of recognition in her eyes. "Assassin!" she hissed. She spat at him and slammed the door.

Wiping his face with a Kleenex, Jim turned around and went down the few steps to the pavement, all churned up. He couldn't imagine that the immaculately dressed woman with impeccable manners was in the habit of spitting at people, which made the insult worse. He kept his rising gorge in check with the reflection that he had no right to be surprised or offended. Who made her a widow? Still, it wasn't all his doing. 'Why, she played as big a part in the tragedy as I did,' he thought in self-defence. He recalled the looks she had given her husband when he was hounded out of *QS* Tower. There was no pity, no sympathy, no support in her eyes, let alone love. Beckford must have felt awfully lonely when he tied his daughter's skipping rope around his neck. Jim guessed that she had realized that she wasn't there for her husband when he needed her and now blamed herself – and if she blamed herself, she would never stop hating him.

Keenly aware that her hostility did not free him from his

debt to the suicide, that he had to keep an eye on the family and had to establish some kind of contact with them, he resolved to give it another try later. Should he write to her? Waiting for a taxi, his thoughts soon drifted to more pleasant things he could do. Mrs. Beckford lost her chance to acquire a powerful protector even while she was watching him from behind a curtain.

14. ELLIE'S WISH

I have been half in love with easeful Death.
KEATS

Jim had never visited Ellie Wade at home, but he had her address. She lived on a treeless side street off the North End Road in Fulham, in a tiny terrace house which she was cleaning over and over again while hoping for the phone to ring about her job applications. Jim counted on finding her at home, certain that in spite of her extreme reliability and competence, the dowdy, plain, middle-aged woman had not found another job in such a short time. Ellie opened the door with a duster in her hand. She looked puzzled, but her face was smoother; Jim guessed that, since her father's death, she had been sleeping regularly.

"Ah, it's you", she finally said. "What happened to you?"

"The same thing that happened to you, Ellie. We've had a rest from the office. It can take off decades of your age."

She led him into a spotless sitting room. There was a vacuum cleaner standing in the middle of the carpet. "I was just about to hoover," she explained. "Exercise."

"You'll have no time for cleaning, you'll be coming back

to work for me."

"Heavens! Do you really mean it?"

"You start today."

She wanted to know what made Jim so slim and so young-looking in three weeks, but the veteran PA knew how to keep her curiosity in check. In any case, the miracle for her was that she had her job back.

"Are we going back to *QS*?"

"No, no. You'll be running a foundation with George Nicholson. He doesn't know it yet; I came to see you first."

"Did you know that Nicholson had a stroke?" she asked.

"No, I didn't. What happened?"

"He was in intensive care the day after you sacked him. I guess it was to be expected. He was your deputy."

Jim sighed. "I'll make it up to him. How is he?"

"I ran into his PA the other day..."

"Heather?"

"Yes. Heather says that Nicholson looks much worse, but his mind is all right. I'm sure I'll be able to get along with him. But let's celebrate your good news first. Let me bring you some wine. Is a red from the Rhineland all right?"

"That would be fine. Thanks."

She picked up the hoover and carried it to its place beside the refrigerator in the kitchen, an extension of the living room. Looking around, Jim saw a montage of old photographs on the wall and went to take a closer look at it.

"That's my family," Ellie said from the kitchen. "My father put the pictures together for me ages ago when my mother died and I came to London. He wanted me to take them and put them on the wall of home wherever it would be. He was big on family. You see three generations of Wades there."

The Wades were serious men and women of Yorkshire, full of pride. Ellie's parents were immediately recognizable. The most striking part of the montage was a big worn photograph of a young couple from the 1920's, judging by their clothes: a girl with bobbed hair and short skirts was showing off her legs, leaning on a solemn young man in a dark business suit wearing thick glasses. Jim assumed he was one of the Wades who had married a floozy from London.

"They're my grandparents from Berlin," Ellie commented as she brought in a tray with biscuits and a bottle of wine and placed it on the coffee table between two armchairs. "They had their newborn baby with them on the cattle car to Auschwitz. That baby was my Mum. On the way my grandparents put their photo inside the folds of her bundle and pushed the bundle through an air hole. Mum landed on a snow bank by the rail trucks; a German railway man picked her up and took her home to his wife and they looked after her till the war was over. Eventually Mum ended up in Canada and married my father. She used to look at that photograph for hours."

Jim took another look at the photo, the only thing the couple could leave of themselves to their baby as the train carried them to their death.

"Jim, did you have a facelift in Florida?" asked Ellie. His interest in her -grandparents encouraged her to be nosey.

Jim realized that if she was to help him, she would have to know everything, but he would scare her if he told her the truth: she would think he had gone crazy. "No, but I learned some techniques which could improve your eyesight. Let me show you," he said, standing up, and indicating that she should stand up too.

Ellie gave a nervous laugh. "Improve my eyesight? That's certainly something I'd love to see."

"Close your eyes."

He massaged her forehead a little for form's sake, then brushed her eyelids. Her bulging eyes sank back to their sockets and her contact lenses fell on the floor. She stepped away from Jim, blinked and stared at the floor, stunned. "I can actually see them," she said with quiet amazement. "I've spent half my life looking for my bloody contact lenses."

"You won't need them anymore."

"What do you mean?"

With Ellie's restored eyesight even her features improved and Jim was struck by the idea that if she were two decades younger, she would be pretty. "Go and look at yourself in the mirror," he said.

Ellie turned to go to the bathroom, but he grabbed her arm and ordered her to wait. He flicked off the small hairy mole from under her chin. "Now you can go," he said smiling, patting her cheek.

A few minutes later, Ellie staggered back to the living room, ready to hear what had happened on the island without wasting his time with too many objections.

"Let's sit down, Ellie, let's sit down. Let me tell you about an amazing kid we met in Florida. I'm sure you'll like him," said Jim and told her everything.

"I'm glad I'm sitting down," Ellie sighed, sufficiently stunned to listen without interrupting him. "How did you happen to go swimming in the middle of the night?" she asked at the end.

Jim didn't mention that he had tried to drown himself and blushed. (At the age of twenty-two, he could blush.) "It didn't seem like the middle of the night; it was the comet's night, bright as day."

"If you weren't so slim, I would think you were raving," Ellie said, shaking her head, still only half convinced. "Did Lesley become young herself?"

"Yes. And it's time for you to be younger, too. To begin with, you'll have a lot of work and besides, you deserve a break. You sacrificed your best years nursing your father; you're entitled to a life of your own."

Ellie shivered at the thought. "I wouldn't want to be any younger, even if it could be done."

"You can't be serious."

Ellie sighed. "Jim, everyone who has ever mattered to me is dead. One lonely life is enough for me."

"If you were young, you'd have a new start and soon have a new family that would matter a great deal to you. You could fall in love tomorrow."

"Oh, God, I'd never go down that road again!" she groaned.

Jim assumed that once she had twenty-twenty vision, she would see sense, but seeing things clearly made her all the more assertive. She absolutely refused to let him muck about with her age. Her mouth dried out from arguing and she emptied her glass of wine. It was a good strong wine, and eventually she relented, ready to enter into fantasy land. "Well, she sighed," if you can do anything, I wouldn't mind dying healthy."

"Don't be absurd, Ellie."

"Even if I had two lives, I'd eventually die, so death has no terror for me. What scares me is being sick. Both my parents died after long, painful, humiliating illnesses. All I ask is that you cure me when I fall ill." She poured herself more wine and emptied her glass again. "I want to be healthy until my last moment," she added with a self-mocking smile.

They both laughed and when they parted at the doorway, Jim took both her hands in his and her swollen veins and liver spots vanished. Neither of them suspected that in less than a year her absurd wish to die healthy would be fulfilled

15. THE CHINESE THREAT

...men age quickly in misfortune.
HOMER

George Nicholson answered the doorbell in his T-shirt and underpants. The lines on his unshaven face had become furrows and he seemed shorter. His head was bent and his shoulders were hunched forward as if he were trying to raise a spoon to his mouth with a shaky hand. Worse, he was strange. True, the central heating was turned up and he was in his own home, but the man Jim knew would have been too dignified to show himself in his underwear, exposing his hairy legs.

"Are you from the landlord?" Nicholson asked querulously, through the half-open door. "I've had a stroke and I need time to recover. Your threatening letter didn't help."

"I'm not from the landlord."

"We can't move until we find a new place."

"What did the doctors say, George?"

Nicholson leaned forward to stare at Jim. "Do I know you?"

"Of course you know me. Jim, Jim Taylor."

"Jim Taylor has less hair than I do."

"Hair transplant."

"How old are you?"

"For Christ's sake, George, all this smooth skin you see came off my ass."

Jim raised his hand to pat him on the back to straighten his spine.

Nicholson drew away as if stung. "Hey, leave off!"

The doorway no longer blocked, Jim stepped in and took off his coat.

"As you find me at home in the morning, I don't need to tell you that I haven't found a suitable job," Nicholson said accusingly.

"That's why I am here, George, that's why I am here. I'm sorry about the whole business."

"Your sorry is no use to me. I'd still be working if it wasn't for you. I'm not going to offer you anything, not even tea." He gave his visitor a violent push.

Jim stumbled and took another look at his former deputy.

"No need to look at me like that," Nicholson objected. "I'm not senile. All the tests show that my brain wasn't affected by the stroke."

Jim wondered whether his wife had left him. "Where is Anne?"

"She's visiting a friend in hospital – Martin's a colleague at Oxfam."

The Nicholsons' flat, like the Taylors', was in an Edwardian mansion block in Chelsea, one of the most desirable parts of central London. Spacious, unfurnished flats like this were impossible to rent any more - they were only for sale

- but the Nicholsons had moved in thirty-two years earlier, when they were only for rent. The rooms seemed to be less cramped than Jim remembered.

"We had to sell some of the antique furniture we inherited from my Guildford grandparents. Not that it matters now - we wouldn't have anywhere to put it in a smaller place." Unsteady on his feet, he was swaying; the stroke had clearly affected his balance.

"What smaller place? What do you mean?"

"We lost our home!" the old man cried out in a weak, trembling voice. "We've lived here for thirty-two years, we've already paid millions in rent but the landlords keep raising the rent. Anne's small salary from Oxfam is our only income. If I were to take the kind of job I could get, it still wouldn't be enough to cover the rent, let alone all our other expenses. Worse, there's going to be a new rent rise next month."

Nicholson was moving and swaying about so jerkily, so unpredictably that Jim had a hard time laying hands on his waist, his back, his legs, but he managed.

"What happened to the money the company paid you when you left?"

"When you sacked me, you mean," Nicholson said spitefully. "We still have some of the money, but both Monica and Josie are at university and it costs a lot. We'll have to move out of London to a smaller place before we become destitute thanks to you, you bastard." He failed to notice that he could stand and walk straight without any difficulty.

Jim was pleased with the effect of his handiwork and wasn't offended that the no-longer old wreck went on to abuse him. "I called you on Christmas Eve..."

Nicholson's grey eyes acquired a yellowish gleam. "Yes, you got the sack, too. It made my Christmas. Will you have to leave London yourselves?"

"No, I had some luck in Florida. I'm setting up on my own and..."

"So you don't have to downsize," Nicholson interrupted and sank into one of the armchairs. The furrows on his face were twisting about like snakes.

Catching Nicholson's hands, Jim began massaging his fingers.

"Yes, it shows. My joints became inflamed from stress."

The massage was soothing and Nicholson relaxed, sounding almost sleepy. "I often think of my father. I dreamed of him the other night. He was standing beside a tank in the desert, just as in the photograph from El Alamein. He risked his life to protect us from a German invasion. I wonder what he would say if he knew that a young German is taking over his son's apartment."

"What young German are you talking about?"

"A German banker with lots of money who's buying our flat," Nicholson said, suddenly wide awake. "He might be a nice guy, but just the same, when it comes to our home, in England, in London, in the capital of Great Britain, I believe Sergeant Nicholson's son should have priority over any German – or for that matter, any foreigner." Feeling stronger and more energetic, he tore his hand away from Jim and an explosion of bitterness propelled him out of his chair. "We've a right to our country ahead of everybody else!"

While Nicholson went on raving, Jim wondered what

made his one-time friend and deputy so different from what he used to be. Was it the loss of his job? The rent? His stroke? "How do your hands feel?" he asked.

Nicholson moved his fingers, a younger man's fingers now, but he had no mind to pay attention to his hands. He meant to ask Jim why he came, but he was too full of rage to stop talking. "I hate foreigners."

"George, the man who ruined you wasn't a foreigner, but a true-blue Englishman, Jeremy Norton".

"And you! Let's not forget about you. I should have had your job and I should have fired you. It's funny you telling me that foreigners had nothing to do with sacking me."

"All right, but before you start hating all foreigners, remember your father."

"He spoke English. Taxpayers didn't have to spend a fortune on translators for him. Besides, Jamaicans came here because they were part of the Commonwealth. And they were Christians. And they weren't all that many. Today all you need is a chequebook or proof that you have nowhere else to go and the government lets you in by the hundreds of thousands. And if you have some contagious disease, all the better."

"Congratulations, George. You may be the only mixed-race racist in the country."

"Racist? Do you think there is still such a thing as a United Kingdom?"

"Whatever do you mean?"

"Where is this United Kingdom of yours?"

"Right under your feet."

"Wrong!" Nicholson exclaimed triumphantly with a

chilling laugh. "We're on Chinese territory. The government gave Hong Kong back to China and gives London to the Hong Kong Chinese. A Hong Kong billionaire bought this building and a German banker is buying our home for 2.5 million pounds. We are kicked out and I might as well cut my throat. Do you have any idea what it's like losing the home where you spent most of your life?"

"Relax, relax. You're driving yourself crazy. Nobody is going to take your home, that's what I came to tell you. Listen..."

Listening was the one thing the younger Nicholson couldn't do. He cut Jim short with the fury of a man who had a lot to say that no one wanted to hear. Getting healthier and younger did not help; it only made him feel his grievances more intensely. His unhappiness was so immense; his dread of a smaller flat away from London so great, that he felt more had to be at stake than his personal misfortune. "Britain is run by traitors!" he shouted. "They surrender the country. They don't surrender their ministerial palaces, of course. They surrender our homes..."

Nicholson seemed to be working himself up to another heart attack and Jim brushed his chest with his hand.

"What are you doing? Leave me alone!"

"George, you don't know your luck."

"Yes, Anne tells me we're still better off than most people. We're certainly better off than the thousands you sacked. Do you have any idea how many of those face eviction? They were left jobless, and the next thing they know they are homeless."

"The next thing they'll know is that their problems are

solved," Jim said with the confidence of a man who had money to burn.

"You mean nobody gets evicted these days?" the former deputy asked sarcastically. *'He's a moron, a moron, he doesn't know anything,'* read his mindscreen.

Jim realised that Nicholson's hatred for him wasn't something that would pass any time soon and decided not to mention the job again. He also gave up the idea of making him too young.

Nicholson couldn't have been more furious if he had known that he had talked himself out of a good job and ten years of a new life. "Nobody cares. You certainly don't care. You can always go home. You don't give a damn what happens to these islands. You're an American."

"George, I'm from Canada. Surely you remember?"

"How could I forget it!"

"Anne shouldn't leave you alone."

"Glad you remind me. Martin, the friend Anne went to see, had his head kicked in and his collar bone broken a couple of weeks ago. He's living with another guy, Peter – they're closer than most couples we know. One evening when they left the pub holding hands, a group of young asylum seekers set upon them. If some of the guys from the pub hadn't come to their rescue, they could have been killed. Two of the attackers were caught. They were from the Sudan and told the police that they just arrived and didn't know that there was a law against beating up homosexuals."

"You're making this up."

"Norton always said that your trouble is that you overestimate people's intelligence. Go to Sudan with your boyfriend and see how you'll do."

"I don't need to go Sudan to meet benighted thugs. We've plenty of them right here."

"All the more reason not to let more of them into the country."

"George, nations and races mix. You know that better than anybody. The mixing of the races is a boon, it enriches the gene pool. Why, you're a living proof of it yourself with your first class Oxford degree."

"My second cousin was blown up on a bus because we don't worship Allah. And a friend of mine was beaten up by young Muslim men because he told one of their women that in this country women don't cover their faces. We shouldn't allow barbarians to invade us."

"Don't you feel different?" Jim asked, having touched him here and there all through the arguments.

"You're right, I do feel different," Nicholson said in a stronger voice. "I'm angry."

"Planes make the whole world one country. Give it a couple of hundred years and we'll all be Earthlings."

No longer stooping, his back straight, Nicholson regained his old height and gave Jim a scornful look. "You talk about a couple of hundred years. Who lives that long? What your kind doesn't understand is that we want to spend our short lives without hordes of newcomers crowding us out."

Jim started slapping Nicholson quite roughly to finish the job and go.

Nicholson slipped and fell to the floor, hitting his elbow. "You too, Jim, you too?" he asked woefully. "I offended your beliefs and now you want to kill me? And in my own home, too?"

"Get up, get up – and put on some clothes before your underpants fall off."

Nicholson lumbered to his feet with a sigh and left the room.

Jim was still waiting for Nicholson's return, when Anne Nicholson arrived back from the hospital. Greeting the faded middle-aged woman and realising that he would have to make her younger, too, if he didn't want to break up their marriage, he wasted no time on explanations and proceeded to pat and stroke her in all the right places, ignoring her screams and giggles. Nicholson reappeared wearing a baggy suit with an open-necked shirt. Seeing her husband looking so much younger than in the morning and feeling stirrings that she hadn't felt for many years, she sank into a chair, not trusting herself to speak.

"So all that talk about plastic surgery was rubbish, right?" Nicholson asked sullenly.

"It's a combination of physiotherapy, reflexology – it's too complicated to explain."

"I was wondering why you kept touching me. Sod off."

The man was still in a filthy mood. Jim couldn't believe it. "George, don't you realise that you have another chance at life?"

"Of course I do," Nicholson shot back, "I'm not an idiot."

"Then what's wrong? You're only thirty-two and you have the experience of an old professional. We'll buy the flat for you and you will also get some money to keep you going until you decide what you want to do. Just give me the name and address of your landlord."

"I have a letter from them!" Anne Nicholson exclaimed, roused from her stupor and jumped up to go and fetch it.

Jim was incensed by Nicholson's total lack of gratitude. "You miserable old bugger, I'm giving you a new start, and I'm a foreigner. How about that?"

As he read Nicholson's mindscreen, he didn't wait for an answer but took the landlord's letter and left. He had come up against the limits of his magic; he couldn't cure rage. After seeing Jim out, Anne Nicholson rushed back. Her husband still stood in the middle of the room.

"George, George, we won't have to move. We can stay! Isn't it wonderful? We won't lose our home. I can't wait to tell the girls." She gave him a quick hug, then stepped back and spread her arms and pirouetted, ready to dance. "Look at me! We're young, George, we're young!"

"So are millions of others," he replied gloomily. "What good is that? Will it give us back our country?"

16. A CRUEL AWAKENING

When I waked
I cried to dream again.
CALIBAN

Nicholson was lucky, he was still alive and he was arguing with ever more vigour, clearly on the mend. The young father who hanged himself with his daughter's skipping rope was beyond help. Having left his former deputy, Jim remembered his own baseness right after Beckford's funeral. He couldn't forgive himself for doing Norton's bidding –– commiserating with him for being stuck with Lady Margaret when he wanted a younger wife.

In the *QS* Tower, in Sir Jeremy's office, to the left of his desk, there was an alcove which hid an enormously wide, black leather sofa accommodating his huge frame; he called it his thinking sofa. He used to nap there after lunch on dark winter afternoons when only underlings were working. Janice had never allowed anyone to disturb him while he was digesting his lunch. Jim Taylor had been the only one who walked past her and barged in on him. But Jim Taylor was gone for good. Sir Jeremy had reached executive heaven: he was head of a profitable company, he had no rivals with threatening energy or ambition and he was earning a fortune even while dozing off. Yet he was dozing off feeling thoroughly wretched.

For all his triumphs, comforts and power, his misery level remained the same. As his business worries faded, his personal tragedy loomed larger in his mind. He had to sit with his wife every excruciating evening; amusing her while she bathed her feet, which had been ruined by her intolerable vanity, by a lifetime practice of squeezing her wide feet into narrow shoes. And now that she was such a wreck that shoes no longer made any difference, he was expected to cut himself off from the world and watch her nursing her little pains. Still cherishing his image of himself as a bull pawing the ground, Norton resented her poisoning his last good years. Stretched out on the sofa, watching the soporific trickle of winter sleet on the other side of the window pane, he wished there was a way to get rid of the old termagant without parting from the Constable gracing the wall behind his desk. Old enough to need a nap after lunch but not old enough to admit it, he half-raised himself when he could no longer see anything in the room - intending to switch on the light - but then changed his mind and sank back again. He felt he could think better in the dark.

In his dream he was in a hospital waiting room with Margaret's sister Bootsie, who was crying copiously. He had his arm around her and concentrated on looking mournful. The family's personal physician was explaining to them that the mastectomy was a simple matter but the anaesthetist had mistaken the dose and, tragically, Lady Margaret had died on the operating table. They agreed that she was irreplaceable. "It was the hospital's fault, you can sue them," said their doctor, while Norton was wondering how long he should wait before marrying again – a young beauty this time.

Suddenly Janice was leaning over him, announcing that finally he could marry her. *"Not bloody likely. If I marry again it'll be somebody new!"* he protested, summing up in his sleep the fate of married men's girlfriends the world over. Many home truths are lost in dreams.

Unhappily, Janice was not a dream: she stood over him, talking in a shrill, agitated voice. All the lights were on, piercing his eyes. He quickly closed them again, to get back to the hospital, to savour the joy of his wife's demise, but it was too late. He remembered that his wife was in perfect health. "Jim Taylor" were the first words that penetrated his consciousness. Jim Taylor? Dazed from sleep, he felt defenceless and, heaving himself up from the sofa, staggered back to his desk, the rampart of his authority. "I'm at a meeting," he groaned.

"He isn't here..."

"I don't want him on the phone either."

"It's not him; I just heard a fantastic story about him." A trim young woman with short hair and sloe eyes, her breasts prominent even under the jacket of her neat beige suit, Janice dressed as a unisex person for the office, but now her dishevelled hair, her makeup, her whole face was disarranged as she leaned across his desk in breathless excitement to report that the Nicholsons were rejuvenated. Janice had just heard it from a friend she trusted, Jacqui, a freelance journalist. "She ran into the Nicholsons in Tesco's and didn't recognize them. The Nicholsons had to insist that she knew them. They were decades younger than the last time they'd met."

Had she got him up for *this*? Now wide awake from sheer annoyance, he berated her for giving credit to childish nonsense.

"How do you know it's nonsense?" she asked, raising her voice. When there were no witnesses, Janice abused their intimacy and argued with the Chairman as if they were equals. "The Nicholsons said that they had a visit from Jim Taylor. He did practically nothing - he just touched them - and they were transformed. Anne Nicholson was raving about Taylor. She said he looks like a young man and isn't fat like he used to be."

"Rubbish! I've never heard such rubbish. What utter rot!" Norton snapped. He refused to believe that his former friend could possibly have the willpower to lose weight. He didn't even consider the rest of the preposterous canard.

"It'll be in all the papers. Jacqui's writing an article about it for the *Sunday Times*. Nicholson told Jacqui he's starting on a new career."

"In Tesco's?"

"He's going into politics."

Norton looked at her grimly, reflecting that he wasn't lucky with her either. She wasn't bright enough to see through a crude practical joke. Was there anything she wouldn't believe?

The executive mistress might have been gullible but she was well versed in power games, in the art of getting even and settling scores. "If Taylor can rejuvenate people, he'll be one of the most powerful men in the world - and you fired him. He'll want revenge." She spoke in her non-committal business voice, but the last vestiges of her office persona deserted her when she remembered. "Oh, God!" she moaned, flapping her hands to her face and collapsing on the sofa. "I marched him out of his office without saying a civil word. He must hate both of us."

Norton shrugged. "What does it matter?"

Janice was growing desperate. "Jeremy, you have to make up with him," she begged, "you used to be friends."

Her absurd fear wounded Norton's sense of his own importance. "What are you going on about?" he asked her roughly, springing to his feet. "What could he do to you? What could *anybody* do to you? You're my P.A."

"We're partners, Jeremy, I worry about you." She wasn't the other woman, she was his partner. He had a wife, but his wife was a necessary evil, a fossil from the Stone Age of marriages, whereas their partnership was 21st century, the real thing. "I wish you hadn't sacked him," she said woefully. "The whole world will be his friend now - businesses, ministers, Brussels - they will do whatever he asks them to do - cancel all our big contracts - he could bankrupt us. You've got to do something. Please." She embraced one of Norton's arms; (he was too big for her to cuddle the whole man). "I don't want you to be hurt."

Norton's face acquired its stony, photogenic dignity. "What do you mean, *hurt?* Am I so easy to hurt?"

"Don't forget, you gave him the job of making people surplus because he was popular. Then you got rid of him because he was unpopular. He'll destroy you... humble yourself if you have to... try to make him forgive you, you can't afford to have him for an enemy. He was your friend and you fired him on Christmas Eve, just as he was leaving for Florida."

She got on his nerves with her offensive fretting and it struck Norton that that she was not only dim but getting old as well: her nose was too sharp, her voice too shrill and her mouth was too thin. Humble himself? Who did she think he was, a schoolboy? And this was the woman who claimed to worship him, who went down on her knees to get his prick up. They were supposed to spend the early part of the evening together, but now the prospect made his groin shrink.

'Talk, talk, you stupid bitch,' he thought, 'I'll never fuck you again.'

Perhaps the fact that his wonderful dream had been so cruelly interrupted had something to do with his unforgiving mood.

17. THE AVENGING ANGEL

I was not stricken dumb,
I was entirely deprived of the power of speech.
CASANOVA
And now the God of Vengeance
lends me his power to punish the wicked!
DUMAS

The Nortons lived in Buckinghamshire, a long way from London during rush-hour but quite close when the roads were clear. Normally this served as a convenient excuse for the Chairman to stay late in town, but today he was happy to leave early. When they reached the motorway, he told his driver to keep to the fast lane, in spite of the heavy rain. He was looking forward to dining with his wife. For once they had something to talk about. However impossible and disgustingly old she was, at least she wasn't an idiot.

"Tell Lady Margaret I'm home," Norton told her maid, Rose, who opened the door. She had a wild look in her eyes but he ignored it; to ask a servant what was troubling her was to invite a request for a rise or a day off. He went to the library, one of those libraries where books are taken off the shelves only for dusting. Though the Georgian country house, regularly altered and renovated, had central heating, logs were crackling in the fireplace for visual comfort. The big library was extended by the lights shining through the tall windows, which pushed back the walls of darkness and made the grass and evergreen trees outside seem part of the room. Norton poured himself a glass of Absolut Vodka, then sat down in his armchair to sip his drink. Margaret's agoraphobia made her avid for stories and now he had one for her. She might spend her days chatting on the phone with half the world but she depended on him for live company. She's soaking her feet again, he thought, I might as well go upstairs.

Climbing the wide, thickly carpeted staircase, carrying the glass of vodka in his hand, he saw that her door was open and raised his voice. "Margaret, I have a funny story for you!"

"I hope it won't take long - I'm in a hurry."

"In a hurry for what?"

"I'm going out."

Norton's steps did not falter; Lady Margaret hadn't left the house for years. Certain that he had misheard her, he continued his climb. "Listen, you've never heard anything so idiotic."

"Can't it wait? It's going to be a long drive in this weather; I don't want to be late."

Norton came to a halt on the stairs. "Margaret?" he called out with a huge question mark in his voice. There was no reply, so he moved on. "Listen, you won't believe this," he said as he stepped into her dressing room and the drink fell from his nerveless hand. He was hit by that invisible tidal wave that crushes mind and soul: total incomprehension. How could this be? Was he hallucinating? Where was the old hag? He had such a vivid recollection of his old wife that he imagined he was seeing her spread out in the armchair with her feet in a washbasin - but then the vision vanished. As a small boy, he had seen a full moon disappear from a clear sky bright with stars; now he felt the same shock and bewilderment. The laws of nature had broken down. His large Chairman's face lost its commanding features and he was breathing through his open mouth like a child.

"I'm sorry I gave away so many of my clothes... I suppose this will have to do."

Half the size that she had been in the morning, Lady Margaret stood in front of the cheval-glass in all the glory of her resplendent youth. She didn't have a single line in her face. A low-cut black blouse showed off to perfection her creamy skin, her breasts in full bloom, and her black tights highlighted her shapely legs. She had been attractive at forty when he first saw her, but now she was breathtaking. Her silky hair, her smell, her luminous eyes, her whole slender figure filled him with awe. Never in his life had he seen such a beautiful woman. And she was his wife!

For Lady Margaret, the Cromwellian nightmare was over. She felt as her 17th century aunts must have felt at the Restoration. She stepped back, turned sideways and walked back and forth in front of the mirror to admire her twenty-two-year-old body from every possible angle. For once, life lived up to her expectations. "Oh, God, old was so boring!" she burst out, stretching herself.

"What... what's going on?" Norton asked in a hoarse, unsteady voice, when he had sufficiently recovered to be able to move his lips and emit sounds.

"Bootsie's having a party - I said I would go... Rose, don't stand there gaping, get me my Russian sable... They'll break up before I get there."

"You don't want to go to a party and meet a lot of strangers," Norton said hopefully.

"It's mostly family and old friends." Lady Margaret bared her sparkling teeth to check them in the mirror. Her luminous eyes shone even more brightly with lust for the kill: she was going to make her entrance and see them all die from envy.

The reappearance of the maid with the coat prompted Norton to assert himself. "Wait, Margaret, I'll go with you."

Rose was helping her into the coat and she didn't seem to hear him. Another minute and she would be gone and every man at the party would want her.

"Margaret, I thought you'd been complaining that I spent too much time away from you."

"I felt lonely, I guess."

"Well, I don't want you to feel lonely."

"All right, come," she said indifferently, her mind on the coat. It was too big, but it couldn't be helped.

Seized by the urgent need to assert his rights, Norton stepped up to her and embraced her from behind, kissing the back of her neck. She smelled so fresh and felt so soft and warm that he stuck to her like a fly to glue. His lingering kiss caught her attention and she frowned, realising that nobody would die of envy if she made her entrance at the party with an elderly husband. And there might be young men there of her own age.

"I can't take you," she said firmly, getting away from him. "They're not expecting you."

"I'm sure Bootsie won't mind."

"Rose, help me find my car keys, please."

"I'll tell you what, Margaret..." Kissing his wife's lovely warm neck inspired happy thoughts. "Let's not go anywhere. Let's just have a nice quiet romantic evening by ourselves."

"Don't be a pest. I told Bootsie I would come alone... I didn't realise that your secretary was going to be indisposed and you'd come home early... "

Sobered by the blow, Norton was breathing through his mouth again; he had never suspected that she knew. Janice hired only middle-aged married men to drive him; they understood the need to be discreet. "Margaret...I..."

"What's the matter? Is she no longer a good fuck?"

"You gave up sex, remember?"

"Did I really?" she asked incredulously.

Norton tried to talk himself out of disaster, his big fleshy face turning purple and white in quick succession. Neither of them was inhibited by the presence of the maid, who stopped rummaging in the drawers and just stood there, listening. The Nortons were fortunate enough to be able to live with servants, since they heeded them less than the cats.

Lady Margaret was excessively bored by her husband's explanations. "It never bothered me in the slightest; I just wish you hadn't lied about it."

"I didn't lie about it. I just didn't tell you. I didn't want to hurt your feelings."

"Aha, there you are!" she said, picking up her car keys. "Don't wait up for me, Jeremy, I might spend the night in London."

Norton grew pale. "What do you mean, you might stay

the night in London?"

"Rose, clean up the mess," she said as she swept out of the room, glancing at the empty glass and pool of vodka on the carpet.

He caught up with her at the foot of the stairs. "She's just a secretary – you shouldn't worry about it."

Lady Margaret stopped, threw her head back, tossing her luxuriant blond hair, exposing her slender neck, her delicate profile, her moist lips, her sparkling teeth, and laughed. Her soft, deep, throaty laugh set his blood racing - it brought him summer and sunshine and turned him into a bull pawing the ground, ready for the ring. He followed her out of the house, pleading. "Let's just stay home, Margaret. Believe me, you have no reason to be jealous."

It was getting so ridiculous, she stopped laughing. Men were such children. Her wrinkles had kept her tongue in check to some extent, but youth and beauty gave her back the freedom to speak her mind. "How could I possibly be jealous of an old fart like you?"

As her Jaguar sped away, it sounded like a roaring beast in his ears. Some gravel swept up by the wheels landed on his shoes. *Old fart?* Her offhand remark shot through the pawing bull's brain and shrank him inside. He was practically paralysed. He remained rooted to the spot, ashen-faced and petrified. Surrounded by the silence of thirty acres of grass and woodlands, he passed out for a moment without falling. The roar of the returning Jaguar brought him back to consciousness. As Lady Margaret jammed on the brakes, the car sprayed more gravel on Norton's feet.

She got out of the car and stood on tiptoe to kiss her

husband on the cheek. (Outwardly he was as tall as ever.) "I'm sorry, dear," she said in a contrite voice. "I was in such a hurry that I didn't thank you. That was mean. I'm really grateful. Darling Jim told me that I owe it all to you. You told him you wished I was young. It was very generous of you, very considerate." He looked so miserable that she gave him another little kiss. "Thomas will cook you a nice dinner, you can watch television, have another glass of vodka, then tuck yourself in and have a good night's sleep. I'll never forget what you have done for me. Don't wait up for me, darling."

She didn't come home that night. In the morning the unhappy husband phoned his sister-in-law, but by then Margaret had gone somewhere else. Where? Bootsie didn't know. Norton's Daimler stood in the driveway with the chauffeur at the wheel, but Norton couldn't make up his mind to leave for the office. He kept wandering from one room to the next, unnerving all the servants, who tried to keep out of sight. At last he came to a stop in front of one of the windows with a good view of the deserted private road leading to the house. He stood there for a long time, perhaps as long as an hour.

When he walked out of the house, doors were held open and heads bowed. He entered his car, got out of it at the basement garage of *QS* Tower and walked to the exclusive lift that carried him up to the executive floor.

Janice jumped up to greet him with submissive affection. It did her no good. He told her sharply that he didn't want to see anybody and went into his office. Janice, tormented by anxiety, couldn't wait long. She came in uninvited and found him standing by the window. She did her sweet warm best but he wouldn't tell her anything and brushed her off every time she touched him.

What had she done? Why was he angry with her? "You were right, Jeremy," she said cajolingly, trying to pacify him. The Sunday Times didn't take Jacqui's story about the Nicholsons. They said it was a hoax, just like you did. You're always right. I don't know why I ever argue with you. Please, Jeremy, don't. Why are you looking at me like that?"

Norton said nothing, suspecting that she too thought he was an old fart.

18. SHORT-LIVED BLISS

April is the cruellest month.
T.S. ELIOT

Lucky enough to have had a heart attack in the pizzeria while Jim sat only a few tables away, the millionaire yachtsman Ward Bunting regained his freedom. Amanda Minton tried to recapture him after Jim had left the yacht. She rushed to him, pressing her exquisite trembling body against his, unable to fathom why he was so remote.

"Rooster, my Rooster," she cooed, "why do you hold me back? You don't have to spare me, my darling; I want to share all your heartaches. Did the osteopath charge you too much?"

"I'll have to cancel your credit card," Bunting said firmly.

"Oh, Rooster, Rooster, don't break my heart, you know I love you."

The oceangoing whore was put ashore with enough money to find another yacht or fly home.

Healthier and stronger, the yachtsman was a new man. A new man of forty-five. Amanda Minton was gone; his headaches were gone. He had a great time cruising down the

Gulf Coast and dropping anchor near attractive beaches. He could swim for half an hour a couple of times a day and felt the better for it. He could eat. Sick of salads, he ate sensibly, but whatever he felt like eating, and it didn't show on the scales. He was sleeping eight hours a night. Having picked up a girl on the beach of Bonita Springs, he threw away the pills, the drugs, his box of syringes and the concoction he had injected into his penis - he didn't need them anymore. Sex was fun again, not a challenge. Recovering from seventy was an indescribable pleasure; he had never known anything like it - and neither had anybody else. It was an exclusive pleasure, which made it twice as enjoyable. Settled comfortably on his deck chair after a delicious lunch, he was in a mood for philosophy and reflected on the vast differences between individual destinies. He thought of the King of Saudi Arabia who hadn't become better off by a single day and shook his head with joyful condescension: "The poor bugger!"

His exclusive bliss came to an abrupt end when he read on his computer that a London fund manager had been cured of his diabetes and made thirty years younger by Jim Taylor for a fee of a billion pounds. Afterwards the fund manager went to his regular doctors for a check-up and they pronounced him cured and considerably younger. It took the yachtsman several sad days to recover, to cheer himself with the thought that he was still forty-five years young and had paid a lot less for it than the fund manager and the others who followed. On the worldwide web, though staying on his yacht in the Bay of Mexico, he followed everything about the business that he could click on.

The osteopath turned out to be a social reformer. Company chairmen and CEOs had to sacrifice seventy-five percent of their wealth for a new lease of life, even if it came to several billions, and had to pledge to limit their yearly income to no more than fifty times the wages of their lowest paid employees – a requirement that made cleaning ladies rich beyond the dreams of avarice. Business journals predicted that business leaders who had been seduced by "such schemes of economic illiteracy" were endangering the economic recovery which could lead to mass unemployment and the collapse of civilization. Indeed a Chairman and CEO declared, immediately after he had become twenty-five years young again, that he had no intention of honouring an undertaking which he had made under duress, and was not going to tie in any way the income of top executives to the earnings of the low paid. In the event that the Osteopathy Foundation sued his company for breach of contract, they would defend themselves "vigorously". A week later the vigorous young executive went skiing in Switzerland. Speeding down a steep slope, he hit a tree and was killed. There couldn't have been any possible connection between not honouring his pledge and a tragic accident; just the same, many of the nouveaux jeunes found it safer to keep their word or give up skiing.

The day Jim's address appeared on twitter, thousands of people converged around his apartment building in London, blocking whole streets. Police cars and mounted police could not hold them back; they broke down all barriers to find the Taylors. Jim and his entourage fled through the basement and disappeared. The search for them was front page news for days, but they could not be traced.

Sitting on his deck chair in a philosophic mood, Bunting found his lot superior. 'Here I am, sunning myself in full view of everybody on the beach,' he reflected, 'I hardly have anything but my boat, but I'm free, while that man, for all his fame and riches, can't show his face.' It hadn't occurred to him to buy more years – with all his outgoings, he could just about to manage with the money Jim had left him. Besides he was only forty-five. It would be a long time before he would be seventy again.

He had nothing more to wish for until the April night when he woke with terrible toothache and a swollen jaw. An infected molar under a gold crown tortured him for a whole week before a dental surgeon in Tampa relieved him of the tooth and a fortune. The wound left by the operation meant that he could have only liquids for days, but that was no hardship. He had lost interest in food - indeed in all the fleeting pleasures of life. He began to suffer from insomnia. His throbbing wound reminded him that he would be forty-six years old in a few months.

19. THE CHURCH WITH A DIFFERENCE

Jesu, Joy of man's desiring...
ROBERT BRIDGES

Toothache and mental pain drove Ward Bunting to write an e-mail to Mr. James Taylor, care of the Osteopathy Foundation:

> *Dear Mr. Taylor,*
> *I trust that you remember me. You saved my life on Magdalena Island. Your rejuvenating treatment was most satisfactory and I offer to pay for another twenty years. I hope you will grant me the same terms as I was your first patient. You can contact me by e-mail and I can come to see you any time you want.*
> *Yours sincerely,*
> *Ward Bunting.*

He waited for a reply for an agonizing week, but no reply came.

> *Dear Mr. Taylor,*
> *I trust you didn't misunderstand my previous communication. I'm not asking for a reduced*

rate. I accept whatever you wish to charge.
Yours sincerely,
Ward Bunting

There was no reply.

"What's your problem?" asked the teenager he had picked up in Bonita Springs. "I don't understand why you're so miserable. You're young for your age and you have at least another ten good years ahead of you. You should enjoy them."

Nothing could have infuriated the yachtsman more. "What do you mean, ten years?" he shouted. "What do you want me to do with ten years? It's nothing, you ignorant hussy."

"You can't talk to me like that," she protested. "I joined you for a bit of fun, not to be shouted at. I can have that at home."

"Get out of my sight."

"Charming." Offended, she flicked her hair back and went below.

'In no time at all, I'll be fifty,' Bunting thought. He ordered the crew to sail for Tampa. He put the girl ashore and flew to London with Bill Nash, a member of the crew who also served as his butler. He bought tourist tickets for both of them, assuming that he might need every penny he had. There was no difficulty in getting to the Georgian mansion in Sussex and he hardly had to wait to speak to one of the clerks who dealt with applicants.

"I can take your details, but there is really not much point," the former project manager at *QS* explained. "There are hundreds of billionaires on his waiting list and he won't get around to treating them either. He treats rich people only when the Foundation needs money to give away. Our job is to sort requests for financial support."

Bunting started drumming on the desk with his fingers to protest. "I was his first client. I gave him his start. I'm sure he would see me."

"Well, if he already treated you once, then he certainly wouldn't touch you again. It would be unfair to the thousands who are waiting."

"But I read that he treats tramps during the night. Would you know what streets he'll choose tonight?"

"If we had that kind of information all my relatives would be on that street. As he cannot possibly treat everybody, you must understand that the only fair way is random."

"Does Mr. Taylor ever see his emails?" Bunting asked suspiciously.

"The Foundation is run by Ms Ellie Wade and she insists that the boss must know about everything. She has a huge staff to read all the mail. "

"All right. I'll write to him again."

> *Dear Mr. James Taylor, my kind Benefactor,*
> *I'm asking you only what you offered me once. You generously offered to make me twenty, charging only a million a month.*
>
> *I hope you don't blame me that I didn't take up your offer at the time. Please remember that I had just had a heart attack and my judgement was affected and I wasn't thinking clearly. It was such a new idea! Considering you are a compassionate man with a good heart, I believe you wouldn't*

give me a glimpse of a second life and then take it away. This would be torture. Worse than torture. You wouldn't do that to a human being.

I am not as rich as some of the bankers you have treated, but I offer you everything I have if you make me a young lad. My house in Palm Beach, my three apartments, one in Mayfair in London, next to the American Embassy overlooking Grosvenor Square, where I'm now staying, my boat, all my holdings because I understand ...

The letter ended with Bunting's Mayfair address and phone numbers.

He stayed in his Mayfair apartment during the day and walked the freezing streets at night, hoping to run into the osteopath healing the down and outs. He got a nasty cold which developed into pneumonia. He languished in hospital for weeks. He sent further emails on his laptop, "humbly informing" his "Dear Benefactor" that he could be found in the private ward of the St Thomas's Hospital. Attached to a drip, Bunting waited and hoped, but his Benefactor didn't come. He was eventually cured, but there was still no response to his e-mails. He had to face up to the fact that after four miserable years he would be fifty and in no time at all he would be sixty and seventy again.

Despairing and full of hate, he sent another email to his Benefactor.

You sadistic bastard, I wish I had never met you!

He flew back to Tampa first class, with his butler Bill Nash at the back of the plane. While up in the sky, way above the clouds, staring at blue infinity just outside the window, he was struck by the idea of God. Life was a con and God alone could help him.

Back on his yacht, he sent off his last email to James Taylor:

You godless jackal, God will punish you!

Bunting searched the internet for God and his hopes were raised by the website of The Church with a Difference. He went ashore to join the revivalist Church and paid his contribution regularly for months. The minister's sermons gave him faith and he learned to pray and sing with the congregation. But once he learned how to be in touch with God, he saw no reason to waste his money. Earthly life was a con, but while he was exiled to this vale of tears, he decided he might as well live comfortably and stay on his yacht. He turned the stateroom into a chapel and he spent much of his days by the altar, praying.

His crew thought he had gone crazy - but then we all believe what makes life easier to bear.

20. BLUE SKIES

There are thunderbolts that strike from blue skies.
OTTHONITE PROVERB

"The rich already have more than one life", Jim said to Lesley one day, deciding to stop treating billionaires. The Foundation's accounts were bursting with big figures, they didn't need more money, and it was more thrilling to rejuvenate the sick, the poor and homeless who had aged before their time. Subsequently, the papers reported that some of those lucky homeless who regained their health and youth were murderers, rapists, violent thieves or otherwise unsavoury characters. They were few in number but they curbed Jim's zeal and he ended up treating only children. Tots had no shady past, no criminal records; and he didn't have to have doubts or regrets afterwards. He showed up in hospital wards during the night, with a security tag on his white lab coat and a stethoscope around his neck, his hands sunk in his pockets, looking like one of the interns. While the tots were asleep, he gently massaged their tiny feet, taking care not to wake them so that, in the morning, they could think they had got well on their own. He liked the idea of boosting their confidence in their fragile bodies. It was pure fun.

One night a nurse at the Great Ormond Street Hospital noticed a young intern in one of the wards who wasn't a member of staff and she called out, asking him to stop. The intern ignored her, got into the lift and disappeared. In the morning many of the sick children woke up healthy and several media reports assumed that the unknown young intern was the elusive former business executive and self-trained healer. New efforts to locate him led nowhere. What made the search for the couple next to impossible was the lack of any photos of their transformation to young adults. The Gulf Views CCTV system had broken down just at the right time for them to hide their identity. Lesley would have been in greater danger of being recognized as she had been teaching and mixed with people who had known for her decades, but a few weeks after the Christmas holidays the discovery of asbestos in the building prompted the abrupt closing of the school for decontamination. The Taylors were safe in their hide-out in Holland Park.

Neb had his own apartment near the Royal Academy of Music, but stayed mostly in the Holland Park house. He preferred to live with the Taylors, as they were the only people, apart from Ellie Wade, who knew who he really was. He regularly raised his fly-whirl disk from under the grass in the park during the night. In cruising gear he could reach any place on earth within minutes and collected musical instruments and folk songs from five continents. He changed the colour of his skin and hair; and when the Taylors joined him on his outings, they wore disguise. But their most effective disguises were the stories and comments which placed them in England. No one expected to run into them in Toronto or Chicago or on the Rialto in Venice. They were curious to discover the wonders of the world – and there were a lot more than seven. Neb photographed them, certain that an exhibition of photographs of our amazing cities, hills, mountains, waterfalls, grand rivers, bays, rain forests and grasslands would create a sensation in the Centre of the Universe. Jim took up painting to record the sites which moved him most. Lesley simply breathed in what she saw; she preserved the wonders of the world by absorbing them.

The Taylors' best moments were when they were by themselves and the child forming in Lesley's womb was the supreme proof. As she grew heavy with child, she became less keen to travel. Which was just as well, because some of Neb's flying attracted too much attention. On a foggy day the fly-whirl disk nearly grazed a ship in New York harbour. All the ships blew their horns to protest. Such incidents gave rise to foolish rumours about flying saucers and little green men. But what if one day somebody made a better guess? It was safer to stay at home.

Neb no longer thought that Lesley was the most beautiful woman in the universe, but they had become good friends. He had brought his father's books to the house and, whenever he had the time, he was teaching her the Otthon language and she kept making notes of the books she managed to decipher with Neb's help and started to write *Life on a Distant Planet*. No doubt most readers, even if they haven't read the book, will be familiar with its often quoted opening sentence: "*To live long you need somebody to love you*".

Lesley frankly confessed that she had never been as far as The Centre of the Universe, but in circumstances "both complicated and irrelevant" she had access to a small travelling library of Otthon books. Lesley found a great deal to praise but her book is not a starry-eyed description of the distant planet. She warned readers not to take her work for some kind of science fiction utopia. "What kind of utopia is it where voting rights are restricted to a minority of citizens? What kind of utopia is it where children are not allowed to enjoy their childhood?" she asked. "Child labour, far from being outlawed, is compulsory between the ages of seven and sixteen; children had to do two hours of community work every day except during holidays, on the principle that moderate physical labour helps them to develop self-discipline and a sense of responsibility and makes them more willing to clean up after themselves. The word for adolescent is *kiskakas-kistyuk*, which could be translated as *a-person-busy-growing-up*. The phrase *to enjoy one's childhood* in the Otthon language is *to enjoy growing up…*

"Otthonites are eons ahead of us in many ways; in other respects they remain barbarians," she wrote. "They still retain the death penalty. While on Earth the list of executed criminals consists mainly of the poor and ignorant, on Otthon most of the unfortunates condemned to die are high officials or members of the government. The cruelty of the judicial system does not stop there: politicians who break their election promises are tortured…"

But Lesley Taylor's seminal work about lives outside our solar system has been published and readers can find the book and read it themselves. She wrote most of it during her pregnancy, in the late spring and summer, away from the madding crowd. Jim had been sighted in various hospitals but nobody could corner him. The Taylors were famous and out of reach. Everybody knew that they were supposed to live in the Sussex mansion, the headquarters of the Osteopathic Foundation. But nobody knew where they happened to be or what they were doing at any particular time.

The Taylors were safe in their four-storey house in Holland Park. The main entrance faced the street, but the windows at the back looked out at the park and from the upper floors they could see the spot where Neb kept his father's spacecraft deep under the grass. No one ever saw them entering or leaving the house. They owned a second property across the street and the two houses were connected by an underground passage. The second house was supposed to be empty, owned by some foreign billionaire who had bought it as an investment and rented out the garage. Jim, Lesley, Ellie and Neb entered and left in cars with smoked glass windows through this garage which had an underground passage connecting it to the house on the park. This all-too-simple stratagem was sufficient to protect them until Jim acquired enemies who were determined to kill him. Hatred has a million eyes.

21. CELEBRITY

Important people are famous.
HELLO MAGAZINE

People tend to keep secrets only until they're at a loss for something to say. Only a few of Lesley's colleagues had known at first that she was married to the sought-after James Taylor and they resisted the temptation to astound others with the news, but their reticence could not last. They told their closest friends about Lesley in the strictest confidence, not to be repeated. When the school reopened, she showed up to teach, not expecting any trouble. The following morning *The Sun* published on its front page an enlarged group-picture of the school's teachers which showed Lesley as she had looked at the age of a youthful fifty-one three months before her trip to Florida, and a Sun photographer's picture of her entering the school as a dazzling young woman. In the accompanying article she was described as "the wife of an osteopath who can cure you if you are sick and make you younger if you're getting old". Within hours of the paper hitting the street, an army of paparazzi descended on the school, followed by a desperate crowd who wanted her to lead them to her husband. They knocked over the guard at the entrance, ran amok in the corridors, opening every door until they found Lesley's class.

"Over here!"

"Don't push!"

"I saw her first!"

"Where's your husband?!"

"Mrs. Taylor, Mrs. Taylor!"

"I'm sure he'd help if you asked him."

"Stop for a minute, listen."

"Take me to him, please!"

"Look at me, it's not fair!

"Don't push!"

"Smile, please!" shouted a photographer.

"Where do you buy your clothes?" asked a journalist working for Vogue. Lesley was wearing a beige skirt and a dark blue silk blouse which set off her lustrous red hair, as Vogue faithfully reported.

In a few minutes more photos were taken of Lesley Taylor than in her whole previous life.

"Here's our card, take it! He could call us at any time."

"Don't let her get away!"

"It'd be so easy for you!"

"Just turn your head, please!"

"Smile!"

She thought she would be crushed to death. Some of her students managed to break through the mob and formed a protective circle around her, but hands reached past the students and pawed her or pulled her blouse to attract her attention. By the time she reached the headmaster's office

- her clothes torn, her hair dishevelled, her face scratched - she looked ready for an A&E Department. The headmaster begged her to spare herself as well as the school. "For God's sake, go, go!" he cried. "I accept your resignation." He hid her in his cupboard and told his secretary to spread the news that somehow she had escaped. The headmaster, who had greater faith in plastic surgery than absurd stories about rejuvenation, felt sorry for his favourite teacher, and once the disappointed mob had left, he drove her out of the school in the boot of his car. He had wanted to take her to the A&E of the nearest hospital, but Lesley asked him to drop her off in a side street.

Having staggered to their secret home in London, Lesley collapsed into Jim's arms. Seeing her in tatters with scratches and dried blood on her face, worried about the baby, he carried her to bed to soothe and heal her. His fingers lingered over the soft skin of her warm belly and bloodied face and her wounds disappeared. The baby was safe. She fell into an untroubled sleep; the unpleasant incident left no unhealed wounds on her body or in her mind. It was different for Jim. On the scale of savagery, Lesley's cuts and bruises, the dried blood on her torn clothes, wouldn't even register, but for the expectant father who had lived through the agony of her miscarriages, it was a profound shock. He felt like killing everybody who had scratched her.

22. THE SECOND WISH

*The more people you kill
the less good it does to you.*
OTTHONITE PROVERB

When Neb came in he found Jim alone in the living room, pacing the floor with his hands behind his back.

"Neb, what's my wishing range?" Jim asked, turning around to face the boy.

Neb looked at Jim's mindscreen and was shocked.

"You'd be a step closer to going home."

"I'm not in a hurry right now." As Gary Clearwater, the spectacularly talented young conductor, still a student of the Royal Academy of Music, Neb had just come from a session with the academy's student orchestra. He had been rehearsing Mozart's *Eine Kleine Nachtmusik*. His fame secured the student orchestra their first concert at the Albert Hall.

"I have my second wish for you."

Neb shook his head "No no. Don't even think of it. Not even my Dad can wish people dead and he's a prosecutor."

"What are you talking about? There's capital punishment on Otthon."

"Yes, some people are condemned to death, but only after a long trial and most of those judgements are commuted on appeal. Even those who lose the appeal are free to take their own lives."

Jim threw up his hands, with a mixture of frustration and contempt. "That's worse. That was the death penalty for high officials in the bloody days of the Roman Empire. That's how Pontius Pilate died, the Roman governor who convicted Christ. Emperor Tiberius sent a messenger to Pilate, telling him that 'the Emperor wants you to die'. That was the formula. Pilate was free to kill himself in any way he liked – but his villa was surrounded, and he had to be dead by the morning."

"For Christ's crucifixion?"

"No, no, for the embezzlement of public funds. Anyway, you Otthonites could wish each other dead."

"Not any more. When our ancestors could wish people dead, we hardly had anybody left. They brought us to the brink of extinction. You *know* that. It's in Lesley's book. Didn't you read it? We had to read a book in school, called *The Funeral Oration of the Otthonites*. It was scary. I still remember how scared I was. Luckily our forebears were scared, too. The survival instinct kicked in and they changed tack. They evolved; they lost the urge to kill. They were too smart to wipe out our species."

"Yes, but we're not there, we're on Earth. And I want the power to wish people dead only for myself, not for everybody."

"Here or there, only you or everybody - it makes no difference."

"I don't want my child shot by a drug addict."

"You've got to wish for something sensible. Killing doesn't work."

"Oh, well," sighed Jim, "then there's no hope for our world."

"I'll tell you what," sighed the young maestro. "I can't help you to kill people but I can help you to make them stink. Is that your second wish?"

23. THE PLAGUE

...the infection had spread itself beyond
all hopes of abatement.
DANIEL DEFOE

The first sign of the plague in London was an exodus of mice and rats from public buildings. The pavements and roads in the city centre were flooded with rodents scurrying in all directions. Office staff, policemen, guards and cleaners ran out of the buildings retching. Later on the same day the birds perching on the ancient buildings of the Houses of Parliament suddenly flew away. In spite of the summer recess, the House was in session, most MPs were present, recalled for a debate on an international crisis. Well into their deliberations, a putrid smell permeated the whole chamber and about two dozen MPs ran out holding their noses, leaving the doors open, letting the stench escape. *"The rankest compound of villainous smell that ever offended nostril"* soon sent everybody fleeing. Researchers, secretaries, caretakers, cooks, waiters, sergeants-at-arms, cleaners were all running, tripping over fleeing rodents, desperate to reach the exits. It was a mysterious stench. No one could understand it, because most parliamentarians couldn't smell anything.

Initially the blame fell on the maintenance people who themselves had fled and it was assumed that the fetid odour originated in the basement, caused by the malfunction of some wiring and electrical equipment, or a gas leak, or the breaking of sewage pipes. The same conclusion was reached about the lamentable condition of buildings in the city, the Law Courts, with additional blame attributed to the system of using unscreened and unskilled casual labour. The first day of the plague was reported in the evening news as a failure of proper cleaning. The government was attacked in the media and the internet for its incompetence, being unable to maintain even its own houses in order.

As a report in the British medical journal *The Lancet* subsequently put it, "the stench is accompanied by an infection of the upper respiratory tracts, *anosmia,* loss of smell. In plain language, the victims cannot smell themselves: they have to be told."

This phenomenon was researched by a young scientist, Anthony Alexander, a dyslexic. In a striking number of cases dyslexia and extraordinary intelligence go together. Anthony Alexander was awarded his PhD from Cambridge at seventeen and became a full professor and the Director of the Institute of Infectious Diseases at the age of twenty-three. Testing the hypothesis that money has a biological impact on the body led him to the discovery that highly-paid underlings catch their masters' anosmia and can serve them without any discomfort regardless of the stench.

Hard-working bankers, politicians, editors who managed the news to keep people in ignorance, prominent lawyers and numerous CEOs were driven home to their families at the end of their day and were greeted with a glad welcome. But their wives and children shrank from them as they took another breath and fled screaming, followed by their terrified dogs and cats. The uncomprehending victims contacted their doctors and ambulances took them to the Institute of Infectious Diseases. They were quarantined in absolute secrecy to prevent panic and the study of the disease began in earnest that very night.

Panic broke out the next day about eleven in the morning in the jewellery section of Harrod's, London's famous luxury department store. Security cameras in every corner of the building recorded the event. It was so sensational, so unprecedented that soon afterwards it was broadcast on television and almost instantly rebroadcast around the world: the capital of the United Kingdom was in the grip of a new infectious disease about which no one knew anything. The video footage showed people suddenly raising their heads, looking left and right with a puzzled stare and, as they breathed in, their faces became distorted with terror and they started running from some invisible menace. Shoppers, sales assistants, security guards stampeded for the lifts, ignoring unguarded counters laden with glittering jewels displayed in all their splendour and available to anyone who would stop long enough to snatch them. Hundreds of people ran past a diamond bracelet worth a quarter of a million pounds which an assistant had been showing to a customer and simply dropped on the counter when both she and the customer fled. No one spared the time to scoop it up. People around the lifts started jostling and fighting; many were injured, some critically. Those who fled by the stairs were luckier but spread the panic to the other floors. You would have thought that the building was on fire.

Doctors and security staff reviewed the videos and identified a dignitary's wife as the cause of the panic. She was the only stationary figure among the runners, who gave her a wide berth. She was quarantined in her own home.

Fetor Syndrome, abbreviated to FS but commonly called the *stinking disease or the BO plague*, caused no physical pain and had no visible effects. Tests showed nothing: no new organisms could be traced in the body, no changes in the composition of the blood or the functioning of the organs - yet those infected oozed a heart-stopping stench from every pore of their bodies, a potent odour of excrement and rotten fish that went through walls. Fetor Syndrome condemned its victims to social death. No matter how highly placed they were in the world, they lost their positions, lost their friends, their families and were treated as pariahs. Many fled and settled in sparsely populated parts of the country to avoid odium. Those who couldn't afford to move suffered isolation in their own communities. The most terrifying thing about FS was that nobody knew what caused it or how it spread. It hit different parts of the capital with large sections between the plague's hot spots remaining unaffected. Within days the *BO plague* spread to other cities, then jumped across the Channel and a tidal wave of fear and anxiety swept the Continent. There was no rush to get on buses or squeeze into crowded trains. The London Underground and the Paris Metro, usually the most crowded in Europe, ran with empty carriages.

There was no prospect of a cure until scientists identified

the cause of the disease. On the assumption that the *BO plague or stinking disease* was caused by exhaust fumes, cars were banned from population centres. Cities, far from becoming paralyzed, came to new life. Millions started using their legs instead of their cars or took to bicycles. However it did nothing to alleviate the repellent odour of the afflicted. As many of the victims worked in offices, several research facilities were testing the hypothesis that, like Legionnaire's disease, it was caused by unclean air-conditioning systems. Professor Anthony Alexander was exploring the possibility that the agent of Fetor Syndrome was genetically modified food. Some of his eminent rivals were trying to demonstrate that the source of the *BO plague* was natural food, poisoned by the food industry with too much salt, sugar and countless chemical additives. None of these scientific efforts yielded any result.

Norton, unaffected by the plague, but worn out and feeling older than his years, sought Jim's help through the Foundation. He tried to explain to the receptionist that he wanted to get in touch with his old friend and colleague.

"Oh yes. You're the man who gave our jobs to Malaysia."

Norton ran the gamut of several former *QS* employees before he was allowed to reach the office of Ellie Wade. He started to explain that he wanted to see his old friend, but Ellie cut him short. "Go to hell, Sir Jeremy," she told him. When Ellie went to see Jim next day she mentioned Norton's visit. "Will you make him stink?" she asked.

Jim nearly said "yes", but then reflected that if Norton hadn't sacked him, he wouldn't have tried to drown himself in the middle of the night and would never have met Neb.

An early morning swimmer would have helped the boy. He wondered whether that lucky person would have thought of the old tale. And if he did, what that stranger's three wishes would have been. And what should be his third wish?

He had been trying to think of other wishes for so long that Ellie thought she ought to rouse him. "Jim?"

"Sorry, I was just thinking."

"Please make Norton stink."

"No, let him be. I think he has enough trouble as it is."

The plague continued to claim new victims every day. To maintain a semblance of normality, the UK Parliament remained in session, ostensibly to debate funding for medical research, but basically to show that the government continued to govern and lawmakers were in their places and smelled nothing unpleasant. Pro-government media stopped referring to the subject; only *Private Eye* magazine continued to report that the stench in the Houses of Parliament was just as strong as it had been on the day when the birds flew away and the rodents fled.

The same magazine, which specialized in exposing rotten people, suggested that the stench was produced by the character of the stinkers. It was meant as a joke. Greed, envy, spite and hate are among the known contributory causes of high blood pressure and coronary thrombosis, but there had never been a single instance of an individual's body odours being affected by his character. Yet the joke happened to hit on the truth. Doctors who dealt with victims of the plague shared their data with the international scientific community and it soon became apparent that the plague affected people from all walks of life and the only characteristic the victims shared, apart from a few puzzling exceptions, was that they were stinkers even before they started to smell. The knowledge of the symptoms, alas, was no cure and in spite of the authorities' attempts to inspire confidence, hopelessness spread as the plague crossed the Atlantic Ocean.

The ravages of the epidemic were not always unwelcome. Some victims of the plague were trying to make themselves likeable to compensate for their repulsive odour. They were so desperate for company that they began to consider the feelings and interests of others. There were rumours of executives who lowered their salaries and went about on bicycles. Many members of the shady professions who were ashamed of their work sought employment in other fields. Stinking drunks sobered up, hoping to rejoin their families. Some lawmakers who had been suffering from the *BO plague* recovered and became much admired politicians. Even stinkers who weren't completely cured smelled less offensively. Gradually it became clear that there was a way to recover from the plague through moral regeneration. However, lawmakers the world over voted billions for research to find a less onerous remedy which would not encounter such deep-seated resistance. An American Senator, like many lawmakers in Europe, argued that there was an urgent need to develop a drug to cure Fetor Syndrome "so people could breathe freely again."

Needless to say, none of the medical researchers found any connection between the disease and Jim. For all the havoc he had been causing in the world, the Taylors were safe.

Clare was born in the Taylors' bedroom in the Holland Park house. Jim himself delivered his daughter, soothing away Lesley's labour pains, stroking her back and her belly. Clare came into the world wide awake. As soon as she was in her mother's arms, she opened her eyes to look at her, then closed them again and began to suck eagerly, patting her mother's breast with her tiny fingers as if she knew that Lesley had longed to feed her for years and years. There was perfect understanding between the baby and her parents. When Jim brushed her forehead and they established eye contact, he felt that he had done something extraordinary.

Jim was in the news that day though he didn't know it. The Taylors had no phones, no mobiles, no computer, no tablet or any other electronic equipment which would have enabled people to trace the whereabouts of their London hide-out. When Ellie Wade saw the headlines, she had no way to alert Jim to the danger other than to drive to London. She had her own keys and when she finally entered the couple's bedroom she was so upset that at first she did not notice the baby. She came to report that Ward Bunting had accused Jim of causing the plague and it was all over the media.

Jim was way beyond worrying about anything. "Relax, Ellie, relax. Nobody would believe that."

"Come and meet Clare," said the new mother. "You've never seen such a perfect creature. Clare will calm you."

Ellie sighed. "Well, I don't want to be a spoil-sport. She's a lovely, beautiful baby. Congratulations."

Realizing that their minds had turned to mush, she drove back to Sussex.

24. HOT CHOCOLATE

Was not his execution rarely plotted?
CYRIL TOURNEUR

Ward Bunting couldn't forgive Jim for ignoring his request to make him a young lad of twenty. He had read on the internet that children in hospitals in New York, Toronto and Chicago had made remarkable recoveries; and police forces in the same cities had caught drug barons who suffered from extreme cases of BO, betrayed by a pervasive stench that not even policemen on the take could ignore. There was no news that the osteopath had ever left the UK, nor were there any previous instances of drug dealers catching the *BO plague*, but Bunting already knew that Jim Taylor came from Toronto and was supposed to heal children, so why not plant the plague on him? With so many powerful people afflicted with the disease, including gangsters, politicians, members of various governments, Bunting felt certain that Jim Taylor would have a very uncomfortable life if they thought he was responsible for their odour.

To give greater weight to his guess, he claimed that he knew it for a fact. "I didn't mention it before because I can't imagine how it is done," Bunting told *The Miami Herald*, "but when Jim Taylor treated me, he told me he could inflict a poisonous smell on anybody he chose." On *Twitter* he posted: "If you stink you can thank Jim Taylor for it."

Anything connected with the epidemic was worldwide news. The very wealth of medical information already available about the disease made the suggestion that it had anything to do with osteopathy and reflexology absurd. Besides, Jim Taylor's fame inspired a great many chancers who claimed to be able to make people healthier and younger, defrauding the credulous of their savings, so that many of those who originally believed the fantastic stories about him decided that he too must be a fraud who couldn't even cure a headache, let alone spread a plague to three continents. Bunting's dubious assertion would have been forgotten in a few days, except that Amanda Minton read about it in New York. She was trying to launch herself as a model and held a press conference to say that she had had an affair with "dear Jim" and foolishly told him that she didn't believe he could make people smell. To impress her Jim made her dog stink so badly that the poor beast had to be put down. She was so angry with him that she sent him back to his wife. Her interview was accompanied by photos of her stunning and barely-clad figure in various poses and received worldwide exposure.

The Taylors weren't bothered, failing to reflect that there are billions who are capable of believing absolutely anything and not all of them are poor and powerless.

Neb had no visible connection with the Taylors. The only time he had been seen with them was on his first day on Earth, in the Pizzeria and the lobby of the Gulf Views Apartment hotel on Magdalena Island. The Pizzeria had no security cameras and something had gone wrong with the hotel's videos and nobody could possibly be identified on it. Neb's visits to the Holland Park house through a garage on the opposite side of the street seemed a perfect cover – all the more so as those houses were all registered to foreigners and the Taylors were supposed to live in the Osteopathy Foundation's mansion in Sussex. As for Neb's trips with his friends around the globe to collect musical treasures and see the sights, their camouflages seemed to them so impenetrable that they did not realise until it was too late that the press's revelations about Neb had anything to do with Jim. A few weeks after Bunting's and Amanda Minton's claim that Jim had caused the plague, *The Cleveland Evening News* claimed on the front page that "Gary Clearwater, the youngest conductor in the world", "the musical prodigy and linguistic genius who talks to every musician in his own language", had given false information about his background. There was no record of his birth in Cleveland or indeed anywhere in Ohio.

"I lie about my name and background," Neb explained in an interview, "to spare my parents who hate publicity."

For weeks he had been preparing an afternoon concert for children at the Albert Hall. Immersed in great music, he was isolated from everything unpleasant, but at the end of the last rehearsal one of the trumpeters came up to him saying, "I didn't want to upset you while we were working," and handed him a nasty editorial from the leading London paper, the kind Balzac called "the ministerial press" for its

423

closeness to the government.

"The young conductor who has become the fashion and who will no doubt fade, like all fashions," read the young maestro with an overwhelming sense of being unappreciated, "told fibs about his background, which endears him to many people who look on it as a youthful prank, but we are inclined to be less indulgent. Mr. Clearwater, if that is his name, not only told 'fibs' but he also carries a forged American passport and other forged documents. These are serious criminal offences. Talent is no excuse for breaking the law nor is it a reason for leniency."

At the edge of the stage two detectives from Scotland Yard were waiting for him to ask a few questions. His very entrails gnawed at by the insult that he would fade, Neb nonetheless answered a couple of questions with ill grace. Seeing on their mindscreens that they didn't believe a word he was saying, he stopped. "I don't like to be pestered," he objected.

"But..."

He looked askance at the detectives. They were sniffing him as though he were a criminal. What if he put them to sleep? For that matter he could have wished the whole of Scotland Yard to fall asleep for a hundred years. He was tempted.

The detectives couldn't read mindscreens, but they could read faces and promptly apologised to the young maestro for bothering him right after the rehearsal. They had tickets for the evening and looked forward to his concert and hoped to see him afterwards.

Disguised as usual when leaving the house, the Taylors celebrated Clare's third birthday (that is, Clare was three months old) by taking her to Neb's concert which, as the programme notes stated, "showcased classic pieces which even babies can enjoy." The young musicians were to play Leopold Mozart's *Sleigh Ride*, Boccherini's *Symphony in G major,* and Haydn's *Symphonies of Morning, Noon and Evening.*

The Taylors had a box on the first floor of the Albert Hall and, as in opera houses, each box backed onto a private room where the guests could rest and be served food in the interval. It was there that Lesley listened to the music sitting on a sofa, breastfeeding Clare and cradling her. They were still clapping in the stalls when a middle-aged waitress with a square, dead face rolled in a table with their pre-ordered interval snack. Noticing the baby, she halted to stare at her. Holding Clare in her arms, Lesley turned a little to give the waitress a better view. People smile when they look at a baby, but the waitress's face remained dead. Lesley couldn't understand how anyone could see Clare and still look grim. 'What a mean face,' she thought.

They didn't tell me about the baby, Jim read on the mindscreen of the waitress. 'What does she mean?' he wondered.

However, they were so surprised by Neb's unprecedented appearance, in spite of their rules never to be seen together unless each of them was in disguise that they forgot about the waitress.

Neb didn't touch the food, just downed a few glasses of water. He wanted to know how Clare had responded to the performance.

"She didn't cry. When I stopped feeding her she seemed to be listening. At times she smiled and made noises – I think she was trying to gurgle to the music."

"I should take her to Otthon," said Neb. "I'm sure Eoz would be crazy about her and when she grows a little she could be in my first symphony orchestra.."

Lesley laughed. "Do you think we would part from her?"

"Well, it's just a thought."

While Neb was talking to the Taylors, the waitress with the mean face poured chocolate in Lesley's cup. Clare grew restless in her mother's arms and strained forward to grab the flowing black stream in the air with her fat little hand. As the waitress stopped pouring, *Cyanide's not for babies* read her mindscreen. Jim hit the pot out of her hand, setting it flying, splashing broken china and liquid chocolate all over the place. The waitress tried to flee, but Jim grabbed her arm and they started to tussle. A man in an usher's uniform rushed in to attack Jim and help the waitress; Jim fought both until the pair suddenly staggered away from him.

Neb wiped the sticky mess off his shirt and his coat tail with a thought. Almost simultaneously the whole box became clean and he wished a mild heart attack on the waitress and the usher, paralyzing their legs.

"The chocolate was laced with cyanide," said Jim, breathing heavily.

Clare started crying and Lesley hugged her tighter, frightened.

Neb turned to calm them. He moved his nose left and right without the help of his hands, which he used to conduct at the same tempo as his nose moved. He made Clare laugh, but he had no effect on Lesley, who held on to her baby with a protective hug.

The audience was filing back into the auditorium and they could hear several musicians tuning their instruments.

"Well, I'm glad Clare liked the music," said the young maestro. "Now I'm going back to join the orchestra and we'll play some lovely Haydn."

Lesley urged him to stay, but Neb left with a wave.

"I want us to get out of here," said Lesley.

Jim bent down to hug both Lesley and Clare. "Relax, Les, we're no longer in any danger. Clare protects us." Straightening up again, he declared with evident pride. "It was Clare who saved our lives.""

"How is that?"

When Clare tried to catch the flowing chocolate, the waitress stopped pouring and I saw her thinking that cyanide was not for babies."

Lesley burst into nervous laughter.

The poisoners were watching them. When they weren't moving, they looked normal. But they couldn't stay still for long. Their legs seemed to be glued to the floor and they tried to free themselves, twisting and straining from the waist, in a kind of silent St. Vitus dance.

Jim turned to the woman. "Are you really a waitress?"

"Please, let us go", she pleaded.

"You didn't answer my question."

"We're part-timers."

"Part-timers for what?"

"We take on any job that turns up. These are hard times."

"Who hired you?"

She looked at Jim defiantly, not realizing that he could read her thoughts: *You should be dead by now, you bastard. I'll tell you nothing.*

Jim turned to the handsome man in the usher's uniform. "How about you?"

"I know my rights!" the man protested."

"Who hired you?"

Lesley snapped. "Don't bother, leave them alone, you don't need them. I'll tell you who paid them. I know exactly who sent them. Let's just go."

She walked out and Jim followed her, but looked back from the doorway. The pair were trying to tear themselves from the floor, straining and twisting from the waist.

"Well, enjoy yourselves," Jim said by way of farewell.

The poisoners didn't cry for help; they didn't want to be caught. Unable to believe that they couldn't move, they strained harder, twisted ever more violently and sweated ever more profusely, getting out of breath.

The cleaners eventually reached the box and found them. They were taken away by a police ambulance.

With Lesley carrying the baby, the Taylors walked home, stopping frequently to check whether they were being followed. It was a long walk in the cold and they didn't talk. They had time to reflect that many stinkers must know a lot about them. They even knew what box they would be in at the Albert Hall, even though their tickets were bought with a French credit card.

'Why did I give in so easily?' wondered Lesley with compressed lips. "Why was I so feeble?' She thought Jim should have stuck to healing children, otherwise they were going to have too many enemies. But in the end she went along with what he wanted.

Jim broke the silence. "You said you knew who sent those two to poison us."

"I can't remember what I meant. I just wanted to get us out of there."

She knew exactly who sent them: it was one of the thousands who wanted them dead. As they couldn't possibly protect themselves from everybody, it made no difference who it was. She could have told him this before they started walking in the cold. Now, she felt it would be too cruel to mention it.

"I'm glad, I'm pleased," said Jim, sounding defiant. "If the stinkers want us dead, it means I'm doing the right thing."

Lesley was shocked. 'How could you say that?' she screamed in her head. 'You nearly got us killed, and you are glad? You are pleased?' But, looking at Jim's face, she saw that he was glad and pleased with a grim face. For a moment she was ashamed. Was she getting hysterical? She didn't want Jim to think that she was blaming him. "You can carry Clare for a while if you want to," she said.

"Come on, our little saviour," said Jim, taking the bundle with huge dark liquid eyes. He carried Clare the rest of the way and Lesley put her arm around his waist. As they walked together, feeling close, they got over their fright and were overcome by the joy of surviving, a sense of elation that they were indestructible.

25. LIVING IN DANGER

When you grow up you know
your life is only a bonus on death
and as it were a found object,
you are ready to return it
at any time
that's why you keep it.
ATTILA JÓZSEF

The same day there was panic at the Sussex Headquarters of the Osteopathy Foundation. The mansion and the surrounding land that Jim had bought were protected by electronic fences and armed guards and visitors were screened, but it was little comfort when the IT team discovered that all their computers and phones had been hacked and monitored. They couldn't determine by whom or for how long. Whoever was responsible had a list of everybody who worked for the Foundation because they had hacked into everybody's mobile as well. As the Taylors had no electronic communication in the Holland Park house which would allow them to be traced, the only way Ellie Wade could inform them was by driving to London. When the Taylors got home, she was standing on the second floor landing with folded arms, waiting for them at the top of the stairs.

"How was the concert?" she asked. "You're home early."

Lesley was carrying the baby once again and it was Jim

who replied. "We were served hot chocolate with cyanide during in the interval, so we left," he said, as they started up the stairs. "What's your news, Ellie?"

"My news is just as bad," said Ellie.

Ellie's words swept away Lesley's joy. She wasn't interested in the details of her bad news and passed Ellie on the staircase with a wan smile. Clare needed changing.

"Actually it isn't as bad as poisoning," Ellie corrected herself, following Jim to his study, "but I didn't think it could wait." She told him that Foundation phones and computers had been hacked.

"Well," Jim said, following an old train of thought, "I still think making stinkers smell is a good idea."

"There can't be any evidence against you. Nobody at headquarters knows about the plague. There hasn't been any reference to it in our communication systems."

Neb walked into the room, still wearing his black tails. He hadn't bothered to change his clothes after the concert, furious with the detectives who tried to question him further without any respect. He wanted to leave right away. He didn't want to linger on a planet where he wasn't welcome.

Jim pleaded for more time.

"You've had a year," Neb protested. "You should ask me to take you all to Otthon. That would be your smartest wish. You would be our principal cellist and you could train the whole string section in my orchestra."

"I can't," said Jim. He wanted to stay where he was born - if not in the same country, at least on the same planet.

"You could introduce your Bach to all the living planets we can reach in the universe. Doesn't that inspire you?"

"Jim can't just leave," Ellie said. "He's responsible for a lot of people. Besides, the family could move out to Sussex, live in the mansion. Our communication system may be bugged, but the building and the surrounding land is well protected. You wouldn't have to worry about what you drink. Actually, on the way here, I was thinking that I should take you back with me to Sussex."

Lesley shuddered. "I wouldn't want Clare to grow up behind fences."

They began to discuss where would be the safest place to live. Where would they feel free? Where was home? They couldn't agree; each of them had a different idea.

They were interrupted by a sudden downpour of hail stones beating against the windows. It was growing darker in spite of the street lights. "Well, think about it," Ellie said. "I have to get back to Sussex. If I was followed, I'm sure by now they've given up. See you tomorrow."

Soon afterwards Ellie's car emerged from the garage on the opposite side of the street and a small Volkswagen parked nearby exploded, shattering windows and hurling chunks of hot metal into the air. Clare started crying.

Jim was convinced that the bomb was meant for him. Braving the assassins who might have been around, he ran out of the house through the rarely used front door, thinking, 'I killed her' but hoping that she was still alive and he could save her. Neb ran out right behind him.

Fate grants our wishes, if at all, in twisted ways. Ellie was spared the torture of a long painful illness and a lingering death. A piece of the Volkswagen's engine cut through the windscreen and crushed her chest, killing her instantly.

26. THE THIRD WISH

Sweet hope and cold fear
Battling in my heart.
JACOPO FERRETTI

It was as if the explosion had blown away the downpour of hail and the clouds. The sky was clear and blue. The cul-de-sac became filled with spectators crowding around the wrecked cars. Ellie's head, which seemed to have grown out of a massive piece of twisted metal, was marked only by a few superficial cuts. Her face was frozen in an expression of surprise and her wide-open brown eyes with their twenty-twenty vision seemed to be staring at something hidden from the living. For all his travels in the universe, Neb had never seen a dead person and he burst into tears.

Police cars arrived. "A lot of people are killed by car bombs," said a detective sergeant. It was a well-meant remark, such as doctors sometimes make to the grieving. "It's quite common."

Jim looked askance at the sergeant and asked Neb for his mobile. He called the Foundation to organise the funeral. It was too late for subterfuge.

Lesley didn't leave the house. She loved Ellie, but

protecting her baby meant more than anything else. She wouldn't have gone to the funeral either, if Neb hadn't given his word that it would be safe.

"But please Neb," asked Lesley, "let's leave right after the funeral."

"Persuade him to make his third wish."

"Don't you want to be here when your book is published?" Jim asked, still reluctant to abandon his native planet.

"And risk Clare's life? Never." Few male authors would have given that answer.

Jim turned to Neb. "I don't know yet, but just in case we do decide to go with you, will you give me your word that you'll bring us back if we want to return?"

"You have my word, but remember, first you have to teach the string section of our orchestra and perform a series of cello concerts."

"But will you give me your word that you'll bring us back if we want to return?"

Neb sighed. "I promise."

It was a cold, drizzly, sunless January day. At least a couple of hundred people followed Ellie's coffin to the Golders Green Cemetery. Neb walked with the Taylors. He had teased Ellie a lot and it hurt him that he hadn't told her how much he liked her.

It is sad when people die and leave their families bereft, but it's sadder still when they leave no relatives behind to mourn them. The dead without any blood ties to the living die the ultimate death – it is as if they had never lived. They leave us with a presentiment of the disappearance of humans, when we will be like dinosaurs, leaving hardly any traces to show that we ever existed. A malfunctioning bomb exploding in the midst of the crowd with a harmless thud intensified the dread of extinction that filled the hearts of the mourners. Hearing the thud of the bomb, Neb and Jim exchanged glances. Neb had Jim's third wish without a word being spoken.

After the funeral Jim transferred the ownership of the Foundation to its employees, and Lesley gave her copyrights to friends. "Earth money would be no use to us where we're going," she told them.

As soon as it got dark, Neb raised the fly-whirl disk from under the grass in Holland Park.

"So my mite, you'll be a fourth generation foreigner," Jim said to Clare, as he carried her aboard the craft. With all the musical instruments on board there was not much room for the Taylor family, but then refugees rarely travel in comfort. Neb locked the hatch, pushed buttons and levers. Leaving a huge crater behind, the silver disk rose straight up into the air, stopped, and started to whirl. They rose above the atmosphere into pure, undiluted sunlight and Neb put the craft on hold, hovering over our blue planet. The Taylors were heartsick and Neb, to his own surprise, felt that he should have stayed longer.

"We'll come back as soon as we're forgotten and nobody wants to kill us," Jim said to give himself courage.

"We were in Venice for only half a day!" Lesley lamented, crying for the whole Earth.

Jim tried to find his cello case with his eyes. When he saw it, he felt less afraid.

They entered the darkness of space, away from the sun. Jim reached out to feel the baby and clasped Lesley's hand. Even Lesley, who had written a whole book about Otthon from written sources, felt that they were setting out for a place she didn't really know.

Neb clicked another set of switches. There was a rushing mighty wind and they whirled away to another world, to the unknown.

There were no new cases of the stinking disease; the epidemic died out. Even the stench of the most revolting characters grew weaker. Like most incredible events in history, people began to doubt that there ever was such a plague. What was it all about? What stinkers? Yet those with fine noses, whom I imagine my readers to be, can still smell them.

About the Author

Born in Hungary, son of a headmaster and church organist, Stephen Vizinczey was two years old when his father was assassinated by the Nazis; two decades later his uncle was murdered by the Communists. During his student years he was a poet and playwright and three of his plays were banned by the regime. One won the Attila József prize, but the police raided the theatre during the dress rehearsal and seized all copies of the play. Vizinczey fought in the defeated Hungarian Revolution of 1956 and fled to the West, speaking about fifty words of English. Since then, "like Conrad and Nabokov, he has risen to the ranks of those foreigners who handle English in a way to make a native Anglophone pale with jealousy" (Leslie Hanscom, New York Newsday), and "can teach the English how to write English" (Anthony Burgess). He learned the language by writing scripts for the National Film Board of Canada, founded and edited the literary-political magazine Exchange and joined CBC/Radio Canada as a writer and producer in Toronto.

In 1965 he quit his job, borrowed money to publish his first novel, In Praise of Older Women (planning to commit suicide if it failed) and distributed it by car and through the post. It became the first and only self-published novel to top the bestseller lists in the history of Canadian literature. Its subsequent publication and success in Britain the following year drew worldwide attention to the novel and it became an acclaimed international bestseller.

In his second book, The Rules of Chaos, inspired by Tolstoy's theory of history and his own experiences of wars and revolution, Vizinczey argued that the chaotic interaction of events renders the conventional belief in power a delusion: "Power is a stick or a mirage of a stick, but it is impossible to know beforehand which it is..." and "the cruelties of power are the rage of impotence." He predicted in a 1968 article in Nigel Lawson's Spectator that America was bound to be defeated in Vietnam, in spite of the massive superiority of American power against an immeasurably smaller and weaker country. "Weapons are means of destruction, not means of control," he wrote. "Power weakens as it grows."

The author moved to London in 1967 and was a lead reviewer in successive decades in The Times and The Sunday Telegraph until the mid 1980s. These reviews, mostly about classic authors, have been translated and reprinted in major newspapers and magazines on both sides of the Atlantic and were finally published in book form in 1985 as Truth and Lies in Literature. It continues to be published and republished in major languages.

Always out of step with prevailing notions of both popular and high art, Vizinczey's second novel, An Innocent Millionaire, was rejected by scores of publishers before it was eventually published in 1983 by Christopher Sinclair-Stevenson in London and Harold Evans in New York. Welcomed by Graham Greene and Anthony Burgess, An Innocent Millionaire was hailed throughout the world by writers and critics, who compared it to nineteenth century classics, notably Stendhal and Balzac. "Vizinczey is one of the great contemporary writers who makes the crucial themes of our times his own and transforms them into the stuff of fiction with humour and passion." (Sergio Vila-Sanjuan, La Vanguardia.)

His books have so far sold seven million copies around the world. Fifty years after publishing is his first novel, Vizinczey decided to return to self-publishing, producing a collected edition of his works in English, starting with his long-awaited third novel If Only.

"If you were compiling an anthology of foreign born writers who make the English writer canon, he would belong, and he is one of the very few who would". (Norman Stone, The Spectator.)

More information can be found on Vizinczey's website: *www. stephenvizinczey.com*

The Rules of Chaos
Revised Edition

"The corollary that we do not control our future is that neither does anybody else."
"We need to free our imagination to understand what is happening."
"All beliefs in power rest on the fallacy that most people do what they are supposed to do."

Originally written in the early 1960's, at the same time that MIT was building computers to define Earth's chaotic weather patterns to improve our understanding of the weather, The Rules of Chaos defines the dynamics of chaotic events to help us to understand and cope with them. Our leading political theories were conceived during the development of the railways which dominated the public imagination. By contrast, this book argues that history is not progressing in one direction like trains, on the iron rails of inevitability, with stations along the way: The metaphor of "the ship of state" sailing on uncertain waters reflects more accurately what is happening. "The difference between seeing the world as orderly or chaotic is the difference between seeing the world as standing still or in motion. The world is not what it is but what occurs. The world is chaotic not because there are no laws but because there are multitudes of incontrovertible laws and their haphazard interplay results in unpredictable outcomes." The book demonstrates that all growth eventually becomes a weakness. "As communities continue to grow past their optimum size they become less coherent, looser, and more disjointed. "There are unions which only divide." The most populous states constitute the most discordant and thus the weakest societies." The book argues that in a chaotic world the ties which hold people together in a crisis – family, language, sense of nationhood, beliefs and coherence - are the most vital. This revised edition also includes the Vizinczey Equation, a mathematical formula to get a grip on the dynamics which determine what happens next, the process by which empires decline and disintegrate.

The Rules of Chaos focuses not only on society but also on individual lives and the psychological reasons for our faith in deterministic views. The Rules: 1.The future is a blinding mirage. 2. Power weakens as it grows. 3. If nothing is certain, nothing is impossible. 4. Delusions kill. 5. You are free and nobody belongs to you.

The first restricted hardback edition of only 100 copies, numbered and signed £120.00

Paperback £14.99

e-book £9.99

An Innocent Millionaire
Revised edition

"I started reading Stephen Vizinczey's *An Innocent Millionaire* and, once I started, I could not put it down. BRAVO. Graham Greene took the very word out of my mouth." (Mary Stewart) "A black treasure hunt for the intelligentsia." (Philip Howard, *The Times*) "Vizinczey's New York attorneys make Balzac's shyster lawyers look like little orphan boys." (Martin Halter, *Berliner Zeitung*) "I haven't experienced so much moral outrage since Nicholas

Nickleby. Vizinczey seems to be as funny as Dickens and as cruel. An enraging entertainment." (Martin Cruz Smith) "So exciting that it is almost unbearable. Vizinczey has written a great novel bringing on stage a multitude of characters, all extraordinarily alive, both good and bad. A *comedié humaine* of the modern word." (Eva Haldimann, *Neue Zurcher Zeitung*) "You gobble it up like an adventure story and savour it like a bedside book. *Un Millionaire Innocent* is also a superb novel about love, sensual and sensitive. A history of the flesh, of the words and the heart." (Michele Gazier, *Télérama*)

"A thrilling and tragic love story. The book literally pulses with life. There is no doubt whatever that Vizinczey is one of the great writers of our time."(Angel Vivas, *Album*) "It shows where the true values lie – not in wealth or the rule of law but in that as yet inviolate sector where a man and woman make love ... the distinction of the book lies in its calm, clean prose style as well as the solidity of the characters, good and detestable alike. I was entertained, but also deeply moved. Here is a novel set bang in the middle of our decadent, polluted, corrupt world that, in some curious way, breathes a kind of desperate hope." (Anthony Burgess, *Punch*)

"A kind of Monte Christo in reverse. With his Mark Niven, Vizinczey has stood Edmond Dantes on his head. Mark ends up with his gold treasure in the mincer of the business machine... the fiendishly clever thing about Vizinczey is that his narrator's bitter, angry comments are fused with a calmly detached, realistic view of things. In his subversive elegance Vizinczey is altogether comparable to Balzac." (Wolfram Knorr, *Die Weltwoche*) "A brilliantly coloured mosaic of crime, adventure and philosophical reflections, which holds the reader more deeply fascinated with every page. The novel sheds light on what holds the world together. This binding force is not firm and incontrovertible, as in Goethe, but something fragile and elusive. A net woven from intrigue, hope and chance determines the fate of mankind. Vizinczey spreads out this net for us in an enthralling manner; he has written a great novel." (Volher Albers, *Deutsches Allgemeines Sonntagsblatt*) "A very funny and serious book, packed with aphorisms... A crescendo of treachery, delay, exploitation that makes Bleak House look like a tea party. It would be salutary to discover why this book, whose messages are unremittingly deflationary, should leave one so elated."(Victoria Glendinning, *Sunday Times*) "Vizinczey has created an authentic social epic which reunites, after an estrangement of nearly a century, intellectual and moral edification with exuberant entertainment." (Christina Monet)

The first restricted hardback edition of only 100 copies, numbered and signed £120.00

Paperback £14.99

e-book £9.99

Truth and Lies in Literature
A Writer's Ten Commandments
Revised edition

Apart from the ever-popular 'A Writer's Ten Commandments', this extended and revised edition contains author's critical work written since the original publication of the book in 1983, which had appeared only in foreign editions. These include 'The Anatomy of Serious Rubbish' (an analysis of the 1968 Pulitzer prize novel about the black slave rebel Nat Turner who, in the book, shows great understanding and pity for the white slave owners while waiting for them to hang him); 'Literary Criticism as the Politics of Literature', 'Goethe – The Genius as a Toady' and Vizinczey's foreword to the French edition of Mark Twain's autobiography - as well as his revised and expanded essays on Kleist, Stendhal and Balzac.

"Vizinczey can make us care about his favourite writers, because the flavour of his own writing makes it apparent, without tedious egotism, that he himself has experienced the raptures of love and reflected on its immutable meaning. In a word, he unerringly knows how to find the weight of experience and states it in unflinching, aphoristic English." (Mark Le Fanu, *The Times*) "The irony, the lightness, the profundity, the naturalness and exactitude of the novelist are found again intact in the texts of the critic. Besides, there is little disparity between the inspiration for In Praise and the inspiration for Truth & Lies. Vizinczey makes love with books with the same desire to understand through pleasure, the same opening up of the mind and the heart, the same freedom, the same lucidity and passion for truth and beauty. Vizinczey's intelligence is so bracing, so contagious, that reading his books plunges you into a bath of joy for at least a week." (Pierre Le Pape, *Le Monde*) "We have to mark with a white stone the discovery of a writer and critic who has no equivalent in France, an avenger of abused truth. This rare bird is called (and perhaps the difficulty of pronouncing and spelling his name is the reason for this belated publication) Stephen Vizinczey. We are indebted to him for two novels: I*n Praise of Older Women and An Innocent Millionaire, and two collections of essays, The Rules of Chaos and Truth and Lies in Literature*, which seem to have earned him an international reputation. Spending his youth under a dictatorship where lies and political cant ruled all forms of life, he contracted an insurmountable aversion to imposture and trickery - an aversion all the more profound because his love of literature is so demanding. Against his own interests, Stephen Vizinczey has the balls to proclaim the scandal of truth. "(Bruno de Cessole, *Valeurs Actuelles*) "The ideas which emerge from Truth and Lies in Literature are the same ones which inspire the author'two very different novels, so reading these essays confers on the novels a mysterious coherence." (Pedro Sorela, *El País*) "The author has the audacity to plunk literature down in the midst of strife, bold and indefatigable, as the articulated conscience of the world. " (Trevor Ferguson, *Montreal Gazette*) "A very uncommon mixture of exuberance and severity. When he loves a writer – such as Balzac and Kleist - he wastes no time on mean qualifications, his intelligent passion to explain why has the boldness and glamour of a cavalry charge." Paul Chipchase, *The Sunday Telegraph*) "A breath of the kind of fresh air that gives academics cold shoulders. The great virtue of this collection lies in its steady concern with serious matters, of life and death." (Frederic Raphael, *The Sunday Times*) "Vizinczey has no patience with trends in criticism which fiddle with word patterns. His concern lies with the portrayal of human characters in the full range of their passions and attitude.). "An intellectual and emotional odyssey. In drawing out the truth (and lies) about reality set forth in literature (he tackles some non-fiction in the process), Vizinczey imparts more about man and the state than a library of scholarly tomes." (Lynn Scarlett, *Reason*)

The first restricted hardback edition of only 100 copies, numbered and signed £120.00

Paperback £14.99

e-book £9.99

In Praise of Older Women
the amorous recollections of András Vajda
Anniversary Edition

"This book is addressed to young men and dedicated to older women – and the connection between the two is my proposition. I'm not an expert on sex, but I was a good student of the women I loved, and I'll try to recall those happy and unhappy experiences which, I believe, made a man out of me. I spent the first twenty-three years of my life in Hungary, Austria and Italy, and my adventures in growing up differed considerably from the adventures of young men in the New World." So begins a young academic's fictional memoirs, which Vizinczey published himself in 1965.

"Here is this Hungarian rebel who in 1957, a landed Canadian immigrant who could hardly speak our language and who even today speaks it with an impenetrable accent and whose name, moreover, we can't pronounce and he has the gall to place himself, with his first book and in his thirty-third year, among the masters of plain English prose." (Kildare Dobbs, *Saturday Night*) "Doesn't offer fantasy sex like Frank Harris, or ribald sex like Henry Miller; he conveys much of the warmth and understanding more common between the sheets than between the covers of novels." (Barbara Saunders, *Library Journal*) "Elegantly erotic, with masses of that indefinable quality, style. It has the real stuff of immortality." (B.A.Young, *Punch*) "Cool, distanced and for that very reason erotic in a subtle and attractive way: it permits us to use our imagination. It has a classic tone, recalling both Casanova and Stendhal." (Robert Fulford, *Saturday Night*) "A masterpiece. Like all great novels, it shows the truth about life." (Pierre Lepape, *Le Monde*) "I was suspicious of In Praise of Older Women, if only because it became a worldwide bestseller. I was wrong. This is true eroticism, which resides in the discovery of and respect for the other person and enriches one's knowledge of oneself." (Maurice Nadeau, *La Quinzaine littéraire*)

"When it was first published here in 1966, a reviewer in Pittsburgh wrote to the publishers, 'I have thrown my copy into the wastebasket, and I hope Mr. Vizinczey will be murdered before he has a chance to write another book.' Although some passages may well arouse the reader, this novel brims with what the Courts termed redeeming literary merit." (Clarence Petersen, *Chicago Tribune*) "One of the most entertaining and wisest books of world literature." (Arbo Widmann, *Perlentaucher der Kultur und Literatur*) "The novel has a dynamism defined by one of its own phrases. Haven't you heard of Einstein's Law? Pleasure turns into energy." (Clara Janés, *El País*)
